I0666704

This is a work of fiction. Any references to historical events, real people, or places are fictitious. Other names, characters, places, and events are products of the author's imagination, and any resemblance to actual events, places, or persons, living or dead, is entirely coincidental.

THE PROPHET
Second Edition, July 27, 2018
Copyright © 2017 Ande Edwards
ISBN: 9781732569201 (Print)
Written by Ande Edwards
Original Cover Design by Matthew David Walling

A Note from the Author.

Encounters with angels and demons seem like something out of a science fiction movie, but the Bible mentions both angels and demons hundreds of times, and Ephesians tells us that we battle against the powers of darkness, not flesh and blood. What exactly does that look like? How do angels and demons fill their days, and what do their interactions with us look like? This book is a feeble attempt to explore that idea.

Before writing this book, I tended to think of demons as beady-eyed beings with jagged teeth. So, I had to spend some time exploring what the Bible had to say about demons and angels. Building from what was there, I let my imagination take over to create one possible view of the spiritual realm. I hope you find it fascinating, but more importantly, I hope it causes you to think about how you see the spiritual realm.

This novel functions on the premise that all demons were once glorious, angelic creatures. The book presumes that at one time, demons (when they were angels) shined with the Light of the King (God). But after their rebellion, that Light was removed. In this book, I have them grow darker as time passes, and they transform further from the angels they had been to the demons they have become. Essentially, a spiritual change first (angel to a demon), and then more gradually, their spirit and physical appearance change to match. This concept is further explored in books 2 and 3 of the series.

This is the first of three books in the Prophet Series. In each book, readers will be introduced to diverse types of angels/demons, each with a unique purpose. I imagine it as a realm where demons retain most of the same powers they had as angels, only now, those powers have been corrupted for evil. In this book, *The Prophet*, I have included the following three primary types of angels/demons:

1. Warriors: The warrior angels fight for the King (God), and the warrior demons fight for the Prince of Darkness (Lucifer). These are battle-ready beings designed perfectly for combat. Consider the many references in the Bible to Heaven's Armies (note that it is plural).

2. Guardians/Destroyers: In the book, I use the term Guardian to refer to angels. Those Guardians who have fallen become Destroyer Demons. As such, instead of protecting humans, they bring affliction and disaster to them. While the Bible is not explicit regarding the existence of guardian angels, I used passages such as Psalms 91 and Matthew 18:10 to build upon.

3. Ministering/Tormenting: These beings in the book can communicate in limited ways with humans. Ministering angels use thoughts, ideas, experiences, and things seen and heard to encourage and build a person up. Tormenting demons use those same things to discourage, tempt, and belittle people—thoughts and ideas from movies, books, music, or those around them

become fuel used either by ministering angels to build up or by destroying demons to tear down. I used passages such as Luke 16:22, Hebrews 1:14, Matthew 4:11, Matthew 17:18, Mark 1:13, and Mark 9:17-22 to support this direction.

4. Archangels: In the book, seven Archangels manage and oversee the angels working on a particular continent. I thought of them as commanders. This idea was based on church tradition and early church references to the seven archangels: Michael, Gabriel, Uriel, Chamuel, Raphael, Jophiel, and Zadkiel.

I took three other important positions in the book. First, while I acknowledge that some people do not believe there are female angels, I used the verse Zechariah 5:9 as a foundation for including some. And it just worked for the story. Second, I used verses such as Hebrews 13:2 and Luke 4:41 to support the idea that both angels and demons can appear to humans in a human form.

Finally, I know that many people believe there is no sadness in heaven. I do not. The Bible tells us in Revelation 21:1-4 that after the end of the earth, once it is all over and the demons are locked away and the earth is destroyed, then…. God will wipe away our tears, and there will be no more sadness. But that day has not come. In this current age, there is much to be sad about and to mourn and so you will see emotions reflected in heaven throughout the series, more so in books 2 and 3.

As an author, exploring how demons and angels may work, what spiritual warfare might look like, and what the fall may have been like was interesting. I explored questions such as, can an angel still fall, or was that a one-time event that can no longer happen? Can an angel die? I do not presume that my ideas are right – they are just one of millions of possibilities and they were fun to think about. I read all I could find in the Bible about angels and demons and their behaviors and attempted to model the story around what I found there. Still, the demons and angels in this series represent my imagination and how I see the spiritual realm interacting with the earthly one. I tried hard not to contradict anything in the Bible, but this is a work of fiction and is in no way meant to imply Biblical truth. I hope you enjoy the story!

ACKNOWLEDGMENTS

I am so thankful to all the people who ventured with me on this incredible journey of faith and discovery.

Thank you to Thea, Nat, Beth, and Melissa for reading, rereading, and reading yet again as I worked on the story and the characters and for engaging with me in endless discussions on angels, demons, and spiritual warfare. Thank you for sharing your experiences and being willing to share your "you're going to think I'm crazy" stories. Your feedback and critique were invaluable to me. This is a better book because of you.

I am so thankful for my Bible study group. You are a fantastic group of people who have inspired and supported me on my journey. You showed me how important it is to have a support system of fellow believers you can entrust with your greatest struggles. You have walked through many fires with me, and I love each of you for allowing me to be my authentic self when I am with you. I tried to model the Wednesday night group after our comradery, and while the characters and their struggles do not reflect ours, their unity and cohesion do.

I want to thank my husband for supporting the crazy idea that I would write a book. I started down this path with great trepidation, but you have encouraged me every step of the way. I could never have hoped for a better man.

To the college professors I know at both state and faith-based schools, thank you for sharing your stories and struggles with me. Your wisdom has never been more needed.

To my mom, thank you for making me strong and resilient.

PROLOGUE

To win a war, you must develop a strategy. Titus once again reviewed the next stage of their battle plan and smiled over its simplicity. Some of the greatest military minds on the planet had spent years developing this plan, and it was paying off. The strategy was simple: do not attract the enemy's attention, be subtle, and pick your targets wisely. It had taken many years to get all the pieces in place, but it had been seamless.

The prince had called in his best, and they had developed a plan so impressive it was destined to succeed. They had lost a great deal of real estate in the process, but some collateral damage was to be expected.

Seneca, the most seasoned warrior among them, offered wisdom and cunning. He had been eager to join, and when he did, the days of losing ground had not only stopped but had turned around. They had been careful to ensure the transition was gradual so as not to attract unwanted attention—and it worked. No one suspected anything.

Titus stood and stretched. It was an unusual practice, but the hairless rats did it so often and with such expressions of comfort that he had adopted the behavior himself. He laughed to think of it.

Walking to the long mirror in the Great Hall, Titus looked at his reflection. He had mastered the mannerisms of the rats. They could not see him for who he was, and his study of their behaviors, such as stretching, made him blend in. But this body was growing old, and Titus saw no reason to remain in a decrepit body. When he had taken over this body, it was young, firm, and athletic, the body of a twenty-year-old. Back then, his black hair had been thick and wavy. But he had been in the body long enough that it was no longer in its prime. When this battle was over, he would find a new one. He smiled knowingly, tucked the manila folder with the latest reports from the field under his arm, and headed into the conference room where Morax awaited his update. Humans were proving to be a relatively easy target.

Chapter 1 - Heaven

Even in heaven, a warrior's heart carried scars. They lingered as echoes, faint reminders of battles fought and burdens borne. Aegeus was no exception. Despite his scars, he moved with the ease of one unbound by time, his stride carrying him through a sea of amber wheat that rippled and whispered in the wind. His hands, calloused from millennia of war, drifted across the soft grain heads, savoring their gentle caress. He closed his almond-colored eyes momentarily, allowing their gentle touch to seep into his soul. The sweet contrast of softness against his battle-hardened skin felt like a gift, precious and fragile. A reminder that even a warrior's hands could know tenderness.

As he walked, each step seemed to draw him deeper into the splendor of heaven that unfolded around him. Light bathed his olive skin, and the scent of lilac—delicate, intoxicating—wrapped around him like a familiar embrace. Its tendrils wove through the air as if binding together moments lost and moments yet to come. He drew a deep breath, allowing the fragrance to saturate him—a lingering memory, an unspoken promise. The King's presence enveloped him, a silent current that warmed his core, whispering of grace and unwavering love.

The glimmering city in the distance pulsed with the King's presence, but Aegeus turned his gaze instead toward the meeting place, the Great Tree standing proud at the heart of the field. The tree stood tall and proud where it had stood for all time. Its bark rough and cracked in a way that was both haunting and beautiful. From a distance, it appeared gnarled, heavy with the weight of ages, cradling stories etched into its surface—whispers of battles won and lost. Subtle carvings emerged from just below the surface, calling to those who would listen, offering messages of redemption and hope, stories of the past, and promises of the future.

The tree's leaves, vibrant and full, danced with the wind, weaving a soft symphony—a hymn of praise carried to the King. The sight stirred something deep within Aegeus's chest—a quiet tightening, a sense of familiarity and reverence. Here, beneath its branches, he felt the unspoken bond between his story and the countless others carved into its surface.

As Aegeus reached the tree, his chestnut-colored hair blew gently in the breeze. He was pleased to see the others had yet to arrive. These stolen moments beneath the tree were his alone, a chance to rest in its quiet strength. Though the tree was said to evoke many feelings, Aegeus had known only peace in its presence, a precious balm for his soul. If it had ever been otherwise, those days were long forgotten, at least by Aegeus.

His hand brushed the bark, rough and ancient beneath his fingers. One memory rose unbidden—the Battle of Pas-Dammim.

He had returned from that battle broken and weary, collapsing beneath the tree's branches. Grief had poured from him like a torrent, and the tree had absorbed it all, its very fruit turning dull and gray, the land beneath trembling with his sorrow. On that day, the King had come and knelt beside him; together, they had mourned. All of heaven had grieved that day, but none so deeply as the King.

Pushing aside the weight of that memory, Aegeus circled the tree slowly as he explored the types of fruit adorning the tree today. He took his time admiring each option before a yellow one with tiny purple dots caught his eye. This one was new. He inhaled its sweet aroma, reminiscent of angelo, one of his favorites.

Sinking into the lush grass at the tree's base, he leaned against its sturdy trunk, listening to its whispers. When he bit into the fruit, sweet nectar burst forth, trickling down his closely cropped beard. He wiped the juice from his chin with the back of his hand. Retrieving his wineskin, he took a sip of wine that perfectly complemented the fruit's sweetness. There was no end to the King's creativity; Aegeus reveled in the joy of being able to experience it. He was going to miss home.

Chapter 2

"You look like you're in heaven," Kfir said, landing softly beside Aegeus under the ancient tree. His wings folded back with a faint whisper.

Aegeus smiled at the familiar jest—a favorite of theirs, though angels were not known for their humor. The golden wheat surrounding them swayed gently in the breeze, the sky above stretching vast and endless, glowing with soft light that pulsed like a heartbeat.

Kfir tucked his wings away and embraced Aegeus, his brother-in-arms. The gesture was warm but brief, a bond forged over millennia.

"Good to see you, Keef. How are things in Africa?" Aegeus asked, leaning casually against the tree, though his tone held genuine interest.

"The people suffer," Kfir began, his gaze lifting toward the shimmering leaves above. He plucked a green and pink striped fruit from a low-hanging branch and turned it slowly in his hands. "But their love is pure, their faith unshakable. It strengthens me, though the burden is great."

His bronze eyes gleamed with quiet pride. "Their prayers are like unbroken hymns, rising to the King—a wonderful aroma to behold. The enemy does not relent, but neither do they."

Aegeus's chest tightened at Kfir's words. His brother's love for humanity had always been unshaken, a wellspring of hope Aegeus did not share. He wondered, not for the first time, if he had lost something vital in the centuries of battle.

Kfir's voice softened as he continued, his fingers brushing the fruit almost reverently. "It is hard," he admitted, "but it is an honor to fight for them."

Aegeus studied him, a flicker of admiration passing through his guarded expression. Kfir's heart had always remained open to humans, a connection Aegeus had long struggled to maintain.

"And the Spirit?" Aegeus asked after a moment.

"The Spirit is ever-present," Kfir replied, a faint smile touching his lips as he hesitantly licked the fruit to sample it. "The people treasure the Spirit, and it knows no bounds."

Aegeus chuckled. "You know it's going to be good. When has the King's fruit ever disappointed?"

"I was in Bethlehem once—" Kfir began, his tone mock-serious, drawing a deep laugh from Aegeus that echoed through the meadow.

Lavi swooped in, his landing seamless, his energy infectious.

"Not the Bethlehem story again," he groaned, rolling his eyes at the familiar banter.

"Welcome, brother," Aegeus said, clasping Lavi's forearm in greeting before pulling him into an embrace.

Kfir grinned and nodded, taking a bite of his fruit. The tartness was sharp but satisfying.

"The trauma was real," Kfir added with a wink, referring to his oft-repeated story, before embracing Lavi.

"And this is why they rarely let you leave Africa," Lavi joked. "Bad things happen when you venture out."

"I leave my mark," Kfir replied with an affectionate shrug.

"Indeed, you do," Lavi said, laughing good-naturedly as he settled under the tree.

Their camaraderie settled into a familiar rhythm born of countless shared battles and victories.

"And you?" Kfir asked as Lavi took a seat beside him under the tree. "Still in Israel?"

"No," Lavi replied, settling into the soft grass. "My charge came of age. I've been on special assignments ever since."

"Ah, the life of a guardian," Kfir nodded thoughtfully, his eyes following Aegeus, who was once again pacing around the tree, his hand brushing over its bark. Kfir sensed something heavy weighed on Aegeus today. It had been a long time since they last met here, under this tree. A place Aegeus seemed to reserve for significant moments.

Lavi glanced toward the shining city in the distance, a longing stirring in him. His soul ached for the presence of the King.

"We'll stop by the throne room before we leave," Aegeus said quietly, sensing Lavi's yearning. "I know you don't get home as often as the rest of us."

Lavi smiled, grateful. "What brings us here?" He asked, eager to move towards the throne room.

"There's a small town in America called Platitude," Aegeus said. "The King has been moving His people there." The weight of his words shifted the conversation, drawing their focus toward the mission ahead.

"America?" Kfir blinked, surprised. "As in the United States?" He had only been to America once, and it had been a disaster, something the other angels referred to as the debacle of 1974. Aegeus grinned at the memory of it.

"There is much to learn, my friend."

Kfir's attention sharpened. "What's happening there?"

"The enemy is planning something," Aegeus explained. "For the past three years, the King has quietly moved His children into place unnoticed. A college seems to be at the center of the enemy's interest. The King loves the place; He has many of His children there."

Kfir raised an eyebrow.

"I always wanted to go to college," he said, smoothing his cornrows with a playful grin. Aegeus and Lavi both shook their heads in amusement.

"Kfir, one day you'll realize jokes are not our strongest suit."

"Speak for yourself, pretty boy. I see no reason that my status as a mighty warrior must mean I have to be serious. Aegeus is stoic enough for all of us." he said, playfully pushing Aegeus.

"Pretty boy?" Lavi laughed, tossing his jet-black hair back with a dramatic flick.

Kfir nearly tipped over as he tried to mimic Lavi's gesture.

Aegeus, with a rare smile on his face and a slight shaking of his head, cleared his throat, drawing them back to focus.

"The King has moved eleven humans into Platitude as part of a team that does not yet know they are a team. They all have a guardian assigned, and some have warriors."

Lavi's brow furrowed at this.

"Warriors typically serve nations." His voice carried an edge of confusion. "To pull warriors from the military and assign them to a town this small…"

"They're not assigned to the town," Aegeus clarified. "They're assigned to individuals."

Lavi's eyes widened at this unusual news. Aegeus continued. "There is one more human that must arrive—the Twelfth."

"The Twelfth, that is an odd name?" Kfir repeated, only slightly disappointed, that the rumors he had heard about the latest way Aegeus was relating to humans seemed to be accurate and lingering.

"It's the order in which they've arrived. First, second, third…and now, the Twelfth." He spoke with an air of distance, a habit born of centuries of keeping himself detached from the humans he fought to protect. He knew it was odd, and he also knew that despite the oddness of it, they would embrace it as Aegeus's way.

Kfir and Lavi exchanged a look, understanding it was how Aegeus coped. They understood the scars that led him to believe that caring too much was dangerous. Those who knew him well could see that Aegeus carried a hint of weariness from centuries of battles fought and difficult lessons learned.

"We would be in trouble if there were too many more," Lavi added with a wink. Aegeus knew it was odd, but he had learned that one day, he may have to fight against the very charge he protected. Keeping his distance was best.

"What do we know of the Twelfth?" Lavi asked.

"Very little," Aegeus admitted. "But I know that the King has personally assigned us to guard them."

"Two warriors and a guardian for one person?" asked Kfir, suddenly intrigued by the mission.

"It is unusual, I know, but I confirmed it with Michael himself," Aegeus said, his voice steady though a flicker of unease crossed his face. He didn't mention the long conversations he had had with Michael—hours spent trying to pass the assignment to another. He had listed a dozen angels, each better suited in his eyes. But Michael had been unyielding. Each time, his response had been the same: The King has chosen you, Aegeus. He has willed it.

"And we know nothing of him?"

"Nothing," Aegeus confirmed.

Meir's sudden appearance interrupted their conversation, her radiant presence drawing their attention. Her dark hair was loosely swept into a bun, and her honey-colored eyes sparkled warmly.

"Meir!" they called in unison, their voices rising with genuine delight.

"How long have you been home?" Lavi asked, standing quickly to greet her.

"I have seen four passes of fruit on the tree," she replied, smiling warmly.

"You will be joining us on this mission?" Kfir asked, barely masking his excitement.

"I will," she said, her wings unfurling slightly in response as Kfir lifted her into a celebratory spin.

"This must be important if the head ministering angel is involved," he said, setting her down gently.

Meir's laugh was soft but full of affection.

"You all have changed so little," she teased.

"You have grown even wiser," Aegeus replied, his tone lighter than usual.

Lavi chuckled, nudging Kfir. "She keeps us honest, doesn't she?"

Kfir nodded. "Always has."

The warmth of their reunion lingered, the bonds between them made palpable in their smiles and shared glances.

"I understand it is of the utmost importance to the King and is being overseen by Michael himself."

Aegeus hugged her next, a smile softening his battle-hardened face. A rare warmth spread through Aegeus's chest. Her presence was a reminder of what angels could be—gentle, steadfast, and full of light. She bore the weight of her assignments with grace, a contrast to the weariness he so often carried. If anyone could remind him of the human's goodness, it was Meir. Her honey-colored eyes flickered with curiosity as they met his.

"Don't do that," Aegeus murmured.

"I can't help it," she teased. "It's a by-product of the job."

Kfir laughed, his tone playful, "What did you see in there?"

Meir smiled; she would no more reveal what she'd glimpsed in Aegeus's mind than she could avoid seeing it.

"I saw piles of muffins from Martha's bakery," she replied with a mischievous wink. They all chuckled.

When the conversation circled back to the mission, Aegeus's pacing resumed, his hand brushing the tree's bark with an almost absent-minded reverence. The vast meadow around them seemed to hold its breath as they spoke of what was to come.

"Tell us about the town," Lavi prompted, bringing the conversation back to the mission, though his gaze lingered toward the city, his longing for the throne room unmistakable.

The tree's leaves rustled softly above them, creating a natural symphony as the golden wheat around them swayed like a tide. Aegeus plucked a colorful bundle of grapes from the tree, offering some to the others. The fruit was sweet and crisp, its taste a vivid reminder of the King's boundless creativity.

When Aegeus finally spoke, his voice carried the weight of their purpose. "There's a small town in America called Platitude," he began, the soft light of the field enveloping them. "Platitude is a tiny town in the middle of nowhere. It is nestled in the Elpída mountain range and is home to a college that draws many of the King's children. It's a place of both beauty and struggle.

"Michael tells me the town has always had a higher-than-normal demon presence because of the college. He says college students tend to attract demons, but Christian colleges get lots of attention as demons try to side-rail the next generation. The college is bright with Light, which has only increased the demon presence. Michael said they've been targeting the students, who are distracted by rules and appearances instead of being honest about their battles. It leaves them isolated, which only strengthens the enemy."

"When you put so many of them in one place, there becomes an unspoken expectation to appear "perfect," Meir added. "When that happens, they become isolated, and shame often follows. The enemy knows how to use that. They no longer share their struggles—not the real ones, those that grab hold of their souls and won't let go. They keep those buried for fear of judgment by their peers. Feelings of isolation and shame are one of the enemy's greatest weapons. But I have seen how kindness, simple, quiet gestures – can break through the darkness. I've seen a smile soften a hardened heart or a quiet word lift a soul drowning in despair." Meir said softly, her eyes distant, recalling countless such moments. Kfir exchanged a glance with Lavi, the weight of her words settling over them.

"Humans seem to need a pecking order. They have an innate need to belong and yet be distinguished. Sometimes, they accomplish that by pointing out the flaws in others. Checklists and legalism help them feel higher in the pecking order." Lavi added.

"The college has been there for over two hundred years," Aegeus said. "Their students are unlikely to grow wealthy, but they will be armed to offer food to the hungry, shoes to the needy, and a drink to those who thirst.

In the past, they made significant strides in understanding and applying the teaching of the Lamb, but the demons have strangled that over the last year. They have begun moving backward. Michael fears they will find themselves right fighters."

"Right fighters?" Kfir's brow furrowed. He had been in many fights; this was a fight he was not familiar with.

"Those who are more concerned about proving they are right than finding the truth," Lavi offered. He had seen it many times on many continents.

"All the more reason we need to be prepared," Aegeus added.

"I trust you've been briefed on the Fifth and the Eighth?" Meir's voice carried a rare note of concern. Aegeus nodded, understanding her unspoken worry.

"I do," he confirmed. "The Sixth worries me the most."

"We'll need extra ministering angels," Meir said, half-request, half-statement.

"Recruit all you need. Michael has cleared it," Aegeus replied.

"I'll form a team and meet you in Platitude." Meir, like Aegeus, was focused on the mission and had little time for unnecessary chitchat. She chose her words carefully because she understood their power in a way few others did.

Unlike Aegeus, Meir had a profound love for the King's children. Her job had shown her their deepest sorrows; she had witnessed the unimaginable damage the enemy could do. Yet she had also learned that kindness could seep into a wounded soul, take root, and save a life. As a result, she understood the immeasurable value of the little things, small words of encouragement waiting for the right moment to be needed. As she turned to leave, Kfir called after her, a playful smile on his face.

"What does heaven smell like to you?"

"Like the King, of course," she replied before vanishing.

Lavi inhaled deeply, letting the familiar scent of gardenias fill him.

"What does heaven smell like to you, Kfir?" he asked.

Kfir's grin was as warm as the sunlight breaking through the clouds. "Today, it smells like freshly baked bread," he said, his tone softening with contentment.

Aegeus, his hand still resting on the tree, glanced toward the horizon.

"Come," he said, his voice resolute. "Let us see the King before we go."

Chapter 3

Cherubim songs grew louder as they walked. Lavi paused often, closing his eyes to let the Light of God wash over him, savoring every second. Guardians seldom returned home, making each breath of heaven a precious renewal for his soul.

Aegeus, too, understood the need to savor their remaining time in heaven. Questions filled his mind—about the mission and the unusual assignment. Aegeus couldn't help but wonder why the King had chosen him for this mission.

As they walked, Kfir smiled as a young child climbed on a lion resting in the tall grass. He felt a surge of excitement for the humans. Their earthly trials were great, but the joy awaiting them in heaven was beyond measure. He loved to be near the new arrivals and enjoy the wonder they experienced when they encountered heaven for the first time, experiencing the King in a way they could not on earth. Their eyes finally fully opened to the glory of the King. Kfir snapped a reed off a plant as his hand brushed against it; he put it in his mouth, sucking on the nectar. He would miss the delights of heaven.

As they neared the city, the King's power and glory intensified, drawing them into reverent silence. Aegeus could feel the power surge through him as if he were made of electricity.

As they stepped onto the streets of gold, a familiar longing stirred within Aegeus—the pull of being near the King. The mark of the warrior glowed warmly against his chest, the sensation heightened by proximity. He pressed his hand over it, feeling the heat and the flicker of life beneath his touch. At that moment, all thoughts fell away, leaving only the love of the King and the honor of being in His presence. At the entrance to the throne room, Michael awaited them.

"He will see you," Michael informed them as he swung the large doors open, revealing the glory of the throne room. The Light radiating from inside filled the space with joy, peace, and love. Not just any love but the complete and overpowering feeling of being loved.

The King had his back turned when they entered. He stood in front of large windows looking out over the city. When he turned toward them, his glory caused Aegeus to stagger. No matter how many times he experienced it, it still overwhelmed him.

"Aegeus." The King's voice, sweet as honey, filled the room. At once, they all dropped to their knees, heads bowed in reverence. The Lamb stepped forward, resting his nail-scarred hand gently on Aegeus's shoulder.

"Rise."

"You are embarking on an important mission," the King began. "Conditions in Platitude continue to deteriorate. It is critical that you protect the Twelfth. Currently, the enemy does not suspect that we know of their movement. A great battle will come, but the Twelfth is not yet ready. You must make sure they have time to prepare. To avoid drawing attention to the Twelfth before it is time, Kfir and Aegeus, you are to wear the uniform of a guardian."

Aegeus and Kfir looked at each other, sure they had misheard. Even Michael seemed surprised by the command.

"Once the Twelfth has been detected, you may once again wear the uniform of the warrior. Lavi, you will assist them in understanding how to pass as guardians." The King winked at Lavi as if they shared a secret.

"My King," Aegeus began. The King smiled, already knowing what was in Aegeus's heart but waiting for him to voice it, something the King highly valued.

"Yes, Aegeus."

"This is a most unusual thing you are asking." Aegeus's hesitation was obvious.

"This is a most unusual situation, Aegeus," the King replied. He crossed his arms behind his back and looked down at the beautiful sapphire floor before taking a few paces toward Aegeus. "I imagine that Joshua must have believed marching around Jericho seven times was a most unusual thing. Naaman thought it was a most unusual thing when he was asked to wash in the Jordan River. Noah found it most unusual when I asked him to build an ark. Certainly, being swallowed by a whale was a most unusual thing. Oh, and Moses? Moses thought it most unusual when I told him to stretch his staff out over the Red Sea. All unusual but necessary. Shall I go on?" he asked gently, stopping in front of Aegeus, his point made.

"No, my King." Aegeus's love for the King was second to none, his loyalty unfaltering. He trusted the King. The King was pleased. He smiled at Aegeus and placed his hand on his shoulder, filling him with Light, strength, and courage. From Aegeus, he moved on to Lavi, putting his hand on him as well.

"You are a great guardian, Lavi. I have entrusted many of my children to you. The Twelfth will be unique, unlike any you have protected before. I am proud of all you have done and all you will do."

Lavi nodded slightly to signify he understood.

"Kfir." The King stood in front of Kfir and smiled widely. "Aegeus will need you on this mission. You have learned many lessons; do not forget them. You will find the Americans different than those you have served in the past. Learn to value them on their own merit. Oh, and Kfir . . ." The King paused as a smile crept across his face, "No hot dogs."

The room filled with soft laughter, and Kfir's cheeks flushed with warmth. The King placed his hand on Kfir, filling him with the Light of God—the angels' most potent weapon and the source of their strength. As he filled each of them, they began to glow radiantly, reflecting their renewed strength.

"I have placed the Third as a power source for you. She is a mighty prayer warrior. Seek her out when you need her," the King offered as they departed.

After they had left, Michael turned to the King.

"You have asked something very difficult of Aegeus." Michael was struggling to understand.

"I have." The King paused. Michael waited.

"When I create my children, I lay out a path for each of them, a perfect plan for their life. But they must learn to listen and hear my voice. They must discover that path and align their lives with my plan. Until they do, they are not who they truly are. In many ways, they are disguised. Aegeus has always known exactly who he was. Since Pas-Dammim, he can no longer understand or connect with the struggle of my children. Until he understands their struggle, he cannot love them."

Michael nodded; it was an unusual situation indeed.

Chapter 4: The Twelfth

The rally point was just over the border between the two states. Aegeus was waiting patiently; he knew how much was at stake. They had agreed to meet at a gas station for the handoff. Sanyi would ensure that the twelfth member would be there. Aegeus looked around at the security detail he had chosen for the day. All warriors disguised in guardian uniforms, fidgeting uneasily.

Aegeus felt the same exposure, a vulnerability that gnawed at him. He tugged at the leather tunic, unable to shake his discomfort. It felt foreign against his skin, a reminder that he was playing a role he did not belong in. Guardians were more empathetic and connected to humans—something Aegeus had deliberately distanced himself from for centuries. His role was to fight with his strength, never his heart. Not anymore. Yet here he was, standing among them, forced into a new identity, and it unnerved him. Every tug at the tunic felt like a tug on something deeper, something he didn't like.

Kfir, as usual, seemed unaffected by the change. As if they were having a dress-up day. But Aegeus had known Kfir for millennia; his pacing and the way he glanced around betrayed his unease as they waited. The summer sun hung high, casting warmth over scattered clouds and a gentle breeze. As Sanyi, guardian of the Twelfth, drew closer, Aegeus could feel his presence approaching.

"Get ready," he called out to the team. "We do this fast and quiet. Any signs of the enemy?"

"Nothing yet," replied Kfir. "I don't think the Twelfth is on their radar."

Just then, Sanyi arrived. His dark hair was cropped closer to his head than Lavi remembered it being the last time they had worked together. Sanyi's facial hair was also shorter, more like a light dusting on his face. His eyes were brooding, but he was not. Lavi stepped forward and offered his friend the traditional greeting of the guardian.

Aegeus turned his attention instead to the car. It was an old family car, wholly unremarkable. Soft drink cans and children's toys fell to the ground as the doors opened in announcement of the occupants' arrival. Aegeus watched as people seemed to pour from the car.

"Which one is it?" Kfir asked.

"The woman," Sanyi answered.

Aegeus, Kfir, and Lavi exchanged glances. None of them had been expecting a woman. A woman. Aegeus couldn't pinpoint why the revelation unsettled him. Perhaps it was the weight of responsibility suddenly feeling heavier. Or perhaps it was something else—a flicker of recognition he wasn't prepared for. Women had always held a unique place in the King's plan, but never had one been thrust into his charge. He felt his heart tighten, an old defense mechanism he had long relied on to keep his distance.

Lavi studied the family closely, his brow wrinkling in recognition.

"Wait…I know them," his voice filled with surprise, drawing Aegeus's full attention.

"Perhaps that is why the King assigned you," Aegeus said more to himself than to Lavi. Aegeus wanted details, but this was not the time —that would have to wait until the Twelfth was safe inside the town.

Lavi checked the car over to ensure there were no unexpected mechanical issues while the family filled the tank, used the restrooms, and walked the dog. Snacks were replenished, and everyone was settled back into the car for the rest of the journey. The entire stop had only taken thirteen minutes. Aegeus gave assignments to the security detail, ensuring they would remain close enough to offer immediate assistance but far enough away to avoid attracting the enemy's attention. Aegeus felt good doing something, returning his mind to the task at hand and not at his discomfort with the uniform or his thoughts about humans.

"Kfir, take the lead until I catch up. You know what is at stake. No mistakes."

"No mistakes, Captain," Kfir assured him as he took the lead in the convoy and then headed east with the Twelfth.

"Sanyi, what is your report?" Aegeus asked when the others had left. Sanyi looked around him and felt the sudden emptiness that always followed handing over his charge. He realized that he missed them already.

"For over a decade, I've guarded the Twelfth and her family, fighting to protect them through every loss and trial. I've come to love them."

Those were precisely the types of feelings Aegeus worked to avoid. How would Sanyi fight against them should the situation change? Would he be able to destroy those he had grown to love if the King demanded it? Would he be able to put his personal feelings aside to do what must be done if circumstances changed? He had long ago learned to separate himself from the humans, he considered it wisdom. Nothing in all of creation mattered more to Aegeus than being in the presence of the King. Love for humans only complicated things, and Aegeus could not reconcile love for humans with unfaltering devotion to the King. He did not respond to Sanyi. He simply waited for what he considered the real report.

"The King has been at work, and she is well prepared. She is tough, Aegeus, but she is tender too," then Sanyi paused, unsure how to continue.

"Aegeus?" Sanyi shuffled a bit, betraying the importance of his words.

"Yes?" Aegeus responded with concern in his voice.

"Aegeus, she has seen me." Sanyi's words hit with a jolt. Aegeus froze, his mind unable to immediately comprehend what Sanyi was saying. This was rare – impossible even. No human could see them unless permitted. Yet, Sanyi's expression was serious, leaving no room for doubt.

"You allowed this?"

"No. She just…. did it."

"I don't understand."

"The enemy was heavy in her neighborhood. One night, when the battle was particularly fierce, it spilled over into her room. She woke up instantly and saw us."

Aegeus tried to make sense of what Sanyi was telling him. Humans could not see them in this form. He could not think of the last time one had been allowed.

"It was just a glance, Aegeus, but it was enough for her to recount the event accurately to her husband the next day. It was as if she could feel our very presence." Sanyi paused, but it was evident he wasn't done.

"There is one more thing you should know." Sanyi paused again because he knew what he was about to tell Aegeus would change everything.

"Yes," Aegeus prompted, wondering what more there could be.

"She has seen the Lamb."

"What do you mean… she has seen the Lamb?" Aegeus's voice was barely a whisper, bewilderment in his eyes as he glanced around them.

"He came to place the mantle upon her, and she woke. She spoke to Him, Aegeus. She spoke to the Lamb." Aegeus felt a rush of concern that he had been separated from the convoy for too long. Surely, the enemy must be aware of her if she had spoken to the Lamb.

"She is a prophet?" was all he managed to say.

"Yes, the King didn't tell you?"

Aegeus, unable to find words, merely shook his head no.

Sanyi paused. "No matter. She doesn't seem to realize it herself yet."

Chapter 5

The convoy reached the house while the morning was still young. The sky was overcast, as it was most days in Platitude. The enemy had moved into the town in such large numbers that their presence muted the sun.

People had gathered to help unload the truck, and Lavi was among them, warmly welcoming each one with words of gratitude and gentle encouragement. His presence seemed to put everyone at ease, his easy laugh blending with theirs as he guided them through the task of moving the truck's contents into the house.

Aegeus couldn't help but notice how the Light of the Twelfth shone brightly, and her husband's too—they seemed to ripple with hope and promise. The warriors observed quietly from the sidelines, their focus slightly shifting as the humans struggled to maneuver a particularly large piece of furniture up a narrow staircase.

Lavi stepped forward. He moved to the front of the group, his hand settling over the Twelfth's with a steady, reassuring warmth.

"Here, I've got it," he murmured as he took the weight from her. His hand pressed gently, not just to lift the physical burden but also to offer comfort through his contact. As he leaned closer to the Twelfth, he added in a low, tender voice, "You are not alone in this."

Aegeus watched closely, his gaze fixed on the woman, eager to see if she showed any sign of perceiving Lavi's words, his support. But she paused only briefly, a flicker of something unspoken in her eyes, before continuing her task, unaware of Lavi's comforting presence.

A faint pang stirred in Aegeus's chest as he observed the interaction. Lavi had a way of connecting with people that Aegeus couldn't fully understand—an unreserved kindness that seemed to flow from him as naturally as breathing. And as he watched Lavi lift the Twelfth's burden, Aegeus felt a fleeting sense of admiration, shadowed by the reminder that, in this realm, Lavi's words went unheard. He wondered what purpose they served.

"She has seen the Lamb," Sanyi had said. The thought lingered in Aegeus's mind. Mortals rarely saw heaven's mysteries. And yet, she had. For a human to have witnessed such glory—it was unheard of. His mind raced. Why her? Why now? Why had the King chosen this woman to bear such a mantle? And why had he been chosen to guard her? Perhaps it was no coincidence. Perhaps this was part of his journey as much as hers. A surge of unease rippled through him; if that were true, then this mission had become far more complex than he had prepared for.

He had served in countless battles and faced enemies no mortal could comprehend, but this? This was different. The word 'prophet' lingered in his mind like an unanswered call. His mind flickered to another mission, another time, a time when he had fought with his heart, and it had almost cost him everything. He wouldn't let that happen again.

He wondered why the King had not mentioned that she was a prophet. Aegeus had not yet mentioned it to the others; he needed time to process it first. Instead, he watched her closely. She smelled of lilac, a fact that made him a little uneasy. She did not seem like a prophet. Perhaps Sanyi had gotten it wrong. That made more sense to Aegeus.

He circled the perimeter of the house—no sign of the enemy. But if the Twelfth were a prophet, it would not be long before the battle began. As the last boxes were unloaded and the family began to settle, Aegeus, his mind on the task ahead, was eager to slip away. At the far northern edge of the mountain range encircling Platitude, there was a small salvage yard full of cars and trucks in various states of decay. The salvage yard sat just outside the town and covered about twenty acres. Humans rarely went there, and as a result, the enemy ignored it completely. Aegeus found the decaying vehicles fascinating. Nothing rotted in heaven, and there was no decay. It was something he only saw while on Earth. He liked to look at each one and consider its story. How did it end up here, neglected and forgotten?

At the back of the property was an aluminum building that, many years ago, had faded to a color that almost wasn't a color. It provided an excellent meeting place. Upon entering the building, he found a small group of warriors and a dozen guardians. Meir and the ministering angels were not there yet. The building was a single room with several giant wooden spools scattered about. Wooden crates also littered the room. The angels arranged the spools as tables and the crates as seats. Kfir and Lavi were sitting on the bench seat from a 1925 Ford T-bucket they had dragged in.

Aegeus cleared his throat and began, "As you know, the Twelfth, the final human, arrived today. Sanyi tells me she has had several years of intense preparation for this task. The training was difficult and involved great loss, but the Spirit is active within her. Because the attacks on her family were so powerful and frequent over those years, she arrives here a little worn down but also full of hope.

"Everyone needs to watch for signs that you need to call in a ministering angel. She does not seem to know what is happening or why she is here. What she knows is that the King has called her to be here. It does not appear she has any idea of why. But it is enough for her. We know that each of the twelve possesses unique gifts that have prepared them for their specific task here. And we know that together, they are an essential part of winning this battle."

Amitiel, a research angel, stood to indicate he wished to speak. Aegeus turned over the floor.

"Many Americans view trials as an indication they are doing something wrong," Amitiel began. "It is quite possible that the Twelfth, and perhaps all of them, will see the last years not for what they were —preparation for this task—but as something else. They may see it as an indication that they were not in alignment with the King's plan. Many of them tell each other that if you feel separated from the King, it is you who have wandered away. We should be sensitive to that."

Aegeus resisted a sigh. He did not understand the King's children. Had they not read the Word? Did they not know of Hezekiah? Had they not learned of Job? He thought he would not be able to understand them even if he tried. Fortunately, understanding them wasn't required.

Lavi leaned forward, his expression earnest.

"It's hard for them, isn't it? Comfort feels like the King's favor to them, but it's their struggles that sharpen their faith." He paused, his gaze softening as it landed on Aegeus.

"We can offer strength, even though they don't see us, even though we are not ministering angels."

Amitiel continued, "It is important that you know some basics about the others because they are all connected even though they do not yet know it; their failures and successes are intertwined. I will walk through them briefly. The First has the gift of wisdom and teaching."

"And how does he use them?" asked Lavi. He knew that while all the children were given gifts, many of them either did not recognize them or did not use them for the King.

"He uses them well," Amitiel answered. "The First and his wife have settled comfortably into the town; The First has found his position in the counseling department at the college to be fulfilling, allowing him to share wisdom and truth with hundreds of hurting students. His wife started a new career as an art curator. Her ministering angel has been working on her, and most of her wounds are healing nicely. However, the arrival of the Strongman will bring unique challenges for them both.

"The Second and the Third work part-time at the college in the department of mission studies. They are acknowledged as people of great faith. They are our primary prayer warriors, and the Third is particularly powerful. If you need to recharge, find them.

The Fourth has done very well in Platitude. Getting him in was tricky because of his divorce, but the Spirit handled that. He is outspoken, which is needed. He is gifted with knowledge and apostleship and has learned to use them well. His colleagues welcome his scientific approach to things, and he is impervious to many of the demons' tactics because he is not easily swayed by emotion.

"The Fifth has the gift of service. But she does not yet know when to say no. She has not learned to listen to the Spirit regarding which opportunities to pursue and which to leave for others. She often overextends herself."

Aegeus was relieved no one had asked additional questions about the Fifth since there was much about her that was unknown, even to him. But what he did know was that her pain ran deep.

Amitiel resumed his report, "The Sixth and the Seventh are best friends. The Sixth has the gift of hospitality and administration. The Seventh has the gift of exhortation, and she uses it very well," he added.

"While I like the idea of them, I don't like the story of the Sixth and Seventh, Aegeus; something seems missing," Kfir said, flipping through the pages of their briefing manual. He looked at Aegeus suspiciously.

Aegeus remained silent—something was missing. The Sixth had a deep secret that she clung to and protected, a source of pain so deep that she had buried it long ago, never daring even to consider it again. But it was not Aegeus's secret to tell, so he remained silent.

"The Eighth," Amitiel continued, "has the gift of compassion. His gift is so powerful that he is often in turmoil. In a way, he can feel the very feelings of those around him. He has had this gift for a long time but has not learned to master it. Often, it masters him. The emotions of those around him often dictate his moods. It can leave him exhausted.

He has found Platitude very difficult. Things have not gone as he had hoped, and his family has started to suffer. Both of his children graduated and moved away to college instead of going to school at the college in the town. His advanced research has required significantly longer hours and more stress. The stress had come home with him, and he began to neglect his wife. He is away from home more than he is there.

"Both regret the decision to move here, and they blame each other. His wife takes frequent trips back to Vermont, where they were from; she stays for longer and longer visits each time.

"The Ninth has the gift of leadership and administration. But she has not yet learned to harness them

"The Tenth has been given a critical job here. One that will determine the overall success of the mission.

Because of her personal experiences, the Eleventh became entirely devoted to women's health issues. She began working in a shelter for battered and abused women. She has cried with many women and shared the love of the Lamb with them in a way only those who have walked the path could understand. Her work with the shelter brought her to the town as a consultant. Once here, they were so impressed they offered her a job."

Done with his report, Amitiel sat down, and Aegeus stood to continue.

"Our first task is to ensure that the twelve encounter each other. We do not interfere beyond necessity - they must have free will and learn to quiet all voices but the King's."

Aegeus paused briefly before continuing. He stood before angels who had served the King for thousands of years and would fully understand the gravity of his next words. He exhaled, a habit he had developed from his limited time around humans. The room quieted; it was unlike Aegeus to hesitate.

"The Twelfth is believed to be a prophet." He could not yet bring himself to declare it. Silence followed, the weight of the words lingering heavily in the room until finally, Lavi spoke.

"Are you sure?" Lavi's voice was quiet, but his expression betrayed a flicker of unease.

"Sanyi was part of the mantle ceremony," Aegeus responded. This caused a slight stir and murmuring among the angels. The responsibility was daunting. Lavi's gaze narrowed.

"Then she must know why she is here," he said.

Aegeus shook his head. "She does not yet know her calling," Aegeus answered. It was unfortunate, but it was the truth. To truly be a prophet, she would have to accept her calling. Lavi nodded slowly, his brows knitting together in thought.

"Prophecy… it can be a lonely burden for a human. If only she knew, perhaps she'd feel more strength, more certainty." His eyes drifted to Aegeus, his words lingering.

"The burdens she carries are many, yet she still moves with such grace. The warmth in his voice showed his empathy for the woman's unseen struggles.

"There is more," Aegeus offered. "She has seen and spoken to the Lamb." That elicited precisely the response he had expected. Excitement rushed into the room, and the electrical charge became palpable. There was to be a great war. This was no ordinary mission.

"How can this be possible? What human can see and speak to the Lamb yet not know they are a prophet?" Kfir asked.

It was a fair question. However, Aegeus knew that as humans had marked off time, many of them had also convinced themselves that prophets no longer existed. Certainly, they were rare, but to deem them obsolete just proved how disconnected humans had become. Some among them further refused to accept that a woman could be a prophet at all, despite the clear evidence in the Word, which Amitiel noted.

Kfir stood to speak. "To recap, this small town is teeming with the enemy. I understand this was previously our territory, but the enemy has been steadily streaming in over the last year, thinking they are undetected. The King has taken significant steps over nearly three years to assemble the twelve.

"Today, the final one has arrived, and we learn she is a prophet. The enemy will learn that, too, Aegeus. Hopefully, she, too, will figure it out in time. But what I know, what we all know, is that this battle will be more than a mere skirmish, perhaps not part of this mission, but a great battle is certainly coming. We are fighting for more than one town. Do we yet know what is happening?

"The King did not mention the prophet or a great war. He told me only that we were to protect the Twelfth. I have no word on the plan other than ensuring the paths of the twelve cross and that there will be the arrival of a Strongman from the enemy," Aegeus answered. "The Strongman will arrive soon.

"We are to protect the twelve from all threats except those allowed by the King for their continued training to make them battle-ready. I want two warriors stationed on the prophet at all times. As long as she remains unaware of her mantle, the enemy may not take notice of her. But once they do, things will escalate.

"Lavi, you said you knew her?" Aegeus prompted, remembering Lavi's comment during the exchange.

Lavi nodded in affirmation. "The Twelfth has many times prayed for additional guardians for her youngest child, which was how I came to be among them. It did not take long on the job to see the reason for her prayers. The child is certainly accident-prone; at least, he was when I was assigned to him. I was an additional guardian to the boy during times of intense prayer from the Twelfth." he murmured, a glimmer of warmth in his eyes. "He was such a small thing then. Fragile but so full of life, always getting into scrapes. It was hard not to smile, watching him stumble and learn. Her prayers for him...they were from the depths of her heart."

Although Lavi found great encouragement in the prayers of the Twelfth, he did not share that detail. He doubted Aegeus would be interested in it since it did not affect the mission. But they had undoubtedly affected Lavi.

Chapter 6

Titus rose to his feet when Morax entered the room.

"Good morning, Titus. I trust everything is moving according to plan?" Titus reached for Morax's hand to offer the customary greeting of the hairless rats—no need to draw attention to themselves.

"Yes, my liege, the Strongman arrives tomorrow." They shook hands and then sat down, Titus on an overstuffed leather chair and Morax in the executive chair behind his oak desk. Titus watched as his commander took a sip of coffee.

"I hate their food," Morax sneered as he put the cup down in distaste. They are horrible creatures. Just look at this body I am forced to wear," he said as he grabbed the handful of extra fat around his waist. "Do I look like the mighty warrior that I am?" he growled with disdain. Titus knew the question was rhetorical, and to answer was to risk his position. He waited patiently for the commander to continue.

"Is he one of ours?" Morax asked, returning to the topic of the Strongman.

"Yes, he is a preacher and a graduate of the seminary we control. He trained under one of our best," Titus offered. The commander stood up and looked out his meager window overlooking the campus. The day was warm, and the air in the room was stale with a slight hint of sulfur.

"Will he be detected?" the commander asked. This was a genuine concern and one they had previously spent much time discussing.

"No, my liege. He is close to the truth in many areas. No one will suspect. But he is one of us, and his position on many things will divide them. He will teach them lies cloaked in truth. He will make them feel isolated and ashamed. His yoke will be so heavy that Depression and Anxiety will be able to take over easily," Titus reassured him.

"And Judgment? We cannot sufficiently castrate them without Judgment and Apathy," the commander reminded him.

"Yes. As you know," Titus began, "the council is meeting now to remove all those with Lights that burn brightly. We are also removing a few of our own, those who were the most distant from the truth and drew too much attention. Those terminations will cause people to be cautious and distrustful and will pave the way for him to speak boldly about restoring truth. He will declare that those who do not walk in Light will not be tolerated and must be removed. He will call on the faithful to watch for those among them who do not walk fully in the Light. He will cause divisions and arguments, and he will sow distrust and fear. He will take a stand on some of the issues we find so easily divide them."

Titus smiled at the thought of it. The rats were so easy to control. Imagine that just a year ago, this town and its Christian college were a threat to them. It had been so simple to erode the foundation. Silence those who had the Light shining brightest and convince the rest to follow the rules. Oh, they loved to tell you how Jesus died to set you free as they chained you to the new rules—their rules. He chuckled to think of it. Yes, this had worked for thousands of years; the rats wanted rules, they lived by the law, and they would die by it.

Morax nodded in agreement with the plan. It was flawless. He had seen lives destroyed over less. He once facilitated the destruction of an entire church using only a disagreement over whether they would sit in pews or stadium seats. The memory of it gave him great pleasure. The rats seemed to worship the Bible over the Creator, yet they appeared to have never read it.

The secret, of course, was to start early, teach them the lies as truth, and perpetuate it for generations. Then, they wouldn't even question it. It had taken years to gain control of some of the seminaries; the Christian universities were proving easier to conquer. One could not argue with the results. Those bearing the title of the King were quick to judge and slow to love, even among themselves. They hid their sins as if they somehow were immune. That served Morax and his team well. Hidden sins festered; they went unchecked, and he and his team were experts at feeding those sins and using them to dim their Lights.

"The Strongman will hire only his own, so the enemy will not be able to bring in anyone else," Titus added.

Before he could elaborate, there was a light knock at the door, and a human opened it as she apologized for the interruption. The council needed the commander. Titus scowled at the rat for the intrusion. Oh, how he hated them. But outwardly, he smiled at her and thanked her for letting him know. Her Light was weak, and watching it flicker with uncertainty pleased him. He was sure that, in time, it would go out.

Chapter 7

Aegeus entered the house as Lavi was running through the tricks he had been teaching the dog of the Twelfth during slow times. Lavi patted the dog's head, smiling at the thought of how the Twelfth had found him—huddled beneath their car in a storm, desperate and alone. He had been living near a movie theater and would come out at night to eat popcorn and candy that he found in the parking lot. Shaking and wet, the soaked puppy had howled out a desperate cry. Now, the little stray had found warmth and love in this home. He was spoiled and loved but not particularly well-trained. Lavi was working on that.

Aegeus lingered just outside the doorway. Lavi crouched down to the dog's eye level, his voice low and playful. "All right, my little friend, let's show Aegeus what you've got." He grinned, ruffling the dog's fur, his touch both firm and tender. "Sit!" he commanded cheerfully. The dog obeyed immediately, tail wagging.

"Good boy," Lavi murmured, his voice softening as he rubbed the dog's head. "You're learning so quickly." He paused for a moment, leaning closer. "It's a lot, I know." There was warmth in Lavi's gaze, a kindness that seemed to pass between him and the dog as if the little creature could understand every word.

"Now, play dead!" Lavi commanded with exaggerated enthusiasm. The dog flopped to the floor, legs splayed in mock defeat, tongue lolling comically to the side. Lavi laughed, a sound as genuine as the light in his eyes.

"Perfect!" he said, clapping softly, his joy evident. Nearly as impressive was that Lavi had taught the dog to freeze in place when commanded, "Stop." From the doorway, Aegeus watched the interaction, a faint smile tugging at his lips. There was an ease about Lavi, an affection that flowed naturally, even in these small moments. It was a gentleness Aegeus had seen many times yet never quite understood. But it was a big part of why they had become friends.

Aegeus joined Lavi in the living room, sitting on the wooden floor beside him. He handed Lavi a cup of wine and a slice of honey bread spread with jam from heaven. Lavi accepted both with a smile. The bread was tender and seemed to disintegrate in his mouth. The jam was sweet and fresh, and the smell teased his taste buds.

"Do you remember Bethlehem?" Lavi asked suddenly, breaking the stillness. Aegeus nodded slowly, a rare smile tugging at the corner of his mouth.

"We never did finish that breakfast," Lavi chuckled. It had been many years since Aegeus had thought about when Lavi had been guardian to Mary. The battle around her was fierce once the enemy discovered that she carried the Lamb, and Aegeus had been called in as part of her security detail. Aegeus and Lavi became instant friends. They had been sharing a meal like this while the holy family slept when an archangel suddenly came to Joseph, telling him to take Mary and the Lamb to Egypt. Breakfast had been forgotten.

Today, the two angels enjoyed a quiet morning, savoring their meal and reminiscing about old times. After breakfast, they wandered outside and sat in the oversized wicker chairs on the wraparound porch to watch the sunrise, a sight that never got old. As they watched the sunrise, Lavi's gaze softened.

"Time's so different here, isn't it? Measured, counted," he mused, as if speaking to himself. "But this moment... it feels endless, like home." The sun did not rise or set in heaven. There was no sun; there was no need for such things because there was no night in heaven, no end to the days.

While angels did not measure time in heaven, they measured their joy at seeing the King's beautiful creation. The King regularly changed the fruit on the trees, the colors of the flowers or sky, and the landscape outside the city. Angels often referred to how many variations they had seen between missions in one of these areas. It was a measurement of the pleasure and joy of watching the King in his creativity. There was no true human equivalent, but it occurred to Lavi that watching this incredible display of the sun was the closest thing humans had, and watching the beauty of a sunrise was something the angels loved to do when they were on Earth. The beauty and artistry of it reminded them of the King. Twice a day, he painted the sky with beautiful colors at sunrise and sunset—no two were ever the same. The sunrise was breathtaking here in the town, with the mountains as the backdrop. The earth was still and quiet at this hour. The birds were just starting to move about and sing their morning song.

Eventually, the sun fully rose, and the conversation turned to the events scheduled for the day. The Twelfth was to meet the Tenth for lunch. The Tenth was the vice president of human resources, and he wanted to welcome her to the community. Lunch was planned for the one local restaurant. It was a small shop just two blocks from the town's main street. Aegeus and Kfir had done a sweep of the area the day before to get a feel for what it was like. They did not anticipate any problems.

It wasn't long before the family was awake, and the house exploded into motion. One of the children was banging on the bathroom door, yelling at the other one to hurry up. The dog was barking and jumping about at the sound of knocking. He ran to and from the front door, clearly confused about where the sound was coming from. Lavi and Aegeus stood near the door, watching the scene unfold. Aegeus stood still, his eyes scanning the bustling scene. Children were a mystery to him, the noise, the unpredictability. But Lavi, he noticed, seemed to thrive in it. He was smiling, his eyes alight with amusement. Aegeus couldn't help but wonder how his friend found joy in such chaos.

In time, the tiny war escalated, and the child in the bathroom opened the door and yelled, "Stop it," at the younger child. While the command had little to no effect on the younger child, the dog froze in mid-movement. Not so much as a whisker flinched. He stood with one leg off the ground and bent mid-stride. The children also stopped then and looked at the dog, baffled by his stance.

"Maybe he's having a seizure," one of them offered. Lavi slapped Aegeus on the back as they laughed.

.

Chapter 8

After settling things down in the house and returning to their version of normal, the Twelfth walked to the restaurant. It was about two miles from her home. Her angels walked just behind her. It was strange to be able to walk everywhere, and she tried to appreciate it. She truly valued the time alone, the peace and tranquility of the walk. She wore her earbuds and put the music on her iPhone on shuffle. It gave her time to think, to plan for her upcoming classes, and to pray. And it discouraged well-intentioned strangers from talking to her. Today, she found she had much to discuss with God, so she prayed nearly all the way there.

As the Twelfth approached the restaurant, her Light seemed to radiate even brighter, as if sensing the importance of this meeting. She stepped inside, taking in the cozy atmosphere—the stone fireplace to her right, the wood floors softened by oriental rugs, and the warm scent of coffee in the air. For a moment, it almost felt like a mountain lodge. The building had high-angled ceilings that reached a steep peak at the top. The entire backside was windowed, overlooking the brook that ran through the town. The back faced a drop-off, giving the impression that the restaurant was floating.

Large, oversized chairs were scattered about on one side, and the tables looked like they had been made from wine barrels.

The other side had traditional restaurant-style tables and chairs. A small stage for live entertainment or poetry readings was on the front wall. The Twelfth loved it instantly.

The Tenth had already selected seats on the side with oversized chairs. The Twelfth was pleased; it was what she would have picked. The Tenth stood to attract her attention, and she joined him at the table, shaking his hand before sitting down. The chair was painfully comfortable, and she had to fight the urge to remove her shoes and curl up. As she settled in, her Light flared brightly, filling the room. Kfir closed his eyes and soaked in the power of the King.

"Aegeus?" Kfir asked quietly, his gaze never leaving the Twelfth. Aegeus felt a twinge of unease. He wasn't used to uncertainty; in battle, he always knew his next move. As the Twelfth's Light flared unpredictably, he found himself on unfamiliar ground.

"I don't know," he admitted, the words sour and foreign in his mouth. He hated not knowing. The Twelfth shifted uncomfortably in her chair, but otherwise, she did not indicate that anything had happened. She chatted with the Tenth easily about moving, preparing for classes, and her family. Lavi leaned in, his eyes soft with understanding. He could sense the weight of the message pressing on the Twelfth and wished he could ease her burden, even if just a little.

"You're braver than you know," he murmured under his breath, knowing his words would never be heard. He longed to help her, to truly know her struggles, but all he could do was watch and hope. Aegeus watched. The Light again flared brightly in her. Something was happening. She squirmed in her seat and glanced toward heaven, but her conversation did not falter.

Kfir stepped closer. He looked around the room to see if the flares of Light had brought additional demons. So far, it had not. He felt a sense of excitement, the feeling you get when riding a roller coaster and you get to the top of a significant incline. You know the drop is coming, and of course, the drop is the whole reason you rode the coaster, but those few seconds in anticipation of something great just before you start the descent are precious and not to be overlooked.

The Twelfth seemed to grow more distracted, but she smiled and nodded as the Tenth spoke. Finally, as if giving in to a highly distasteful task, the Twelfth took a deep breath. The angels leaned in with anticipation. Aegeus caught himself holding his breath and waiting. He chastised himself for getting so drawn in and started trying to distance himself, once again focusing solely on the mission.

She hesitated, her fingers trembling slightly as she took another deep breath. "Sometimes, God tells me things," she began, her voice barely above a whisper. She felt the heat of her own Light intensify, crackling in the air around her. "And right now," she continued slowly, "he is telling me to tell you something."

She paused so as not to say it so quickly that she looked more like a freak than she was sure she already did. He was the head of human resources, for goodness' sake, and she had only met him one other time during one of her interviews. She was sure he would think she was certifiable.

"Okay, well, let's have it," he said. The Twelfth was stunned by his nonchalance. She wasn't sure what she was expecting, perhaps something more like him backing from the room with eyes wide and finger-pointing. She sighed.

"I don't think you are going to like it. It doesn't seem positive," she explained.

He sat quietly, looking at her expectantly. She sighed again, then decided it was best just to plow through.

"You are embedded with a holy passion like Phinehas, son of Eleazar. Like Phinehas, you will need courage and strength to carry out God's task for you, but so far, you have taken the safe route. You must be bold, not just for your purpose but for God's. You have a sin that has mastered you, but you must master it; otherwise, you will never confront the spreading plague."

With the message delivered, she sat uncomfortably, staring down at her lap. Her Light caused the air to crackle with the power of heaven. The angels looked at each other pleased. Kfir danced about in sheer joy.

The Light of the Tenth also burned brightly. His heart tightened as she said—Phinehas. The name struck a chord too familiar, too close. He swallowed hard, willing his face to remain impassive. On the outside, he sat calmly, looking at the Twelfth. He noted she was utterly unimpressive to look at. Her hair was a dull shade of brown. She was not particularly attractive. She was a person you would walk right past and never notice. She was bright but not brilliant. There was nothing remarkable about her, with one small exception. She had a quality that made you immediately feel comfortable with her. He couldn't explain it, but he certainly had noticed it during her interview.

During the interview, she had been honest and sincere. She was polished without seeming practiced. She had no sense of pretense, and she spoke to the interview team as if they had all been friends for years and were merely having lunch together—all while maintaining a professionalism that could not be questioned. He had been impressed; all of them had been captivated by it, lured in. Some shared personal information with her that had not been shared before. It alarmed him, and thus, he secretly feared her.

A power such as that—something that made people feel comfortable enough with you to share their secrets—could be dangerous. What if he slipped? He had decided right then to avoid her as much as possible. He could not afford to let his secret get out. He was making a fresh start; things were going so well. People wouldn't understand; he would be fired, and his family would be humiliated. Thankfully, her office would be far from his, and there was no reason for their paths to cross again other than this one obligatory lunch. Now here they were sitting in this restaurant, and she knew things she should not. He had not even had to reveal his secrets for her to know them. He pondered the idea that God had told her this message, then concluded that there was no other explanation. How else could she have known about the Phinehas thing? She looked very uncomfortable as she waited for him to respond. He felt sorry for her, but he also wanted to get away from her—and quickly.

"Who is my Goliath?" he asked her.

She looked up, startled and a little confused. "Your Goliath?"

"Yes, who is my Goliath? You know, the person I will stand against. Will anyone stand with me?"

"I don't know," she paused to consider his question. He appeared genuinely disappointed that she didn't seem to know. She appeared equally disappointed.

"Phinehas stood alone. I don't know what it means, but I believe you do."

He couldn't afford to let her see the truth—not here, not now. The truth was, he knew exactly what it meant, but he did not intend to tell her that. She sat painfully still, obviously feeling uncomfortable.

The Tenth eased the conversation back to safer ground until he could end the lunch without it being awkward. When the time came, the Twelfth put her earbuds in and started the long walk home, arguing with God all the way there. Lavi walked beside her, his steps light, a proud smile lingering on his face. He marveled at her courage, his heart swelling with hope. Kfir practically bounced, unable to contain his excitement. But Aegeus remained a few paces behind, his eyes scanning the surroundings, his mind focused on potential threats. The battle was only beginning.

Chapter 9: The Tenth

The Tenth leaned over the edge of the bed, feeling sick. He honestly thought he might vomit. He looked back over his shoulder at the woman in the bed. She was beautiful. Even with her hair disheveled and her makeup smeared, she was beautiful. They all were. That was the problem. He gathered his clothes from around the room, dressing as quickly as possible. He suddenly felt the need to escape, to run from the room and never look back. She woke up as he turned the knob to leave.

"You're leaving," she muttered in a sleepy voice.

"I have to; I have a meeting." He smiled at her to cover the regret.

"When will I see you again?" she asked, concern starting to pepper her voice.

"Soon," was all he could muster as he left the room and headed to his van. When he pulled into his parking space at work, his wife was there waiting. She did not greet him; she merely launched into complaints about the traffic, a strange sound the car was making, and something their son had done that morning.

He wasn't sure he had heard her correctly, but if so, their son had eaten his cereal with Coke in the bowl instead of milk. He wanted to laugh, but he knew his wife would not see the humor in it. She didn't see the humor in anything these days. He looked at her as they walked across the parking lot toward his office. He had no idea what she was talking about, but he let her prattle on because it required less of him.

They met when he was in graduate school at Cornell, working on his MBA in human resources. She was one of the few women in the engineering program. They dated for two years before he proposed. One night, when they were celebrating the end of finals, things had gotten a bit out of control. They were already engaged, so he didn't see the big deal in having sex a few months early. At the time, she had agreed.

But the next morning, he awoke to find that her heart had changed. She regretted what they had done, and she blamed him for it. She was angry—angrier than he had ever seen her. She cried, she screamed, she threw things, she called him names. He sat naked on the bed, too shocked to speak. Eventually, he tried to comfort her, but there was no comfort to be had. She was so ashamed and filled with regret that she did not want a wedding. They went away for a long weekend and eloped. That was twenty-five years ago.

His wife had never gotten over what she considered to be a betrayal. She had become someone different than the woman he had known and fallen in love with. They had one child, whom she adored. But after she had their son, marital relations had ended. She had gained weight with the pregnancy, and she didn't feel beautiful or desired anymore. He agreed. The affairs began five years later.

Each time, he hated himself for what he had done. He didn't want to want other women. He didn't want to have affairs. He wanted his wife to be the woman he had met and fallen in love with, but that woman was long gone. He told himself he deserved an award for all the women he had not had an affair with but could have. In his darkest moments, he told himself he was justified. But if he was justified, why did he feel so sick?

For many years, his shame had kept him from the church. He couldn't bring himself to sit among the righteous. What if they learned of his secret? His wife did not understand why he wouldn't go to church with her, but she continued to go faithfully. He often wondered why.

But his heart yearned for communion with the saints. He never ceased communing with God. He prayed fervently, repeatedly asking for forgiveness, yet never feeling forgiven. He begged God to remove these desires from him, to help him desire his wife. Sometimes, it worked; sometimes, he would make it a year before slipping again. Then, his guilt and shame would be renewed. But never, in all those years, had his relationship with his wife improved. He stayed with her only to fulfill his commitment to God. He didn't like her and was no longer attracted to her.

When they arrived at his desk, he turned to look at her. For just a moment, his eyes were opened to see her for who she was. She looked sad. Rejected. Like a woman who was trying not to notice that her husband had affairs. She looked like a woman who knew she was unloved by her husband. The truth of it was overwhelming.

"Let's move," he blurted out before he realized what he was saying.

"What?" Understandably, the suggestion shocked her.

"Let's move; start over. It would be nice to get a fresh start." He pushed on. At that moment, he wanted nothing more than a fresh start. A place where none of their history existed. Where they could be new, he knew he sounded crazy, perhaps even frantic, but he wanted so desperately to be free of his past, of their past. His eyes looked at her longingly.

"Sure, let's move; that will fix everything." The sarcasm dripped from her lips. Hatred stained her face, but in her eyes, he saw hope. Her eyes reflected all the sadness of the years and yearning for things to be better. In her eyes, he saw his feelings. He walked toward her and took her hands in his. Shock registered on her face; it was the first time he had touched her in years.

"I think this would work. We could start over." He was sincere, his eyes pleading with her.

"I just came here to trade cars with you. I need the van. As far as moving, you do what you think is best." She pulled her hands from his and stepped back from him, suppressing the sudden flood of emotions that she felt. She did not trust him. She hadn't trusted him for many years, and she doubted he would do what was best for her. She couldn't remember the last time he had.

He understood, but it hurt just the same. She extended her hand for the keys. He handed her the van keys, and she left.

"Are you coming to the meeting?" his secretary stuck her head in his door.

"Yes, sorry I'm running late." He forced a smile and followed her into the conference room. He entered the room to find it full of middle-aged men in suits and one woman. The woman had wild red hair pulled into a tight bun, giving her the look of a librarian. She wore stylish glasses that almost hid her green eyes. Being the only woman in the room made her stand out. Having red hair sealed the deal.

He greeted everyone and sat down to begin the meeting. The woman did not speak, but she looked at him in a way that made him feel uncomfortable, as if she knew him and the secrets he hid. It was not condemning. On the contrary, she exuded a gentle, warm feeling. But it was as if she could see his very soul. As the meeting was nearing its end, she finally spoke.

"The landscape is shifting around us. Continuing to do the same thing you have done will not bring new results—only disappointment. You have been given unique gifts that should be used wisely. But like Phinehas, to stop the plague, you must first have courage; you must stand up and intervene. You must confront Goliath. Identify your Goliath. Then, you can begin to make progress. Like Moses, you will need help. Your Aaron will meet you along the path, but when the time comes, you must stand alone."

She spoke with such authority that it made the Tenth question everything that had been said during the meeting. It made him question himself and his very direction in life. He felt a sense of joy to have even heard her words as if they were spun from gold. But the context was so odd that he needed a moment to consider it and delve into the philosophy behind it. He felt like she was speaking directly to him. No one else in the room even looked at her as she spoke. They did not respond. The meeting ended.

The woman rose from her chair and walked purposefully from the room. The Tenth tried to follow her, but one of the men in the meeting stopped him to ask a question. The delay was long enough that she was gone when he left the room.

"So, this is how she brought him to Platitude?" Lavi was curious about the Tenth, the angels knew him to be the one who was to eventually challenge the Strongman.

"Yes. The seed was laid. His cousin is the Eighth. When the position for VP came open, the Spirit led the Eighth to recommend him. The timing was right, and he readily accepted." Aegeus answered.

"I see the sin the enemy has found for him. Remind me of his gift?" Kfir asked.

"Knowledge and teaching. He has excellent insight into the Word. But Shame covers him, and so he rarely shares his knowledge.

Lust has been with him since adolescence. He clings to it, both despising it and keeping it close.

"I once had a charge in Persia who found a baby tiger. The tiger did not know its own strength and often would hurt him. The man clung to the tiger. It grew, and his injuries became greater, and yet he would not let it go. Eventually, famine came to the land, and the tiger devoured him." Lavi looked at the others with a sense of understanding.

"You let your charge get eaten by a tiger? What kind of guardian are you?" Kfir laughed a deep, roaring laughter that made Aegeus laugh, too.

"You miss my point!" Lavi laughed, giving Kfir a gentle brotherly shove.

"Oh, I heard your point; the Twelfth is doomed!"

"Only if she gets a tiger," Lavi countered.

Chapter 10

As the Twelfth stepped outside, the sweet scent of honeysuckle wrapped around her like a warm embrace, offering a moment of calm amid the lingering chaos inside. The summer air was warm, with the promise of a cool, cricket-filled night to come. The old Victorian, still packed with half-open boxes, felt more like a storage unit than a home. From within, the children's shouts echoed off the half-painted walls.

"Mom, where's my superhero cape?" one of them called out, rummaging through a box labeled *kitchen*. The Twelfth shook her head with a tired smile. "We'll find it... eventually," she muttered, knowing it was probably buried beneath winter coats. The kids, brimming with energy but lacking friends and familiar routines, darted from room to room in search of something—anything—to hold their interest.

The house was old and desperately needed renovation, but a fresh coat of paint would have to do for now. The Twelfth was determined to get the youngest child's room unpacked. She haphazardly pulled her hair into a ridiculous excuse of a bun with random pieces sticking out in most directions. The kids had camped out in the den, the only room that wasn't giving birth to boxes. She decided to let them sleep in.

"Coffee?" Her husband asked, handing her a hot cup as she stood in the doorway to the youngest child's room.

"You are so good to me." She let out a sigh as she took the cup from him. *How did I get so lucky?* she thought as she gently sipped the coffee.

"What's on your list for today?" he asked.

"I thought we would paint this room and get it unpacked. The boxes are driving me crazy. I can't stand it." She took another sip of coffee. "I am so thankful that God made the coffee bean. Specifically, the ones used to brew this very cup," she added, smiling.

Aegeus and Lavi looked at one another in amusement. Aegeus could not recall ever having encountered a charge quite like her; of course, he had never been assigned to a prophet before. He thought fleetingly that if she were a prophet, there would be little chance he would ever have to fight against her. But he shook the thought from his mind almost immediately—there was great danger in becoming connected to humans.

"Let me go get a drop cloth and the painting supplies. You work on moving these boxes out of here so we can get in the room," her husband directed, then left to retrieve the necessary supplies.

"And where exactly do I put these boxes? In the yard?" she called after him, adding a mock-serious tone to soften the complaint.

"You'll figure it out!" he called back. Before she had moved many boxes, her husband returned without any painting supplies.

"The welcoming committee is here," he whispered to her.

"What?" she whispered back, not knowing why she was whispering.

"Neighbors. Come on." He had that desperate look he got. Meeting new people was not one of his favorite things to do.

"Look at me! I look like a raccoon who lost a wrestling match," she whispered, glancing down at her paint-splattered clothes.

"Perfect first impression, don't you think?" she whispered, gesturing to her disheveled appearance. He shrugged, pushing her toward the back door and laughing.

The Twelfth opened the door to an older couple standing there, beaming warmly. "We brought you something," the woman said, holding out a picnic basket filled with lunch, snacks, and the comforting smell of homemade bread. The Twelfth blinked, momentarily overwhelmed by the gesture.

"Wow, thank you," she managed, her smile widening despite her disheveled appearance.

Kfir had gone to do a patrol, but Aegeus and Lavi followed the Twelfth to the door. Aegeus, dressed in the traditional guardians' uniform, mostly leather coverings and arm guards—arrived first.

"Voog, guardian of the King, sent to the earth to oversee his children." Voog, the guardian of the Second and the Third, stepped forward, extending his hand to Aegeus and offering the traditional greeting of the guardians. Aegeus stood befuddled for a moment.

"You are not a guardian; you have no ring," Voog assessed quickly.

Aegeus glanced down and realized he did not have the stand-in osmium signet ring, an essential part of the uniform. It, of course, was not the real thing; he was not a real guardian, and therefore, the King had not bestowed upon him the true version of the ring, but the one he had been given would have passed as long as no one looked too closely. That is, if he had remembered to put it on. Aegeus stood awkwardly for a moment, unsure of what to do.

"Lavi, Holy is the King." Lavi stepped forward, extending his hand to complete the traditional greeting.

Voog accepted the greeting from Lavi but looked more closely at Aegeus. "You are a warrior," he said in astonishment and confusion. Aegeus shifted in discomfort.

"It is that obvious?"

"You are covered in the markings of a warrior," Voog said as he stepped back to look more closely.

"Wait…. Aegeus?" Voog questioned after a moment more. Upon recognizing Aegeus, he erupted in laughter. "Aegeus, if you are to pass as a guardian, we must work on your greeting. And your uniform—look at you," he chuckled. While Aegeus and Voog had not previously met face to face, Voog knew of Aegeus—most angels did.

"You should see Kfir," Aegeus offered in a desperate attempt to deflect the attention from himself.

"Kfir as a guardian? Next, you'll tell me I'm meant to wear a tutu," Voog roared, slapping Aegeus on the back.

"We've all got our roles, and Kfir's just isn't 'blending in.'"

Voog had served in Africa many times and knew Kfir well.

"He is on patrol, but you must be sure to see him as a guardian when he returns." Aegeus smiled. Voog was right: warriors did not make good guardians. The leather tunic chafed at his shoulders; it felt binding to Aegeus, as if the uniform itself rejected him, a constant reminder that he was playing a role not meant for him. He felt like an imposter. As others discovered the truth, he felt embarrassed and awkward. The King had created him to be a warrior. Anything else was an identity that was not his own. It was confining both physically and mentally.

Aegeus was happy to turn their attention back to the humans whose Lights were gradually burning more brightly. The Light in the Twelfth now burned bright enough that she was emitting gentle currents that the angels could feel the power of the King. Aegeus looked at her. He suspected the Twelfth must be offering praise to the King—which would explain the Light.

"I hear she is a prophet?" Voog asked, hope tainting his question.

"We hear that as well, but we have not seen the evidence ourselves." Aegeus tried to sound matter of fact; he was not yet ready to declare the prophet. One message was not enough for Aegeus to be sure. Besides, she was not a prophet until she realized it herself. He wondered how long she would wear the wrong uniform before the discomfort of it caused her to be who she truly was.

"We would love to have you stop by," the Third said. The dog, who had been sniffing the Third with great interest, suddenly froze. The Twelfth noticed immediately. She tried not to be distracted from the conversation, but seeing the dog standing there frozen was bizarre.

"We should be going, dear," the Second offered as the men, who had wandered out to the garage, rejoined the Third and Twelfth. He, too, noticed the dog, but he tried not to draw attention to the bizarre sight. "They have lots to do; we don't want to keep them." He gently placed his hand on her lower back, directing her toward the door. His wife had never met a stranger. He knew her well, and she would undoubtedly spend the day communing with the Twelfth if left to her own devices.

The Second and Third returned to their home, and the Twelfth and her husband climbed the stairs to resume painting.

"They were so kind, weren't they? I loved them." The Twelfth had a smile on her face and a prayer of thanksgiving in her heart as she climbed the stairs.

"I could tell," her husband offered, pleased to see her happy again after the trials of the last two years.

"How incredibly kind of them to bring that basket." She was a bit overwhelmed by it. "I am never going to fit in here," she lamented.

"You just did," he offered in reassurance.

"No, I mean, I am not that thoughtful. If everyone here is that 'good,' I will stand out as not belonging."

Doubt, attracted to the home by the Light of the Twelfth, slithered up through the floor, his dark fingers wrapping around her ankle. He began clamoring up her leg, moving like a lizard toward her head before he noticed Aegeus and Lavi. When he saw them, he froze, a bit startled.

Aegeus's hand instinctively reached for his weapon, but Lavi's warning gaze stopped him. A gaze that said *that is not how guardians do it.*

Before the darkness could take root, the husband of the Twelfth walked over to her and wrapped her in his arms, trapping the demon between them. He leaned down and kissed the top of her head.

"They are going to love you. You'll see." He kissed her gently again. "Now, let's get this painting done." The Twelfth smiled, grabbed a paint roller, and said a quick prayer that sent the demon flying from her.

Aegeus laughed at the sight of the demon being shot from her body by a burst of the Light.

Lavi placed a gentle hand on Aegeus's shoulder, his voice warm but firm.

"You know, Aegeus, guardians protect with presence as much as with weapons. Try to hold back, even if it feels strange. if you are to pass as a guardian, you must act as a guardian," Lavi offered in gentle correction.

"Acting like one is the problem," Aegeus said, shifting uncomfortably in his borrowed uniform. Aegeus did not want to pass as a guardian—it was not who he was—but he accepted the correction, acknowledging it was the task the King had given him.

Just then, Kfir burst through the door, his face lit with anticipation. "Did I miss any paint disasters? Or did Aegeus accidentally smile again?" he teased, earning a playful glare from Aegeus.

"The Second and the Third dropped by," Lavi offered.

"And I think they may have noticed something odd about the dog," Aegeus laughed.

Chapter 11: The Second and the Third

The Second and Third arrived at the town together. They had met and fallen in love in the sixties. They were married in 1969 and left for the mission field in 1972. They had traveled to more than seventy countries in their work. The Third gave birth to three children: two sons and a daughter.

Over the years, their children grew up and moved back to the States, pursuing their own lives and having their own children. Their oldest son became an architect, the second son was a linguist, and their daughter had heard the call to ministry. She began speaking in churches in her twenties and was now regularly invited to speak to those of faith around the world. She was not a preacher—she did not shepherd a church—but her choice to speak in churches was often met with criticism and reprimand. She knew she had been called on this path, but knowing in no way made it easy. She frequently prayed that God would call someone else, but she loved his people and longed to encourage them with his words.

Four years before moving to Platitude, the Second and the Third served in the Middle East. Terrorists raided their village one night to rid it of all Christians. They were dragged from their home, and the Third was shot in front of her husband and left for dead. The Second was bound and taken into captivity.

The Third had been found in a mass grave, clinging to life. She was stabilized and flown back to the United States, where she spent a year recovering. She prayed that her husband would be found alive. Four months into her recovery, the first video of him emerged. He was blindfolded and wearing an orange jumpsuit—beaten, frail, and thin, but he was alive.

She began to pray more diligently for his protection and God's provision. When she recovered enough to move around the hospital, she regularly visited the chapel and organized prayer warriors, who each committed to praying for five minutes daily. Soon, she had enough people that someone was praying for the Second every minute of every day.

After eighteen months, on a beautiful spring day, the Third was working in her garden when she heard a knock on the door. There had been a raid on the captors to rescue several hostages, including her husband. During the attack, one of the attackers had attempted to kill the Second, slicing his throat. First responders had been able to save his life, but they were not sure of his prognosis.

Waiting for his return to American soil had been difficult. Then, she was not allowed to see him for some time after his arrival. He required numerous surgeries. His condition was critical, and he was not expected to live. But the Third had come too far to give up hope now. She would stand outside his room and, placing her hand on his door, pray until God saw fit to let her in the room. Day and night, she prayed. She thanked God for getting them both this far.

She thanked him for bringing her husband home even if he had been brought home to die.

The day finally came when she was allowed in to see him. The Third stood over his frail body, and her foundation was shaken. He weighed just ninety-eight pounds. He still had bruises, and his body was covered in scars. His head looked as if it had been cut off and sewn back onto his body. She placed her hand over his and prayed for forgiveness for the hatred she felt toward those who had done this. She prayed for their souls. When she finished praying, she stepped out of the room and let herself cry.

Months passed, and the Second began to regain his strength. Shortly before he was released, he and the Third planned a short visit to the hospital garden for a little fresh air.

The Third had pushed his wheelchair around the hospital, and they had been laughing at their apparent state of going in circles.

"Do you need some help?" a woman asked, her wild red hair escaping from the clasp she had used to pull it back.

"We're trying to find the garden," said the Second.

"Ah, yes, so many are searching for the garden. I'm going that way; I am happy to show you," she offered, her green eyes sparkling. The three of them chatted as they made their way to the garden. The Second and the Third talked easily with her about their experiences.

"Our histories are so interesting," observed the woman. "But more important is where we are right now and where we are going. What will you do now?" she asked, her hair further slipping from the clip.

"Oh, we're retiring," offered the Third. "We are headed to Florida as soon as he is released."

After settling them in the garden, the woman went farther into a more secluded spot, and they did not see her again. They sat comfortably in the garden, enjoying the sun and each other. As the warmth of day gave way to the cool of night, they decided they should begin their journey back inside to the Second's room. As the Third pushed the wheelchair back toward the hospital doors, she ran over something, and the wheel stuck. Bending down, she picked up a small broken hairclip engraved with the name of a college that was hidden in the mountains, in the middle of nowhere.

Chapter 12

Days turned into weeks, and summer seemed to fly by while the boxes remained stubbornly stacked. The house was still a maze, each unopened box a reminder of how little she'd accomplished. The Twelfth stared at a lopsided shelf, trying in vain to make it fit against the wall. She sighed, pushing a stray lock of hair behind her ear.

"Nothing in this house makes sense," she muttered. The couch was too big for the living room, and the kitchen table wobbled on the old wooden floorboards. She wondered, not for the first time, why she hadn't just sold everything and started over. She sat on the floor in what would one day be the living room, surrounded by boxes and covered in random dirt she couldn't quite identify. Her husband had already started his new job, so she was on her own to get the house back together. Perhaps trying to paint before unpacking was a bad idea. She had lost her steam, so she poured herself a large cup of coffee and plopped down onto the floor. She sat thinking about nothing in particular.

"Aegeus, she has been sitting on the floor for over an hour. We are warriors, not sitters. Where is the battle?" Kfir lamented. "Lavi, how do you do this?"

Lavi had been leaning against the wall, staring out the window and dreaming of heaven. He looked over at Kfir and smiled. He could only imagine how difficult this must be for Aegeus and Kfir. They were accustomed to more action.

"We have done our job well," Aegeus answered.

"Is there nothing we can do to get her moving? What would Meir do?" Kfir pondered.

"Meir would walk in, put her hands on her, and the Twelfth would get up and solve world hunger," Aegeus offered with a chuckle.

"That's true, that's true." Kfir nodded consent.

"Why don't you get her husband? Bring him home, and we will see if we can get her going again," Lavi suggested to Kfir.

"How am I supposed to get him here?" Kfir questioned.

"Be creative." Lavi smiled at him.

Kfir looked at Aegeus; his eyebrows raised in question. Aegeus nodded his agreement. Kfir flew from the room, happy to have a task. Aegeus busied himself with once again patrolling the perimeter.

Lavi sank to the floor beside the Twelfth, watching her with quiet compassion. He could almost feel the heaviness in her heart, a tiredness that seemed deeper than mere exhaustion.

"What happened to the fire in you?" he whispered, wishing his words could reach her, could remind her of the strength he once saw blazing so brightly. It had been several years since he first met her. She had changed. Age had been kind to her skin, but her hair was streaked with hints of gray. The years had added a few pounds to her. But there was something else, something more profound. When Lavi had met her before, she had had such fire, such passion. Now, she seemed worn and tired. She wore it like an undergarment, something no one was meant to see, but it was there all the same. Lavi watched her with a longing he couldn't quite explain. How he wished he could do more than guard and observe. But that wasn't his role. He wondered, not for the first time if perhaps this mission was meant to teach him as much as it was to protect her.

"What happened?" he asked her again as if she could hear him. She sighed deeply in response.

"God, where are you?" Her voice cracked, the words raw and unexpected. The suddenness of it startled Lavi.

"Why aren't you here?" She leaned back against the wall. Lavi's heart clenched at the sound, and he wished, more than anything, that she could feel the presence surrounding her. The air seemed to thicken with her desperation, each word carrying a quiet power.

Lavi laid his hand on hers. He wanted so desperately to let her know that the King was there; he was always there. He wanted her to know that the King had sent an entire team to care for her. He hated that she felt alone. At the same time, he was glad that Aegeus and Kfir were not here to hear her; it would discourage them to hear her thoughts.

"I felt so sure you were sending us here, but since we got here, I can no longer feel you. Did we do the wrong thing? Did I bring my family here outside of your will? Because right now, this feels like one long, messy mistake." She spoke into the room. The room filled with her prayer crackling in power and Lavi soaked that aspect of it in. If only she knew how much the King was with her, if only she could understand how many were working together for her good.

"Looks like you're making progress," her husband's voice cut through the silence. She jumped slightly, startled by his sudden arrival, but quickly replaced her frown with a tired smile. She was pleasantly surprised.

"You're home!" She got up from the floor and hugged him. Reality struck her, and she stepped back, perplexed, "Why are you home?"

"Some kind of fluke power outage. The whole block lost power, so they sent us home."

"That's great!" she said, her tired eyes lighting up.

"You can help me paint." But the thought of more work made her shoulders sag, and her face fell at the thought of it.

He took her hands in his and smiled. "I got a free pass; let's not paint. Let's sit on the back porch and pretend we're on vacation," he suggested, his grin contagious.

"I'll even burn the hot dogs for that authentic 'camping trip' vibe." She laughed, the sound a welcome break from the day's weariness.

"Deal," she agreed, already feeling lighter. "I like the way you think."

"Power outage?" Lavi asked Kfir.

"He's here, isn't he?" Kfir said with a smile. Aegeus returned from the perimeter sweep.

"She's up." He said, obviously pleased.

"They are having something called a barbecue," Kfir offered. "The Twelfth seems pleased by this."

"Excellent. Now, see if you can get the First here," Aegeus directed Kfir. Kfir raised his eyes in alarm.

"You know I'm a warrior, right?" Kfir asked, a sly smile on his face.

"You'll do fine." Aegeus smiled. Kfir started to exit the room.

"Keef," Lavi called. Kfir looked back over his shoulder.

"No electricity." He winked as Kfir left.

Aegeus was sure he didn't want to know what that was about.

Chapter 13

The Twelfth and her family were playing Frisbee in the backyard while their lunch cooked on the grill. The smell wafting toward heaven made the angels think of burnt offerings, a scent pleasing to both the angels and the King.

A small dog came running into the yard, followed by a slightly flustered woman. The Twelfth positioned herself in the dog's path, stooping down to stop him when he got to her. He rushed toward her, and she reached out, ready to grab his collar. But she didn't have to catch him. Kfir stopped right in front of the Twelfth and knelt, placing his hands over hers. The dog stopped directly in front of her and sat down. He licked her hands and squirmed as she picked him up to give him back to his owner.

"Thank you," the woman offered, out of breath from the run. "I don't know what spooked him; he just freaked out and started running."

"Seriously?" Lavi laughed at Kfir. "You tricked a dog into chasing you here?"

"I made myself smell like bacon," Kfir admitted. "Then I ran just far enough ahead of him that he couldn't get me. It was all I could think of."

"Only you, Kfir," Lavi chuckled, shaking his head. He shot Aegeus a knowing look.

"This is the First?" Lavi asked, looking at the woman who carried so much hidden pain.

"No, this is his wife. He is on his way, he got tangled in the leash as the dog ran by. His guardian was not thrilled," Kfir added, making a face. "You may have to smooth that part out."

"Leave it to Kfir, winning friends," Lavi chuckled.

"Would you like to join us for lunch?" the Twelfth offered the wife of the First.

"Kfir, fan the smell of the barbecue over here; no one can resist it. They'll stay for sure," Lavi called. Kfir rolled his eyes but flew over to the grill and blew gently on the smoke, sending the smell directly toward the wife of the First. It worked perfectly. She agreed to stay.

"Looks like Kfir's bacon trick worked. Maybe he should handle all our diplomacy from now on," Lavi quipped with a grin, nudging Aegeus gently in the side. Aegeus smiled reluctantly.

Shortly after, the First arrived with bandages on his knee, forehead, and elbow from the fall. Otherwise, he was unharmed. Aegeus and Lavi looked at Kfir, who flashed a sheepish grin and shrugged.

"Feel free to leave that part out of the report, Aegeus," Kfir joked.

The Twelfth brought out extra place settings, and they all sat at the table. Conversation flowed easily; the two couples had much in common. As afternoon turned to early evening, and the lightning bugs began to dance about the yard, the First and his wife got up to head home.

Suddenly, the Spirit within the Twelfth flared brightly, attracting the attention of the angels. While outwardly she gave little sign of what was happening, a sudden wave of sorrow, sharp and inexplicable, washed over her, leaving her blinking back unexpected tears. It was as if she could feel the wife's heartache—the years of trying, the rooms that remained empty, the quiet acceptance that was both strength and sorrow. But she said nothing, offering only a warm, genuine smile to the woman.

"Did she get a message?" Lavi wanted to know his face suddenly serious.

"What happened, Aegeus? That was a very bright flare. Did you see how she looked at the wife? What was that?" Kfir was very interested.

Aegeus walked closer to the couples. He said nothing. His eyes narrowed slightly as he focused on the Twelfth and the unfolding scene.

Lavi, too, stepped closer, his eyes softening as he leaned in as if to study the wife of the First.

"What is your story?" he asked as if expecting a response. His eyes softened as he observed a smile that was forced, a smile he suspected was hiding a great longing of unmet hopes and dreams.

"We are planning to start a small group once a week. Just a few families getting together each week to fellowship. Have you met your neighbors?" the First asked as they were leaving.

"We have; they're great," the husband of the Twelfth answered.

"Oh good, they're part of the group; it will actually be at their house, so you wouldn't have to go far. If you would like to come, we would love to have you join us." The Spirit again flared within the Twelfth. Her lips parted; the words formed before she could catch them.

"We would love to," she answered.

"Great, we'll see you then." And he and his wife left.

"We'd love to?" her husband asked when they were back inside, and there was no risk of the First and his wife hearing.

"I don't know why I said it; it just came out." She smiled at him. He sighed in response and smiled at her, shaking his head in disbelief. Maybe it would be great, but he doubted it.

"Maybe it's exactly what they need," Lavi whispered to Kfir with a grin. "A little hope and some laughter go a long way."

Aegeus was pleased with the development. "What happened, Aegeus? What is it she knows about the wife of the First?" Kfir asked. Aegeus shared the story of the First and his wife.

Chapter 14: The First

The First had such high hopes when he graduated from medical school. He was going to find a wonderful medical practice eager for a soft-spoken psychiatrist, and he and his wife would settle in a lovely coastal town. His wife had waited patiently for him to finish school so they could fill their home with children. All she had ever wanted was to be a mother.

But God had other thoughts. As his classmates moved away to begin their careers or ministries, his opportunity came in a different form. A small clinic that provided counseling to low-income families asked him to join them. The pay was minimal and the hours long, but the mission was noble. After considerable prayer and many discussions with his wife, they agreed that the clinic was where God was directing them. The coastal town would have to wait. Instead, they moved to a small Alabama town.

The First and his wife bought an old antebellum home in need of considerable work. But it was within their price range, and they began to plan for their family. His wife began pouring herself into repairing the house to prepare it for what she hoped would be numerous children. But children were apparently not part of God's plan for them either. The First watched helplessly as month after agonizing month, his wife wept to discover that she was not pregnant. After a year of trying, they conceded that something might be wrong. She went to the doctor and received a clean bill of health; there was no reason she could not get pregnant. And so, they continued trying until it was no longer enjoyable to do so.

He watched as his wife began to age before his eyes. Her once beautiful smile faded. The shine in her eyes was replaced with the glistening of tears. Her once patient and gracious manner was overcome with sadness and frustration. Daily, he went to God on her behalf, begging that she would become pregnant—worried that she never would.

Five years passed, and their home, once so perfect and full of promise for a beautiful family, now seemed vast and empty. The empty rooms seemed to scream reminders to them constantly. Instead of nestling children in their bosoms, the rooms were used to host visiting missionaries or guests as they came to the church. But even that seemed to be a reminder of her failure.

The First watched as his wife painted a smile on her face and poured her energy into caring for others. She became heavily involved in their church, serving on numerous committees and missions. But in private moments, her anguish was real. She wanted to be a mother.

And then the fateful day had come. The grant that had funded his job at the clinic was not renewed; the clinic would be closing. That same day, they received news that the fertility issue was his. He was unable to give his wife the children she had so earnestly sought.

That night, they cried together late into the night. He poured out apologies to her that he was not able to give her what she wanted most. His anguish poured out over her suffering, and he begged her forgiveness. And then, something happened. A strength he had not seen in her in years filled her. She wiped the tears from his eyes even as her own continued down her cheeks.

"You are the love of my life," she began. "God has given me all that I ever needed. He has given me his son, and he has given me you." She kissed him gently. "I wanted so badly to be a mother. But that is not what God has planned for me. Now that we know, we can move on together."

Two days later, the First was carrying a box from his office to his car when the bottom gave way, sending books toppling out. A woman with wild red hair was passing by and stopped to help.

"Need help?" she said, stooping to help him retrieve the books.

You have no idea how much help I need, the First thought, but "thanks" was what he managed to say. There was a genuine kindness and warmth about her that was comforting, and the First found himself telling her about his position there at the clinic and how they had lost their funding.

She listened intently with wide green eyes that seemed to peer into his soul. As he gathered the books, she managed to repair the box. After the books were secure, the woman with the wild red hair picked up the box as if to carry it.

"I'll take that," said the First, attempting poorly to reach for the box, his own arms already full of other items.

"I'll help; I'm heading that way," she said, smiling. "If you don't mind, I can walk with you."

They chatted as they walked across the parking lot. Her kindness disarmed him a little, and he felt himself wondering when he had last stopped to help a stranger. He learned that she was just passing through on her way to a conference at a small college. There was someone in his office building that she had stopped to meet along the way. *A college, now that would be a great place to work*, the First thought. He decided he would explore options at universities. The Light within him burned a little brighter.

Over the next few months, the First noticed that his wife seemed to be walking straighter, with a small skip in her step. A smile returned to her face for the first time in years, and she set about packing their home as he searched for a new job. A burden had been lifted from her heart.

Moving day arrived, and they stood together on the lawn of their home, looking at it for the last time. The First slid his arm around his wife and kissed her gently on the cheek. He was pleased to be leaving, starting fresh. They had found a modest house in their new location. Something small that would not be a reminder that they would never fill it. He felt this move would be right for them both, a place where they could start over. With one parting glance, he led his wife to the car, and they drove away to start a new life at a small Christian college hidden in the mountains.

Chapter 15

Wednesday morning was rainy. The Twelfth hit the snooze alarm and rolled back over, snuggling further into the bed. They had finally gotten the frame assembled for their bed—no more sleeping on just the box springs and mattress on the floor. She had enjoyed her first night of proper sleep in their new home.

The idea of getting out of bed and facing another day of unpacking and painting had no appeal; her bed did. She had concluded that she had been foolish to insist on painting each room before they unpacked it. Each room had floor-to-ceiling wallpaper that had to be removed; the walls had to be sanded and primed before, finally, she could paint. *What was I thinking?* She mused before stilling her mind and drifting back to sleep.

She stood in a field of amber-colored wheat. The stalks were soft like silk to her hands. The air smelled clean with a hint of lilac. The ground beneath her feet was cool and soft, like freshly turned earth, while a light breeze caused the tree's leaves to rustle gently, their whispers almost intelligible, like forgotten words on the edge of memory. Birds, somewhere in the distance, sang a beautiful song. Her heart felt as if it knew the words. It swelled with a longing she could not explain, a deep desire to join the song that felt etched into her being, and yet her soul struggled to break free from her humanity and sing along. An abundance of love washed over her. She was at peace. There was no rush, no hurry. Slightly in front of her was an enormous tree. The tree stood with a majesty she could not explain. It seemed to beckon to her, inviting her in with whispers of hope.

As she walked toward the tree, she noticed there were three men underneath it. The tallest among them stood slightly apart, his stance steady and watchful. His wings, though beautiful, had a sense of restraint, as if he were prepared for battle even in this peaceful place. His wings glistened in the light. They were not made of feathers like those of a bird; instead, they were made of a nearly translucent material that captured and reflected the light. It was stunning. His eyes were piercing, with a depth that seemed to hold both sorrow and wisdom. The second man had an unmistakable warmth, his face radiating kindness. His laughter rang out like bells, infectious and joyful. His wings shimmered as if reflecting the joy of creation itself. The third man's wings seemed to ripple with mischief as if the light itself wanted to dance around him. His eyes sparkled and his movements had the easy comforts of one who was always at home no matter where he was.

The men seemed to know each other well. From where she was, she could not hear what they were saying, but she could see them picking fruit from the tree. Each time one of them would select fruit and pull it from the tree, the tree would emit lights that reminded her of the aurora borealis. It was as if the tree itself celebrated the act of providing for them. It was so beautiful and captivating that she willed them to eat more. A deep guttural laughter erupted from one of the men, a laugh so contagious that she laughed with him—the stress and anxiety of her life all but forgotten. She felt an inexplicable familiarity, as if she were somehow connected to them as if she were witness to their strength, their joy, their purpose. It was as if they were a part of her story, even if she couldn't quite grasp how. A strange sense of longing filled her, not just for the peace of the place but for their presence. She began to walk more purposefully towards them.

Her alarm went off again, abruptly pulling her back to reality. She stretched lazily, not ready to release the dream. It had given her such peace and had seemed so real. She wanted it to be real. And she longed to return to that place. The smell of coffee hit her nose and made her smile. She rolled over and found a steaming hot cup next to the bed.

The Twelfth pulled herself up to a sitting position and reached for her Bible. She had started one of those "read the Bible through in a year" programs when she moved here. It was interesting. She had read it all before, but she found a new layer of God every time. It had become her favorite time of the day.

Currently, she was reading Leviticus, and she had to admit it was not her favorite. Nevertheless, each day, she found a small nugget of something beautiful, a treasure God had left just for her. Today, she read about the sacrificial system and the law regarding one being unclean after bearing a child. This did not sit well with her, so she took it to her father.

"God, how come you think women are dirty?" she spoke out into the empty room. The woman with the wild red hair sat unseen on the end of her bed.

"Where do you get that idea?" she asked back.

"Right here, in your word. Give birth to a male child, and you are unclean for thirty days, but give birth to a girl, and you are unclean for sixty days." She spoke out again, looking toward heaven. The woman with the red hair could not contain her joy at the comment.

"And if today, you received thirty days of parental leave for birthing a son and sixty days when you birthed a daughter, would you still feel like girls were devalued?" she asked the Twelfth. The Twelfth had never considered it that way.

"What about the animals?" she asked. "To atone for sin, it normally had to be a male animal sacrificed. Doesn't that make them more valuable?"

"How many animals were sacrificed in what you read today," the woman asked her.

"Thousands."

"What would happen to the herd if we killed thousands of the females in one day?"

The Twelfth sat frozen, her Light blazing with new understanding.

"But you make most male animals the beautiful ones, and the females are normally dull, like the peacock, for example, or the duck."

The woman with the red hair could not contain her laughter. "Which duck is easier for the hunter to see?"

"The male." Realization began to dawn on her.

"And if a female duck had the colorful plumage of the male, how would she protect her nest?" And just like that, the matter was settled. The Twelfth closed her Bible and got out of bed, ready to tackle the day.

The day passed swiftly, and before they knew it, it was time to go to the Wednesday night gathering. The group members had decided to each bring a covered dish to share. The Twelfth was not much of a cook and had spent most of the day reviewing recipes and comparing the ingredients list to what she had in the pantry. Options were limited. She eventually settled on a Mexican dish that she hoped would be well received.

The Twelfth and her husband made their way to the neighbors' house. Aegeus, Kfir, and Lavi joined them. The group hit it off immediately, laughter bubbling up as they found shared stories and mutual quirks. The Twelfth, balancing a precarious plate of enchiladas, grinned sheepishly.

"Well, I'll be honest," she said with a chuckle, "I had to google 'easy potluck recipes' this morning. Cooking is not my spiritual gift."

The Eleventh let out a warm, knowing laugh. "Trust me, it's a skill I'm still praying for," she said, nudging her husband playfully.

"Trust me, I'm praying for that too." Her husband added before dodging a playful elbow.

The home of the Second and Third was lovely. The Third had a refined taste that was elegant and upscale without seeming stuffy. She used warm colors and lighting to bring an inviting feel to the home. The décor was classic but had pieces from all the countries they had been to during their travels.

The room had beautiful chairs around a rustic wooden table made from a boat that had sunk off the coast of Sierra Leone. The Second had been onboard at the time. The table was beautiful, but the story was better, and listening to him tell it captivated the group, drawing them into the circle. There was something about the Second, something distinguished that made you feel important. He had a quiet strength that was peaceful and comforting.

The Twelfth admired the eclectic decorations as she took in the room.

"Is that really a piece of the Berlin Wall?" she asked, her eyes widening.

The Second nodded with a modest smile.

"Yes, from a mission trip we took years ago. A reminder of hope and perseverance."

"I'd love to hear that story sometime," the Twelfth said, her voice genuine. "It's incredible how the simplest things can carry the most profound messages."

The warm lighting and elegant furnishings made everyone feel at home, encouraging a sense of ease and connection. As the night wore on, the laughter deepened, and stories flowed effortlessly. The Twelfth realized, with a warm feeling spreading in her chest, that these were the kinds of moments she had been missing— simple, honest, and filled with unexpected joy.

The angels watched as the King's children laughed and enjoyed one another's company. While Lavi got quickly sucked into the story, Aegeus focused on being one step closer to the mission. He was pleased to see them bonding. He knew the group was not quite complete, and a few more would be added over the next several months, but tonight's gathering was an important milestone for them. It was small and intimate, and the Twelfth would leave tonight with a support system in place, something she hadn't had when she woke up that morning. This group surrounded her with those more experienced and wiser. Those who could mentor and support her. People, she would call friends.

Aegeus looked around at them, and a sense of sentiment filled him. He knew that each of them would benefit from being together. Tonight, a bond would begin that would become a lifelong connection between them. But of course, they did not know any of that yet. All they knew was that they felt the King in this place, they felt wanted, and they had enjoyed being together and breaking bread.

The Third had a natural talent for hosting, and she kept the conversation flowing smoothly. They laughed together and shared stories to get to know one another. The conversation eased organically into a discussion of their faith, which tended to happen when a group of the King's children were together for any length of time.

The angels relished the Light as it poured from the group and filled the house with the Light of God. They felt almost drunk with its power. They watched as the lights intermingled, making glorious colors before melding together into one. The angels seemed to be enjoying the evening as much as the humans.

The angels, too, were chatting amicably and sharing stories of old when Aegeus noticed that the King's children were discussing their thoughts on demons and if they thought "the devil made me do it" was a clever ploy or if demons actually roamed the earth. This got his undivided attention. It was fascinating to him to listen to them discuss the spiritual realm.

The angels positioned themselves around the room and listened intently to the discussion. The Eleventh was adamant that demons did indeed exist, but she gave no proof to support her conviction. The Twelfth suggested that if you believed the Word regarding demons, then you would have to conclude that demons did indeed roam the earth.

Aegeus wasn't sure which of them brought up the question of angels, but when they did, the angels shifted in their seats, both uneasy and amused. It was a strange sensation to listen to someone debate if you existed while you were sitting right there. Soon, Aegeus realized that he and the other angels were wholly engaged in the discussion the King's children were having.

Lavi leaned forward, his wings twitching with excitement. He wanted to jump in, to shout, "Yes, we're here!" Instead, he exchanged an amused glance with Kfir, enjoying the rare moment of connection with the King's children.

Aegeus noticed the other angels were answering questions that were being posed and cheering when one of the humans said something correct—almost as if they were watching a sporting event.

As Aegeus watched, it was as if they really were all in the room together. He had never felt so connected to humans. But of course, he knew that was not the situation. He tried to pull back— to separate himself—but the experience was so powerful, the King's love so overwhelming in the room that he struggled to disengage. He wanted to hear what they were saying, to be part of the moment, and yet…. history had taught him that engaging with them led to heartache. Abruptly, he stood and walked to the back of the house; he would do outside patrols while they finished up. It was safer to battle demons than to sit with humans.

The evening ran late, and the families made plans to meet again the following week. They each bid their good-nights and headed out toward their own homes. As they were walking out, Aegeus rejoined them just as the Twelfth asked the Eleventh, "How are you so sure there are demons?"

"You are going to think I am crazy, but...," the Eleventh hesitated. She had had such a great time that evening, and she liked the group, so she didn't want to say anything that would make them avoid her. The angels all leaned in. The Twelfth looked at her with anticipation, waiting for the end of the sentence. In her experience, sentences that started that way were the start of a great story. The Eleventh plunged on, "I have seen them."

Kfir and Lavi looked at Aegeus with raised eyebrows.

Chapter 16: The Eleventh

The Eleventh sat on the side of the tub, the cold porcelain serving as a witness that she was awake. She stared at the pregnancy test. This could not possibly be right; why would God let this happen? She closed her eyes tightly, willing it to be a mistake. She picked up the box the test had come in and once again read the directions. She had followed them, and it was hard to misread the word "pregnant" on the digital display. She sat in stunned silence, her mind blank, the word "pregnant" blinking like a neon sign in the darkness of her thoughts. It didn't feel real—not yet.

Nausea overwhelmed her. Not the nausea of pregnancy but the kind of nausea that hits you when you find yourself in an unbearable situation. Something so horrible that you have only one course of action: throwing up. She dropped onto the floor in front of the toilet and threw up until she thought her very insides were coming up. Tears poured down her cheeks, wails of sorrow flooding her and filling the room. She collapsed on the floor sobbing and begging God to undo this thing that had been done to her. The cold tiles pressed into her skin, unforgiving and rough, a harsh reminder that there was no escaping this reality. Her stomach heaved, her sobs echoing off the walls as if the room itself was weeping with her. She fell asleep on the floor in front of the toilet.

When the Eleventh woke up, she was slightly disoriented, not quite sure where she was for just a moment. The room had grown dark. Then, it all came flooding back as she looked at the pregnancy test still clutched in her hand. Her eyes and throat were sore from crying, and her nose was stuffy. She stood to her feet, her legs unsteady. She left her hope on the floor.

The Eleventh made her way to the sink and ran cold water to rinse her face. The water felt refreshing. She looked up into the mirror as it dripped down her face and back into the sink. Her eye was black, her mouth busted, and the bruises on her cheek and on her forehead were still there. They had transitioned from the black/purple they had started to a green/yellow mix. How could this have happened? Wasn't it enough that God let her be raped; must she be pregnant too?

Fresh tears ran down her face. How could she ever survive this? She had one more semester of graduate school after this one. Walking into class, beaten and bruised, had been hard enough. All the questions, all the prying eyes. How many times had she been asked what happened? She had created a vague story about being in a car accident. No one questioned it when she couldn't remember the details.

But she had not been in a car accident. She had been beaten and raped in her own home. She had gone over it a thousand times in the days since it happened. Coming home from her run, she found two strangers in her apartment. They wore masks, but they knew her name. They had left her bleeding on the floor. Her first instinct, whether right or wrong, was to shower—she felt so dirty.

She just wanted it to be over. She wanted to forget. She wanted to scrub the smell of them, the touch of them from her body. Perhaps, if she scrubbed hard enough, she could reverse it. She had clawed and scrubbed at her skin until the water ran cold. Then she sat down and cried until she had no tears left. But life didn't stop just because she had cried herself out.

She supposed she told people she was in a car accident because she didn't want to have to admit out loud what had happened. She didn't want to say it over and over again. She didn't want their looks of pity. She didn't want it to be real. It was embarrassing, and she felt great shame. She lived in constant fear since the incident. Someone she knew, someone who knew her name—had done this. Who? Every man she encountered was a potential suspect. She no longer felt safe in her own home. She was angry with God. And now? Now, she was pregnant.

After another hot shower, she double-checked the locks on the door, making sure the chair she had wedged under the knob was still secure. She triple-checked the windows and then made it to her bed, exhausted physically, emotionally, and mentally. She crawled into bed and cried. But sleep was elusive. Eventually, she gave up and got out of bed; she felt too vulnerable. She took her pillow and a light blanket and went to the back corner of her closet. With the closet door closed and her back against the wall, she was finally able to doze off, but it wasn't long before the nightmares began.

Two months passed. During that time, the Eleventh moved from her apartment into a smaller apartment off the back of an old woman's home. It was much smaller, and she felt safer there. Her visible bruises and cuts had almost healed, but it was still evident that something tragic had happened to her.

For weeks, she pretended the pregnancy wasn't real, but her body betrayed her. A swell, a tenderness—constant reminders of what she couldn't erase. The reality pressed on her, leaving no space to breathe or escape. She just couldn't deal with that on top of the rape, and so she tried desperately to pretend it wasn't real. But over the last month, she had been forced to acknowledge it.

You couldn't say that she decided on an abortion. She didn't think about it. She wouldn't allow herself to think about it. She merely acted as if it were the natural course of things. It wasn't a baby; it was a reminder. It was like having the rapist inside of her still.

The drive to the clinic was uneventful. They had told her to have someone drive her, but she didn't. She couldn't. Who could she tell? She came from a very devout Christian family. Her friends were all believers. How could she tell them? And so, she drove alone, not sure what she would do afterward except finally be free.

When she arrived at the clinic, there were protesters out front. Every step felt like a betrayal—of herself, of her past convictions, of everything she had believed. But the baby wasn't hers; it was a symbol of violation, of everything taken from her. She felt both anger and grief, shame and relief, all tangled together in a knot too tight to unravel. She thought about times she had gone and protested, holding signs and pleading with women not to commit murder. Now, as she walked the long sidewalk from her car to the clinic and they yelled similar things at her, it didn't seem very loving.

What did they know of her pain? Which of them had bothered to know anything about her at all? How could they stand in judgment of her? She walked with her head down, not looking to the left or right. Had she bothered to look, either way, she might have seen the woman with the wild red hair and beautiful green eyes holding the door for her. The woman's hand gently brushed her own as she walked in.

But she was so lost in her pain that she didn't notice any of that. She walked past the woman into the waiting room. The waiting room was dark; thin black smoke filled the room. Not enough to choke you, but enough to cloud your vision. The smell of sulfur hung thick in the air. That's when she saw them. Demons. Demons were hanging about in the waiting room, clinging to the other women there. Their red eyes fixed on her horror-stricken face when she walked in. Their eyes glowed red, burning through the smoky darkness like embers of hatred. Their twisted shapes seemed to blur at the edges as if they were both real and part of the shadows. One of them giggled in glee, its mouth widening unnaturally. She stood frozen where she was, her eyes wide in horror.

The woman with the wild red hair and green eyes that seemed to look straight through you walked up from behind and stood beside her, looking at the demons, too.

"Do you see them?" the Eleventh finally whispered.

"Oh yes, I see them," the woman answered, her voice bringing comfort and peace, something the Eleventh hadn't known in quite some time.

"What are they?" she whispered again, not daring to move from her spot.

"They are tormenting demons," the woman said with confidence.

"What are they doing here?"

"They are everywhere. Anywhere people are, they go." The answer seemed so simple.

"How come I can see them?" The Eleventh wanted to know.

"Perhaps you needed to be able to see them," the woman answered. She stepped slightly closer to the Eleventh so that their arms barely touched. The woman's skin was warm against the Eleventh's icy fear. Her voice was sure and soothing – like the sun after a bitter winter.

"Do not be afraid. I am with you," the woman said gently. A surge of power and electricity pulsed through the Eleventh. Her fear was gone.

The demons, too, were standing very still, anxious, and unsure of what to do now that the woman with the wild red hair had entered the building.

"Let's leave here," the woman suggested. Nodding in agreement, the Eleventh turned and walked from the clinic with the red-haired woman. With each step away from the clinic, the weight that had crushed her seemed to lift. The red-haired woman's words lingered, echoing within her: *"Do not be afraid. I am with you."* For the first time in months, she felt a glimmer of hope—a chance to reclaim her life, one step at a time. From that day on, the Eleventh was able to see demons. In many ways, it was terrifying, but in some ways, it was also liberating. She found it easier to fight what she could see.

Chapter 17

Aegeus called a meeting of the team covering the Twelfth. They met once again in the old salvage yard. He wanted to lay out a plan. The air was thick with the scent of rust and oil, a fitting backdrop for the looming battle. Shadows lingered among the wreckage, hinting at the demonic forces that swarmed the town above.

Now that the twelve were all in place, he wasn't sure how much longer they could conceal them. The sky over the small town had darkened even more over the last two days, which could only mean one thing: the arrival of the Strongman. The demons swarmed the sky, forming a canopy of evil and deception over the town. The streets were clogged with them, but nowhere was their presence more noticeable than at the college.

Aegeus knew that his small fleet of warriors was grossly outnumbered. Soon, the demons would know they were there, and more importantly, they would understand why. The King had begun to call other angels to the battle, and Aegeus looked forward to their arrival. But getting through the demon swarm to the town would not be easy, and that battle could delay them. The demons had become confident in their position, and as their confidence grew, their activity grew.

Lavi arrived at the meeting first.

"You've got that look again, Aegeus," Lavi teased as he arrived. "You're thinking too hard," Aegeus smirked, but his eyes held a hint of affection.

"Someone has to."

Kfir and Adiel entered next with a nearly silent swoosh.

Kfir grinned as he caught sight of Adiel's struggle with the guardian's tunic.

"Still not a fan of the guardian uniform, are we?" he teased, his tone light.

Adiel shot him a withering look, still tugging at the constricting leather. "It's like wearing a cage," she grumbled. "How do you even fight in this thing?"

Lavi chuckled, adjusting his own tunic with ease. "It's not so bad when you're born to wear it," he said, a hint of pride in his voice. "Besides, it's meant for function, not fashion."

"Function?" Adiel scoffed, finally managing to untangle her braid from the collar. "I've seen better range of motion from a straitjacket."

"Oh, come on," Kfir jumped in. "At least it's an upgrade from that fiasco in Damascus—"

"Say one more word, Kfir, and I'll make sure you regret it," Adiel shot back, but a mischievous glint lit her eyes.

Lavi grinned. "Just don't rip it. We are far from our type of seamstress, you know."

"Trust me," Adiel retorted with a wry smile, "if I rip it, it won't be by accident."

Aegeus observed the exchange with a faint smile, appreciating the camaraderie despite the gravity of their mission.

Adiel's eyes, sharp and alert, scanned the room. She was clearly uncomfortable in the guardian's tunic and continued tugging at it with mild irritation. Yet, there was a calm authority in her stance, a reflection of centuries spent in battle.

As she continued to tug at the tunic, her long braid again caught it in, making her wince and mutter under her breath.

"Blasted tunic," she grumbled, untangling the strands with an annoyed tug. "I'm more likely to strangle myself with this thing than face a demon."

Lavi chuckled softly, stepping closer. "Careful, Adiel. We can't afford to lose you to wardrobe malfunctions before the battle even starts."

She smirked, finally freeing her hair. "I'm a warrior, not a princess. Wardrobe or not, I will be in the battle."

Aegeus's lips twitched in the faintest hint of a smile, but his focus remained serious.

"Let's hope it doesn't come to that. I'm glad you're here."

"Aegeus," she finally said in way of greeting.

"Adiel. How is Greece?"

"Strong. It seems strange to be anywhere else. How are things here?"

"I have received more information regarding our mission. Aegeus continued, "This nation was once founded on the basis of freedom of religion. It was once a holy nation that trusted in our King. They prayed and remembered the one True God." At the very mention of his name, the angels began to emit strong electrical energy and to shine ever more brightly.

"But the nation has lost its way, and those who follow the King have grown silent. In place of the love that the Lamb called them to, judgment, fear, and lies fill their hearts. They have become meek and afraid to speak the truth. When they try to speak the truth, they do not do so in love but out of fear and ignorance. The Lights of many have dimmed, and they have resorted to the same hypocrisy as the Pharisees.

"The truth is being lost," Aegeus said quietly, his eyes narrowing. "The enemy's grip is tightening, and we are standing at the edge of what could be a final stand for them. We have been assembled here to preserve what is left. If we lose this town, Lucifer will send deception, hatred, and judgment out from this place cloaked in the truth. He has already placed thousands among them who falsely bear the name but not the Spirt. They are becoming the loudest voices. A voice of lies. The twelve are the key to reigniting truth and love in this place. They will have to work together. But the Tenth, as you know, is to be the one to confront the Strongman".

"The intense demon swarm signals the Strongman's arrival. We're currently outnumbered. Meir arrived last night; she is visiting each of the twelve today to get a better understanding of their needs. Ayo and Berhanu, the rest of our allotted ministering angels, will be joining us over the next few days after they finish an assignment in Africa. We are hopeful to figure out how to get them into the town without having to reveal our positions."

"We need to make sure all twelve are feeding truth into their soul so that Meir's team will have something to work with. Meir tells me this can come from reading the Bible, listening to music, or interacting with others of positive influence, particularly those who love them and are kind. Basically, the goal is for them to hear or see positive, uplifting things."

"Kfir, survey the town and find the Strongman. We need to know where and who he is. If the Strongman consolidates power here," Aegeus continued, his voice low and intense, "he'll spread lies disguised as truth, and the mission could be over before it begins. We can't afford to lose this ground."

Adiel, try to find the meeting place for the demons. Find out anything you can. We need to know their plans. Lavi, visit the church and the coffee shops to get a measure of where the people are spiritually. We need to know what we're up against and who, other than the Third, we can count on for prayer cover."

"I'll handle it," Lavi said with a grin, though his eyes held a somber depth. As Lavi prepared to leave, he turned back toward Aegeus.

"You know," he said, "I have a feeling something big is coming." Aegeus wanted to respond, but the words felt too heavy. Instead, he simply nodded, the silent understanding between them needing no words.

"Aegeus, some battles leave a mark no matter how they end." Aegeus's jaw tightened, but he forced a nod.

"Just make sure this one doesn't leave more than it should."

Lavi gave a small, rueful smile, his voice softening.

"As the King wills, so shall it be."

As Aegeus watched Lavi head out, a rare pang of unease settled in his chest. He trusted Lavi's instincts implicitly, but something about this assignment felt heavier, more dangerous. He pushed the feeling down, knowing there was no time for hesitation.

Chapter 18

Lavi headed for the coffee shop that was on the way to the church. The smell of freshly roasted coffee beans flooded from the shop and spilled into the street, welcoming him as he got closer.

It reminded him of Heaven's comfort - warmth, peace, and the King's presence. After the mission, he would be there again to renew his strength. But not yet. Working amid the warriors, who spent most of their time in heaven, reminded him how much he longed for that. Time on earth was draining. But the distinct aroma of freshly ground coffee beans was one of the small pleasures that Lavi enjoyed on earth. He found the smell aromatic and a reminder of the comforts of home. But as he rounded the corner, the smell of sulfur quickly overpowered the smell of the coffee beans.

Demons stood like sentinels in the doorway of the coffee shop, sliding their hands over each person as they entered. Lavi knew it was one way for them to determine who was worth further attention. A young couple walked into the coffee shop just ahead of Lavi. One of the demons ran his hands over the girl's long hair, lingering only a moment before letting out a hideous hissing sound and holding his hand as if it had been burned. The girl's Light exploded in intensity because of the unwanted touch. She seemed to shiver imperceptibly and looked in the direction of the demon. She could not have felt him, and yet the Spirit was strong inside her and had given a clear message to the demon.

The boy, however, did not have the Light, and the demon found him to be a more willing host. Very quickly, in the time it took the boy to open the door for the young lady, the demon used one of his long talons and pierced it through the boy's head. A black stream of evil thoughts and desires passed from the demon to the boy. The demon laughed in glee as the boy moved into the coffee shop.

Lavi put one hand on his sword as he approached the doorway where the demons were standing.

"Easy there; you know the rules. This is common ground," said the demon who had just retracted his talon from the boy.

"I know the rules," Lavi said grudgingly. He would not defy the rules of the King to satisfy his own desires, but he would defend himself if needed. That was his angelic right. The temptation to engage in battle was strong, but his love for the King was stronger. Lucifer had once placed his own desires above the King's, and the rebellion that followed left a lasting scar on creation—a scar that still burned in every demon's hatred for humanity. The King had created a prison for them. He specially designed hell to contain the demons who rebelled against him. But then Lucifer tricked Adam and Eve into disobeying the King, and man's fate had been sealed to share in the destruction and punishment intended for Lucifer.

But the King offered a solution, a way for the humans to avoid hell. He knew the road would not be easy, but for those who would persist, death would bring about eternal life. The King's son volunteered to take the punishment intended for humanity. He would be killed to pay their debt. The King had not made a similar provision for Lucifer and his followers. For this reason, Lucifer declared war on humans. He could not touch the King, but he was committed to doing all he could to destroy those created in the King's image, those he called children. Lavi knew well the end that was in store for the demons. The demons knew it, too, and it fed their hatred for the humans.

Lavi stepped through the threshold of Perks to see that the coffee shop had brick walls inside with large, rounded windows. The walls were decorated with antique coffee relics sparsely placed along the walls throughout. The six baristas stood behind a long black counter with a solid marble top. A huge chalkboard hung behind them with the menu written on it. Someone had put a considerable amount of time into writing it, complete with chalk drawings of the different coffees randomly throughout.

Bistro tables were scattered around the shop, each having a marble top with either two or four bistro chairs. A small bakery case on the side wall contained a selection of baked goods like scones, bagels, or fresh quiche. According to the sign stuck to the front of the case, everything was baked fresh daily by the local bakery. The coffee was served in plain white coffee cups on plain white saucers. For those in a hurry, there were traditional to-go cups.

The smell of sulfur thickened, twisting into the comforting aroma of coffee, turning the shop into a battleground masked by earthly scents. Shadows deepened, making the air heavy with malice, the demons' dark energy infusing the atmosphere. Lavi scanned the room quickly. Many of those present had the Light of God, although some of their Lights were very dim. There were tormenting demons in the coffee shop, making their way from table to table and whispering suggestions or feeding thoughts to the occupants. Sometimes, the unwanted thoughts and ideas would be met with a flash of Light that would burn the demon or send him flying backward, depending on how active the Spirit was within the person.

But for those who did not have the Spirit, the human was left to fight the thoughts themselves. Some of the humans embraced the thoughts and ideas offered by the demons while others struggled against them. The demons were relentless and continued to feed their poison into the crowd.

There were three guardians already in the coffee shop. Two of them were in the back corner chatting. The third guardian stood very close to his charge. He was protecting a college student from the demons. The guardian had wrapped his large wings around the young man so that the demons could not touch him. The demons were not foolish; they knew they could not break through the wings of the guardian, so they directed their taunts to the angel himself.

The guardian stood firm without even blinking. A look at the young man would never reveal the sorrow that was in his heart.

But as Lavi walked closer to him, he could see that the boy had considerable pain. He wore a smile on his face and laughed at all the right times, but his soul felt great sadness. As Lavi moved closer, he could feel the depth of the boy's sorrow reaching out to him.

The proximity of the two guardians made the demons move farther away and redirect their attention to other patrons. Lavi noticed them latching on to a high school girl who did not have the Light.

As they began to pour darkness into her, she accepted it willingly; she did not have the strength to fight. Her soul cried out as her mind embraced the lies they fed her—lies of her worthlessness. Lavi's heart ached to lift that burden, to shield the girl now slipping under the demons' grip, but he held fast to his purpose.

He felt his anger begin to rise at the sight. But angels were neither friend nor foe of the humans—they served the King. They defended those the King told them to and fought those whom the King declared enemies. More than once the King had directed the angels to fight against his chosen people, Israel. Long term, it had always worked to the advantage of the Israelites, but Lavi was sure they had not seen it that way at the time. Humans did not tend to understand the ways of the King.

Lavi looked up to see that the guardian had not taken his wings from around his charge.

"Lavi, guardian of the King, sent to the earth to oversee his children," stated Lavi in the tradition of the guardians.

"Octar, holy is the King," responded Octar, finishing the traditional greeting.

"Have you been assigned to him long?" asked Lavi. As he greeted Octar, a flicker of pride filled him; they were all here for the same purpose, all tied by their devotion to the King. It was a loyalty forged in battles across millennia and bound him deeply to his fellow guardians.

"His mother became worried and prayed me here," Octar replied.

"And she has maintained you since?" Lavi asked, impressed. Human mothers held a power that even angels respected. Lavi had been called to countless assignments by the prayers of mothers alone.

"What is the boy's condition?" Lavi asked.

Just then, the demons erupted in laughter. Lavi turned to see the situation and noticed the girl without the Light was now crying. Her face had grown red, and she jumped from her chair, sending it crashing to the ground. The metal bistro chair collided with the well-polished stone floor, making a tremendous sound and attracting the attention of all the patrons in the shop.

The outburst brought more demons streaming into the coffee shop, and Lavi realized he and the other guardians were now outnumbered four to one. Demons continued to pile in, eager to join in the tormenting. The girl did not have the Light, and she had no guardian. She had little to defend herself with.

The demons had climbed onto her and wrapped their arms around her throat. Anger had sunk his talons into her temple, and Worthlessness had grabbed her heart. Insecurity had covered her mouth and was spewing dark thoughts through her open mouth and nose. Spittle flew from her mouth as tears streamed down her cheeks. She was yelling things at her tablemate that made no sense to Lavi and didn't seem to make much sense to the tablemate.

The girl at the table with her—her sister, from what Lavi could tell—was trying to calm her. Her face flushed from the scene developing around her. Everyone in the coffee shop watched. She spoke words of apology and encouragement to the girl, but they were swatted away by demons who refused to let them in.

Patrons in the coffee shop began to grow increasingly uncomfortable, and the demons grew increasingly jubilant. Lavi felt anger rising within him, but he was severely outnumbered, and he had not gotten the order to protect the girl. Lavi's heart broke for her; she had no defense against the darkness, no hope unless someone intervened.

Progressively, more demons swarmed the coffee shop, piling onto the girl. Her anger and despondency grew greater and greater. The smell of sulfur became so overwhelming that Lavi wondered how the humans could not smell it.

The guardians in the room began to move strategically around the room to position themselves for the best possible attack should the order come. Except for Octar. He remained steadfast, wrapping his wings even tighter around his charge. Lavi's hand hovered near his sword, every instinct urging him to intervene. But the King's silence held him back, a quiet command to wait. His heart ached at the sight of the girl, her Light flickering as the darkness closed in. He forced himself to hold back, to trust in the King's wisdom, even as his love for humanity cried out for him to act.

Lavi surveyed the room and found that as the demons had piled in, they had launched full attacks against many of the patrons. He fidgeted in his position as the demons bumped and shoved him in their eagerness to get closer to the girl. He wanted to strike, to drive them out, but he held back, restrained by the King's command. Loyalty meant trust—trust in the King's timing, even as the darkness closed in.

Where was the prayer? Why was no one praying for this girl? Did they not realize the signal was powered by their prayer? Lavi searched the room for those with the Light. He had to believe that one of them would plead with the King for this girl. Did they not know they had the very power of the King inside of them?

In the corner sat the girl with the long hair who had deflected the demon upon entering. Her Light began to burn more brightly. Her eyes were open, but she prayed. Her Light got stronger, more powerful until finally, she closed her eyes and bowed her head—even more fully committed to her purpose. As the Light grew, others in the room finally joined her until, slowly, the room was full of the Light. And then the signal came.

The guardians drew their swords simultaneously in one swift motion. Lavi grabbed the demon closest to him and thrust the sword straight through his back. The demon let out a scream of pain, and an electrical surge left his body as his corpse dropped to the ground. Lavi's blade sliced through the air, meeting demon after demon with relentless force. His muscles burned, and his breath came in short gasps. Pain lanced through him as a talon scraped his shoulder, hot blood soaking his tunic. But he pressed on, knowing every swing brought him closer to freeing the girl.

Lavi ducked just in time to miss a poorly aimed sword being wielded by an untrained demon. He grabbed the sword, spun around, and stabbed him with his own sword. The air crackled with the released power of the demon as he fell to his death.

A long-haired warrior demon with a deep scar moved to position himself between Lavi and the girl. Lavi could see the other two guardians slashing their way through the demons toward the girl, but they were not yet close. Lavi knew that he was little match for a well-trained warrior.

The girl, oblivious to the battle around her, knew only of the battle that raged within her. Her anger had reached a fevered pitch, and her sense of hopelessness and worthlessness had overwhelmed any sense of propriety. She raged on, having thrown her hot coffee from the table; she was now ranting at other clients, hurling accusations that made little sense. Her eyes had taken on a frantic look of pain, anguish, and not understanding her own actions.

Her hair flew about in the unkempt manner of an animal. Lavi thrust his sword at the long-haired demon with the scar, who easily dodged it. The long-haired demon smiled a knowing smile as if he were part of some elaborate secret, then tipped his head slightly to Lavi and vanished just as another demon thrust his sword deep into Lavi's stomach.

Lavi stumbled to his knee, momentarily dropping his sword. Clutching his stomach, his angelic blood quickly covered his hands and dripped onto the coffee shop floor. He reached for his sword and pushed himself to his feet, desperate to free the girl from the demons that encompassed her. He slashed his way toward her, striking down demons in his path, his blood gushing from his wound as he went. Pain lanced through his side, the searing heat of the demon's sword burning with each movement. Blood—gold and shining—dripped to the floor, but Lavi fought on, each strike slower than the last, his vision blurring. He looked around, assessing the room as he tossed a demon aside. The remaining demons far outnumbered the guardians. But they were not warriors, they were tormenting demons untrained in the art of real combat. Lavi swung around, slashing a demon as it prepared to jam its talons into the girl's back. At the same time, he felt a sword pierce through his back. He looked down to the tip of it emerging from his chest.

He sank to the floor beside the girl, knowing this was his last battle, but he was not yet defeated. For Lavi had one weapon that demons did not, the most powerful of all weapons, the Light of

God. Something the demons had lost with their rebellion. Lavi forced himself to stand up and spread his wings as wide as they would go, summoning the last reserves of his strength; his wings unfurled, each feather blazing with a pure, radiant Light that filled the room.

'For the King,' he whispered, letting the Light of God erupt from him. The walls seemed to tremble. The demons were hurled from the shop. Only one demon remained. A small tormenting demon scorched and charred from the Light had dug his claws into the girl, and just as Lavi reached for him, he darted inside the girl, where he was protected. The girl had no defense now.

The smell of burnt demons lingered in the air. As Lavi collapsed to the floor, golden blood poured from his wound. As he lay waiting for Aegeus, who he knew would come for him, a quiet warmth washed over him, a presence so familiar it soothed his pain. The King's touch was gentle and reassuring. Lavi's spirit swelled with peace, knowing he had served well.

Chapter 19

The blast of the Light of God did not go unnoticed by Morax. He summoned his leadership team to his office at the college. Titus brought one of the tormenting demons with him to testify to the situation at the coffee shop. Morax glared at the demon and demanded an explanation.

"You have evoked the Light of God in this place!" he yelled, sulfur pouring from his mouth and filling the room.

"Don't worry, Lord," the demon responded without fear. "It was only a few guardians. No real cause for concern."

Just a few guardians? Just a few guardians!" Morax's voice was low and deadly, his words dripping with venom. Sulfur billowed around him, thickening until the air grew stifling. In one swift move, he lunged at the demon, clamping his hand around its throat. "Those 'few guardians' just blasted a hundred demons from our stronghold," he hissed, his eyes flashing with an intensity that sent a shudder through even his hardened team.

The room had grown dark with sulfur, and Morax found his human eyes starting to burn from his own essence.

"You have given away our numbers; do you not realize they will wonder why there are so many of us here? They will have reinforcements by morning," he snarled.

"But . . . but—" the demon sputtered, realizing his position was perilous. "We destroyed one," he blurted out, hoping to help his situation.

"You have destroyed one?" Morax asked, an uneasy calm coming over him. His eyes became glassy, and his stare cold. The rage from only a moment before was instantly gone, and the hand clutched around the tormenting demon's throat began to tremble.

"Yes, Lord; I saw him collapse in his own blood," the demon added, his confidence returning. "And we took possession of a girl," he added, sure that he was advancing his position.

Morax released the demon, shoving him as he did so. "You are an idiot," he snarled with a cold hatred that was shocking even to the demon. "Kill him," he said to Titus. Without hesitation, Titus drew his sword and decapitated the tormenting demon in one swift motion. The demon's body jerked slightly and then collapsed to the ground, dissipating in black smoke.

Morax stood in front of his office window, looking out over the campus. His office was large and spacious, precisely the type of office a man in his position at the college would warrant. But his window was much too small for his liking.

"One guardian destroyed. One. Do you realize what that means?" He turned to Titus.

"This death will draw more angels than we have seen here before. They will bring Light with them—too much Light. And human prayers—such an irritant." His voice dripped with disdain.

"A single faithful whisper can ruin weeks of our work." We must proceed cautiously, even if it means slowing down."

He remained silent for a long moment as he watched the demons darting in and out of buildings around campus. They had taken control of this campus, being careful not to attract attention. Tormenting demons were common. They were the most common type of demon, and their presence on a college campus would be expected. The demons had controlled the hiring and removed anyone who posed a problem to their plan.

They had sought zealots, those who loved the Word more than the Creator—those who would adhere to rules above clinging to love. Those who were timid and would not speak up or sacrifice their own comfort to defend the truth. Those who knew of the King but did not actually know him. But these things had to be done slowly over time.

While the strongest among them had been eliminated, there were still many who had the Light. And thousands of years had taught Morax that those with the Light were unpredictable. If the guardians attacked the demons in the coffee shop, it was because they had been given orders to do so. The death of a guardian would bring many angels to the town. Morax walked from the window to his desk and sat down, looking across at Titus and his team.

"I believe we all know what is at stake here," Morax began. "This small college is our ticket to taking over America. We will defeat this town using the Strongman, and we will send false religion under the cloak of truth out into this nation. We are so close to destroying this generation. The Strongman will rise in notoriety, and we will progress to phase two of our plan." He looked at each of them in turn.

"In mere days, the students will begin classes. We have laid a flawless foundation," Morax said, his voice calm but filled with conviction.

"New faculty members, trained in our seminaries, control the Word here. They will sow the right seeds of confusion, mixing just enough truth with lies. Rules, judgment, and shame will bind them—until they no longer even recognize the Spirit. We will flood the campus with Depression, Anxiety, Guilt, Distrust, Worthlessness, and Shame. Suicides will rise, breakdowns will rise, and they will feel despondent over their sin, but they will not repent because we will convince them they are not worthy. They need not repent if they read the Word more. That will save them, we will say.

We will teach them to say the right things while understanding those things the wrong way. We will strangle them with rules and checklists of what 'good Christians' do. They will lie and heap judgment upon each other.

"We will enervate the faculty members who contain the Light. They will not know who to trust, and so they will remain silent. We will fill them with the fear of losing their jobs and convince them that they will not ever work again. Our version of the truth will be close to the truth, and they will wonder if they are the ones who are wrong. We will shame them if they speak of the Spirit. We will fill their days with what is good to keep them from doing what is best."

The demons in the room smiled at the thought of it. It was a brilliant plan.

"We have done our research," Morax continued. "The Strongman is getting settled and acclimated. He is preparing opening remarks that will stir their hearts and confuse them greatly. It will divide them and make it easy for us to determine who will be trouble. But we need more time. We must not attract unnecessary attention. The angels will flock to the town over the death of their own. So, we will pull back, all of us. Everyone is to leave for three days.

"Titus, gather all the tormenting demons and move them to neighboring cities. Leave only a few. We'll need a few to observe and report. Their job is to blend in, to watch the movements of the guardians."

Morax turned to Titus, his eyes sharp.

"And they will report directly to me. Three days is all we'll need," Morax said, calculating. "Just long enough to quiet the guardians' suspicion before we close in again. Let them believe they've secured the town," Morax sneered. "We'll return with more force. Our strength doubled. When they're complacent, we'll tighten the noose. This town will fall one way or another."

Titus nodded his head at the command and stood, signaling to his team that it was time to depart.

Chapter 20

Lavi's decision to use the Light of God to defend the girl and his fellow guardians did indeed draw the attention of all the angels—just as Morax had predicted.

All the guardians and warriors in the town flooded to Perks when they saw the Light. Aegeus was the first to arrive. Upon entering the building, he was prepared for a battle, but he was not prepared for what he found: Lavi's lifeless body lying on the floor, unseen by the humans. Lavi was covered in golden blood. Aegeus froze at the sight, his heart plunging as he took in the golden blood staining Lavi's tunic.

"No… no, no, no," he muttered, dropping to his knees beside his friend. His hands shook as he tried to staunch the flow, to pull his friend back from this fate.

"Lavi!" he cried, shaking him roughly. He tried to cover the wounds, to stop the immense flow of blood, but it did not seem to help.

"I saw the Light. I came as quickly as I could. What happened?" Kfir asked as he joined Aegeus. The coffee shop had filled with angels who now stood silently looking on with great sadness at their fallen brother. They formed a protective circle around him, keeping out any stray demons; although the demon's presence was sparse, most had fled or been flung far from the coffee shop with the blast.

"I don't know," Aegeus answered, still trying to control the bleeding.

"You must get him to the King. It is his only chance."

Aegeus scooped up his friend's body and headed for heaven. As Aegeus ascended, Lavi's body held close, a mix of sorrow and denial surged through him. Each beat of his wings felt heavier, and he found himself dreading the finality of the King's verdict. But deep down, he knew.

He landed at the tree where he and Lavi had first stood with Kfir and discussed the mission. He could already feel the tree celebrating the life and service of Lavi. Streams of golden light poured from the tree's branches, encircling Lavi's lifeless body. Aegeus cradled Lavi's body close before reluctantly laying it gently on the soft grass. The tree's light spun around Lavi, a vibrant swirl of color that danced in honor of his spirit. Aegeus sunk to the ground and rested his hand against the tree. As Aegeus's hand met the rough bark, memories surged forward—Lavi's laugh ringing out over fields of battle, his lighthearted quips during missions, the countless times they'd fought side by side. Each memory pulsed through him, intertwining their lives as one.

"NO!" he yelled, yanking his hand from the tree." He was unwilling to let memories be all that was left.

The King arrived and knelt beside Aegeus, his presence gentle yet filled with quiet strength. The air around them warmed as the King placed his hand on Lavi's body, and though grief still tore at Aegeus's heart, he felt a surprising sense of comfort flow from the King's touch.

"Well done, my good and faithful servant." With those words, the sky erupted with images of Lavi's life. From his creation to this death, his life was displayed in moving pictures in the heavens. The tree erupted in golden light that sparked and danced around Lavi, surrounding his body until there was nothing left but the lights.

"No," Aegeus said with less vigor, more like a request than a command this time. His pleading eyes met the Kings.

"He is the fifth, Aegeus." The King offered. "He knew his part in this mission, and he chose it willingly."

"Find a way to honor him and to help the others do so as well. They will need you to lead them through their grief." The King added before laying his hand on Aegeus's back and infusing him with power, comfort, and strength.

"The Ceremony of Remembrance will begin soon." The King said, stepping back to give Aegeus a moment alone.

After a moment, Aegeus carefully selected a variety of fruits from the tree and placed them in a wooden pestle. He sat quietly under the tree and crushed the fruit, making juice. The simple act brought him comfort and peace. He leaned back against the tree; he could feel Lavi.

When the day of wrath was upon them, Lavi would again walk the streets of heaven. Knowing that encouraged Aegeus, but it could not remove his pain. He would miss his friend. In time, he felt Michael arrive at the tree before he saw him, and he knew that others would soon follow. Michael remained silent, standing a few paces behind Aegeus, waiting for Aegeus to initiate.

Aegeus rose slowly to his feet but did not turn around to face Michael.

"Why must it cost so much?" he muttered, his voice raw. Michael stepped forward, laying a firm hand on Aegeus's shoulder, though he did not answer.

"Do we lose this battle?" he asked, his voice barely above a whisper. Michael's gaze was steady.

"In human terms, perhaps. They see only the immediate struggle, the loss. But in heavenly terms... no, we never lose. Every Light added to heaven strengthens our cause."

Chapter 21

The fall of Lavi left a large hole in the team and in their hearts. Aegeus entered the abandoned building in the salvage yard, where the other angels sat quietly. They looked to him for leadership. He cleared his throat unnecessarily. At that moment, Aegeus felt an overwhelming love for them. He stood silently, looking at each of them in turn, remembering battles fought together and shared moments. As Aegeus's gaze passed over each angel, he felt the weight of Lavi's absence like a missing piece in a mosaic. Lavi's warmth and unshakable loyalty had been woven into the fabric of their brotherhood, and without him, they felt somehow incomplete.

The angels, completely comfortable with silence, sat motionless, their expressions a blend of grief and pride, each knowing the honor of Lavi's sacrifice. Silence was no stranger to them, but today, it felt heavier, charged with a sense of loss that reverberated through their ranks.

Aegeus took out a glass decanter etched with a Celtic cross, the ancient symbol of the guardian. He poured himself a glass from the decanter as though he were offering a piece of his heart in memory of Lavi. The liquid sparkled in the decanter. It had an iridescent quality, highlighting the colors of each of the fruits he had used to make it – reminders of the King's promise. He passed the decanter around, and each angel carefully poured a glass of the heavenly concoction that Aegeus had made while in heaven. Aegeus raised his glass, steadying himself as he spoke, though his voice wavered with grief and pride.

"We have lost one of our brothers." he began each word bearing the weight of their shared sacrifice. "But Lavi was the fifth angel, he gave his life in service of the King; there is no more noble honor. He fell, fighting to protect a human girl, a girl who does not yet have the Light. If she were to be lost, her suffering would have no end. But because of Lavi's sacrifice, she will live to have another chance. He gave his life to protect one of the King's beloved. The King loves his children. He sent us to defend and protect them. Lavi's sacrifice also reminds us of the King's timeline," Aegeus continued, his gaze steady.

"Seven angels will fall before the Day of Wrath, and Lavi was the fifth. Our journey grows shorter, and each step takes us closer to that final battle. Our journey will continue to be difficult, but we will not waiver from our path. We will not turn our heads to the right or the left but will run the race set before us. To Lavi, the fifth angel."

"To Lavi." The other angels said in agreement. A hushed reverence filled the room as they drank the sweet nectar in honor of Lavi. Each angel held his glass for a moment longer, the taste of heaven mingling with the memory of their fallen brother. In silence, they felt Lavi's spirit, his courage urging them forward.

Chapter 22

The Twelfth was relieved to be headed to campus for her first official day. Despite the summer heat, the Twelfth decided to walk to campus, eager for the fresh start the day promised. As she made her way toward the school, she listened to music and prayed. The last two years had been especially difficult.

As she walked, a mix of excitement and dread churned in her stomach. Working somewhere that felt like it had a higher purpose—that was something she'd longed for. But if anyone here knew just how many times she'd failed, they'd see she was not fit for this place.

As he walked beside the Twelfth, Aegeus felt Lavi's absence as a quiet, unfamiliar weight. Lavi's way of carrying Light, of reaching beyond himself, had balanced the fight in all of them. Now, that steadiness felt less certain. Aegeus kept his gaze forward, forcing himself to focus, but Lavi's loss lingered in the back of his mind, a reminder of the cost they all bore. Aegeus was still dressed as her guardian. Wearing the uniform of the guardian in light of what happened to Lavi made him even more uncomfortable. He tried to reframe it, to view it as an homage to his friend, but he felt like an imposter. He scanned the streets for any sign of demons, but the town seemed quiet. The Twelfth turned her face toward the sun and closed her eyes for a moment as she walked. Aegeus couldn't help but think how much stronger the light was in heaven and how one day she would have the honor of feeling real light upon her face.

He also found himself hoping that she would not trip and fall because he wasn't actually a guardian, and he was ill-equipped to serve as one. She needed a proper guardian, not a warrior disguised as one.

Her Light flickered quietly as she prayed. Aegeus thought about how much easier it would all be if he could hear her prayers. But, of course, prayers were not meant for him. The red-haired woman arrived quite suddenly, as she usually did. She placed her hand gently on Aegeus's back and smiled at him. Then she moved so that she walked just behind the Twelfth, out of sight. She laid her hand on the Twelfth's shoulder and kept it there as they walked toward the campus.

Aegeus looked at her and smiled. Things were always better when she was here. As they rounded a corner, Aegeus saw the Fifth approaching from a side street with Haywood. In a matter of seconds, the Fifth and the Twelfth had converged and were walking side by side but not speaking. The red-haired woman laid her other hand on the shoulder of the Fifth. Their Lights flared, but neither woman spoke. Aegeus and Haywood greeted each other as they, too, walked toward the campus.

"It is strange to see you dressed as a guardian," Haywood chuckled uneasily to Aegeus.

"It is strange to be dressed as such," Aegeus said, smiling down at himself.

"How is the Fifth holding up?" Aegeus asked, changing the subject. He knew her past, and he had real concerns.

"She carries a heavy burden, but she resists any ministering angel that comes to her. It is as if she does not want to release it. Her body carries the effect of her soul. She prays often, but because we have had to battle to get in and out of the town, our response has been delayed, and this has caused her to feel distant and unheard. In her darkest days, she feels abandoned by the King and alone."

Aegeus sighed. This was such a common attack from the enemy. He again thought of Lavi, who had just given his life in battle to protect a child of the King. His mind wandered over the other brothers he had lost over the centuries. All the battles, the time away from heaven, all in service to the King for his children, who didn't even know they were there. Children who cried out, feeling abandoned and alone when Aegeus and those like him were there fighting and dying. Then, he remembered how the Lamb had also felt abandoned in his darkest hour.

"Aegeus?" Haywood's voice broke through his thoughts.

"Yes?"

Haywood hesitated. "I think she believes she deserves to be abandoned by the King. I think it is why she fights the ministering angels so strongly."

Aegeus could not understand this; he made a mental note to discuss it with Michael. The two women had begun chatting and were engrossed in whatever it was human women talked about as they all approached their building. From the outside, there was no indication of the anguish that was within the Fifth. The King's children were good at concealing their pain. Perhaps this developing friendship would help both women. The women parted ways inside the building, each heading to her respective office. Hayward and Aegeus did the same.

When Aegeus was satisfied that the Twelfth was settled safely in her office, he decided to walk the perimeter of the building. Low-level demons were darting about in the halls, looking for people to torment or taunt. Most of them were just reaching out and touching a person, leaving a stream of black smoke behind and the thoughts that went with it.

Aegeus watched as the Light would flair in some of them, rejecting the thoughts immediately and sending the demon howling in pain. But occasionally, a demon would land on a target that had not been feeding their soul. The demons would latch on to those and dig their talons deep into their minds, feeding them messages from the enemy. The other demons would cheer at their success and rush to join in.

He witnessed one such attack on a student who had stayed on campus for the summer to work on research—or so that was the story she was telling people. She was walking out of the bathroom when Aegeus first saw her, and she was covered in demons. Despair had the firmest hold on her, but she was covered in Self-doubt, Worthlessness, Lies, and Shame. Additional demons latched on to her as she walked the halls silently, wearing a smile that said everything was great. But Aegeus knew the damage demons could do. Intrigued, he followed the girl at a distance.

The Twelfth came around the corner carrying an empty coffee cup in her hand. Her Light flared brightly when she saw the student, and she stopped suddenly. The Twelfth smiled at the girl.

"Am I heading in the right direction for coffee?" she asked, lifting the cup slightly as if she needed proof of her intentions.

"The faculty break room is that way." The student gestured down the hall, smiling as she did. She gave no outward indication of her demons.

"Thanks." The Twelfth started in the direction the girl had pointed and then paused and stood very still. Aegeus watched; he loved to see the Spirit at work. The Light in the Twelfth was burning brightly, but he could see her face was wrestling with what she had been called to do. The girl had already turned and started the other way. The Twelfth's heart raced. She could sense the Spirit's nudge, urging her to reach out, but what if she was wrong? Her fingers tightened around her empty cup as she tried to calm her nerves. Finally, she took a deep breath, turned, and called out to the girl.

"Hey," she called, "would you like to get a cup of coffee with me?"

The girl was about halfway down the hall; she stopped and looked back at the Twelfth, considering the offer briefly before answering.

Aegeus watched as she struggled, too. His frustration simmered beneath the surface. They needed a ministering angel, not a warrior. He felt out of place, as though he wielded armor too heavy for a job that demanded something gentler. The girl's Light flickered and flared until, finally, she answered.

"Sure."

The two of them walked together to the faculty break room. Aegeus followed. Their initial conversation was superficial. They introduced themselves and shared safe things, such as where they were from. But as Aegeus watched, the woman with the wild red hair arrived and whispered to the Twelfth. Her Light filled the room with warmth and power. Aegeus lifted his face to soak it in. He thought of the Twelfth doing the same this morning as she walked, and he again wished she could know how much greater this was than the sun. The power of the King surged through him, strengthening him. His wings began to unfurl just slightly from the compartment where they were tucked when he didn't need them.

And then, without warning and with a boldness Aegeus had not seen in her before, the Twelfth spoke a message from the King.

"God wants you to know that you are not alone. He has not abandoned you. He sees your pain; he knows what happened to you as a child and what is happening to you now. But what man has meant for evil, he will use for good." The Twelfth paused, full of the Spirit and a little anxious at the same time. She nervously waited for the girl to say something.

"Who are you?" the girl asked, looking nervous. The demons that clung to her also grew still and silent as they stared at the Twelfth. Aegeus moved into position. He could not allow the demons to leave and alert others to what he now knew was indeed a prophet.

"I'm nobody. I'm new here," the Twelfth stammered.

"Who told you those things?"

"God. He tells me things sometimes." This was the part where she expected the girl to reach the conclusion that she was crazy and excuse herself from the room. That was usually what happened; the Twelfth didn't blame people for thinking it.

The demons, who had been shocked into silent stillness, were still staring at the Twelfth when they suddenly realized the situation. Their eyes met Aegeus's for a moment, and then the room erupted into motion. The demons scurried for a way out. The air grew thick, tinged with a faint stench of sulfur. Shadows danced along the walls, cast by the dim light, as if the room itself was closing in on them. Aegeus moved swiftly, his sword flashing with each strike, cutting through Lies and Shame with a single blow. Kfir, drawn in by the Light, dropped from the roof of the building onto the table where the Twelfth sat drinking coffee with the girl.

He grabbed Worthlessness, who squirmed in his hand. Black smoke spewed from Worthlessness as he fought to escape. Aegeus thrust his sword into Worthlessness and turned his attention to Self-doubt. Self-doubt had a talon caught in the girl and could not break free. Aegeus walked slowly forward.

"You must have been with her quite some time," Aegeus said as he slid his sword back into its sheath.

"You are no guardian," the demon accused as he squirmed to break free of the girl. Kfir jumped down from the table and positioned himself behind the girl and the demon. Self-doubt twisted around, trying to see what Kfir was doing. Free of the other demons, the girl's Light began to burn brighter—bright enough to start burning the demon. He started to squeal in pain, tugging the stuck talon. He put both feet on her face and pulled with all his might, but he could not free himself.

"I am Aegeus, warrior of the King, protector of his children," he said, stepping closer, his voice steely with resolve.

"She is a prophet," the demon spit the words from his mouth as if they were poison.

Kfir grabbed the demon and destroyed him with his bare hands. The demon dissipated into black smoke, except for his talon. It dangled from the head of the girl, making it appear as if she had a horn.

"I saved you," Kfir teased.

"What? I totally had this." Aegeus scoffed, feigning indignation.

"I'll remember this the next time you're the one in over your head." Kfir joked.

"How long will she have that horn?" Kfir couldn't help but chuckle. Aegeus walked over to the girl and tugged on the talon. It was stuck deep inside her head.

"No telling."

"I am Aegeus, warrior of the King," Kfir said in his best Aegeus voice. He puffed his chest out and strutted forward a few steps before being overcome with laughter at his own joke.

Aegeus shook his head and playfully shoved his friend.

The Twelfth finished her coffee with the girl, who interestingly didn't run from her. Instead, the girl was quite intrigued by the whole thing. She was not entirely convinced that God saw her, but something about the experience gave her hope and left her feeling a little lighter.

What if it were true? She wondered. What if God did see her? What if he really did know what was happening? What if he hadn't forgotten her as she had told herself for so many years? What if he did have a plan to use all her pain and sorrow for good? Well, that would change everything, wouldn't it? The idea was powerful. The girl was not sure she was ready to believe it, but she was at least interested enough to sit with this strange new professor and consider it.

After coffee, the Twelfth returned to her office and unpacked the few items she had brought with her; then, she began the process of figuring out the computer system. She checked e-mails, set up her voicemail, and then poured herself into creating her courses. She wanted them to be great. She had been working for several hours when a light knock on the door snapped her from her concentration. Her head popped up.

"Am I disturbing you?" the Fifth asked sheepishly.

"No, please, come in." The Twelfth gestured toward one of the chairs in her office. But the Fifth didn't come in.

"I didn't bring lunch; I thought you might want to walk over to the cafeteria with me?"

"I would love to." The Twelfth's heart lifted. It was hard being the new person, and the Fifth's invitation felt like a lifeline, an unspoken welcome in a place where everything else still felt unfamiliar.

Haywood, the guardian of the Fifth, joined Aegeus and Kfir for the walk to the cafeteria.

"You are in for a treat, boys," he teased as they got closer. "The smell in this place is not soon forgotten." He shook his head in disgust. A few taunting demons fluttered about the campus, but overall, things seemed quiet. Suddenly, out of the corner of his eye, Aegeus saw a quick movement. He stopped and looked in the direction of the clock tower. Nothing moved. Aegeus felt a chill ripple down his spine, his gaze fixed on the clock tower's shadow.

He couldn't see anything, but a presence lingered—watchful, calculating. The air grew heavy, and he could sense the familiar weight of an enemy's gaze. He held his breath, muscles tensed, scanning for any sign of movement.

"Aegeus?" Kfir stopped too.

"Someone is there," Aegeus offered. "A warrior."

"One of ours?" Kfir asked.

"No." An ominous feeling settled over him.

Chapter 23: The Fifth

The Fifth stared at her reflection in the mirror. These pep talks were becoming increasingly necessary. She looked deep into her own watery eyes and let out a slow, deep breath.

"You are a smart woman. You know what you're doing. You have managed this lab through hundreds of research projects. You can do this."

The speech was simple, and it usually worked. Today, she wasn't so sure. Another deep breath.

The chemicals from the morning research project caused her eyes to sting and demand a cry to flush them out, but she refused. There was no time for that.

"You are a smart woman. You know what you're doing. You have managed this lab through hundreds of research projects. You can do this." She repeated. The ministering angel leaned closer.

"*It is all meaningless, a chasing after the wind.*" The Fifth shook her head at the thought as one might shake something sticky from their finger. Where did that come from? She asked herself.

She stared at her reflection, feeling the urge to cry slipping away and the frustration returning, which seemed to be her new normal.

She would walk into this meeting and show them why she should be selected for this promotion. She stood up straight and walked confidently from the bathroom to the conference room. The ministering angel shook his head. *They will have ears but will not hear,* he thought.

The board was convened around the large conference table, and they rose when she walked in, a tradition that was nearly lost but one she appreciated.

"Gentlemen," she said in greeting as she took her seat.

"Thank you for joining us," the chairman began. And so, the interview started. The Fifth enjoyed interviewing; she thought she excelled at it. She had been interim director of the lab for more than two years, the very job she was applying for. There was nothing they could ask her about the job or their research that she would not know. She had worked with these men, and they knew her; they already knew her strengths and weaknesses. This should have been a formality—and yet it wasn't.

"How is your daughter?" The question would have been reasonable had they been walking down the hall or standing over a set of microscopes, but during an interview, it was out of place. The Fifth paused for a moment.

"She is doing well, thank you." She sat up even straighter in her chair, glad that she had chosen the black suit and worn her hair up in a strict bun today.

"And how does she feel about you getting this promotion?" the board member continued.

The Fifth tried to imagine how this line of questioning had anything to do with the interview. How was this appropriate? And yet, she hesitated to say anything. She told herself to let it play out and see where they were going.

"Are you concerned, being a single mother, that she will be alone for too long each day if you get this job?" the board member pressed. The Fifth sat stunned as if she had been slapped. She would have preferred to be slapped.

"I have been doing this job for more than two years. Being granted the official title of the position will not change my schedule, nor should it impact my personal life." She tried to answer the question without mentioning her daughter. Her daughter was none of their business.

Although she had been doing the job flawlessly, she did not get the position. Instead, they selected a recruit, fresh from medical school. Someone she had hired—someone she had been training. He would become her boss, and she would step back to the job she'd had two years ago, his current job. The board requested that she continue to teach him. Train her own boss? For the very job she wanted? She thought not.

And so, the days dragged on. She tried not to think about why she had not gotten the position. Instead, she began to pour herself into church activities. She would serve others to help her forget about her own pain. She tried to look on the bright side, to focus outwardly.

One year after she had been told she would not be given the title for the job she had been doing for two years, the US Office of Research Integrity showed up. The trainee they had promoted instead of her was missing, along with millions of dollars in grant funding. A formal investigation was launched, and the lab was under considerable scrutiny. The Fifth was once again asked to step in as interim research director.

The records were disastrous, and the investigation grueling. The Fifth worked tirelessly with the investigators to restore order. Early mornings and late nights became her new norm. When she wasn't in the lab, she was serving in her church. Church had become both a haven and a distraction. She buried herself in committees and volunteer work, hoping to outrun the growing hollowness she felt. But the emptiness remained, waiting for her whenever she was alone. Sleep became a commodity she could not afford.

After six months, the investigation was complete, and the Fifth had restored order to the lab. She had written reports on every project and accounted for all the spending. All except, of course, what her boss had embezzled. The board requested to see her.

This time, she walked into the conference room in her scrubs and lab coat. She hadn't given herself a pep talk—she didn't need it. She had worked tirelessly to prove to the Office of Research

Integrity that it was one rogue researcher who had falsified data and stolen funds.

But an hour later, she again emerged from the conference room without the title of director. She had once again been asked to train someone else to do the job, her job. The Fifth walked purposefully from the room, picked up her keys, and headed out the front door. She spoke to no one. She was numb. The ministering angel sat in the car beside her and laid his hand on her shoulder.

"It is a chasing after the wind; it's all meaningless unless it is for the King." He spoke gently but distinctly. Her Light flickered. She didn't know where she was going—she just drove. She drove until the numbness became rage. She drove through the rage until the pain surfaced, and then she drove until the tears ended and she returned to numbness. Night had fallen, and her phone had rung many times, each one ignored.

As she began to regain clarity, the realization that she had neglected all her responsibilities flooded over her. Then she also realized the car was losing speed. Pulling to the side of the road, the Fifth realized she was out of gas. She was lost, and her cell phone battery had died hours ago.

Night had settled in, and she began to feel foolish. There was nothing she could do about her dead phone; she hadn't brought a charger. No phone meant the cavalry was not coming. Opening the trunk, she found a small gas can, and she uttered a silent prayer of thanks. She wrapped her lab coat around her to block out the chill of the evening, and she started walking.

Walking helped her clear her head, and she found herself singing worship songs as she made her way mile after mile. Just when she felt her feet might refuse to take her another step, a small car pulled up beside her. The Fifth tensed involuntarily. The window of the car rolled down, and a woman with wild red hair leaned over from the driver's seat.

"Need help?" she asked with a voice that was soft and warm.

"I ran out of gas," the Fifth offered, holding up the gas can as unnecessary proof.

"I'm heading that way," the woman said. "I would be happy to help."

The Fifth hesitated. Everyone knew not to get in the car with a stranger. And yet the woman had a presence about her that made the Fifth feel comfortable and safe. She knew her options were limited, and right at the moment, she wasn't sure she cared if the woman was homicidal.

"Thank you, I would appreciate that," she said, easing into the woman's car. The car was warm, and the woman had a faint scent of vanilla that filled the small space. The Fifth relaxed almost despite herself, soothed by the gentle hum of the car and the woman's quiet presence. It was as if she'd been given permission to let down her guard. They drove several miles to the gas station. The two women made small talk on the way to the station. When they arrived, the Fifth got out of the car and thanked her for the ride.

"You will need a ride back to your car," the woman offered. "I am happy to help you get where you need to go." Her kindness was radiant, and the Fifth could not seem to say, "No, thank you." The truth was, she did need a ride. She looked at the woman and was struck by how willing she was to help. She didn't seem rushed or flustered. In reflecting on the drive to the gas station, the Fifth would have to admit the same was true. The woman had been wholly present in the moment.

"Thank you," was all she managed in response. She filled the small gas can and got back in the car. As they were driving back, the woman asked her, "How did you find yourself in this predicament?"

The Fifth shared the heartache of the last few years. She vented her frustration over not getting the position she wanted, and she shared how much it had hurt her to feel rejected by the very people she had worked so hard for.

And then, she did something she never thought she would do. She told the woman about her daughter. Tears flowed freely down her cheeks as she shared the story—her story, her most precious and protected story. She shared her feelings of failure, inadequacy, guilt, and loss. Her Light began to burn more brightly. The woman with the wild red hair said nothing. She simply drove the car, allowing the Fifth to pour out her heart uninterrupted.

When they arrived back at the Fifth's car, the woman pulled to the shoulder and stopped. She looked at the Fifth and smiled. That was not the response the Fifth was expecting.

"What has all your work and sacrifice accomplished?" asked the woman.

The Fifth sat there a little stunned. She took a deep breath and whispered words she had not been willing to admit to herself.

"Nothing. It has been meaningless." She said it more to herself than to the woman. The truth was that the last five years of her life had been the hardest she had ever endured. She had carried an enormous burden, and she had used work as a way to lighten it. But it left her feeling empty. Work could not return her love; it only took from her and left her feeling empty.

The woman looked at the Fifth and smiled. As she pushed a stray hair away from her face, she said, "It is meaningless—unless it is not. When you work for more than yourself—when it is lasting, when it is eternal—then you find meaning and fulfillment."

The Fifth felt the words sink into her soul. She knew these words to be the truth. The word tasted bitter, but she couldn't deny it. "Meaningless," she whispered. Everything she had fought for felt empty like sand slipping through her fingers. And yet, admitting it aloud brought a strange, fragile peace, as if finally acknowledging the wound was the first step toward healing.

There was something about the woman that made the Fifth want to stay there with her, but they were back at her car, and she knew that she needed to go. She thanked the woman for the ride and got out, her Light burning brightly, filling her with hope.

The Fifth did not return to working in the lab. Instead, she spent time in prayer and fasting, seeking out the King's will. In time, she found a teaching position at a small Christian college hidden in the mountains. There, she believed she would find meaning in her work, and it would have eternal consequences.

Chapter 24

Aegeus was pleased to see that the Twelfth was settling into the town, making friends, and feeding her soul. She walked to the college most days, praying along the way. She often prayed aloud, allowing Aegeus to hear her heart. But her prayers were around, hiding her Light. She asked the King to silence her daily, allowing her to blend in. She prayed fervently for this.

As she walked, Aegeus noticed the slump in her shoulders, the weight of her whispered words hanging between them. Her plea to "blend in" was a daily refrain, but today, he sensed a thread of fatigue woven through her prayer—a quiet surrender that gnawed at him as if her Light were dimming from her own will rather than any outside force.

"Doesn't she know that salt that is merely called salt is worthless? You must actually be salt to be beneficial to the kingdom," Kfir observed one day as she made her plea. But Aegeus did not think she knew. Like many of the people in the town, she put on a smile and went to work and tried to ignore her humanity. She felt like she wasn't enough—not good enough, not holy enough, not righteous enough. This was one of the great weapons used by the enemy, and it worked well.

Multiple times over the summer, the King had given her messages to deliver. In each instance, she had wrestled with the message. She had argued and protested and questioned, and then she had delivered the message exactly as the King had required. Yet, during a conversation with the Fifth and the Eighth about spiritual gifts, she declared she had none. Aegeus had searched her face for an indication of false humility, but it was not there. She didn't know. Twice, Aegeus had gone to the King filled with frustration because of her, but the King had smiled and answered, "Be patient, my good and faithful servant." Despite his numerous requests, the King would not reassign him.

In resignation to the King's will, Aegeus returned to the salvage yard for the shift change. He arrived in the abandoned building they were using as a meeting area to find that Kfir already had breakfast laid out. Manna was one of Aegeus's favorites. He picked up a bagel-shaped piece of manna and carefully spread a light coating of honey on it. Kfir handed Aegeus his wineskin, and Aegeus poured himself a glass of wine to go with the manna. He surveyed the room where the next shift was finishing their own breakfasts.

Amitiel, engrossed in a novel, was sitting in the corner on an old wooden crate. Aegeus took a long swig of his wine and walked over to him.

"What are you reading?" he asked as he tapped the book with his free hand.

"This Present Darkness."

"Ahh, Peretti, one of my favorites," Aegeus said, smiling. "What have you learned?" he asked.

"About Peretti or about the twelve?"

"About the twelve," Aegeus answered.

"They are not holding up well, Aegeus," he said, "but I have researched their backgrounds extensively, and I believe we will be able to break through to them. It just takes time."

"Indeed," noted Aegeus.

Aegeus walked to the head of the room and cleared his throat. The other angels stopped chatting and waited for him to give them the morning report.

"We had another quiet night. The college has a meeting today that is required for all employees. So, all twelve will be in the same room for the first time. The Strongman will be there as well, so this will be our first real look at him. Kfir, stay close to the Twelfth and see if you can tell if she recognizes him for what he is."

When Aegeus mentioned the Strongman, a hush settled over the room. Even the most seasoned warriors among them held their breath, their eyes narrowing as they prepared. They all understood what the Strongman represented—a force of corruption cloaked in influence and charm that could twist even the brightest souls.

"Has she carried any messages?" Adiel asked, interrupting the silence.

"Yes. She has delivered messages for the King over the summer," answered Aegeus. "She knows they are from the King, and she has told the recipients they were from the King, but she still does not recognize she is a prophet."

"This makes no sense," Paki, a guardian angel recently joining the team from Africa, interjected. "How can she carry a message from the King and not realize she is a prophet?"

Amitiel, as the specialist in researching customs and cultures, jumped in to help.

"Paki, in America, many of the shepherds have convinced the people that prophecy is no longer one of the spiritual gifts. Furthermore, among many denominations, even if it were a gift, it would never be given to a woman. The Twelfth has been told this her entire life. She does not even consider prophecy as an option. Someone will have to tell her this is her gift. She will not believe them, but it will plant a seed, and the Spirit will water that seed until she is forced to see what is there."

Paki nodded his head, but he did not truly understand. How could anyone read the Word and conclude that prophecy was no longer a gift? Was it not listed in the lists of spiritual gifts? Were there not multiple places that spoke of it? Did the King not say that he was the same yesterday, today, and tomorrow? But Paki knew that generations of misinformation could indeed lead people astray. It was hard to ignore what you had been taught to believe and even harder to use untainted eyes to see what was in the Word.

Prophecy's too much for them," Kfir chuckled, clapping Paki on the back. "Some think it's ancient history—others say it's a threat to the status quo. Americans prefer their prophets in books, I think."

Paki shook his head, looking bemused, and Kfir just smiled.

"The Eighth is struggling; we may lose him," Aegeus continued. "He is essential to encouraging the other eleven, but he is so discouraged himself that he is of limited use. Understanding the history of each of the twelve will be important. Amitiel, prepare a file on each of them for tomorrow's briefing. Keep to the essentials. Our reinforcements will be here by then, and we can get everyone caught up at the same time. For now, we will focus on the encounter with the Strongman. The demons are returning to the town, causing the sun to be muted, and many of the humans are impacted by the lack of sunshine."

"I have heard them refer to the demon cover as 'the dome,'" Kfir added. "They know it is there even if they don't fully understand what it is."

"Dome sounds less ominous than demons," chuckled Paki, still trying to understand the Americans and their view on spiritual things.

"I do not know what the Strongman will say in today's meeting," continued Aegeus, "but we must be prepared for anything. The King is sending the army, and they will arrive when the time is right. A squadron will come as part of the advance party. He is sending in additional ministering angels, guardians, and common angels. They will begin arriving today during the speech. The demons will be distracted then, and we expect a good number of them to be in the Great Hall when the Strongman gives his speech. That should allow the angels to arrive with little notice. The King's army would bring with it a tide of strength they could not afford to be without. If they were to reclaim this town, if they were to resist the Strongman's reach, they would need every weapon and every ally heaven could send. We will do all we can to remain undetected until that is no longer possible." Aegeus finished his wine and licked a small trace of honey from his fingers. Oh, how he missed home.

Chapter 25

The Great Hall was teeming with demons, mostly low-level demons whispering anxious thoughts and doubts to the people gathered there. Aegeus and Kfir watched as the Twelfth and the Eighth entered the hall. The Strongman was mingling about the hall as people entered. He was shaking hands and offering conciliatory introductions, smiling, and laughing. He referenced the King repeatedly and how grateful he was to be in the service of the King. He told person by person how pleased he was that the King had brought him here and provided this opportunity for him to further the kingdom. It made Aegeus's skin crawl, but the humans seemed to believe him.

The Twelfth and the Eighth drew near the Strongman. They were positioned to greet him next when Aegeus noticed the Light in the Twelfth suddenly erupt. She stepped back from the Strongman and stared at him, her eyes opened wide in horror or shock—Aegeus could not tell which. He was mesmerized to watch the Spirit work in her, and he was a bit caught up in the surge of power he felt from heaven as it happened. Kfir elbowed him, breaking the moment.

"Look," Kfir whispered. Directing Aegeus's attention to the Strongman and away from the Twelfth. The demon inside the Strongman was raging. He fought against the flesh and blood body that contained him and reached for the Twelfth. The Strongman recognized her for what she was: a prophet of the Most High.

While the demon struggled to reach her, sulfur roaring from his mouth, his arms reaching desperately for the Twelfth, the human body of the Strongman continued to smile. He continued the charade of greeting each new person while reciting his speech about advancing the kingdom.

The Twelfth stood still, just looking at him, unable to see his true form but sure that something was wrong. An icy warning settled in her heart as if a profound wrongness lurked beneath his smile. The Spirit whispered to her.

"It is not God's kingdom he is here to advance." She took another step back from him. Aegeus moved closer to her, positioning himself between her and the Strongman.

"Do you smell that?" asked the Eighth. "Smells like someone farted." He chuckled as the sulfur reached his nose.

"That's awful; we should get out of here." And he and the Twelfth moved on to find seats near the Fifth, who had come by herself. The Twelfth couldn't help but wonder why the Fifth hadn't come over with them. Aegeus looked over at Kfir, who was snickering like a child.

"What is so funny?" he asked, starting to chuckle just at the sight of it.

"He thought the demon smelled like farts," Kfir laughed. Aegeus just shook his head and took his position near the Twelfth.

The Strongman took the stage, positioning himself in front of the large cross that served as a backdrop to the pulpit. The Great Hall had many purposes at the college, but once a week, the students, staff, and faculty gathered in it to worship the King. In years past, this had been a beautiful time, and angels would gather on the roof of the building to hear the songs of praise coming from the hall. Five thousand voices strong singing songs of worship was a beautiful sound to the angels and the King alike.

"Let us open with prayer," said the Strongman, kneeling in front of the group. Prayer was normally a source of power for the angels. But the Strongman's prayer was not to the King but to the Prince of this world. The angels in the room became antsy to be in the presence of such darkness. The warriors had been in this situation before, but the guardians and ministering angels were less used to such forms of evil. They shifted uneasily, feeling the full burden of being close to such filth. For an angel to stand in the presence of such evil and listen to a prayer to the Dark One was a true test of their self-control.

Aegeus looked around the Great Hall to see how well they were handling it. Paki was horror-stricken and shaking with rage; he had unknowingly gripped his sword. He appeared as if he would vomit—if angels did that sort of thing.

Aegeus sent calm and peace to Paki, who feeling the gift, lifted his eyes, searching the room for the source. His eyes met Aegeus's, and he nodded to acknowledge the gift. Aegeus looked around at the humans, who had all bowed their heads and closed their eyes, a tradition the Americans had when praying. But the Twelfth did not have her head bowed or her eyes closed. She was staring at the Strongman with the same look of disgust that Paki had displayed only seconds before. Aegeus smiled, feeling pleased with her. Somehow it made him more aware of the empty space beside him where Lavi once stood. How he would have despised the Strongman's hollow prayer.

The Strongman concluded his prayer, which had consisted of a mini-sermon for the sake of convincing those present of his piousness and dedication to the King. He had worked up tears and allowed them to pour down his face and strangle his voice, so he seemed wrought with emotion over his passion for the King. The problem was that it was not the King he was passionate about. He stood from his kneeling position and made a show of wiping the tears from his face. Then he turned to the crowd and began his well-rehearsed speech.

"My family and I are so honored to be here," he began. "I feel God has blessed me in innumerable ways by giving me my dream job. I love that we are a community of faith and that we are pouring into the next generation to send them out on fire for the kingdom. I still remember the first time I set foot on this campus; it was years ago, and I was struck by the way it felt like home, like a community bound by a shared purpose. And now, standing here as your leader,

I feel a renewed sense of that purpose—to protect what we hold dear and guide the next generation."

He put his hands in his pockets and looked down at the ground as he began to pace a few steps on the stage. The pause was dramatic enough to cause a short moment of silence and create the effect he was after without being too long. "Now I understand you have had some trouble here," he continued. "The board brought me in to clean house and remove those among us who were not true to the faith—radicals who had strayed from the truth."

He paused again to let that sink in, then he removed his hands from his pockets and stared out at the four hundred faces looking at him. "It was not easy terminating people, but I am committed to keeping our mission pure and our path straight. If any of you are not in agreement with our beliefs, I will remove you as well." The threat lingered in the air and seemed to have the effect he was looking for.

The tormenting demons squealed with pleasure at that comment and began to flit about the room, spreading fear. Lights all over the room started to flicker and dim. The room grew stifling, as though the very air vibrated with the undercurrent of fear and doubt. But the Twelfth's Light began to shine more brightly, her righteous anger beginning to simmer as she shifted uncomfortably in her seat.

"In two days, five thousand young college students will descend on us, and we have the great privilege of shaping their futures. Our students are precious, and they trust us to guide them toward truth. It's our sacred duty to shield them from dangerous ideas that could lead them astray, ensuring that they become torchbearers of faith who will stand strong, unwavering, in a world of shifting values. I take this responsibility very seriously. We will pour into them; we will saturate their minds and souls with the truth. We will not let them be swayed by the lies of the culture. We will teach them to stand firm for the faith, to oppose what our culture is telling them, and to fight for religious freedom!"

This statement elicited applause from the crowd, although Aegeus noticed that a few did not join in.

"We will put God first in all that we do, and we will teach the students to do that as well. We will restore this institution by setting things right and removing the cultural creep that has set in. I have great plans, and I am hopeful that you are the right team to come on this great journey with me."

More applause.

"I want us to trust each other. So, I would like to open things up for questions," he continued.

Early questions were silly things about where he had moved from and what types of things he liked to do in his spare time. He answered each question graciously and tried to seem likable in the process. A small woman in her early fifties rose from her seat, her Light burning brightly as she made her way to the microphone. She was flanked on both sides by ministering angels giving her courage and offering affirmation. The Spirit was ablaze inside her.

The demons, seeing her Light, became nervous and repositioned themselves throughout the crowd. But the Strongman seemed to know what was coming, and he smiled at her widely, inviting the question. He signaled almost imperceptibly to the demons who moved to try to silence her. This woman had not been part of the plan. Morax sat in the back of the room and shifted in his seat; he did not like this at all.

"In researching your background," she started, "it looks like there is a considerable amount of controversy surrounding your position on women. Could you clarify your view of women?" she asked.

"Of course," he answered. "I love women; I love their cooking. I even have one of my own," he said, laughing at his own joke. Chuckles filled the room.

"But seriously, I value the soft perspective a good woman brings to a situation. I want to be sure we have women involved in all appropriate areas of the college. We need them to mentor the young women on campus and teach them about becoming godly women. The Word tells us that our older women need to teach the younger women how to be good wives and mothers. I fully support that as should you all."

"And when you say, 'all appropriate areas,' what does that mean to you?" the woman asked as a follow-up.

"Well, we all agree that God created men and women differently. Women were designed to complement men, to be their helpers. Paul tells us that it is not appropriate for women to be over men or to teach them. Now, culture would tell us that is not right. Culture would have you believe in this whole feminist movement. But as believers, we know that God has established order, a hierarchy if you will, and that he has told women to submit to the leadership of men.

"It is crucial that we hold tight to those truths and not let Satan draw our young women away from the truth and God's divine plan for them. In accordance with God's law, we will not have women speak in chapel, we will not have women preach—nor will we have women in leadership positions that could cause them to violate any of the aforementioned rules.

"We will make sure our young women hear that God has a great calling for them, the greatest calling a woman could ever hope for, the call to be a good mother and wife. When you get a dog, it is not truly yours until you name it. But once you name that dog, you have dominion over it. You are given authority over the dog. In the Bible, you see that Adam named Eve, giving him dominion and authority over her. These are not my rules; they are God's rules, and we will honor them. Now, in the past, there have, unfortunately, some Corinthian women among us, but they have been removed. There is no place for that here."

A murmur settled over the room as people looked at each other and commented to their neighbors. The demons giggled with glee; the plan was working exactly as they had hoped.

"But those are rules for the church, and we are not the church," she countered.

"The church is the body of believers, those who join to worship God. It is not a building; surely you know that," he responded with a slight sneer.

"One last question," the woman said, her Light burning bright and her rage causing her hands to tremble slightly. She could feel the tension in the room, but she held her ground as she prepared her next question.

"Of course," the Strongman replied.

"One report I saw said that you advised an abused woman to go back to her husband and simply pray more. You reportedly told her that if she would just submit more, her husband would not beat her. Is there any truth to that?"

The room went silent; the demons even paused in their glee to look at the Strongman. Morax was not pleased that things had gone in this direction. This was not the subtle plan they had discussed. This was too much; he feared they would be undone by this woman on the very first day. Everyone waited for the Strongman's response. A smile spread wide across his face.

"That is one of my favorite stories. There is nothing simple about praying. Is there anything better than a story of redemption? The Word tells us that the shepherd will leave the sheep to go search for the one that is lost. And this is a story of him finding and redeeming a lost sheep.

"We are taught to turn the other cheek when someone strikes us, to pray for those who do evil to us. To love those who persecute us. And that was what I advised that woman. Her husband's very soul was on the line. And what is more important, salvation by grace or a few rough nights?

"God had put that woman under the authority of her husband, and she had the incredible privilege of showing her husband God's unfailing love by following God's command for her to stay under her husband's authority and submit to him.

"God never says to obey his commands only when it is easy or when we like the results. He commands us to turn over our lives to him, take up our cross, and follow him. Sometimes, that means making sacrifices. Now, I am not condoning violence against women; I don't want you to hear something I am not saying. I abhor violence against women. We are not called to violence. But I lift that woman up for staying in a situation that was hard and following the command of the Lord."

The Strongman ended the discussion and then closed the meeting with another kneeling prayer. Some in the room remained unfazed, nodding along, while others exchanged uneasy glances, their Lights flickering with uncertainty. He thanked God for a group of people who loved the Lord enough to sacrifice their own comfort to take the gospel to the ends of the earth. He thanked God for a people so dedicated to doing his will and so unified in mind. He thanked God for ridding them of those who would tell lies and divert the path in honor of the ways of the culture, and he asked God to give him discernment so that any other distractions among them could be rooted out and eliminated.

Aegeus looked around the room and noticed that the Twelfth was not the only one who did not bow her head and pretend to pray. Now, at least, they knew his hand.

Chapter 26

As the faculty and staff exited the Great Hall, the hallways buzzed with whispered doubts and half-formed questions that never found a voice. Those who'd been unsettled by the words grappled with their own thoughts, reluctant to speak for fear of seeming rebellious. The demons flew about, assuring that the men were not overly concerned, given it did not apply to them. Most of them had tuned it out and couldn't even tell you exactly what was said. Those who had listened dismissed it immediately as something that would not make any difference to the everyday functioning of the college, so there was no need to get worked up.

The women were reeling from the comments but did not want to be seen as "Corinthian women," so most of them remained silent, wrestling internally with the remarks and concerns about what this meant for them and their jobs. What he had spoken was so close to the truth. Perhaps it was the truth. Maybe they were the ones that were mistaken? What if they were being rebellious; after all, the abused woman's husband did get saved, and wasn't that the most important thing? Divorce was a sin unless your spouse was unfaithful.

The Strongman was an ordained preacher; he had been to seminary and earned a Master of Divinity degree. He had overseen numerous churches. He was a man of God. Who were they to argue with him? And yet, something didn't feel right. Most of them tried to stifle it as their own pride and rebellion.

The Fifth said she had to go across campus for something, leaving the Twelfth and the Eighth to walk back to their building. Upon entering the Great Hall and encountering the Strongman, the Twelfth had been sure he was not of God. After hearing him speak, she felt even more certain. And yet, she too feared this was her own selfish pride. Didn't Paul say those things that the Strongman had quoted? Didn't the Word tell women to submit to their husbands? The Word was clear about the qualifications to be a shepherd. She did not want to be rebellious, and yet the thought that the God whom she loved so much would love her less than another just because she was a woman was a sickening thought.

Could this be true? The same King who had crafted her so lovingly—could he truly want her to stay silent, to submit so blindly? If the Strongman were right, it left her feeling like an intruder in her own faith. The idea that her Creator had made her to be second class was something she was not prepared to digest just yet. Was she a rebellious woman? She agreed that the Bible said a woman was not to shepherd a church, but this was not a church; it was a college. Could a woman not speak? Were those same rules of leadership applicable outside the church structure? Despite what he had said about the church being the body, weren't those rules for organized church meetings? Was a woman forbidden from preaching? What about Anne Graham Lotz or Beth Moore? She just couldn't believe those women were violating God's law. If this was the truth, why did it feel so wrong? Why did the love of her King feel so far from these words?

The Eighth, whom the King had adorned with intuition and an abundance of compassion, could feel the conflicting emotions of the Twelfth. He had spent months getting to know her over the summer, and they had bonded as friends. He was "normal," and she liked that about him. He was honest, real, and imperfect. He got angry, he struggled, and he hadn't always done the right things—he still didn't—all things that made the Twelfth more comfortable around him. He seemed to understand her, and he seemed to know what to say to make her feel better. Gifts the King had given him. He slowed his pace slightly and offered a gentle glance as they grew closer to their building.

"I don't think he should have advised that woman to stay with her husband," he said, hoping to safely open the topic. But this subject was so raw for her, so intimate that she was not quite ready to talk about it.

"I don't either. I would never advise my daughter that way. But maybe that is because I am a woman; perhaps I should go home and ask my husband what to think," she quipped. She knew it was snarky, but she felt incapable of responding any other way. The Eighth could feel her pain. He could feel all of their sadness and anger. Sometimes it served him well to know the feelings of those around him, but sometimes, it was an overwhelming burden. As the anger and sorrow grew around the town, he felt their burdens; he carried them in his soul. He and the Twelfth walked the rest of the way in silence. He could feel the silent tremor of the women's doubts and frustrations in the hallways, their thoughts tangled in uncertainty and fear. Normally, he would have said a silent prayer for them, but things were not anywhere close to normal for him.

Chapter 27: The Eighth

The Eighth looked around at the small campus as he walked from his car to the building whose address he had scribbled on the notepad. It wasn't a bad campus—it was immaculate and relatively new compared to his own. But he was used to a much larger school; this one felt too small and suffocating. He flipped over the paper he had been carrying with information about the ribbon-cutting ceremony and saw that the college boasted five thousand students. He couldn't help but feel a little superior.

The college was opening a new physician's assistant program, and he had been invited, along with hundreds of others, to the ribbon-cutting for their new building. As he walked toward the building, he wasn't sure why he had even agreed to come. No one had ever heard of this school. It was in the middle of nowhere, hidden in the mountains, and it was a competitor to his own program. Well, if you could even call it that. As he walked toward the building, he once again wished that his wife would have been able to come with him, and even as the thought entered his mind, he wondered what had brought it on.

He reached the door of the building, and a woman with wild red hair was coming out. She smiled at him and held the door. "Need any help finding your way?" she asked, clearly detecting that he was a visitor.

"I'm here for the ribbon-cutting," the Eighth said, noting that no one had ever held the door for him at his own campus. He could feel the warmth and genuine kindness radiating from the woman. It disarmed him a little.

"Oh, that's right around the corner," she said, gesturing in the direction he should go, which was not the way he was headed. "I'm headed that way, too; if you would like, I can walk with you."

"That would be great." The Eighth felt an urge to stand up a little straighter and straighten his tie. He wasn't used to such courtesies. That never happened on his campus. The Light within him began to burn more brightly.

The ceremony was simple yet elegant. Much nicer than the Eighth had expected, and the people were so sincere in their joy over the new building. They had been working for years to start the school and having a new building of their own just seemed something tangible they could point to. Everything was state-of-the-art. A small pang of jealousy swept over him as he thought about how much research he could do in a lab like that.

Several months passed, and the Eighth had long since put the visit to the small school behind him. His days were once again filled with his own students, his own school, and his own research. He was happy; things were going well.

One evening, as he was leaving the office, the phone rang. He hesitated; if he answered it, he might be stuck there for much longer than he wanted to be, and he had promised his wife a night out. Reluctantly, he reached his hand out, saying a silent prayer that it would not take too long.

"How was your day?" his wife asked as they sat across from each other in the restaurant later. They had been to a movie and were having dessert after, a tradition they had started in college.

"Something strange happened," he offered, easing into the conversation that had ended his day. He told her about the call from the small school hidden in the mountains. The dean had called and offered him a job. He would be able to do more advanced research and would have a reduced teaching load, but the pay wouldn't be quite as good. They discussed the offer and what an honor it was, but they also agreed they weren't interested in moving, and so he would decline.

They finished their ice cream without thinking any more of the offer. They chatted about the movie, their children, and their dreams. And then they walked hand in hand to the car for the drive home. The Eighth leaned down, kissing his wife on the head. Things were good. He was happy just the way they were. There was no reason to change anything. The small school was forgotten.

They arrived home late and ready for bed. The Eighth was waiting in the bedroom for his wife to finish her nightly routine.

"Perhaps this night may end with my tie on the doorknob," he chuckled to the empty room. His wife walked into the room, her toothbrush still hanging from her mouth, toothpaste starting to drip from her lips. She reached up with her left hand to catch it as it fell.

"Maybe you should consider the job," she garbled through the toothpaste.

"What?" He understood the words, but he was surprised. She held up a finger to give him the "wait a second" sign as she went to spit out the toothpaste and rinse her mouth.

"I've been thinking about that offer since we discussed it," she continued when she got back in the room. He had not thought about it again.

"Maybe it would be fun to move and start over," she said as she climbed into the bed next to him. "I mean, the kids are old enough to adjust well. And if you teach less, you will have more time at home. We're adventurous, aren't we?" she said, smiling at him. He was struck by her beauty. She had aged so well, and he reached up to stroke her face without thinking about it.

"Next time, we don't go to an adventure movie," he said, teasing her. She laughed easily at his joke.

"I just think we should pray about it before we discount it completely. There's something about it I like," she said, putting the topic to rest for the time being.

Chapter 28

The next day, the campus was transformed from a virtual ghost town into a bustling community filled with young energy. The students flowed into the dorms and filled classrooms. They were full of hope for a new year and dreams of a future.

As was the college's tradition, the opening day involved a worship service as part of the convocation ceremony. The ceremony was held in the Great Hall. Every student, staff member, and faculty member were required to attend the midday service. The demon presence was thick, and the day was overcast with a haze that could only be explained by the sulfur oozing from them. Thousands of tormenting demons filled the rafters of the Great Hall. Several hundred warrior demons were also present, some of Titus's best.

Aegeus and his men found themselves severely outnumbered once again. The ministering angels had been busy encouraging parents to pray for their children as they dropped them off. This led to the arrival of more guardians, which pleased Aegeus. But the arrival of the guardians had raised alarms for Titus, and he had doubled his warriors swarming over the town, completely sealing the dome of demons. All of them were destroying demons. Now, every angel that arrived would have to battle their way in. The demons far outnumbered the prayers that were calling the guardians in.

The faculty, donned in their academic regalia, filed into the Great Hall behind the mace, as was the tradition. The service started with singing to the King. Their voices filled the room with the sweet sound of praise. It overwhelmed the space and charged the angels. The demons screamed in protest, covering their ears and swarming the room as they worked desperately to distract the humans.

"Wow, that girl is way off-key," one whispered to an unsuspecting male who could then only hear the off-pitch sounds coming from behind him. The distraction would keep him from focusing on the King and draw all his attention to wishing that the off-key girl would stop singing.

"Look at what he is wearing," another demon suggested to a girl. "Were his eyes shut when he got dressed?" This, of course, led her to check out what others were wearing and even rethink her own choice for the day.

"Check her out," another enticed. It would draw the eye to a girl he found attractive. "Imagine what her skin must feel like," the demon offered. "Imagine touching her hair, gripping it in your hands, and breathing in her scent." It was all that was required to start his mind down a path of lust. The demon could then leave him and attend to another.

But as the tormenting demons approached some and reached toward them, the Light would burn the demons, sending them scampering to find someone else to tempt and torment. The warrior-demons found this particularly amusing and laughed riotously from their posts. The warriors were there for one reason only: to fight. They did not bother with petty tormenting; they were bred for war.

As the singing ended, the Strongman walked confidently to the podium and called those assembled to pray. He knelt on one knee. "Lord, we are so honored to be in your house with the freedom to worship you. We are so thankful that you sent your son to die so that we may live. We ask, Lord, that you guard our hearts and minds as we begin this academic year. We know how tempting sex can be. We know how tempting it is to rebel against your plan. We know that the call of alcohol can be loud, but we ask, Father, that you deliver us from these evils. Please don't let us be tricked by those who would speak against your words or try to twist them for their own purposes. Give us discernment when we encounter those who have sacrificed your truth for a modern culture so that we may rid them from our midst." The subtle threats and warnings of his position wrapped in righteous packaging and delivered, he rose and began his first address to the students.

"I know that for some of you, this is your last year here at the institution, and some of you are just beginning. But I am so thrilled for all of you to have the opportunity to be here. I wish I had had this type of experience. I did not go to a faith-based school. I had my priorities all wrong. I went to a secular school, and you know how those are—everyone is doing drugs and drinking and having sex. There are no morals or values, and it is easy to get pulled into that. We are called, as you know, to be in the world but not of it. We must engage culture to show them where they have gone wrong, but we must not embrace it. We must fight against the lies that we are being taught about marriage and family and the new normal. But the good news of the gospel will free you from those temptations. I was very blessed that God delivered me from those evils and preserved righteousness in me.

"You are in a wonderful position here to find a spouse from among this impressive collection of believers." Applause erupted from the students.

"Seniors, if you haven't been blessed with the gift of singleness, you only have one more year to find a spouse. After this, you will be searching for diamonds among thorns.

"Ladies, you need to find yourself a good God-fearing man to lead you before you graduate. A man who will love you as Christ loved the church and will lead you and your family.

"Men look around at these ladies. They are good, Christ-loving women who will honor you. They understand that the biblical role of women is to submit to their husband's authority and care for their children.

"You will not find that outside of here. Women in the world are feminists. They will tell you that women can have it all. They have convinced the culture that women should put off marriage and pursue their careers. We see that happening across the nation.

"An education is a good thing—look where we are—but it is not a woman's highest calling. Bearing children and caring for her family is her highest calling. Good Christian women, those in this room, recognize that. They know how to show respect to their husband; they understand that they should not make more money than their husbands. Doing so is a blatant sign of disrespecting your husband.

"Ladies, you must guard your bodies and not lead men into temptation by wearing provocative clothes; yoga pants and sleeveless tops have no place in the Christian woman's wardrobe. Now I know the devil will tempt you this year. He will tempt you with the desire for sex. But for you to have any hope of a successful marriage, it is vital that you are a virgin when you marry. Don't let Satan destroy your chances of finding a mate and getting married by giving away the most precious gift you have to offer your husband.

"Gentlemen, if the cow will offer you the milk before the wedding night, it is not the right cow."

Laughter filled the room. These were teachings most of them had heard many times. But a select few sat stunned, offended even.

"I was fortunate to find a beautiful Christian woman when I went to seminary. She is a strong woman, and she does a great job of caring for our children and home. Now, I don't think she will mind me telling you that she went through a bit of a rebellious stage about two years after we got married. We had just had our son. He was not sleeping much, and my wife was getting up with him about every hour all night. This had been going on for about two months, and as you can imagine, she was tired. When you get too tired, you become vulnerable to the temptations of Satan, and she fell prey to his tricks. Selfishly, she asked me to alternate getting up with her so she would get up once, and then I would get up the next time, and so on. Now, don't judge her —don't judge her—she is a good woman. But the devil got her while she was weak. Then, she would sometimes forget to prepare dinner or take too long in the market. But again, it's not her fault—just Satan sowing seeds of rebellion, and it's my job to remind her of her true path. By the grace of God, I can help her find her way back to obedience, and she has been blessed by it, as we all have.

"But, men, I knew my calling to love my wife and my responsibilities to lead her. I pointed out her selfishness and reminded her that God had given me a brand-new church to disciple, and I had to be fresh and rested to do his work. And at the same time, God had given her a family to care for. How beautiful that he had chosen her to bear our son and care for him, this precious gift from God. I loved her and would never deprive her of fulfilling her divine calling, nor would I expect her to try to keep me from fulfilling mine.

"We each have our God-assigned roles. She recognized the truth in it and apologized to me, asking my forgiveness for her selfishness. Men, you need to offer your forgiveness to your wife; don't withhold it. Well, years passed, and God saw fit to bless us with six more children. After they all started school, my wife once again fell victim to temptation. That time, it took a little longer for her to repent; the devil had his talons in her deep. But we are out of time today, so I will save that story for next week. Let's close in prayer."

When the Strongman was done praying, he dismissed the congregation and sent them out for their educational pursuits. The tormenting demons immediately latched on to any student without a guardian. There was so much material from the Strongman's speech for them to work with. As the students poured out of the Great Hall, the tormenting demons set to work like hungry wolves, targeting every lingering doubt and insecurity the Strongman's words had planted. To the girls, they fed whispers of shame and inadequacy. For the boys, they twisted the understanding of what it meant to be a godly man, what true leadership looked like, and a sense of disgust and judgment over any girl who might dare to challenge "the order." The demons swarmed in the students' minds, wielding the Strongman's words like daggers. But Aegeus noticed that it was not just the students. The tormenting demons also grabbed the faculty and staff who had attended. The Twelfth was among those leaving the Great Hall. Her rage burned bright, but her Light grew dim.

Chapter 29

The Twelfth, the Fifth, and the Eighth had attended the service together. They remained silent as they exited the Great Hall and were relatively clear of students' ears. Then, the Twelfth eased into the subject.

"I went to a secular school. It wasn't evil," she started.

"That was your takeaway from this?" the Fifth asked, a little shocked. The Twelfth shifted her weight, wrapping her arms around herself as if bracing against an unseen force. Her heart pounded, not from what she believed, but from what she hoped they wouldn't affirm.

"I did too," the Eighth added quickly. "It was trite to suggest that secular schools were nothing but evil." Having found a small slice of common ground, the Twelfth ventured out to more dangerous territory.

"Do you think God created women to be second class?" she asked hesitantly, secretly desperate for them not to agree with the Strongman's statements. Desperate for affirmation that she wasn't a rebellious woman who didn't know her "place."

"That isn't exactly what he said," offered the Eighth cautiously. He could sense how delicate this situation was. "He didn't say God made you second class, just that God made men to lead."

"So, women can't lead?" asked the Fifth, not pleased with the answer. Aegeus watched as tormenting demons swooped in beside the Twelfth and began whispering to her. But Aegeus had been warned that this test was necessary, and he did not interfere. The Twelfth would have to learn to listen to only one voice. Learning to silence the lies and hold on to the truth was valuable training. And so, he stood at a distance, watching the situation unfold.

"No, that's not what I'm saying," said the Eighth, immediately regretting that he had said anything at all. Did anyone ever win this discussion? He could feel their anger, but mostly, he could feel their pain. The comments of the Strongman had damaged their souls, leaving them feeling underloved by a God who loved them dearly.

"I am not saying I agree with him," he continued. "And certainly not with the way he put things. But he didn't say that women were loved less or held less status or importance with God. He just said there is a hierarchy in the family and church, and in that hierarchy, men are the leaders." He paused there because he knew they both already knew that.

"Yes," said the Fifth, "but what he said wasn't that simple. It was offensive and degrading. He likened us to cows!" She felt repulsed at the idea. If all she had to offer a man was servitude and virginity, she was in trouble. The idea that her sole purpose was to be a good wife and mother dug deep into wounds she thought had finally scarred over. But with only a few distasteful words, they had been ripped open, and anguish poured from them.

"It was indeed offensive, but I think what he was trying to say was biblical—his delivery was just poorly executed. I don't think he was trying to be offensive."

"You can't be equal if there is a hierarchy. If the two are to become one, how can one of them be over the other? You would have to still be two," The Twelfth noted.

"And yoga pants are evil? Seriously?" The Fifth wanted to move the conversation toward safer ground—something they could more easily agree on.

"And the whole idea that what a woman brings to a marriage is virginity is awful. Why was that directed to the women anyway and not to both?" The Twelfth wanted to hash this out. She needed to discuss it, to hear other perspectives, to be challenged or affirmed.

"I think you might be taking that out of context." The Eighth just didn't hear it the same way they had.

Neither woman was convinced. The Twelfth began to doubt herself even more. The tormenting demons jumped onto her back and dug their talons into her head, leaning close and whispering in her ear. The demons' whispers slithered into her mind, each lie sliding into place like a piece of a puzzle. The words weren't foreign—they echoed her own doubts, drawing out fears she'd tried to stifle. Her head throbbed, and the familiar heaviness settled over her like a shroud, fogging her thoughts.

"You are not a good woman," they told her. "You are violating God's will for women. You are selfish and think you should have an equal say in your family. God hates your rebellion against him. Your husband wishes you were more submissive. God created you to be led."

The demons stayed attached to her throughout the day, continually feeding her messages of anger and despair. "You have no say in your life anymore; you have gotten married. Therefore, you have given up your freedom. You are like a child who needs a man to tell you what to do." They badgered her throughout the day, leaving her distracted and grouchy.

If this school promoted those types of beliefs, perhaps she was in the wrong place. Her soul ached for answers and reassurance. She sat at her desk, trying to focus on preparing for class. There was only an hour before she was to stand before her students, and she believed firmly that the first day set the tone for the entire semester. She wanted it to go well, but she just couldn't quite get her head straight.

"You have a second?" The Fourth, the head of her department, stuck his head in her door. She stood and welcomed him in. There was something about the Fourth that she liked. He was a massive man, the kind you would expect to find on the football field, not in the classroom. He was no-nonsense and shot straight from the hip, both characteristics she valued. But more importantly, she could feel the presence of God when he was around.

He walked into her office and took the seat directly across from her. He paused for a moment, taking time to see her, to read the concern in her eyes. She sat a little uncomfortably with the silence and the intensity of his gaze.

"What did you think about the message this morning?" he asked without any conversational cushioning. She sat frozen, trying not to let her face reveal her sheer panic at the question. She said a quick prayer before she started.

"As a woman, I suppose it is only appropriate that I defer to you to tell me what I should think of it," she said gently. The sarcasm was obvious but conveyed hurt, not anger. The Fourth understood the statement precisely for what it was.

"And the rest of the female faculty in the department? They, too, are waiting for us mighty males to tell them what to think?" he asked, playing along.

"Those who have spoken. Many remain silent—after all, we want to adhere to Paul's rules." She winked at him. He leaned forward in the chair that suddenly seemed much too small for him.

"You know we are not a church. We are a school. I have no desire to get into this conversation, but I want it very clear that here—in this place—there is no male or female. We are all here working toward the same goal. What happens in your home, between you and your husband, is between you, your husband, and

God. It has nothing to do with me, and I want to keep it that way." He peered at her over the top of his glasses.

"Understood." She left it at that. He rose from the chair, considering the matter completely settled. "Good, I don't want any distractions." He walked to the door, his shoulders sagging just slightly. Over half the department was women; he had a lot of offices to visit.

Chapter 30: The Fourth

The sunshine was bright, and the little umbrella in his drink almost made the Fourth forget the week he had had. He closed his eyes, letting his other senses soak in the feel of the warm sun on his skin and the sound of the waves lapping against the shore. The smell of the beach wafted through his nostrils, bringing him a soothing feeling of nostalgia. He hadn't been to the beach in years—not since before the divorce when things with his wife had been good. He shook the thought from his mind and refocused on not thinking at all.

The week had been tough; he deserved the break. Lounging here at the beach, listening to the ocean, almost allowed him to forget that he had changed the course of his life this week. He let his mind wander to days gone by, but it insisted on landing on unpleasant memories, memories of dropping his son off at rehab—again. Memories of his wife telling him she was having an affair. Memories of his son being arrested. Memories of his wife refusing to go to counseling and insisting on a divorce. He took a sip of his drink; this mini vacation wasn't working out.

The week had started with a summons to the dean's office. Never good. A female student had reported an unwanted advance from one of her professors. At large state schools, this was not unheard of—not okay, but not unheard of. The student had declined the professor's advances; the professor had failed her. This was medical school. Failing could be a death sentence. But for the college, it meant a possible lawsuit. The accusation had to be investigated.

The Fourth had heard all sorts of accusations over the years. Many were found to be things students said to get better grades, only a few were founded in truth. But all of them were investigated. The faculty member accused was one of their best. He was a top-notch cancer researcher, receiving millions in funding every year. His research was innovative and could one day save millions of lives. He had been at the institution for years, married, with grown children.

But something in the girl's eyes had told the Fourth this was not going to end well for the professor. The Fourth was not driven by emotion. He was a man of science, and he moved methodically. He was fair and unbiased and searched out the facts of the situation.

When the week was over, the faculty member had been escorted from campus by security. Apparently, he had had inappropriate relationships with many students over the years in exchange for grades. The Fourth had been made to resign as well. As the chair of the department, he was told he should have known what was happening.

The Fourth left campus Friday and drove east until he hit the ocean. He just needed some fresh air and time to think. He began to wonder if he should leave academia and go back into full-time practice. But getting up from his lounge chair reminded him why he had gone into academia in the first place—an old football injury. College football had taken a toll on his body, and age had magnified that toll. Full-time practice was no longer an option, but a swim in the ocean might be just what the doctor ordered. He chuckled at his own joke as he eased into the warm ocean water.

After what seemed like a very short swim, evening started to set in. The Fourth remembered having once heard on Shark Week that sharks came close to shore around sunset looking for dinner. As tiring as the week had been, he decided dancing with a shark was not how he wanted to end it.

He made his way back to gather his things and find a hotel. He rubbed his knee as he struggled to get his chair folded and his towel back into the small drawstring bag he had brought with him. Getting things gathered up was easy; carrying all of it across the sand was a little less easy with his knee acting up.

The Fourth was fumbling with the chair, shoes, and bag when the bag slipped off his arm, hit the shoes, and sent them flying in two different directions. A woman in sunglasses and a big sun hat appeared like a wisp of air, her wild red hair blowing in the ocean breeze.

"Let me help you," she offered. Her smile was so radiant and warm it brought with it a sense of peace and belonging.

"Thanks," said the Fourth, accepting her help. He reached for the shoes she carried over to him.

"You seem to have your hands full," she said. "I'll carry these for you," she offered as she fell into step with him.

"Oh, that's okay; I can get it," he said, not wanting this woman to carry his shoes.

"Don't be silly; I'm going that way," she said with confidence.

"Are you a local?" the Fourth asked, knowing from her pale skin that she probably wasn't.

"No, I just made a quick stop here on my way to Platitude College, a small little school hidden in the mountains," she said.

"Oh, are you a professor?" the Fourth asked, happy that he would perhaps have something to discuss with her as they walked. Small talk was not a skill he was good at; in fact, it exhausted him.

"The people there are of great interest to me," she offered. They reached the car of the Fourth, and he put his chair, bag, and towel in the trunk. The woman handed him his shoes and smiled. The Fourth thanked her and turned to get in his car. He turned back to wish her luck with her interview, and she was gone. The beach was oddly quiet, a hush falling over the usual bustle. He scanned the shoreline, but there was no trace of her. His interest piqued, the Fourth found a hotel room, and once settled in, he looked up Platitude College. Much to his surprise, they were hiring. *Why would you ever name a college Platitude?* He wondered.

Chapter 31

The Twelfth put on her lab coat and headed to class. It was her first class, and she had prepared carefully. She was teaching first years about the transmission of infectious disease and had gone into the room early to put germ powder on the doorknobs and all the table surfaces. Once it got on them, they would pass it on to everything they touched. It was an excellent tool for teaching disease transmission and handwashing.

She had positioned posters of the different stages of the disease cycle around the room with QR codes that would take them to short, interactive games on each topic. She planned to start by asking the students to get vitals from five students not sitting near them. Then, they were to peruse the posters to gather the lesson information and group back up. She would do the grand reveal, and using UV light, she would show them how contaminated they had become during the short class session. Then, she would cover proper handwashing for the clinic and finish the class by going over the syllabus. The scent of antiseptic lingered faintly in the room, mixed with the sterile smell of lab equipment. Students shuffled in, grabbing seats and trading awkward first-day glances, unknowingly passing along the invisible germ powder the Twelfth had strategically applied.

Aegeus and Adiel went to class with her while Kfir patrolled the hall. Tormenting demons clung to the students and swarmed about the room. When she began class, the Twelfth called on a small blond-haired girl in the front to pray.

"Wouldn't you rather ask a boy?" the Ninth quipped. A demon clung tightly to her throat. The Twelfth was a bit taken aback.

"Why would I do that?" she asked.

The girl went from looking angry to looking tearful in an instant.

"Men are here to lead us, so have them pray." She was angry. The Twelfth did not like the direction this was going, and yet she instantly admired the girl's spunk and courage. Adiel looked up at Aegeus, shock on her face.

The demons in the room howled with laughter, flitting about the place, whispering in the ears of students, stroking their hair, or brushing against their hands. Occasionally, one of them would have a Light that would flash and send the demon scurrying away.

"Yeah, but they can't seem to be responsible for anything when you're dating. During that phase, we are the ones who must be in charge. But say 'I do' and forget it," another girl in the back chimed in.

"What do you mean?" the Twelfth asked.

"Oh, you know, girls have to be the ones to say no all the time. We are responsible for protecting "our honor". A boy can't be trusted to do that. You can't trust him not to 'try to milk the cow' because you are wearing yoga pants, but he should be in complete control of you once you're married. How does that make sense?"

She put the stress on the Strongman's own words, air-quoting them, so there was no question. The girls were hurt, and their pain was seeping out as anger and resentment. But the Twelfth knew that it was not about the boys. It was not about anger. The Twelfth's heart twisted as she listened. She could see the hurt simmering beneath their sarcasm and the mistrust tangled with their faith. She wanted to offer reassurance, to remind them of their worth, but it was like grasping at smoke. She looked at the males in the room.

"Gentlemen? What say you?" she asked, her lesson for the day temporarily forgotten.

"I'd say today is not a good day to be a guy thinking about asking someone out on this campus," a young man with a full, thick beard said, eliciting laughs from the entire class.

"I don't care what a girl is wearing. If I think she's hot, she could be wearing a potato sack. I'm still going to think she's hot. If I don't, she could be naked, and I am not going to be interested," one brave guy in the back of the room offered. Others nodded in agreement.

"Do they teach you how to deal with lust?" the Twelfth asked sincerely.

The males all nodded no.

"No tips; they don't ever direct you what to do to help combat it?" She was truly shocked.

"No, of course not," a female in the back row offered up. "That's the girl's job. It's our lack of modest dress that causes the problem. Men have no control over that; they can't control themselves but should have full authority over us after marriage, but we are the ones who must be in control of premarital sex. Wait till you've been here for a while, Doc. The 'purity' talks are all about how important it is for you to save your virginity for your husband. Your husband! Do you hear that? What about saving it for your wife? Trust us; that never enters the discussion."

"Why do you suppose that is?" she asked them.

"Genesis 3:16," the girls said in near unison. "Women are to be led—not lead," was the consensus. Adiel shifted uneasily. Her own history was rooted in centuries of the King's love and his presence. But here, the pain was so raw and unresolved. She tugged at the guardian tunic, better understanding why Lavi had developed so much love for them. This discussion made her feel sick inside.

Puzzled, Aegeus gently shook his head. He could not figure out how a verse about the curse of man related to sexual purity. It just wasn't coming together for him.

"That argument doesn't make sense. Besides, the Bible is full of women who were leaders," the Twelfth noted, taking the conversation in a slightly different direction. The Twelfth thought about the strong women she'd known—some who stayed home and others who led classrooms, companies, and ministries. To suggest that any of them held less value to God was beyond her comprehension. How did it honor God to imply they were "less than" simply for being women?

"Not in the important parts," a boy murmured under his breath. A few people around him chuckled.

"What about Athaliah?" she questioned.

"Who?" they asked.

"Athaliah," she repeated. "She was a monarch who ruled over Israel/Judah. Note that I said monarch. She was the ruling queen. There was no king—she was it. Now, she was considered evil, so let's be clear on that. But it wasn't because she was a woman. It was because she worshipped other gods, as did most of the male monarchs. She ruled over Israel for seven years."

The class sat quietly. They had never heard of Athaliah.

"That doesn't mean God approved of her being in charge," a boisterous boy in the back threw out.

"If you believe the Bible, it does." She stated it matter-of-factly and then waited for just a beat before going on. "The Bible says we are not to revolt against our leaders since there is no one in leadership that God did not put there. So, if you believe that, then you must believe that God put Athaliah in as the queen to rule over his chosen people—women and men alike."

"So, if Bowlinger is elected, we have to honor him as president?" a student from the left of the room questioned.

The class laughed. The Twelfth laughed, too.

"Yes, whoever our president is, we are to respect that person. God says that he appointed them himself."

"There are lots of examples," the Ninth offered. "Lydia owned her own business; Phoebe was a deacon in the early church. Acts refers to women prophesying. Galatians says we are neither male nor female.

"But all of that seems to get lost because Paul also said that he didn't let women instruct—never mind that he qualified it as his practice and did not offer it as a command or even condemn those who did it differently. None of that matters. His one statement is enough to keep us wily women in our place—the kitchen. Stay here long enough, Prof, and you'll figure it out," the Ninth finished. Her pain was evident, but worse, her spiritual struggle was great.

The Twelfth was a little stunned. She did not want these students to walk away from her, thinking that women had no purpose. Being a mom was a hard job. There was great honor in that. It was a thankless job—at least for the first twenty years or so—but it was a beautiful responsibility.

The Twelfth loved being a wife; she loved her husband. But there were also many women who had neither a husband nor children. Were they not just as valuable as the women who had children or husbands?

And what about the role of the father? Wasn't the father just as important? Was a mother to be valued over or above a father? Having a loving father in the home was invaluable. The world was full of examples of the damage an unloving man could do to the life of a child. She believed her value was from being a child of God—that was who she was.

Despite the difficult topic, the Twelfth was impressed with the students' knowledge of the facts of the Bible. But she feared that while they knew a lot about God, they did not seem to know God. Class time was quickly evaporating, and she doubted she would be able to cover all that she had planned.

"Well, if there's one thing we can all agree on," she said, glancing over at the UV light, "it's that germs definitely don't care who's leading. Let's get back to why handwashing's going to be your best friend in the clinic." By abbreviating the activities, she got through the most crucial items before time was up.

The students were surprised to see their glowing hands under the UV light, and she was able to use it to look at their faces and demonstrate how many times they had touched their eyes, noses, and mouths over the course of the class. It proved to be a success despite the rocky start.

The Ninth, who had started the entire discourse by refusing to pray, came to the Twelfth's office later that day to apologize for her behavior in class.

The Twelfth immediately liked the Ninth. She was a strong young woman who had a great passion for the Lord. But her path was not an easy one, and over the next six months, she would spend many hours with the Twelfth, pouring out her heart, sharing her anguish and her struggles. They would celebrate her successes, and the Twelfth would comfort her when she cried.

On one particularly stressful day, shortly after the Ninth's father died, she looked up into the eyes of the Twelfth and made her promise that she wouldn't leave the town until the Ninth graduated. The Twelfth hesitated. This place was not what she had expected, and she did not plan to stay beyond the year. But the Ninth did not break eye contact, fresh tears in her eyes.

"Please," she pleaded. "Please promise." The Twelfth felt a surge of love for the girl that she could not explain—all that she had endured, all that her young life had brought her way. She took a deep breath, not wanting to make a promise she could not keep. Staying until the girl graduated would be a significant commitment. The Twelfth felt her heart swell with affection for the Ninth—this resilient young woman carrying more hurt than anyone her age should. She hesitated, torn by the uncertainty of her future here. But looking into the girl's pleading eyes, she laid a hand on her shoulder and gave a gentle nod, her heart making the promise her mind wasn't yet   sure   of.

Chapter 32: The Ninth

She had always known she wanted to be a doctor. As a small child, she had stuck Band-Aids on all her stuffed animals and applied slings to her Barbies. When other little girls talked about being nurses, she dreamed only of being a doctor. She would boss around the nurses, letting them know that as a doctor, she was in charge. Looking back, she realized that the other girls never even considered that they could be doctors. She was grateful to her parents for raising her to believe she could do anything.

Then, of course, all her classmates dreamed of being teachers. They would play school, with each of them taking turns being the teacher. She never wanted to be the teacher when they played; instead, she insisted they pretend they were in "doctor school."

When she was five, her uncle bought her her first doctor's kit. She loved it. It came with a doctor's coat, a stethoscope, a thermometer, and a hammer to check reflexes, all packed in a plastic, bright yellow doctor's bag. It became her most precious possession. She wore her stethoscope everywhere.

At church, she would listen to the hearts of anyone who would allow it. Placing the earpieces in her ears and listening to the thump, thump, thump of their hearts was exhilarating. The day she realized it was a prerecorded heartbeat had been devastating. She felt duped.

High school came to her easily, and she graduated at the top of her class. She volunteered at the local hospital as soon as she was old enough. She wanted to learn all she could about what it was like to be a doctor. She shadowed different types of doctors, spending time in a variety of specialties—some in the hospital, some in private practice. When she headed off to college, she had no doubts about what her goals were.

She planned to attend Johns Hopkins for premed and then complete the bridge year before starting medical school. Premed had been challenging, and she spent many long hours studying, but she also found time to be involved in a sorority and served on the student council. She was well-rounded, she was focused, and she had a plan. Everything was going as she had planned.

Two hours after finals in her fourth year, her cell phone rang. She was lounging on the lawn in front of the Eisenhower Library, soaking in the sun with friends before packing up. Emotion choked her sister's voice, her words almost indiscernible. Almost.

Time stood still for one fleeting moment. That moment when everything changes. One of the moments that becomes a time marker in your life, and everything else happened either before or after it. This became one of those moments for her. She looked around at everyone else—unaware, unaffected—and she resented that their lives had not just changed in an instant.

The campus swam around her; the words did not make sense. She pieced together that her father, a paramedic, had been on a call when his ambulance was hit by a semi whose driver had fallen asleep at the wheel. He was still alive, but the prognosis was not good.

The drive home was agonizing. The week following was even worse. Her family stood vigil in the hospital, praying for a miracle. The days turned into weeks, the weeks into months. The fall semester approached, and her father was still in the hospital. Returning to Johns Hopkins now didn't seem possible. Her father, if he ever woke up, would be paralyzed.

Her mother had gone home to take a shower. The Ninth sat quietly by her father's bed. She thought about her family, about how young her brother still was. Her sister was a senior in high school. Her mom would need her. Her heart settled on the reality that medical school at Johns Hopkins was no longer in her future. But the tragedy of giving up her dream of being a doctor on the same day she gave up the idea of dancing with her dad at her wedding seemed like asking too much.

A team of doctors entered her father's room, and the head physician presented her father's case and asked them questions. While they discussed his situation, one of the physicians, a woman with beautiful red hair pinned back in an unruly yet professional bun, read his chart.

She smiled at the Ninth, her bright green eyes seeming to pierce through the sadness and heartache. The woman spoke about her father in such a way that made the Ninth feel as if she knew him personally. He was not just a patient on their rounds—he was a person. The woman felt his pulse, smiled brightly, winked at the Ninth, and then led the group of physicians from the room.

When they left, her father stirred. Groaning slightly, he opened his eyes and looked at her; he was groggy. He closed his eyes again. The Ninth jumped from her chair and ran into the hall to find the physicians. They had all moved on to the next room. All but the woman with the wild red hair. She stood in the hallway talking to a young man. The woman looked up and smiled at the Ninth, the kind of smile that is usually reserved for dear friends whom you haven't seen in a while.

"He opened his eyes," she offered excitedly.

The woman with the red hair walked purposefully into the room. She called the man's name, and he opened his eyes and looked at her. He smiled at her and then closed his eyes again. The woman placed her hand over his and called his name again very gently. A toothy grin spread across his face, and he once again forced his eyes open. The woman smiled throughout, seeming pleased with what she found.

"Is he okay? Will he be okay?" the Ninth asked, hope streaking her voice for the first time. The woman, stepping slightly away from the hospital bed, turned her attention to the Ninth.

"He is exactly as he should be," she said with a smile. "Are you?" She looked at the Ninth as if gazing into her soul. The Ninth felt a small jolt of electricity as if a static-filled carpet had shocked her.

"I . . . I . . ." She wasn't sure how to respond. The woman with the wild red hair waited patiently as if there was nowhere else she needed to be, nothing else in all the world more important than this discussion. "I am supposed to be in medical school at Johns Hopkins," she stammered.

"But you are needed somewhere else?" the woman said as if she understood the predicament. And yet the Ninth couldn't help but feel as if the question were a statement. As if the woman were telling her that she was needed somewhere else—somewhere other than here, somewhere other than Johns Hopkins. It was a statement she would think back on for many years.

"I suppose I am," she said, looking down, tears starting to fill her eyes. Saying it aloud made it seem more real.

"Sometimes, being where you are needed leads you to find what you need," the woman answered. She smiled again and walked from the room. The Ninth stood still, trying to digest what the woman had said. It seemed so meaningful, and at the same time, it made no sense at all.

She walked into the hall to find the woman, and she was gone. But the young man she had been speaking to earlier was still there, standing near the nurses' station. He was a PA student from Platitude College, not too far from where they were. The Ninth thought that perhaps she might have hope after all.

Chapter 33

Titus and Morax joined the Strongman in his office. The Strongman seemed pleased with how well the last few days had gone. Morax was less sure; this had not been the gradual, subtle attack they had discussed. In fact, it seemed to Morax that it was two days of all-out offensive against on the female "rats." But he decided it was better to bridge that issue slowly.

"That was a wonderful opening to the year, sir," offered Morax as he settled on the ornate leather couch positioned in the seating area of the office. He looked around the room and felt a tinge of jealousy that the Strongman's office, including the big windows that overlooked the campus, was so much better than his own.

"I was concerned that you may not be up to the task, but you have done a marvelous job," Morax offered as affirmation. He turned to Titus to ask, "What do you hear from the troops?"

Titus was still standing, recognizing his position as the lowest-ranked in the room. "It is early, my liege, but reports are that the rats left confused and besieged. The males are largely complacent, and the females are anxious. Some of them have swallowed the pill whole, while others are struggling. He has certainly created doubt and fear. They do not trust each other."

"Do not grow overly confident," the Strongman warned. His tone darkened at the memory of the close encounter with the prophet. "What of the prophet?" he demanded.

"Prophet?" asked Morax, concern evident in his voice.

Titus, too, shifted his weight at this news.

"Yes, the prophet that was in the session with the faculty and staff." The fact that Morax and Titus seemed unaware of the presence of a prophet made him feel more concerned. "How did a prophet slip through?" His anger began to seep out.

"Are you sure?" Morax asked. The idea that there was a prophet among them was so surreal that he was having trouble believing it. Who could this man be? When did he arrive? A prophet among them would be trouble.

"Yes, I am sure!" the Strongman nearly shouted. "I recognize a prophet when I see one."

Morax turned to Titus, who gave a little shrug and a look, letting Morax know this was news to him.

"Did he speak to you?" asked Morax to the Strongman.

"She did not." He spat with emphasis on the word she.

"A woman?" Morax asked, astounded, the notion sounding absurd. The presence of a prophet among them was shocking enough, but the idea that it would be a woman was nearly laughable.

"Why do you think I changed the plan and came out so fiercely about women from the beginning?"

Morax began to laugh. The Strongman did not see the humor in it, and his anger burned as sulfur began to pour from him.

"The King sent a prophet—a female prophet." Morax laughed so hard it nearly brought tears to his eyes.

"We have little to fear," suggested Morax. "You were right to change our approach and begin the process of demeaning the position of women. You have made it clear that women are not to be listened to or in leadership. We just need to make sure we continue along that line. Hammer it home. There will be little to no resistance to that idea here.

"We can add sermons on how prophecy is no longer a spiritual gift, and we can speak about how the women prophets in the Word were not real prophets. Talk about how God only uses women when he is desperate and there are no available men.

"In fact—" Morax was getting excited about the change of plan now, this would be so much easier. "Do an entire series on women in the Word as a way of celebrating their contribution. Share the stories, stay close to the truth, but diminish the effect they have. Be condescending without seeming so."

Morax thought this would work very nicely. A prophet could be trouble, but a female prophet in this environment would be easily dismissed. In fact, the whole issue of the role of women would serve as the perfect distraction. The rats would be so consumed arguing over it that they would lose sight of what was truly important. Yes, Morax decided this would work out quite nicely. They would refocus on this issue; it would be the perfect distraction.

"Should her voice grow strong," he concluded, "we will label her a Corinthian woman and send her on her way." The plan was wonderful. He didn't know how this woman came to be in the town, but he would relish destroying her. Listening to them preach lies would eat at her soul. She would not be able to stay quiet for long. They would flush her out and crush her.

"Did she recognize you?" he asked.

"I don't think so," answered the Strongman.

"Did she have a warrior with her?"

"No, she was flanked by two guardians."

A prophet with no warrior was even better news to Morax. It was almost too good to be true. He opened the door and yelled down the hall to the Strongman's assistant. She hurried into the room without making eye contact, clearly upset by the Strongman's prior comments. Good, Morax thought. Let her be offended. Let her offended spirit turn her from the Word and the King.

"Bring us a pictorial directory of all the faculty and staff. The president would like to learn their faces and names as soon as possible," he ordered. She nodded her head and left the room, bile rising in her throat and Insecurity clinging to her back and laughing. After she left the room, he closed the door and looked at the Strongman. "Look carefully through the pictures and identify the prophet. We will deal with her."

"Titus, when we find her, we will assign her her very own tormenting demon and a destroyer. Double the warriors we have on standby. If there is a prophet, the King will send warriors. Thicken the dome; they are not to get in. Tell your men to keep an eye out for any prophetic activity."

"Yes, my liege," Titus answered and left quickly. He did not believe the prophet came to be there by accident. If they had missed a prophet, what else was inside the dome that they had missed? But Titus did not see any reason to voice his concerns to Morax or the Strongman.

Chapter 34

Aegeus sent out a message for the angels to again convene in the salvage yard. He needed an update on each of the twelve. Their team consisted of twelve guardians, one for each family. Ayo, Berhanu, and Meir had recently joined the ministering angels to make five in total. Including Kfir, Adiel, and Aegeus, there were fourteen warriors assigned to the twelve. Undoubtedly, more would be needed when serious combat began, but keeping the ones here hidden had been difficult.

The new demon dome would make it more difficult to get others in, but the angels had never been afraid of difficult. Eventually, all the angels in the town would need to attend the updates. But for now, just those directly assigned to the twelve were included in the meeting. It drew less attention that way.

The increased size of the team necessitated a larger meeting space. In the back of the salvage yard, nearly hidden from sight and long ago forgotten by human eyes, was an old shed. The shed was sufficient size for the current group and allowed some room for growth, so Aegeus moved the meeting there.

ChiBreeze was the guardian assigned to the Eighth, and Aegeus decided to start with him.

"Chi, how is the Eighth?" Chi stood before the group to give his report.

"Not well. Meeting and befriending the Twelfth has given him someone to talk to and some support, but the enemy is attacking him heavily. A destroyer named Kali has been working day and night to undo him. He has had two car accidents, a cancer scare, and possibly a pregnant daughter. The situation with his wife has not improved, and he is slowly losing steam. He has not mastered his gift and, therefore, carries the burden of all those around him. As the town crumbles, he crumbles. He is currently depressed. I fear we may lose him." Chi sat down to signify he was done.

"Ayo, spend a few days with him and see if we can get him better positioned."

"As the King commands, so shall I do," responded Ayo.

"As the battle nears, we will need more ministering angels; they are on the way. With prayer cover, as you know, we will get resources faster. I trust the ministering angels are encouraging that," Aegeus reminded them. Meir merely nodded in affirmation.

"Haywood, an update on the Fifth?"

"The Fifth does not sleep," Haywood looked troubled. "She was distraught by the Strongman's speech to the students. She carries their burden on her very body. Her heart has remained tender, and she has gone nearly unnoticed by the enemy. My concerns for her are all physical. It has been many months since she slept more than a few hours a night. The lack of sleep is taking a toll." Haywood finished and sat.

"Why isn't she sleeping?" he asked.

"I believe she is overextended, sir. She will not ever say no. As a result, it is not until the rest of the world sleeps that she can attend to her own needs. She does not dream, nor does she have trouble falling asleep. No tormenting demons are living in her home. She just seems overextended," he replied.

"Berhanu, perhaps you could tackle that?" Aegeus suggested.

But even as he asked, he knew it would take much more than a ministering angel to deter an over-provider. The Fifth had the gift of service, but it sounded like she still had not yet learned to hear the call of the Spirit regarding which acts of service to perform and which to leave for others.

"Remind her that his yoke is easy and his burden light." Meir offered. Aegeus wasn't so sure that her only concerns were physical.

"As the King commands, so shall I do," responded Berhanu.

"Voog, what of the Second?" Aegeus continued until the door crashed open.

An angel burst in, his face stricken. "Aegeus, they're scouring homes, looking for the prophet."

The announcement shot through Aegeus like lightning. His chest tightened. If they found her… the cost would be unimaginable.

She might not yet understand the full extent of her role, but the enemy certainly did.

"Adiel, Kfir, you're with me. We are going to the Twelfth. The rest, scatter and slow the horde however you can—report back once you've confirmed their position."

Without hesitation, the angels burst into the skies, wings slicing through the night as they sped across the town, each one watching, scanning, prepared to meet the horde head-on. *The prophet must not fall,* Aegeus thought, his wings straining as he pushed himself faster. She has no idea how many lives hinge on her survival—or how close the enemy is to finding her.

Chapter 35

The house of the Twelfth was silent, veiled in the stillness of night. Only a faint light in a small sitting room below cast shadows across the walls, where her husband worked on a jigsaw puzzle. Aegeus flew upstairs and found her looking in the full-length mirror in her room. Two tormenting demons were clinging to her tightly and were startled by the sudden entrance of an angel. Intuitively, Aegeus drew his sword.

"What is this?" one of them asked with a snarl. "A guardian draws his sword?" hissed the demon as he dismounted from the Twelfth to face Aegeus. Aegeus's grip tightened on his sword as he watched her fight herself. He knew the demons fed on her self-loathing, twisting her perceptions to see only flaws. But he was bound to protect, not to intervene—unless the King willed otherwise. Aegeus's hesitation convinced the demon that he would not attack. The tormenting demon knew he would never win in one-on-one combat with a guardian. But he also knew that guardians did not engage in battle unless absolutely necessary—they were protectors of their charge, not warriors. He knew guardians fought only as required to protect their charge. Knowing this, he thought it may be fun to goad the guardian a bit before getting back to the human. The demon walked closer to Aegeus but not close enough for Aegeus to easily reach him. Aegeus maintained his stance, ignoring the demon's sneering words. The urge to strike was strong, but he held back. The King's orders were clear: only defend if the Twelfth's life was in immediate danger. The demon's confidence wavered slightly under Aegeus's unblinking gaze.

"There is something about you," the demon said as he circled Aegeus, scrutinizing him to detect just what it was that was not right.

He strained to see Aegeus better in the dim light. Aegeus turned his attention back to the demon that was still latched to the Twelfth. She stood before the mirror, looking at herself in disgust. She was randomly pinching and poking areas on her body with a sense of hostility that only a demon could invoke. From her mouth, she spewed hate speech to herself. The demon laughed in glee as the Twelfth became increasingly discouraged, finding fault with her body.

Aegeus put his sword away angrily and flew from the room to the roof to get out of the prying eyes of the tormenting demon and survey the situation. Kfir joined him.

"Is she okay?" he asked.

Aegeus sighed; his frustration evident. "Two demons are taunting her, and she is not fighting it. She embraces their lies and is feeding them. We have not been cleared to defend her from them since this is training for her. She must learn, Kfir," he said, more as a reminder to himself than Kfir.

Kfir and Aegeus waited on the roof, listening to the glee of the demons in the room below. Aegeus was grateful they didn't seem to know she was a prophet. Ezekiel landed on the roof.

"The horde is two streets over; they will be here shortly," he updated Aegeus.

Finally, the order came, and the King cleared them to act. As Aegeus unfastened the guardian's tunic, he felt a momentary weight in his chest. The uniform was a reminder of Lavi. It had become a tribute to his friend's unwavering commitment to protecting those he loved. But tonight, shedding the disguise brought a sense of homecoming. He breathed in, letting the cool air settle over his shoulders. Aegeus welcomed the familiar weight of his own armor, as he shed his guardian form.

His stance changed, his heart steady as he drew his sword and let out a call that cut through the night—echoing for his brothers and sisters to hear. Tonight, they could be who they truly were, who the King had created them to be. Tonight, they would answer the horde.

Aegeus's eyes met Kfir's, and he knew there was no one he trusted more in battle.

"This is only the beginning," he said as he let out a battle cry. Finally, they battled.

Chapter 36

A long-haired demon with a scar led the horde. He smiled at Aegeus with a sense of familiarity.

"We are here for the prophet," he said, the smile never leaving his face. He sauntered slowly forward.

Aegeus scanned the horde, thousands strong, mostly destroyers and tormentors. Few among them had the skills of warriors.

"You cannot have the prophet," he answered, careful not to shift his weight or move too suddenly. He knew the battle would come—and to be honest, he was looking forward to it. Aegeus steadied himself, a calm rising within as the thrill of battle stirred his spirit. Finally, he could fight without restraint. For too long, he had worn a cloak of guardianship; the waiting had been challenging to him, and now he welcomed the battle. His blood surged as he prepared. But wisdom and strategy were necessary, and so he waited just long enough to give his team time to move into position. They were indeed outnumbered, but fortunately, the enemy had sent the wrong type of demons.

"We will take the prophet," said the long-haired demon. "And when we are done destroying her, I will personally come back for you." His eyes were fixed on Aegeus.

"It is unwise for a warrior drawing his sword to boast like one who has already won the battle," Aegeus said, quoting the Word as he drew his sword.

The long-haired demon swung his sword at Aegeus, and the horde rushed forward. The sheer number of them made the battle difficult. But it felt good to Aegeus to be fighting. He grabbed a destroyer demon and used it as a shield against the more-well-trained warrior. Then he threw its body to the side as it dissipated into black smoke. This seemed to amuse the long-haired demon.

Aegeus looked over his shoulder and saw Adiel and Kfir both in battle. Kfir had a massive smile on his face as he slashed at tormenting demons and threw them from the roof of the house. A human walked by with his dog. The dog barked at the ensuing battle, but the human was oblivious and tugged the dog along, shushing him for fear the barking would disrupt the quiet evening. The absurdity struck Aegeus as funny, and he was chuckling when a blade suddenly sliced into his arm. The pain of the cut brought his attention back to the battle. The long-haired demon stood still, watching him, a grin on his face.

"Come now, Aegeus; don't make it so easy for me," he taunted.

"Who are you?" Aegeus inquired.

"I am the one who will destroy the great protector," he said, using Aegeus's angelic name. He once again swung his sword at

Aegeus. Aegeus tensed, momentarily thrown by the strange familiarity.

Their swords clanked together, and the demon threw his weight into Aegeus, knocking him through the roof and into the house. They landed with a crash in the room of the Twelfth. The long-haired demon was on top of Aegeus, pinning him to the ground, the sulfur pouring from him almost imperceptible in the nearly blacked-out room. The smoke of hundreds of demons filled the room. Aegeus had not seen them entering the house. He turned his head, desperate to find the Twelfth.

His eyes locked on her. She was on her knees on the floor, her head touching the ground. Sobs shook her body as hundreds of demons piled on top of her. They clawed and bit at her in a near frenzy. Her Light was dim, flickering from the effort. There were too many for her. Aegeus's eyes met the eyes of a taunting demon as it leaned over and licked her face and then dug its talons deep into her. She wailed as the talon sank into her.

"Would you like to watch her die?" the long-haired demon hissed into his ear, sulfur filling Aegeus's lungs. More demons poured into the room, piling onto the Twelfth, biting, scratching, and cutting their way to her.

Aegeus struggled under the weight of the long-haired demon. He reached for a small dagger he kept in his boot just for such occasions. With a swift, calculated thrust, Aegeus plunged his dagger deep into the demon's side. The demon let out a raging scream and shifted his weight enough that Aegeus could free himself. He knew the injury was only enough to anger the demon, but it bought him time and leverage. Clasping his wound, the demon snarled, 'Another day,' before dissipating into the shadows.

"Aegeus!" Kfir yelled as he entered the room. He pointed to the Twelfth.

"I know. Go for Meir; we will need her!"

Aegeus rose to his feet and grabbed the demon closest to him, throwing it from the house and fighting his way to the Twelfth. Meir would be close, waiting for the call, but she would not be engaged in battle.

With the long-haired warrior gone, there were only tormenting and destroyer demons to fight. Aegeus continued slicing and flinging demons as he worked his way to the Twelfth. There were so many on her. As he got closer, they began to tear at him, leaping onto him and ripping at him, slicing him with their talons. He fought on, slashing and tearing them from his body as he inched closer to her.

Adiel crashed through the floor on top of two demons. She stabbed through them both at the same time and smiled at Aegeus when their eyes met.

"Need help?" she asked, winking at Aegeus. The two of them began to make their way through the demons, but more poured in. Aegeus gritted his teeth as talons raked across his arm, his focus unwavering. The Twelfth lay smothered, her Light fading. He would cut down every demon in this room if he had to. Nothing—no power in this dark horde—would keep him from reaching her. As Aegeus fought through the fray, he caught a glimpse of Kfir battling with fierce joy, laughing as he tossed demons from the room. They fought as one—brothers in arms—and Aegeus knew they would hold this line together.

And then Aegeus heard it, the ram's horn blast. The sound of the ram's horn cut through the chaos, a clear, ringing note of defiance against the darkness. A stunned silence fell as the room blazed with the arrival of reinforcements. Warriors flashed into the fray, their Light piercing the darkness with renewed fury. The reinforcements had arrived. Soon, the room was filled with warriors, and many of the demons became streaks of black smoke as they were tossed from the home or dissipated. The Twelfth was nearly hidden beneath the mass of demons, her trembling form swallowed by darkness. Her Light, flickering weakly, was smothered under layers of claws and twisted limbs that pulled at her, taunting her broken spirit. Tears streamed from her closed eyes, and she muttered pleas, half-formed, lost in her desperation.

Kfir arrived with Meir but kept her out of the fray. The demons would need to be removed from the Twelfth before Meir could minister to her. Meir, like all ministering angels, had no weapon other than the Light of God. Her role required something different—something more tender and delicate, something that could reach a human soul. Aegeus pushed through the swarming demons, his mind flashing to the sacrifice of Lavi. This was why they fought—in service of the King, and Aegeus relished being back in the role he was made for.

Aegeus and the other warriors fought off the last of the demons, clinging to the Twelfth, leaving her soul frayed and battered. Meir stepped forward, and the warriors formed a protective circle around her and the Twelfth. Aegeus watched as Meir draped her iridescent wings over the Twelfth, enfolding her in warmth and Light. For a moment, he marveled at the strength within Meir's gentleness—she was a warrior of a different kind, wielding comfort as fiercely as any sword. Meir leaned close, whispering truth into the Twelfth's ear. Gradually, her Light began to glow brighter, flickering weakly.

"Kfir, check the others; report back," Aegeus ordered.

"Adiel, get a team of warriors and secure the perimeter; I don't want any more demons getting in here!"

"How is she?" he asked as he glanced over his shoulder at Meir. She waved him away. Looking at the Twelfth's crumpled body stirred something in Aegeus. He decided instead to focus on Meir. Her blue hair was cropped short and wispy today, glinting with a quiet radiance even in the dimness. Aegeus found himself mesmerized by it; how was light bouncing off her hair in this dark place? He studied her flowing top made from a light material he could not quite place—perhaps it was something new the King had created.

Paki appeared beside him, his gaze fixed on the blood seeping from Aegeus's arm.

"You're bleeding," he said matter-of-factly. Aegeus looked down at the gash on his arm. He had forgotten about it. Paki walked over and touched it, healing the wound.

Aegeus nodded a thank-you.

"How is she?" Paki asked.

"I don't know," was the only answer that was honest. He certainly didn't want to admit that he didn't want to look. Hundreds of demons piling on a person could do much to destroy them.

Meir curled around the Twelfth on the floor. Her wings created a cocoon of warmth around the Twelfth, the darkness receding as Light enveloped her. Each whisper of truth, each memory of comfort she wove into the Twelfth's mind, chipped away at the demons' lingering shadows. It was a fierce, silent battle of restoration.

She delved deep into the Twelfth's mind to find scripture and song lyrics she could use to encourage her. She filled the Twelfth's mind with memories of encouraging things her husband had said to her, things she had read in her daily devotional, memories of things the Spirit had told her, anything she could find to soothe her battered soul. It was working. Slowly, her spirit began to settle.

After some time, the Twelfth got up from the floor and moved to her bed. Meir followed her, wrapping herself around the Twelfth, offering her comfort and peace. In time, when she felt the

Twelfth was stable, Meir rose from the bed and laid her hand on the alarm clock. Aegeus looked at her with a question in his eyes.

"She wakes up to NPR every day and listens to the news. Tomorrow, she'll wake to praise and worship songs from the local Christian station. NPR will be missing from the dial—at least for a little while." Meir said with a sly smile and a wink.

"How is she?"

"She is strong, and the Spirit is strong within her. Worthlessness and Doubt had the strongest hold on her, so she will need reassurance over the next few days. They convinced her that she was not good enough, not thin enough, not smart enough to be here.

"They also filled her with lies about her husband not loving her, not wanting her. Her husband is her earthly stronghold, the one person here that keeps her grounded, the person who makes her feel loved, so attacks that cause her to question her marriage are particularly vicious."

She paused as if unsure whether to continue.

"What is it?" Aegeus asked, sensing her hesitation.

"She has always been able to feel the angels. She doesn't realize that is what it is—she just knows she senses heaven, her connection to Sanyi is very real, and she has been able to feel his presence for a long time. Now he is gone." She paused slightly.

"She cannot feel you, Aegeus, and so she fears that she is somehow further from the King."

"I don't understand that." Aegeus shook his head. "I am a different type of angel than Sanyi," he said as if to defend himself.

"Besides, humans can't normally feel any of us," he said, equally defensive.

"I know that, Aegeus," Meir said, laying her hand gently on his arm. "But she doesn't. It is not criticism; it is simply what is happening. Paired with the conditions in the town, she is very unsure of herself. I will stay with her for a day or two to make sure things get back on track." Aegeus sighed heavily once again, wondering why the King had chosen him for this mission.

Meir started to leave the room and then stopped. Aegeus looked at her expectantly.

"Aegeus, you have more in common with her than you think." Meir paused.

Aegeus looked puzzled. He stood silent, waiting for her to go on.

"She is a warrior, Aegeus." Meir met his eye briefly before leaving.

The word lingered: *warrior.* He looked at the Twelfth, still trying to reconcile the image. How could this fragile, wounded human carry the heart of a warrior? Yet Meir's words echoed within him. He looked at the Twelfth and tried to see her as a warrior, but he could not.

Chapter 37

Titus pulled open the heavy door of the old church. The door creaked loudly as it swung outward on its hinge. The smell of mothballs wafted out to meet him. Wooden pews with red velvet bench cushions filled the sanctuary. Stained glass windows lined the room. The windows had no particular pattern, no scenes from the earthly life of the Lamb.

Titus preferred them plain. The hues were mostly blues, purples, and greens. Titus loved old churches. He smiled at the irony of a demon enjoying entering a church building, but it held some nostalgia for him. The wooden floors announced his arrival. The sun was streaming in through the stained-glass windows, giving the church a glorious light.

Morax sat in the front of the sanctuary with another demon. Based on the long black hair and size, Titus assumed it was Seneca. If Seneca was here, it was not a good sign.

Morax stood as soon as he heard Titus approaching. Seneca stood with the lazy confidence of one who knows they are in charge and that their very presence brings trembling. He smiled a slow smile at Titus. They did not offer the traditional greetings of the hairless rats. There was no need; they were alone.

"You have failed in battle." Seneca was not one to mince words.

"I was not in the battle," Titus offered, trying to sound more confident than he felt.

"Your demons cannot kill a simple woman," Seneca snarled.

"Yes, I am disappointed in that. Tell me, Seneca, what happened in the battle? I understand you were there—in the very room with the prophet. The battle must have been intense indeed. What went wrong? I will find the guilty party and make sure they are punished." Titus knew he was risking his life by goading Seneca, but he could not resist. He began to sweat slightly from his boldness.

Seneca walked confidently toward Titus, his smile never wavering. Titus stood tall and still. Seneca approached until they were face-to-face.

"You reek of fear," he said quietly into Titus's face.

Titus did not flinch, but his insides trembled, and he was sure that he did indeed reek of fear.

"Seneca," Morax spoke only his name, but it was enough. Seneca was a warrior; he lived for nothing more than to kill. He was a great warrior and had seen many battles. But he respected Morax, as most demons did. Seneca stood motionless glaring at Titus, and then his mouth softened into a snarl, but his eyes remained fixed in hate. Morax put his hands in his pockets and looked at the ground for a moment. Titus was struck by how well Morax could emulate the hairless rats.

Morax spoke calmly, but the ice in his tone was evident.

"The prophet is proving to be a problem, Titus. Your demons have failed to overcome her. Warriors of the King now protect her. How did they get in?"

"They were already in Platitude, my liege. Reports are that they have been here for some time disguised as guardians." Titus stood unmoving.

Seneca leaned against a church pew, looking at Titus as if he were a junior demon.

"Kill the prophet," Seneca said softly.

"I assumed you had," Titus began.

Seneca moved with great speed, covering the short distance between them, and grabbed Titus around the throat. His demon breath poured into Titus's nostrils as their noses pressed together. Titus began to feel himself suffocating. But he refused to indicate weakness.

"Seneca," Morax said again. Seneca released Titus begrudgingly.

Seneca spoke softly but not gently. "Cover the prophet in demons, Titus. Put an entire team of destroying demons on her. Find a way to kill her. She has many weaknesses; send taunting demons." Seneca conveyed a quiet evil that caused Titus to feel a shiver.

"The Strongman will continue to undervalue women and speak lies into the town that will upset them. This will weaken her.

Cover the students in taunting demons and send them to her. Overwhelm her with them, so she will be exhausted.

"Keep her so preoccupied that she has no time to care for herself, no time to eat or rest or feed her soul. She will tell herself she is doing the King's work. Fill her office with hurting souls until she carries so much of their burden that we can easily destroy her."

Morax smiled at the plan; it would work.

"And what of her warriors?" Titus asked, reminding them all of the obvious.

"Aegeus and Kfir are but two. We will reach her. I have secured the town, and no further warriors will arrive from the enemy without us knowing. More demons arrive daily, and soon, the dome will be complete—too thick to be penetrated. I will kill Aegeus personally."

The idea of the dome made Seneca smile; it would block off the entire town from the Light.

"If you cannot cover the prophet with demons, then cover those around her—her friends, her family, her coworkers, cover her neighborhood, block out the sun because the demons are so many." Morax wanted the objective to be clear.

Titus nodded his understanding. then left the church to continue the attack.

"Seneca, are you up for this?" Morax turned to him as he asked.

"You forget your place, Morax," Seneca said with the same quiet anger he had been using with Titus.

"This is personal for you. We can't afford to make mistakes." Morax spoke with confidence, almost in a fatherly tone, but he did not overestimate his position. They had mutual respect, but Morax knew that Seneca was dangerous.

"Do you question me, Morax?" Seneca walked closer to Morax, sulfur beginning to ooze from him.

"I have no doubt of your greatness in battle." Morax did not move. He did not fear Seneca the way Titus did. Morax was sure of his position. "What I question is if you will see clearly when it comes to Aegeus."

"I will kill the prophet." Seneca looked directly into Morax's eyes. "And then I will rip the wings from Aegeus and deliver him to the King."

"Our King or his?" Morax asked, unflinching.

"There is but one King, Morax—even the demons acknowledge that. You worry about your job. I will do mine." Seneca flew from the church, leaving Morax alone.

Chapter 38

"I don't know how they eat this," Kfir muttered, spitting out bits of popcorn that clung to his beard as he and Aegeus followed the Eleventh and Twelfth out of the small movie theater. The November air hit them with a sharp chill; their breaths rose in faint plumes as they stepped into the dimly lit parking lot. Aegeus noted the hush that had settled—only the distant hum of traffic and the rustle of a few dry leaves scuttling across the pavement.

Kfir's interest in the strange human snack vanished the moment he sensed it: demons everywhere. They felt like a ripple of shadows spreading through the night. He drew his weapon, the metal gleaming under the flickering light of a lone streetlamp.

"Steady," Aegeus ordered, his voice low but firm. He slipped his own sword free, scanning the perimeter. Taunting demons and destroyers ringed them, twisting the darkness into something menacing. Aegeus's stomach tightened at the sheer number of destroyers. Their presence meant something grim was brewing.

Just ahead, the Eleventh and Twelfth stopped next to the car. The Eleventh's voice dropped to a shocked whisper:

"Do you see them?"

"See who?" the Twelfth asked, peering around and seeing nothing but empty spaces and silent cars.

"Demons," the Eleventh replied, her tone trembling. "Hundreds—if not thousands."

The Twelfth's eyes widened, but she perceived only the quiet darkness. She offered a silent prayer of thanks that she couldn't share her friend's terrifying vision. Without lingering, the women climbed into their car and pulled out of the lot, their taillights fading into the distance.

Aegeus exhaled softly when the women pulled out of the parking lot unharmed, but he didn't relax. Kfir glanced at him, brow furrowed; taking to the skies, they flew after the car, determined to ensure the women's safety on their journey.

A short while later, the Twelfth slowed the car to the shoulder of a narrow mountain road. The night had deepened, and the temperature had plummeted. She realized something was wrong—maybe a flat tire. When she and the Eleventh stepped outside, the cold needled their skin. They stood at the car's rear, thin moonlight gleaming off the metal frame. The Eleventh crouched down, brushing her fingers over the flat tire's worn rubber.

"Oh, great," sighed the Twelfth, hugging herself against the cold. She regretted not bringing a coat; the chill seeped into her bones. The land around them was quiet and isolated, with steep drop-offs plummeting into darkness on either side of the road. Not a single house light blinked in the distance, and the silence pressed down, heavy and expectant.

Suddenly, the eerie quiet fractured. Demons descended like a swarm of locusts. Their dark shapes streaked through the night, thickening the air with malicious intent. Adir, who had been concealed, burst forth from the car's roof in a flash of movement. Sword drawn, he slashed at the demons, trying to keep them at bay. Aegeus and Kfir arrived moments later, weapons raised, forming a defensive line in the shadows of the trees. Yet the demons kept coming, more and more pouring from the woods, their laughter a high, chittering mockery.

The Eleventh could see them all too well. Demons whooshed past, tangling their bony fingers in the Twelfth's hair as if testing her, only to yank their hands back as if burned. The Twelfth felt only strange gusts at her head, her hair whipping wildly though no wind blew. She shivered, terrified but uncertain why. The Eleventh swatted at the creatures, eyes wide with horror, as twisted faces and gleaming teeth lunged at them. She stumbled backward, instinct driving her toward the edge of the embankment.

Adir strained to push the demons back, but their sheer number was overwhelming. The Eleventh, disoriented, took a step too far and slipped down the steep slope. With a yelp, she tumbled, twisting her ankle painfully as she landed on a ledge of loose stones and sparse brush. She cried out, verses of Scripture tumbling from her lips, her voice ragged with fear.

Above, the Twelfth stood rooted in shock, unsure what was happening. Terror—a powerful demon—swooped in from behind.

Talons dug into the Twelfth's spine, causing a searing pain she couldn't explain. Kfir lunged forward, slicing through the demon's form. Terror vanished in a puff of darkness, but the Twelfth remained frozen, caught between fear and confusion.

With a soft whoosh of wings, Meir arrived. Kfir's eyes narrowed. "What are you doing here? It's not safe!" he shouted over the shrieking wind of demon wings.

Ignoring him, Meir placed a gentle hand on the Twelfth's shoulder. She whispered softly—words lost beneath the clamor—but whatever she spoke sent warmth coursing through the Twelfth's spirit. Meir slipped away, her mission complete, leaving the Twelfth suddenly flooded with an inner Light that flared like a shield. Strengthened, the Twelfth rushed toward the embankment's edge.

"Are you okay?" she called down to the Eleventh, who lay below in the ditch, clutching her injured ankle and shivering. Adir dove down and spread his wings over the Eleventh, covering her from above as best he could, shielding her from the worst of the onslaught. The Eleventh's breath came in sharp bursts, eyes huge with fear and pain.

A strange sound drifted through the trees, muffled but growing—a distant roar. The Twelfth turned her ear toward it, brow crinkled in confusion. Kfir, hearing it too, leapt to the treetops, scanning for the source.

High on Elpída Mountain, Titus commanded a pack of destroyers. They hacked at ice and snow, forging a sudden flood.

Titus smiled, picturing the chaos below as a wall of freezing water would crash into the vulnerable humans. Tonight, he would kill the prophet.

"Aegeus! A flood, two hundred yards out, coming in hot!" Kfir yelled the warning down to Aegeus. Concern flickered in Aegeus's eyes. The women were too far from the car, boxed in by the cliffs and the demons. There was no time to outrun the flood. The narrow road and the steep drop ahead meant they were trapped, with only seconds before the torrent hit. He tightened his grip on his sword, frustration simmering beneath his calm as he watched the demons close in.

"Get them in the car!" Aegeus shouted to Adir, swinging his sword through a cluster of leering demons. But the Eleventh was on the ground, reciting verses through chattering teeth, and the Twelfth stood tense with uncertainty. They had no time. Terror's lingering touch and the swarm of demons pinned them down.

A moment later, the flood crashed down the gorge, a roaring torrent of icy water that snatched the women off their feet as if they were rag dolls. Adir tried to shield them with his body, but the current was merciless. It swept debris along with it—branches and stones that battered them. The Eleventh's cardigan snagged on a submerged limb, dragging her under. Her lips tinged blue as icy shock gripped her lungs.

Adir spotted the Eleventh's pale face beneath the turbulent surface. He dove down, shoving her free. She emerged coughing, sputtering, and gasping, her eyes filled with terror. Aegeus caught a glimpse of them—Adir struggling to keep the women afloat as demons pressed in from all sides. His adrenaline surged, and he plowed into a mass of shrieking forms, his blade a bright arc in the moonlight. Not again, he vowed silently. He would not lose anyone else.

The Twelfth slammed into Adir under the water. He grabbed at her shirt, forcing her up for air. Desperate, she reached out wildly, hands finding the rough bark of a tree trunk protruding from the embankment. Her fingertips bled as she clung to it, legs swept behind her by the current. She hugged the trunk, sobbing breaths ripping from her throat, ignoring the pain as bark tore at her skin. The Eleventh drifted by, flailing, and managed to grab the Twelfth's leg. Adir added his grip atop hers, forming a tenuous chain against the raging torrent.

Demons circled overhead, hurling heavy branches at them. The makeshift missiles struck the Twelfth's hands and shoulders, leaving welts and bruises. The Eleventh prayed hoarsely, voice cracking between coughs. The roar of water and laughter of demons filled their ears, and time seemed to slow into a sickening crawl.

"I can't hold on!" the Twelfth cried; voice barely audible over the crashing water.

"You have to!" the Eleventh pleaded, panic edging her words. "If you let go, we'll die!"

Adir could not reach the hands of the Twelfth from where he was to help secure them. He strained, gripping both women as best he could, but the angle made it impossible to reinforce the Twelfth's hold on the tree. He saw the despair in their eyes—and the choice looming before him if she slipped. The Eleventh was his charge, but the Twelfth was vital to the King's plan. Would he be forced to choose? He clenched his jaw, channeling peace and strength into them, willing them to hold steady.

Aegeus's heart wrenched as he caught sight of Adir, barely holding onto the two women as demons tore into him. Rage and fierce protectiveness surged within him. A memory of Lavi's face flashed in Aegeus's mind, sharpening his resolve. He barked orders to Kfir, his own sword flashing as he cut down demons swarming his brother. Demons shrieked in rage as he cut them down, sulfur-laced breath hissing in his face.

Below, the demons converged on Adir. They jabbed at him, tearing into his back and hands with their talons. Demons swarmed, their talons relentlessly tearing through him. He cried out in agony, his grip faltering as blood pooled beneath his fingers. His suffering energized the demons, and they swarmed faster and faster into the frenzied scene, stabbing him over and over while others clawed desperately at his wings. He cried out, agony and frustration colliding in a raw sound. Blood slicked his grip, and he felt the world blur at the edges.

Still, he held on.

Chapter 39

"I've got her." The voice drifted through Adir's fog, familiar and comforting, yet distant, as though carried on a fading echo.

"Adir, let go. I've got her," Aegeus repeated, his words steady, urging Adir to release his grip. Adir tried to focus, to latch onto that voice. It stirred a memory of safety and loyalty, but his thoughts floated just out of reach. He blinked, vision blurring, shadows pooling at the corners of his eyes.

"Aegeus?" he managed, voice weak and uncertain.

"Yes, let go, Adir" came the gentle command. "You have done well. You are seriously injured. You must let go of her so that Kfir might heal you."

Adir tried to focus; he had to be sure. He turned his head toward the voice. His vision blurred, shadows dancing at the edges. The voice reached him through the haze, comforting yet distant, like an echo through water. Aegeus's face began to come into focus, concern etched in his eyes. Relief fluttered in Adir's chest.

"My charge?"

"We have her; she is safe. You have done well. Now, just let go," Aegeus assured him. At last, Adir let go.

Below, the Eleventh gasped as she felt a sudden upward tug. A stranger had seized her from the raging flood as if plucking a doll from a puddle. His strength was effortless—otherworldly. He said nothing, face set in stony silence, as he also lifted the Twelfth with ease. He walked through the torrent as though it were no more than a shallow stream. His grip was firm and unyielding, one hand on the Eleventh's arm, the other grasping the back of the Twelfth's shirt.

No words, no glance, no explanation. He simply trudged onto dry land and released them, both women collapsing onto the cold ground. With a casual brush of his hand over their car's metal flank, he kept walking, disappearing into the dark.

They knelt there, coughing and shivering on the shoulder of the road, both too stunned to move at first. The icy air bit at their damp clothes, and the cold felt even sharper now that the adrenaline was wearing off. The Twelfth cradled her torn hands, wincing at the sting of raw scrapes and bleeding knuckles. The Eleventh shifted, gasping as pain flared in her swollen ankle. She wrapped her arms around herself, teeth chattering, and looked to her friend with eyes that mirrored her bewilderment.

"What... what just happened?" she managed, voice trembling.

"I—I don't know," the Twelfth answered, peering around as if expecting to see their silent rescuer lingering nearby. There was no sign of him—just darkness, distant headlights, and the fading roar of the water still rushing below. Everything felt unreal, as if they'd stumbled into a nightmare that refused to make sense.

"Are you okay?"

The Eleventh swallowed hard, shivering so fiercely her words came out in stutters.

"I'm f-freezing… and my ankle…"

The Twelfth fumbled for her car keys, her hands shaking almost too badly to hold them.

"Look, let's just… get in the car," she said softly, struggling to sound calm. "It's got to be warmer than out here."

A shaky laugh slipped from the Eleventh's throat, half relief and half disbelief. "Warm sounds good."

The Twelfth offered her an arm, helping her stand.

"Start it up," she urged through chattering teeth, pressing the keys into the Eleventh's hand. "Get the heat going—I'll try to change the flat."

She popped open the trunk, retrieved the jack and tire iron, and trudged to the passenger side. But when she crouched to inspect the tire, confusion struck. The tire was fine—fully inflated. She circled the car, checking every wheel in the thin moonlight. Nothing. All the tires were intact.

Nearby, Aegeus, Kfir, and Adir observed, invisible to human eyes, yet very much present. A faint smile tugged at Kfir's lips.

"Nice touch fixing the flat," he said quietly, glancing at Aegeus. He gave him a gentle nudge.

"If I didn't know better, I'd think you were worried about her."

Aegeus's jaw tightened slightly.

"Just doing my job. We are neither friend nor foe," he replied, voice carefully neutral. "We fight for the King."

Yet even as he spoke, he felt a subtle warmth in his chest, a crack in the protective wall he'd built around his heart. He had been worried—truly worried—about the Twelfth. This was a slip he had not intended, a softening he thought himself beyond after millennia of war and loss. He remembered too well the agony of watching someone turn against everything he held dear. He would not repeat that mistake. Certainly, he had slipped; he could admit that, but he promised himself that this moment of concern was a single lapse, nothing more.

Inside the car, the women huddled, waiting for the heat to penetrate the dark chill of the night; their voices trembled as they offered a prayer of thanks. They spoke of their protector, never knowing their words reached his angelic ears.

Aegeus stood in front of the car, pressing his palms to the hood. Warmth coursed through the metal, filling the interior with heat. He listened to their grateful voices, odd and unexpected in his long existence. In all his centuries, he couldn't recall anyone giving thanks for him. The realization settled like a faint glow in his chest, one he both welcomed and feared.

Shaken, injured, but alive, the two women drove off into the night, heading for the hospital. Above them, Aegeus hovered, sword sheathed, heart guarded, and destinies entwined.

Chapter 40

Titus stood staring into the night. They had again failed to kill the prophet. The rage boiled inside him. The knowledge seethed inside him, igniting a rage like dry tinder. He remained unmoving, his silence heavy, letting the fury coil tighter in his chest. His breaths came slow and controlled, savoring the taste of his own hatred, a flavor he had not relished in ages. Soon, Seneca would learn of his failure, and that thought fanned the fire even hotter.

Around him, demons began to gather, drawn to his fury. They hovered anxiously, awaiting orders, but Titus neither opened his eyes nor acknowledged their presence. He stood like a statue of wrath, every muscle taut, rage rising to a fever pitch.

One demon dared to step forward and speak. Titus's eyes snapped open—wild and burning—and in a swift, brutal motion, he wrenched a dagger from its sheath and plunged it deep into the creature's body. He twisted the blade, snarling through clenched teeth, his scream tearing through the darkness. At that cry, thousands of demons across the town took flight, blotting out the stars as they spread like a disease.

Titus raised his voice, sharp as a blade drawn across a whetstone:

"Swarm the prophet's home! Cover her husband, plague her office, suffocate her students in darkness! Give her no rest—no peace! Flood her days until they clamor for her counsel at every hour! Find her family and shroud them in torment. Destroy as many as you can!"

With that, a legion of demons scattered in a frenzy of smoke and fury. They spilled into the town's streets and alleyways, carrying his hatred on their wings, eager to obey the command.

Chapter 41

The college was covered in soft white and blue icicle lights on every building. On the first Friday of December, two weeks before the Christmas break, as was the long-standing tradition of the college, the students, faculty, and staff gathered to decorate the big evergreen outside the Great Hall.

Students stood out in the cold night air, clutching the warm mugs of hot cocoa provided by the Science Department. Little marshmallows, shaped like DNA, floating in the cups would stick to their noses if they weren't careful. Warm snickerdoodle cookies greeted all those who braved the cold. The Bible department provided a nativity reenactment complete with live animals. Professors played the part of Mary, Joseph, and the shepherds. They used a doll for Jesus.

Each department brought ornaments to help decorate the tree. After which, there was a tree-lighting ceremony. The tree shimmered with blues and silvers, the angel at its peak aglow, a beacon against the night sky. Christmas carols began, voices mingling in the crisp air.

The angels meandered easily among them, enjoying the joyous nature of celebrating the birth of the Lamb. The King's children were never as full of his Light as at Christmas. There was something about the innocence of a baby, the newness of life, the vulnerability of God incarnate that stirred them. All of heaven remembered that night; all of heaven and earth had paused to watch and celebrate the birth of the Lamb.

The tree in Platitude was spectacular. The night was quiet and carried their voices beautifully throughout Platitude. The angels stood among the humans, turning their faces toward the King as his children sang classic Christmas carols. Thousands of voices singing to the King on that cold night stirred him. One by one, angels from all over Platitude arrived. Together, they joined the King's children in praise. But Aegeus did not. He stood silently; his heart stirred with each note of *Silent Night*. The song's haunting simplicity mirrored the quiet humility of that night in Bethlehem, where the King lay in a cradle of straw under a canopy of stars. Thousands of voices joined in harmony, lifting the song heavenward, and Aegeus stood silent, overwhelmed by memories. The Light emanating from the gathered angels around him was so profound that he closed his eyes, his throat tight with reverence. Christmas brought out the best in Platitude.

Aegeus had been there. He had watched in awe as the Lamb confined Himself to a tiny, vulnerable body, each breath a miracle of humility and strength. Heaven's power flowed from that child, radiant and uncontainable, yet there he lay, unable to lift his own head. In that one beautiful moment, Aegeus glimpsed the true depth of humility. He remembered Mary's gentle touch, the way her eyes softened as she stroked her baby's cheek, her heart swelling with love. Standing by the campus nativity, he felt the echoes of that night, though he knew no earthly reenactment could ever fully capture its power.

But the presence of so much Light agitated the Strongman who climbed the stage and took the microphone in an attempt to end the singing that had brought such beauty. He could not bring himself to speak of the birth of the Lamb. Instead, he discussed the sanctity of marriage. He spoke of the union of Adam and Eve as the model. He reminded everyone that God had created man first, giving him dominion. Then, he spoke of the marriage of Joseph and Mary. The words stuck in his throat as said them. He despised the holy family.

His hatred for Mary was so great that even her name made his skin crawl. If only she had been unwilling to bear the child or to bear the burden of being an unwed mother or the stigma associated with it. And Joseph? Why had Joseph been willing to overlook her pregnancy, refusing to send her to the stoning that she deserved? If there was anything the Strongman hated more than a righteous woman, it was a righteous man. A righteous man was a force he could never control—a threat he loathed.

But outwardly, the Strongman appeared to preach with such conviction. He trembled, and to those who watched, he seemed to do so out of overwhelming reverence. He took this opportunity to diminish the role of Mary to nothing more than an incubator. He used the story of the Lamb to rail against abortion and premarital sex—to pour out guilt. He took the beautiful story of how heaven came to earth to bring hope and peace and turned it into an opportunity to offer condemnation and judgment. Aegeus's fists clenched as he listened, his heart heavy with sorrow. This night should have been a celebration of love, hope, and peace—a reminder of the King's sacrifice. But the Strongman twisted the beauty of the Lamb's story, wielding it as a weapon to condemn rather than comfort. As the Strongman's words filled the night, the Light around the tree seemed to flicker, a reminder of the battle still raging,

Chapter 42

It had become the practice of the Fifth, Sixth, Seventh, Eleventh, and Twelfth to meet during lunch once a week and share their struggles, praying together and offering each other insights, advice, and encouragement. Their meetings had become a safe place to admit their doubts and share their collective wisdom. A place where they could be honest and raw with each other. Mostly.

Yet even in the safety of their group, each of them held their deepest needs close and did not share those. They did not yet trust each other enough to lay out their innermost pain—some pain was too deep to share. And so, the prayers, while powerful and a delightful aroma to the King, were never as strong as they might have been, so they could never find real freedom.

The women had chosen to meet in the office of the Sixth for their final gathering of the semester. Unseen by the women, Adiel, Kfir, and Haywood stood guard outside the door. Aegeus went inside the room with them as an additional level of protection.

The women sank into the chairs around the perfectly decorated room, eager for the spiritual encouragement these meetings tended to bring. The last month had been particularly difficult. Their offices had been flooded with students whose souls yearned to hear that they were loved. The students' sadness seemed palpable and had seeped into the women, exhausting and distracting them, just as the Strongman had intended. Their souls were heavy from the burden the Strongman had placed on them over the semester.

It seemed that no matter how many students they saw, there was still a line of them waiting. Their stories ranged from divorcing parents, unexpected illnesses, pregnancy scares, or marriage problems. The women were not only physically and emotionally exhausted, but they had begun to doubt themselves. So much of what the Strongman was saying seemed right. His condemning and judgmental words were taking a toll on them.

They exchanged glances of weary camaraderie, each bearing the sting of judgment. In that quiet moment of shared fatigue, the Fifth cleared her throat, determined to show how the strongman's influence touched more lives than just their own.

"One of my students this week told me she called off her engagement with her fiancé. She was just devastated. But her boyfriend was going into the ministry, and she knew that as a physician assistant, she would make more money than him. Her Bible professors apparently told her she could not be a good Christian woman and make more money than her husband. So, she decided to remain unmarried. She said to marry, she would have to seek out a husband based on his income, and she didn't feel right about that."

"Oh! I had the boy in my office," exclaimed the Fifth.

"He, too, was devastated. He said he didn't care how much money she made. He said he told her he didn't believe she would have to give up her independence or make less than him. He told me that her independence was one of the things he loved most about her—that he viewed marriage as something they did together and that he believed the Bible told them to submit to each other, meaning neither would rule over the other but that they would walk together.

"But it didn't seem to matter. He said she told him that while he might feel that way, if the Bible said otherwise and they got married, then she would constantly be sinning. And while he might not care, she was not willing to spend the rest of her life violating God's law," the Fifth concluded, sadness and anger evident in her eyes. Something about the Fifth's eyes cried out. They implied that perhaps her anger and pain came from somewhere deeper than just this story.

"I think the word 'submission' should be better defined," suggested the Twelfth. "I think the church has messed that up. And honestly, why do we all ignore the verse that says we are to submit to each other? It isn't just about women submitting; husbands are also called to submit to their wives and to God. Submission is meant to be mutual; why do we ignore that?"

"My husband knows I hate it when he leaves the toilet seat up. So, he puts it down. That is submission. He quit smoking years ago because he knew I didn't like it. That is submission. I pre-rise the dishes on my night to do them because I know he likes it. We submit to each other daily out of love—not out of fear or demand.

"I hate that we have been taught to associate submission with the idea that one person gets to tell the other what to do. We aren't dogs. Marriage is give and take; both have to give. It is about harmony, not hierarchy. When you learn to let things go, and you love someone enough to avoid things they don't like and do things they do like, it makes for a more harmonious home. Both people have to do that. And that is submission." The Twelfth stopped.

The Eleventh picked up there. "And, of course, when you can't agree on something, your husband has the final say."

"I don't agree with that," said the Seventh. "I know I'm not married, but I don't think it works that way. If you can't agree, I think you should both pray about it. And God will give you an answer. But if you still can't agree, then I think you should think about your motives. Are you doing what you think is in the family's best interest? Are you doing what is in alignment with God? Are you being selfish? I don't think you have to concede to do things your husband's way just because he is a man and you are a woman. Look at Abigail in the Bible. If you recall, Abigail was married to Nabal, who was something of a jerk. Nabal offended David, and David was going to kill him. Abigail went to David and smoothed things out behind Nabal's back. Nabal had a stroke and died when he found out what she had done. She did not just go along with her husband Nabal; she did not just submit to him and was rewarded for it."

"The typical answer to that is always that the exception is if your husband tells you to do something contrary to God's law. Then, and only then, can you disobey him," the Sixth responded.

"But Nabal was just being rude; he was not violating God's law, so that argument doesn't stand," the Seventh countered.

"What I want to know is if marriage is just about giving a man control of your life—clearing the path so he can accomplish his goals while giving up any goals of your own—and letting him tell you what to do while you wash his clothes, clean his house, and birth his children, what value is there for a woman to get married?" asked the Eleventh.

Aegeus shifted uncomfortably. The King had declared from the beginning that it was not good for man to be alone. He had created a woman so that he wouldn't be. Aegeus thought back to Adam and his search for a companion. The King had created Eve; Adam had been overjoyed. He celebrated her arrival, a day never passed in the garden that Adam had not expressed that joy to Eve. Aegeus wondered when that had gotten lost.

"He will provide for you financially and guide you spiritually," the Sixth answered, sarcasm dripping from her lips.

"I don't need anyone to provide for me financially or guide me spiritually. So, I guess my student was right: you should only get married if you need someone to take care of you. I guess that is why we see that trend in the country," the Fifth retorted.

"According to our college administration, that would then make you a rebellious woman because a woman's calling is to get married and have children. Not doing so is a sign you are rebellious and selfish," the Sixth fired back.

"What?" the Twelfth asked, baffled by the statement.

"That's what he said." The Sixth let the facts speak for themselves. "Naturally, as a nonmarried woman, I can never fulfill my calling. I suppose I shouldn't have waited for the right one to come along. I should have married for money years ago," she said, causing the group to laugh.

"They are telling the students in the Bible classes that if a man doesn't make enough money to support his family, he can't call himself a Christian," the Fifth offered.

"Based on what?" asked the Seventh.

"They are basing it on 1 Timothy 5:8," she offered, pulling up the Bible app on her phone to read the passage to the group.

"I don't think that is what that means," offered the Twelfth.

"The students say they are taught that a man's biblical role is to be a provider. In accordance with God's role for him, he must provide for his family, and his wife must bear children—that is her biblical role," offered the Sixth, starting to feel a bit sick to her stomach.

"Well, you don't want your husband to be a deadbeat, but I don't see where "provider" means the sole provider or that it has to be the primary financial provider. And what if God gave the woman a job making a lot of money in order to support a husband going into the ministry who won't make anything?"

"Out of alignment with the biblical role of men and women per the current administration." The Fifth shook her head in befuddlement, as did Aegeus.

Aegeus marveled at how little understanding they had about how the King worked if this was what they thought. The King created each of them to be unique. Each of them had a purpose that only they could fulfill. Each of them had a path and journey just for them. Certainly, females were designed to be able to bear children, but that didn't mean that was their sole purpose in life. He felt a pang of sadness as he watched them grapple with words twisted into chains. These terms were never meant to bind but to guide. He wished they could sense the King's heart—a heart of unity, not division. But he remained silent, knowing their questions would lead them closer to the truth.

"So, what if you don't want children?" the Seventh asked. She had been thinking for years that she did not want to have children. She felt God calling her to the international mission field— places that could potentially be dangerous—and she had no desire to take children into that setting. It just wasn't a yearning she had.

"Then you are selfish and are rejecting God's gift of children. Of course, there are those women who cannot have children. They can never fulfill the great calling of God. They apparently have no purpose, nor do women who remain unmarried.

Or perhaps God will find them a secondary purpose, but their lives will be less important than those married with children." The pain in the Sixth was evident in her comments. The other women shook their heads in disgust at the idea.

"I wonder if Esther realized that saving the entire Israelite civilization was not her 'great calling'?" the Eleventh suggested. "I mean, did she have children that we know of?"

"She did, later. What about Deborah?" the Twelfth asked.

"Oh, well, you should know that Deborah was not a judge over Israel like the other judges—the 'men' judges—she was just a good luck charm, and she was only used because no man was available. Apparently, when God gets desperate, he will resort to using women—at least according to what my students tell me they're being taught," the Fifth said.

The Twelfth shifted in her seat. The conversation had nearly become too much for her. She struggled, and she prayed, and she questioned. She had read the verses over and over, and she didn't see them the way they were being taught. She wanted to know the truth.

"What about Sheerah?" she asked. Aegeus nodded his head, excited that the Fifth had thought of Sheerah. He had not thought of her for a long time.

"Who?" asked the Sixth.

"Sheerah, from 1 Chronicles. She was a woman who built three cities, naming the third one Uzzen Sheerah— 'listen to

Sheerah.' Do you think that she didn't command men? Do you think she didn't rule over them as she built her cities? And we know nothing else about her. We don't know if she was married or if she had children. What we do know is that she built three cities. Oh, and we know that God used one of her cities to throw hailstones down on the Philistines while time stood still."

"I've never heard of her." The Eleventh looked puzzled and pulled up her Bible app to look up the passage.

"There are many women in the Bible you may not have heard of," noted the Twelfth. "The genealogies are full of them. Pay attention to the ones that say 'sons' compared to the ones that say 'descendants.' Often, the ones that say 'descendants' list both males and females. First and Second Kings list the mothers of all the kings except for two, specifically giving the names of both the father and the mother.

"Most scholars believe the queen mother was an actual position of authority within the royal family. We know from Solomon that his mother had a throne right beside him in the throne room.

Aegeus looked at the women in the room. They were women with many talents and beautiful souls. They were in various stages of life and relationships, and he hated the idea that even one of them would leave this room feeling as if their life and their future did not have meaning if it did not involve marrying and having children. Those things did not define you or your purpose. Being a child of the one true King was what defined you.

"God himself called Job the most blameless of all men. He was described as a man of great integrity, the finest man on all the earth. If you look at how he managed his family, I think you get a great model of what a father and man should be." The Fifth offered.

"What I find interesting," she continued, "is that at the end of Job, when God once again blessed him, we are told the names of his three daughters but not the names of his sons. We are also told that Job treated his daughters as equals to his sons, including them in his will. If that is how the finest man on the earth behaves, shouldn't that be our model?" she concluded.

The Twelfth wondered why she had never heard that pointed out from the pulpit. Aegeus felt proud of the Fifth despite his best efforts to remain neutral.

The Eleventh looked at the Twelfth and asked, "Do you believe the man is the head of the home?" Certainly, they all recognized how loaded this question had been in the media recently.

"I do. The Bible says the man is the head of the home. I think the issue is what we think that means. I believe a husband is supposed to be a servant leader, as was Christ. Christ never forced anyone to do what he wanted. He was never selfish in his leadership, and he sacrificed his very life for the church.

"I don't think it means he's 'the boss' because the Bible also says a husband and wife become one. How can you be one and yet be divided into rank? It is a dichotomy I can't quite explain, like the Trinity. I just have to accept it in faith. I'm pretty sure it also says he should deal with intruders and/or bugs," she said with a smile.

The other ladies laughed at the joke, and Aegeus also smiled.

"Perhaps the church should focus more on teaching men what it means to be the head of the family rather than focusing entirely on telling women to submit to their husbands," Added the Eleventh.

"A husband has a responsibility to love his wife as Christ loved the church. To care for her and protect her with his very life. He is responsible for helping her be the best version of herself by loving, supporting, and walking with her. He has full authority to do that. In that way, he is the head of the wife. But that responsibility, that authority, does not translate into him being the boss of her or having the authority to command her what to do – that level of authority is reserved for God alone. At least that is how I understand it", the Twelfth said.

The women's Lights burned brightly as they struggled with these ideas and concepts and worked to understand what the Word said. Aegeus tried to remain impartial, but he found himself cheering for them in their success and wishing they could hear him when they had it wrong.

"What about that 'helper' issue?" asked the Seventh, circling back to a prior conversation.

"Anytime I have ever had to call for help, I am ecstatic to have help arrive. I did not see that help as inferior to me but as someone who could do what I could not. Men cannot do it alone. They need women. God said it was not good for man to be alone. Why would you undervalue that? It is a partnership," the Fifth offered.

The Twelfth's light flared, filling the room, and she suddenly realized that the Fifth had indeed known great love. She wasn't sure what caused her to think it exactly, but she knew that the Fifth had once loved a man deeply.

"I heard a great sermon on that once," the Seventh offered. "I'll e-mail the link to everyone." She pulled her phone out and started looking for the link. "I honestly think the issue is one of nomenclature. It is how we define 'submission' and 'helper', and 'head' that brings about the problem. Perhaps it can only truly be defined within the confines of marriage. Perhaps it is personal and will look different for everyone. Perhaps no standard answer will fit every marriage. So much of the Bible is personal."

"And isn't that the whole purpose of the Holy Spirit? To convict us? To teach us? To interpret scripture? Maybe you're right. There is no one answer," the Twelfth offered.

The others considered this possibility. They had indeed had prior conversations about how the Spirit led some people not to drink. For them, drinking was wrong because the Holy Spirit told them not to. Just as in the Bible, some had been called to special diets or to not cut their hair. It was not about rules but obedience, and sometimes, that looked different for each person. Perhaps submission looked different in every home.

"Are you suggesting there is no one standard of truth?" the Sixth asked, alarm rising in her.

"Not at all. There is indeed truth; I am just suggesting that in some things, perhaps it is more personal than that. In some things, it is about conviction." The Twelfth stopped because she felt concerned. They were going into dangerous territory. She was not trying to imply there were no absolutes.

Their time was over, so they prayed together before each left to get back to work.

"I see their Lights are all burning brightly," observed Kfir as Aegeus exited the room. "I trust it went well?"

Aegeus nodded consent. "It was an odd conversation about marriage and children and what particular words meant. They were in alignment with the Word regarding men being the head of the home. But they are not sure what that means. They have been taught many conflicting ideas, some of which come from the Strongman and are, of course, designed to demean and hurt them. But they seek the truth, and the King will show them that." Haywood could see that the Fifth was distraught after the discussion, and her face was flushed. He worried about her. Perhaps he would call Ayo again tonight to try to minister to her. He bid the other angels goodbye and left to walk her back to her office.

"Haven't the Eleventh and Twelfth both been married many years?" asked Adiel, already knowing the answer.

"Indeed." Aegeus nodded, starting down the hall after the Twelfth.

"And aren't they happily married?" Adiel followed.

"Indeed," Aegeus answered again.

"And they have not yet figured this out?" Adiel asked, baffled by the ways of humans.

"Knowing and knowing that you know are not the same thing," Aegeus answered.

Adiel nodded knowingly. That she understood. And marriage was, as Paul had put it, a great mystery.

"Think of it this way," Aegeus said, "warriors, guardians, and ministering angels are all different. We meet different needs and are designed for different things. Is the warrior better than the guardian or the ministering angel?" Aegeus asked.

"Of course not," Kfir answered. "We are all needed. We are all necessary. We are equals and work together as a team."

"And who is in charge?" Aegeus asked. Kfir laughed at that.

"The King is in charge," Kfir said as if to a child.

"Am I in charge of you, Adiel?" he asked. A look of shock spread over Adiel's face as she tried to comprehend the question.

"None but the King is in charge of me," she replied.

"Am I in charge of you, Kfir?" he asked, turning to Kfir, who roared with laughter.

"None but the King is in charge of me. You are in charge of this mission, but not me. I am free to make my choices and to do what I think is best, and I answer to the King for those choices. Being in charge of the mission and being in charge of me are two different things."

Aegeus nodded. "Exactly. That's the truth these women seek, even if they don't know it yet."

Chapter 43: The Sixth and Seventh

The Sixth and the Seventh were six months apart. They had grown up together, neighbors and best friends since third grade. The Sixth was the older of the two. She liked to think she was also the more responsible one. She had spent her life playing by the rules. She wore a rough exterior, but it covered a tender heart—one she was petrified of being broken.

She was tall and beautiful and attracted the attention of many men, but she intimidated most of them. The Sixth liked to take the safe road. She weighed options, considered consequences, and always tried to do the right thing. She feared punishment, and although she would never admit it, she feared the rejection that came from it.

The Seventh was originally from the Dominican Republic, but her family had moved to California when she was young. The Sixth had taught her English and about American culture. She quickly became the protector of the Seventh.

The Seventh was adventurous; she followed her heart and paid little consideration to the consequences. The Sixth bulldozed trouble from her path. But the Seventh rarely noticed. She wasn't much of a rule-follower, but she did have an overactive conscience that kept her from going too far astray.

The girls had grown up knowing the Lord, but each had chosen her own path when committing to becoming His children. They were as close as sisters. They had gone to the same college, the Sixth, studying accounting, and the Seventh, pursuing art. Now, they shared an apartment in a bohemian town, just outside Platitude.

The Sixth wore crisp, clean lines, with well-pressed suits and heels, her curly hair always painstakingly straightened and pulled into a tight bun. The Seventh wore flowing fabrics with patterns and dangling bracelets, and her hair was loose about her shoulders.

The Sixth was recruited first. She was working in an exhibitor's booth at a conference in Tulsa. A wayward handcart rolled into her display, sending things sprawling across the exhibitors' hall. As she scrambled to pick up the pieces, a woman with wild red hair approached her.

"Let me help you," the woman offered with a kind and gentle smile. The Sixth was frazzled by the incident and from working at a job she hadn't liked in years. If she were honest, she would have to admit that she had lost a little respect for herself for even working there. But bills didn't pay themselves, and the Seventh was often late with rent since sculpting did not provide a steady paycheck. She smiled at the woman, accepting the help gracefully.

When the display was back in order, and all the materials she had brought with her were once again in neat rows on the table, the woman with the red hair stood quietly looking at the display. The

Sixth found herself growing a little uncomfortable. The woman with the wild red hair smiled at her in reassurance.

"You could do better." It was not a question but a statement. The Sixth looked down momentarily, and then a slight fleck of anger sparked inside her. The woman stood firm, not flinching.

"Thank you for your help. I truly appreciate it. But if you will excuse me, I have to get back to work." The Sixth felt unexplainable anger, and yet when she looked at the woman, she couldn't help but feel like the woman's green eyes were looking right into her soul.

"Indeed, you do. You have many talents; I am a talent expert," the woman said. "You are wasting them, and you know it. Leave what is good for what is better." She reached into her jacket pocket and pulled out a small business card with nothing but a logo. Handing the card to the Sixth, she allowed their eyes to lock briefly and then walked away.

The Sixth put the card quickly in her pocket, intending to throw it away once she was back in her hotel room. She felt flustered by the woman's abruptness. She smoothed down her suit jacket, pasted on a smile, and threw her mind into her work—even if it was work she hated. *How could this woman have known?* She wondered. *Who had put her up to this?* When she returned to her room later that evening, she threw the business card in the trash.

"How was your day?" the Seventh asked as they were chatting by phone.

"Oh, I'm living the dream," the Sixth said with a snicker. She went on to tell her about the encounter with the woman and the odd business card.

"How mysterious! What is the logo?"

The Sixth attempted to explain the design to her, but it just didn't translate well. She fished the card out of the wastebasket, snapped a picture with her phone, and sent that instead.

It took the Seventh nearly six weeks to determine that the logo was for a college hidden in the mountains, in the middle of nowhere. With her encouragement, the Sixth reviewed their job site. They had an opening in the accounting department that was perfect for her.

After she had been working there for just over a year, the art department had an opening, and she recommended the Seventh.

Chapter 44

The last day of the semester finally came, and the Twelfth was looking forward to the long break. Christmas was in two weeks, and she had not done any of her shopping. She had been so busy with students and grades that she had let things at home go.

Her Wednesday night group was planning a progressive Christmas party, and she had lots of cleaning to do to be ready. She was thankful for a few weeks to focus on her family. She bundled up, put Christmas music on her iPod, and started to lock up her office to begin the walk home. Just as she was walking out the door, a young man from her afternoon class asked if she had a minute.

Aegeus immediately noticed the demons that clung to him—demons that had been with him for a long time. Most tormenting demons were opportunistic. They tormented their charge for a season but did not remain long-term. But just as the King had knitted each human together, providing them with all the gifts they would need to find him and fulfill his perfect plan for their life, Satan too took a great interest in the birth of a human child. Each human would be assessed shortly after birth, and Satan would determine the sin that would work best for that individual. He would assign tormenting demons to them based on his findings.

For some, it was lying. Certainly, all humans lied. But some people lied for no reason. They lied about everything. Some people lied just because lying was their default setting. They justified their actions by calling them "white lies" because they didn't hurt anyone. Once the sin became part of you, it was easy to convince yourself that it wasn't a sin at all.

For some, it was gossip. They lived for a juicy bit of gossip. If there weren't any, they made some up. You could hardly tell a gossip that they were gossiping. They would tell you they were just telling you what was happening. Often, gossip was disguised as prayer requests, which somehow justified it.

For others, it is gluttony, jealousy, lust, selfishness, or pride. Ah, pride, that was one of Satan's favorites and one of the hardest to overcome. Those demons dug deep. Their talons sank deep into the person's heart and would fester if the human did not remove them.

When the person accepted the Spirit, things got more complicated. The Spirit would rail against those sins and burn and scorch the demon. The demon would cry out in pain but cling tightly, anxious to keep its charge.

The Spirit would be grieved that the person clung so tightly to the demon. Often, the person would wail and beg the King to deliver them from this sin, yet they would cling to it desperately—perhaps even unknowingly because it was so much a part of who they were. This young man had one of those demons dug deep into his chest.

The Twelfth invited the young man in, and they sat together in the small seating area. She offered him some water, but he declined. She could see immediately that he was uncomfortable. He shifted uneasily and didn't make eye contact.

She said a quick prayer, asking God to give her wisdom regarding whatever the young man wanted to talk about. She asked that God give him courage and help him feel comfortable.

Meir entered the room silently. She looked at Aegeus and smiled. He smiled back. If the Twelfth had summoned Meir, it meant she was making progress. Meir positioned herself between the Twelfth and the boy and laid a hand on each of them. Aegeus kept a watchful distance, his posture unwavering as he silently pledged to shield both their hearts from any further darkness. He marveled at the Twelfth's gentle strength, knowing the significance of this moment.

The Twelfth gently prompted the boy. He looked down at the floor and unknowingly placed one hand across his chest, pinning the demon to his body. A single tear ran down his face. He remained silent as he struggled to control his voice. The Twelfth prayed for him. His hand trembled slightly as he clenched it over his chest, pressing down as if to hold something back. For a moment, he looked as if he might walk away, but then his gaze settled on the

Twelfth's calm, encouraging expression. He drew a deep, shuddering breath.

"I....I have a secret that I have carried for many, many years," he started. "I have carried it alone, but now I am afraid it has gotten too heavy. I have been praying, and I feel like God has directed me to share it with someone. And after praying about it for a while more—well, here I am." He paused as the Twelfth waited.

Her chest tightened with the ache of wanting to ease his burden. She longed to reach out, to let him know he was seen and understood. In his posture and trembling voice, she saw not only a student but also someone's beloved child. She wanted him to feel safe and valued. She continued to pray silently while she listened. Her Light blazed brightly within her. The red-haired woman arrived and placed her hand on the back of the Twelfth. Power filled the room. Kfir saw the Lights and came to stand guard at the door.

"It is important to me that you know that I love the Lord," he went on. "I was raised in a Christian home by good Christian parents. I go to church, I pray, and I read my Bible daily. But as long as I can remember, I have been gay." He stopped there. His heart laid out bare and unprotected—his vulnerability palpable. The demon clinging to him hissed in anger that he had told anyone. He looked down at the floor, not daring to meet the eyes of the Twelfth.

"Am I the first person you have ever told?" she asked him gently. He nodded yes in response.

"Thank you for trusting me with something so big." She felt honored that he had come to her and petrified that she might say the wrong thing.

She ached for him and longed to hug him as a mother. She thought about her own son and what she would want someone to say to him if he confided such a significant secret in them.

"Do you think your sin is any different than mine?" she asked him.

He looked up then, a puzzled look on his face. She waited.

"What is yours?" he asked, genuinely interested.

"Self-centeredness has always been my struggle," she confessed, a soft sadness in her voice.

"But you are always listening to people. You are always asking how we are and investing in us?" He said it as a question since what she was describing was not how he saw her.

"It's my default, the place I drift when I'm not careful. Yet I'm most at peace when I'm here, with others, looking beyond myself. It's a daily choice to pull away from that dark comfort and open myself up to the world around me. I have to remind myself every day to look outside myself—because, honestly, I am happiest in moments like this when I am sharing in your life and helping others face their struggles. But when I am not careful, I lose sight of those around me and get overwhelmed by my own needs and my own issues. And when that happens, I find myself sinking into a quagmire.

"Our sins are the same. In God's eyes, our sins are equal. I sit here before you broken over my sin. But there are moments when I embrace it. I soak in it; I rub it all over me, breathing it in and justifying my own self-absorption. I have battled it as long as I can remember."

She smiled at him. He smiled back. More angels flocked to the office, surrounding it, protecting it, for this was a holy conversation, one in which all of heaven was invested. He looked up slowly, his brows furrowing, searching her face as if for reassurance.

"Really?" he whispered, his hand easing from its tight grip on his chest. Her simple honesty was like a balm, beginning to soothe a wound he hadn't realized had been so raw.

She smiled at him, her eyes soft with understanding. "Yes, really," she said gently, her voice steady. "You're not alone in this, and you don't have to carry it by yourself anymore."

"I don't want to die an old man alone," he blurted out, emotion strangling him. His hands fidgeted, twisting together in his lap, and he stared at the floor as if it might hold an answer.

The Twelfth reached out, resting her hand gently on his.

"You are not alone now, and you never will be," she said softly. "God sees you, loves you, and has a path for you, even when it feels unclear. Let's keep walking together, trusting that He won't leave you without hope, even in the moments that feel the darkest."

Aegeus yearned for the final battle. He longed to see Satan defeated and humanity restored and free from the pain and anguish of sin. He did not think the humans understood how much heaven grieved for them—how intricately involved heaven was with their daily lives and their development. Shaking the sin that Satan had assigned you was difficult. Few humans ever fully rid themselves of it. Most faced a lifelong struggle against it. If only they could see that the King's love was unchanging, beyond every shame or fear they carried.

Did the humans understand that all of heaven cried out for every young man and young woman like this one? Did they know how much it grieved all of them to see the King's children struggle so much? Did they understand that the King did not cast blame for the temptation that Satan laid before them? Aegeus found himself a bit surprised by his own reaction to the boy.

The Twelfth and the boy sat for more than an hour discussing his fears, his struggles, and his courage. Carrying his secret had been a heavy burden, and every day, he was overcome with the fear that someone would find out and he would be dismissed from school. It was a lot for a person to shoulder alone. Now, she would help carry it. She would pray for him daily and serve as someone he could come to when he struggled.

She encouraged him to share with his parents what he had shared with her. She again thought of her own son and said a little prayer for the man he would one day become. She asked God to place people in his path that he could confide in if he ever needed to. She prayed that they would have the wisdom to encourage him to come to her with his struggles, and she prayed that she would handle whatever it was well when he did. She reassured the boy that he was not alone, something he desperately needed to hear.

His struggle was no different than her own or that of any other Christian on the planet. As much as we like to rank our sins, there is no rank, no hierarchy; they are the same. She reassured him that he was loved and valued for who he was and that he didn't have to be anyone other than that. He did not have to earn love; God gave that freely. She assured him that his secret was safe with her. When they were done, they prayed together, and the boy left. The Twelfth sat for some time, praying over the conversation, and that she had said the right things—things that allowed the young man to see and hear God, things that would encourage and build him up. Then she locked up her office and began the walk home.

Chapter 45

The sky had darkened early, and a biting wind swept across the quiet streets of Platitude. Though Christmas lights twinkled cheerily from porch railings and front windows, the night felt cold and unwelcoming beneath the glitter. The Twelfth trudged along the particularly icy sidewalk, determined to reach her house where the Wednesday night group had already gathered for a progressive dinner. She slipped once, tumbling onto her knee and soaking her pants.

Unbeknownst to the Twelfth, Kfir hovered nearby, invisible to human eyes, flitting closer every time she lost her footing. On her second slip, he attempted to nudge her away from a slick patch of ice, but instead caused her to flail wildly, arms pinwheeling as she barely remained upright. Had she glimpsed him, she might have wondered what strange force was keeping her from face-planting into the slush. Kfir winced as she let out an exasperated groan, then gave a small grin of relief—no serious harm done.

Kfir swooped in as the Twelfth's foot slid on a patch of black ice, but he fumbled trying to catch her elbow. She spun awkwardly, nearly toppling over. Under his breath, Kfir let out a low chuckle.

"This is exactly why I'm not a Guardian," he muttered. "Months in their uniform, and I still can't keep anyone upright."

Aegeus shook his head, allowing a smile to tug at his lips. "If anything, we have learned that merely wearing a uniform does not make it yours, Kfir," he said quietly. "Steadiness of spirit must come before steadiness of hand."

By the time she reached her porch, she was bruised and soaked through, mumbling under her breath at the biting cold. Inside, however, warmth and laughter radiated into the street. She heard the low hum of Christmas carols and felt her spirits lift just a little as she stepped into the glow. Voices called her name, rising in a mixture of concern and merriment. The Third teased her about her soggy clothes, urging her upstairs to change before she caught a cold.

Aegeus quietly followed as she climbed the stairs, ensuring no demonic presence lurked in the house. Over the past few months, he had grown increasingly vigilant; the Strongman's influence had taken a toll on the entire town. Despite the season of celebration, darkness still lingered.

Satisfied that no threat had followed them inside, Aegeus descended quietly. The First and his wife stood near the fireplace, talking quietly. The Second and Third exchanged travel stories from their days on the mission field, drawing exclamations of laughter from the Fifth, who was perched on the sofa. Nearby, the Eighth and his wife sipped cocoa, leaning against one another in a comfortable hush. The Eleventh and her husband gathered plates and napkins for everyone, managing the logistics of the progressive dinner with ease.

When the Twelfth returned in dry clothes, she found the living room full of familiar faces. Her reappearance drew the group's attention. A few rose from their seats to greet her, while others paused their conversations to check on her well-being. In that subtle stir, the living room's arrangement shifted—enough for Aegeus to slip in quietly, keenly observing the new clusters around him. Aegeus stepped in closer. This group had formed a bond unlike any other in town, a source of mutual support the King had orchestrated. Aegeus could sense the underlying fatigue, though—months of battling the Strongman's lies had worn them down.

He noted how the First's wife avoided certain topics, having been wounded by the Strongman's words about a woman's supposed role. Aegeus admired the First's devotion to protect her from those toxic ideas, though he couldn't entirely shield her from them. Aegeus admired how the First prayed for the students at the college, doing all he could to counteract the corrosive effects of condemnation and shame.

Nearby, the Second and Third regaled the group with tales of their time on the mission field. Aegeus often found himself captivated when the Third spoke—her stories glowed with an almost tangible warmth. She and the Second radiated wisdom, and though they had heard the Strongman's lies, they dismissed them outright.

Aegeus appreciated how their solid partnership acted like a protective shield against the gloom spreading through the town.

Across the room, the Eighth and his wife sat quietly, close but not entirely at ease. Aegeus recalled how the Eighth's research partner had become an unwitting pawn of jealousy—one of Satan's favored tools. As a result, the Eighth had nearly lost his marriage. Tormenting demons had tried to convince both spouses to leave; for a while, the wife had indeed gone. Adir and a handful of ministering angels had fought fiercely on their behalf, and by the King's grace, she had returned. Aegeus couldn't help but feel a swell of gratitude each time he saw them together, drawing strength from the group's prayers. He felt a flicker of relief seeing them side by side this evening.

The Fifth and the Twelfth sat together, laughing one moment and conversing in hushed tones the next. From what Aegeus had observed, the Fifth busied herself constantly as if movement alone could keep her thoughts at bay. Haywood, one of the ministering angels, had spoken often to Aegeus about her; they both worried about her well-being. Tonight, however, her eyes brightened, at least for a moment, as she and the Twelfth exchanged tales of campus life.

Soon, the group wrapped scarves around their necks, preparing to move to the next house for the rest of the dinner. They spilled out onto the porch, boots crunching in the snow. Christmas music followed them into the night, blending with their chatter. The angels, positioned themselves around the humans, watchful in the softly swirling flakes.

Aegeus stayed back, watchful for any lurking demonic presence set on disrupting the evening. Meir walked alongside the Eighth, offering subtle reassurance. For a moment, it was almost peaceful. Aegeus savored that calm; he knew the battle was far from over. Once again, the Twelfth nearly slipped on a hidden patch of ice. This time, Kfir nudged her just in time—her arms flailed, but she remained upright. She glanced back, puzzled at her sudden balance, then laughed it off, cheeks reddened from the cold.

Even when the Twelfth slipped on the slick path, she laughed with her friends as they helped her up. Aegeus couldn't help but smile—these humans were steadfast, enduring life's trials with a measure of grace and humor that left even angels in awe. He smiled faintly to himself. This was a rare lull in the ongoing battle, a brief respite of fellowship and holiday cheer that reminded him there was hope in the King's plan.

For now, they would walk from home to home, sharing laughter and stories, leaving footprints in the snow. Aegeus let the sound of their camaraderie fill him, a soft assurance that though the Strongman's lies lingered, they could still find joy—and that bond might be enough to see them through the darkest days ahead.

Chapter 46

Demons knew no holidays, so Christmas had been anything but restful. Demons swarmed the town, casting a dark shroud over Platitude. The residents hadn't glimpsed the sun in weeks, and discouragement ran thick, permeating every corner. Aegeus and his team had fought non-stop, barely holding back the tide. The husband of the Twelfth had been covered in demons, and although he fought against them, there were so many that when he shot one from himself, another replaced it.

Eventually, no one could withstand that. Discouragement seemed to have the strongest hold. Aegeus, Kfir, and Adiel had been fighting non-stop, but even that had only kept the demons to a minimum. Several times, the Twelfth smelled the sulfur, but no one else smelled it, so she dismissed it as her imagination. The twelve did at least have time free from the messages of the Strongman.

The Wednesday night group continued to meet over the Christmas break. Things were going well. Aegeus looked forward to their gathering each week. He found it fascinating to listen to them wrestle with the Word, and he particularly liked the way the angels would listen in and join in the conversation even though the King's children could not hear them.

They cheered when one of them got something right after a long struggle and sighed when they had it wrong. It got exciting at times, but the energy and power of the King that always came from those gatherings was something Aegeus had never experienced before. It had become his favorite thing about earth because it created a feeling that he knew nowhere else but in heaven.

With one week left before the students' return, Aegeus convened a gathering of the angels in the salvage yard. They met not just to share updates but to prepare. The Strongman's influence was spreading fast, and they would need to be ready. He entered the meeting location in the salvage yard and was pleased to see the other angels were all there. The angels milled about chatting, laughing, and sharing a meal. Aegeus stood and just soaked it in.

Haywood approached him, bringing with him a full wineskin. He poured some into a small wooden tumbler and handed it to Aegeus along with a piece of aina, a tender plant similar to pineapple, its flavor a bit more savory.

Kfir stood in the back with a steaming cup in his hand. This puzzled Aegeus. There was only one hot drink in heaven, something similar to apple cider, but it was made from the fruit on the trees, which often varied, so the drink was different every time you tried it.

Aegeus took a long, deep breath in to smell what Kfir had. His eyes flew open in surprise as the smell of coffee hit him. He sniffed again. Coffee? From the smell of it, robust coffee. He walked toward Kfir. The smell of the coffee grew stronger as he approached.

"Kfir, are you drinking coffee?" Aegeus couldn't help but laugh at the idea of it.

Kfir looked up with a big smile on his face, excitement in his eyes.

"I thought I might try it; it smells so good." His smile was infectious, and Aegeus laughed despite himself. "It's called Death Wish coffee and is trendy at Perks."

Berhanu and Emeka goaded Kfir, daring him to try it. As long as Aegeus had walked the earth, angels had dared each other to try the food. Before the fall, the angels had eaten freely from the garden. But Eden had been destroyed during the flood.

Food on earth was different from the food in heaven. Eating the things on earth that the King had made was reasonably safe, but it was eating the items made in factories that became the angel equivalent of a triple-dog dare.

By far, Kfir had tried the most things. This was impressive, considering how much more time guardians and ministering angels spent on earth compared to warriors. He had many stories of mishaps. He once ate something called a hot dog at a baseball stadium in 1974. No one was quite sure what it was, but Kfir spit it from his mouth so far that it hit a spectator in the back of the head. The man convinced himself that it was a fan from the opposing team. And before the angels knew what was happening, a riot broke out in the stadium. The assignment had been simple, and the riot was not part of it.

Kfir's food tasting led to another riot at another stadium just one week later, one of the most significant riots in baseball history. As a result, the warriors had to spend three additional weeks on earth sorting it all out. The angels referred to it as the debacle of 1974.

Kfir lifted the steaming mug of Death Wish coffee to his lips, wincing slightly at the intense, almost acrid scent that rose to greet him. Thick whipped cream crowned the top, already drooping over the sides. The other angels crowded around, their wings brushing together as they chanted Kfir's name in exaggerated encouragement, some patting him on the shoulder, others grinning in anticipation. With a theatrical flourish, Kfir took a sip—and immediately scrunched his face as though he'd swallowed a hive of bees. His right eye slammed shut, his tongue poked through his lips, and a dollop of whipped cream stuck to his nose like a badge of honor.

For a moment, he just stood there, blinking and sputtering. Then he cleared his throat with a dramatic cough, finally declaring, "Mmm... delicious, but oddly... a bit on the chemical side." The angels erupted into laughter, a few doubling over at the sight of the proud warrior reduced to a cream-faced coffee critic.

Aegeus called the meeting to order. He wanted to get an update on what had been happening with the twelve. He saw some of them regularly, so he wanted to start with those he knew less about. He began with the Fourth. The angel of the Fourth stood and gave an update.

"The Fourth is the direct supervisor of the Twelfth. His son was in prison for four years on a drug-related charge, but he was recently released. The boy was too ashamed to face his parents, so he was living on the streets.

"Somehow, the boy's mother found out, and she called the Fourth, asking him to find the boy and take him in. The Fourth told no one; he merely took a few days off and went in search of his son.

"He found the young man hungry and dirty but otherwise unharmed. The Fourth brought his twenty-four-year-old ex-convict, recovering addict son home and celebrated his homecoming but told no one in the town. He felt it best to keep personal matters private.

"This burden has proven to be heavy. Demons swarm his home, trying desperately to get to his son. But the Fourth has prayed a hedge of protection around the young man that is so thick with heaven's power that only the son himself can fail.

"The Fourth and the Twelfth are getting along very well. The Twelfth trusts him. He values her and her contribution to the department, and he has made sure she knows it. The King selected the Fourth because the King knew that it would take a very particular type of man to manage the environment that the Strongman would create.

"The King knew that the Twelfth's first reaction would be to leave since this was not a battle she wanted. It is a topic that makes her very uncomfortable. And he knew that she would need to be surrounded by people that would encourage her to stay.

"The Fourth is uniquely positioned to do that, he has broad shoulders that will not stoop under the pressure of the Strongman— he will lead the department well."

"Berhanu, make sure you are making regular trips to both the Fourth and his son. Let's get a couple of warriors on them as well." Aegeus did not want to risk it. "What of the Tenth?" he asked.

"The Tenth works in Human Resources. He has a lust demon that clings to him from his youth, and though he battles daily, he has not yet been able to break free. Since moving to the town, he has done well resisting temptation. His wife is covered in tormenting demons, and in this environment, she is sinking into depression. Ayo comes to minister to her often but freeing her from the demons enough to receive ministering has proven a challenge.

"The Tenth has a great deal of knowledge regarding the Word and is passionate about the Spirit. He fears the Twelfth and, therefore, avoids her. His avoidance is evident, although the Twelfth does not understand it. She has incorrectly interpreted it to mean that he is concerned with her performance and regrets allowing her to be hired.

"It causes her concern, and if left unchecked, it will develop into distaste and then disdain. He is, however, fascinated by her in a way he cannot explain, and he monitors how she is doing. He respects her but fears her greatly because he can see that she is a prophet."

Aegeus was concerned about this development. The Tenth was to be the one to finally challenge the Strongman, but he would never fulfill that role if he continued to avoid the Twelfth.

"Meir, see if you can get the Fourth and the Tenth in the same room for a discussion regarding the Twelfth. Perhaps the Fourth can ease the Tenth's concerns about her," Aegeus suggested.

Meir nodded in agreement.

"What of the Sixth and Seventh?" Aegeus continued.

"The Sixth is very distressed over the Strongman's statements. Worthlessness has found her a willing host and has dug talons deep into the girl. She is actively seeking a way out of the town. I fear she may not last through the year.

"The Seventh is doing well. But the call to her from the mission field is strong. Her time here is not long."

Aegeus nodded in understanding—this mission was taking a toll on them all. He asked Amitiel, the research angel, to share any insights he may have that could help the angels better serve their charges. Amitiel provided additional insights about each. He did not rattle through them as if they were the mere numbers by which they were called but told their stories as children of the King. He shared insights that painted a somber picture and spoke of each human's story, of the silent battles and scars that were unseen by earthly eyes. But as he reached the Twelfth, he paused, his expression darkening.

'Her resolve is strong, yet the Strongman's influence has frayed the fabric of her belief.'

As Amitiel finished, Aegeus felt the weight of what lay ahead. These twelve carried burdens meant to refine them, and Aegeus sensed that each victory or failure would reverberate beyond their lives. He found himself drawn closer to them, perhaps understanding, for the first time, the fragility and strength of human faith in the face of darkness.

Chapter 47

The spring semester started without considerable fanfare. Like the fall semester, the first day of classes included a noon service that everyone attended. The Strongman made his way to the podium. He smiled at the students and then began.

"Welcome back." His voice echoed through the hall, a warmth on the surface that did little to mask the chill behind his words.

"I trust you spent quality time with God over the break, praying, reading your Bible, grounding yourselves in faith. We all know a 'good Christian' meets with God daily. Neglecting this?" He shook his head, casting a slow, disappointed look across the hall.

"Some people would tell you that you don't have to do that, that it is something nice to have but not a required thing. But we know that isn't true.

"We know that you cannot know the Father if you do not spend time in prayer and studying his Word. One of the signs of a good Christian is daily quiet time. Giving in to the temptation to skip it will destroy you.

"Our nation suffers, our town suffers, and right here on this very campus—we suffer. Depression, suicide, anxiety—these come from a lack of faith." He paused, letting his words settle. "The world will tell you to turn to drugs for help, to trust in medicine, but I am here to tell you—trust in God. You don't need chemicals; you need Christ. I got a report over the break from the counseling department that I found troubling. My heart breaks to hear such reports, and I have been praying diligently for you over the last few weeks. We have a real issue on our campus, and I would like to spend this semester addressing it. Will you let me do that?"

He waited for the congregation to offer affirmation. The Twelfth clenched her hands as the Strongman spoke, each sentence twisting into a tighter knot of dread. Beside her, the Eleventh's eyes widened, and she began to pray urgently. The Twelfth looked at her and mouthed, "demons?" and the Eleventh nodded. She could see thousands of demons soaring through the room, touching and brushing against students, faculty, and staff. The room filled with their smoke. But the angels stood stoically around the perimeter. It was not yet time for battle.

"The problem we have here is a lack of faith," the Strongman continued. "This is evident in the fact that we had a record number of students in the counseling department last semester for depression. We had numerous suicide attempts on campus. We even got a report from our insurance that faculty visits for depression were up. How can this happen on a Christian campus?"

He let the question linger in the air with a look of consternation.

"I mean, the joy of the Lord is our strength. If we do not have the joy of the Lord, we need to spend more time in prayer and Bible study. Some people turn to drugs for depression and anxiety, but I am here to tell you that you just need to turn to God. God is your anti-depressant. God will take away your anxiety.

"What I see here is a sin issue. The Bible is sufficient for all your needs. We don't need to medicate; we need to meditate! If you are here today and you are depressed or anxious, you lack faith. You have a sin problem, and we need to get to the heart of it.

"I am going to be working with the counseling department to make sure they are using Christ-centered counseling and not relying on secular wisdom to solve spiritual problems. Because I have to tell you that you can't have the Spirit of God inside you and be depressed!" He nearly shouted the last part.

The room was silent except for the jubilant cheers of the demons. They watched as Lights dimmed and flickered. The demons swarmed the students, filling them with doubt, deepening their depression and anxiety, and pouring on guilt.

"I am going to make a promise to you. I want you to listen; I want you to hear what I am about to say because I am going to make a very important promise. If you let me challenge you spiritually over the next fifteen weeks, I promise you that you will leave here free from depression, free from anxiety, free from mental health issues.

"Those are the work of the evil one. I will give you the verses you need to free yourself from them. I will arm you with the spiritual tools for you to walk away from depression and anxiety. Is that okay?

"Can I walk this journey with you? Can I help you free yourself from these demons? My goal for us, listen close, my goal is for us not to need a counseling center anymore! I want to arm you with everything you need so that when depression comes knocking on your door, you will know exactly how to rid yourself of it.

"You will declare the promises of the Lord, and you will be free! There will be no more depression; there will be no more anxiety; there will be no more mental illness!" He shouted it out to the group.

The demons surged forward, writhing through the room in dark waves as the students clapped. Glee twisted their demon faces, delighting in each Light that dimmed and flickered under the weight of guilt.

The Fifth looked as if she might throw up. The Fifth, Eighth, Eleventh, and Twelfth walked out of the Great Hall together. The Twelfth couldn't help but wonder what the First must be thinking about this. When they were away from the student's ears, the Fifth opened the topic for discussion.

"How many people do you think he damaged today?" she asked.

"Too many," said the Eighth, a sadness settling over him.

"Did he just say that you couldn't be a Christian and be depressed?" the Twelfth asked, unsure that she had heard correctly.

"That's what I heard," the Fifth agreed. They all muttered agreement. It was indeed what they had heard. As they walked back to their building, they explored the idea that depression could be a sin issue.

The Twelfth felt so shocked she could not even be angry yet. "Can you even imagine how you would feel if you were in that room and suffering from depression?" she asked. "Do you know how dangerous it is to suggest that medication is unnecessary? Can you even imagine the ripple effect of the things he just said?"

As she finished her questions, the Twelfth did not notice the quiet resolve that had taken over the Fifth, but she did notice the Eighth, who had grown quiet.

When they got to their office building, the Twelfth separated from the others and began the long walk to her own office. The Eleventh caught up to her.

"There were thousands of demons in that room," she whispered to the Twelfth. The Twelfth stopped walking and turned to look at her.

"Thousands?"

"Thousands," she confirmed. "They were jubilant. I wonder if he did it on purpose. Do you think he is evil, or do you think he is clueless?"

They had not had this conversation before, and the Twelfth was slightly hesitant to say what she thought. She paused, subconsciously pressing her lips together as they stood in the seating area outside the Twelfth's office.

"You think he is evil?" the Eleventh said, half as a statement and half as a question. Panic streaked her voice just enough to make the Twelfth nervous.

"I do. But that doesn't mean he is. I have tried to think he is just clueless or insensitive. I have even tried to believe he was right, and I was the issue. But I keep coming back to the same conclusion: he is evil. He is not a good man who is confused. He is an evil man who is intentional. He is trying to destroy our campus for some reason." There, she had said it. And in many ways, it felt good to lay it out there.

"Oh no," the Eleventh shook her head in dismay, concern covering her face. Her Light flared brightly, filling the area with light. Aegeus and Kfir basked in its power, wondering what the Spirit was telling her.

"Well, I could be wrong; I mean, just because I think it doesn't make it right," the Twelfth said.

"No, you're not wrong. You're a prophet—you would know."

"What?" The Twelfth was genuinely shocked. She stared at the Eleventh, not believing what she had just heard.

"I am not a prophet." She emphatically stressed each word individually. She shook her head and took a step back.

"The Eleventh tilted her head, a faint smile softening her expression. "Of course, you are. You didn't know?" She didn't wait for an answer, turning down the hall as though she'd just given the most ordinary answer in the world.

The seed had been planted; she had been exposed to the truth. She would reject it, of course. The question was for how long. But now that the seed was there, the Spirit would take over and water it until the Twelfth accepted the truth. Now, they could make real progress.

The angels celebrated—it was the only good to come from the Strongman's speech. Kfir danced about the hall, looping his arm with Aegeus's and swinging him about. They both laughed and celebrated; it was a wonderful moment. Students filed by as they rushed to class, unaware of the angels celebrating the birth of a prophet. As Kfir shouted for joy, Aegeus laughed, but a thoughtful glint entered his eyes as he glanced down the hallway where the Twelfth had disappeared. The journey ahead would demand everything from them—and from her.

The Twelfth tried to put the entire conversation out of her mind. She had a class to teach. She dashed into her office, grabbed her lab coat, and rushed to class, pushing away the strange, unsettling conversation with the Eleventh. Yet as she walked, a quiet sense of urgency overcame her, a sense that something was coming, something she didn't fully understand but couldn't ignore.

Chapter 48

The students slouched at their desks, quiet and unfocused, their usual chatter absent. She could almost feel the weight of the Strongman's words pressing down on them. If only she could undo the damage—but instead, she took a deep breath and focused on today's lesson.

She was covering how to perform pelvic exams. She had the male students take turns in the stirrups, a hands-on way to cultivate empathy to help them understand how vulnerable their future patients might feel. A few chuckled nervously, but the lesson was already taking root in their quiet responses as they looked around, newly aware of the importance of dignity in their work.

Because this was the introductory day for this skill, she had them divide into groups of three. One person took the role of the patient and climbed into the stirrups. One of them performed the mock procedure. They were required to know the names of the instruments and equipment and to go through the steps in the proper order.

The third person was responsible for documentation and assisting. Each person would do a walk-through in each role. Tomorrow, they would use manikins and perform the procedure, getting a sample that would then be analyzed for them to read, interpret, report, and document. For today, they just needed to get comfortable instructing the patient in a professional way and make sure they knew the steps and equipment.

While they were working, the door creaked open, and a female student slipped in, her wet uniform clinging to her as she darted toward an empty seat. Her hair hung limp, covering her face but not enough to hide the bruise near her eye. She smelled strongly of bleach, and just under the edge of her long-sleeve undershirt, well-formed bruises were visible. Her eyes were red and wild. Her late entrance caused considerable disruption, and the entire class stopped to see who had come in.

The Twelfth's Light burst forth from her, shooting the straggler demons from the room. She looked to the Ninth and asked her to take over monitoring the class. Then she looked at the young woman and said, "Come with me."

The young woman walked silently behind her down the hall. She began to panic. She knew the penalty for being late, and this was not her first offense. Fear that she would be dismissed flooded her. They walked through the hall and entered another lab. Without speaking, the Twelfth opened a cabinet and searched through it.

"Professor, I am so sorry," the student offered. "My husband got angry. He didn't want me to come to school today. He threw my uniform in the toilet and poured bleach on it. When I tried to get it out he shoved my head into the toilet and poured bleach on me. He knew I couldn't come to school without my uniform. I know

I am a mess. I am so sorry, please. Please.... I...I can't be kicked out"

The words poured from her mouth. Fear and panic strained her voice; her plea was heart-wrenching. Rage simmered beneath the Twelfth's calm exterior. Her fingers tightened around the fresh uniform she had pulled from the cabinet as she turned, her voice steady but fierce.

"He doesn't get to win—not today," she said as she looked the young lady directly in the eyes and handed her the uniform. She walked from the room before the girl could speak. Once outside the room, she stopped and leaned against the wall. Her hands shaking, tears burning her eyes. She took a few deep, steadying breaths to compose herself. Then she rejoined her class already in progress.

The young woman rejoined the class in time to get through one rotation. The Twelfth did not see her again until classes were done for the day. The young woman walked into her office once again in her bleach-stained clothes and handed the Twelfth the new scrubs neatly folded. The Twelfth stood when she entered the room.

"You can keep those," the Twelfth answered, sorry that she hadn't made that clear earlier.

"No, I can't. If I take these home, he will destroy them too." She held them out to the Twelfth. She spoke without sadness—she was past sad. She accepted that this was her new life.

"Then I will keep them in my office," the Twelfth said, taking the scrubs from her. "And each day, you will come in and get them. You can change here at school and leave them here at the end of the day. I will take them home and launder them for you as needed." She, too, spoke without emotion, without any illusion of options. This simply was how it would be. The student nodded.

"I suppose you want to know," the girl started, looking a little uncomfortable.

"Only if you want to tell," the Twelfth replied.

"Perhaps another day," the young woman said. "I don't think I am up for it today."

The Twelfth reassured her that she was always happy to help. She made sure the girl knew the resources available to her before she left. As she was leaving, the student paused and looked back. She hesitated at the door, her voice barely a whisper.

"Professor? Do you think he hits me because I am not submissive enough?"

The question cut through the Twelfth, leaving her breathless. She wanted to say so much, wanted to shake the girl free from this lie. Instead, fighting against her emotions, she steadied her voice and chose her words carefully.

"No. He hits you because he has control issues and needs help; it has nothing to do with you." After the student left, the Twelfth closed her office door and sank into her chair. Her hands were still shaking, and her heart ached with the weight of her student's pain. She felt helpless as if her words could never be enough to undo the Strongman's lies or soothe wounds so deep.

Quietly, she cried out to the King, pleading for strength—for herself and for the young woman.

Chapter 49

The weekly meeting began in the Twelfth's office, where the Sixth, Seventh, Eleventh, and Fifth settled into their seats. Their lunches sat untouched on the small table, and a strained silence hovered—each person reluctant to break it with forced small talk. The weight of discouragement was palpable, etched into their tired faces and slumped shoulders.

At last, the Eleventh cleared her throat, her voice slicing through the hush. "The Twelfth thinks the Strongman is evil," she blurted. "I told her I trust her judgment as a prophet."

"I am *not* a prophet," the Twelfth protested, rolling her eyes. A faint flush crept into her cheeks, and she wished the Eleventh hadn't said such a thing in front of the others.

"Of course, you are," the Seventh said, looking surprised that the Twelfth denied it. The Twelfth looked at her, stunned, and shook her head no.

"You didn't know?" the Seventh asked, astounded.

"Prophets are old men from the Bible. No one does that anymore, and certainly not me." She felt embarrassed to even be having this conversation.

"It makes sense," the Fifth offered, looking as if she had just considered it. She, too, was completely ignoring the Twelfth's protests.

"No," the Twelfth said, looking from woman to woman. "No," she repeated as if by saying it twice, it was settled. "First, that isn't true; second, saying things like that here will get me fired. Let's talk about something else. Let's talk about the idea that depression is a sin issue, and we don't need anything but the right Bible verses to resolve it."

They all groaned at being reminded. The women expressed heartbreak that such a thing had even been said. They were in agreement that it would isolate those who were depressed even more. The Fifth pointed out the obvious: all the people in the Bible who suffered from depression—Abraham, Jonah, Job, Elijah, King Saul, Jeremiah, the prophet.

What about King David?" the Fifth said, her voice rising with frustration. "He was tormented by depression, too. Half the Psalms are him crying out in despair. Are we really saying he didn't have enough faith?"

"And what about Proverbs when King Solomon, the wisest of all people to ever walk the earth, asked who could bear a broken spirit?" the Eleventh asked.

"Certainly not Elijah. He was so depressed that he wanted to die. God had to send angels to attend to him," the Sixth added.

"But of course, that doesn't happen anymore. I wonder why he doesn't send angels anymore."

Aegeus and Kfir exchanged a look, shaking their heads in dismay. Aegeus exhaled in exasperation.

"I think he does," the Twelfth ventured.

Aegeus and Kfir leaned in as she shared the story of when her son saw the angel on the roof. The story of Sanyi. Aegeus was interested to hear the story from her perspective. She had been gardening in the yard with her children. Her youngest, under the care of Lavi, had asked her who the men on the roof were.

The Twelfth had looked and seen no one. Her son had described a warrior with a sword fighting against two bad guys. She didn't see anyone.

Aegeus, of course, knew Sanyi was a guardian, not a warrior, but the child did not know this. He also knew that Sanyi reported that she had seen him herself on another occasion, but Aegeus noted she had not shared that story. He couldn't help but hope she would since he would like to hear it.

While they trusted the Twelfth, it was still hard to believe in something you could not see. The Sixth shifted uneasily in her seat; her Light burned brightly, but Aegeus could see that she struggled against it.

"And..." the Twelfth hesitated, glancing at the Eleventh, her voice low, almost reverent. "I know it sounds strange, but during the flood—I'm sure that was an angel. The way we were saved, I can't explain it any other way." She felt a mix of awe and vulnerability, saying it aloud.

The room was quiet except for Kfir. "Did you hear that?" he asked, jubilant.

Aegeus stood stunned. It was a strange sensation to hear her talk about him—for her to recognize that he was an angel. It caused a stir in his soul he couldn't quite explain.

"Then why do they let terrible things happen? If angels are here, why don't they protect us? Why do they let children get hurt? How do you explain that?" The Sixth spit out the words. She tried to hide her anger and hurt, but she failed.

As the Sixth spoke, the Twelfth's Light flared instinctively. A wave of knowing washed over her, the kind that only came from the Spirit, and a deep ache filled her heart. She sensed something broken and hidden in the Sixth—something she'd guarded fiercely and carried alone, an old wound that left shadows of mistrust. It was as if the Sixth's words themselves were a silent plea, her voice betraying scars that time hadn't healed. The Sixth had been sexually abused as a child by someone close to her family, someone she trusted. She had kept that secret from everyone but the Seventh. She suppressed the pain. If you had asked her about it, she would say that she had dealt with it. But in reality, she feared men because of it.

She wouldn't say she feared men—she may not even know it. But she feared them and found fault in every man who tried to get close to her. She did not trust them, none but her own father. She put on a brave front—a hard front—but in her heart, she longed to marry but knew she could never do so because she could never trust a man. Not just for herself but for her future children.

She certainly was not willing to ever again let anyone have complete authority over her—male or female. God alone had that position. To hear the Strongman say that this was a faith issue—that it was a sin issue, that she just needed to read more Bible verses—left her feeling sick.

It was not a lack of faith in God but a lack of faith in men. Was it sinful for her to feel hurt and betrayed? She had wounds deep in her soul. And per the Strongman, she had nothing to offer a husband anyway since her virginity, her most prized offering, according to the Strongman, was stolen when she was only eight years old.

Aegeus wanted to be able to explain. He wanted her to understand. It wasn't just about the angels. There were demons, too. And prayer, why did so few of the King's children pray? Did they not understand the power of prayer? Aegeus wanted to ask his own questions.

Aegeus's frustration mounted. He wanted to tell them, to make them see—it wasn't the King or the angels who had brought evil into the world. He remembered Eden's quiet beauty, unmarred by sin, and how easily it had all been lost. Now, they fought tirelessly to hold back the darkness, but evil still found ways through. Would the humans ever understand how it pained even heaven to see them suffer? The King had promised tranquility and paradise in Eden. But Adam and Eve had opted out. Was that the Angels' fault? Adam and Eve had let evil onto the earth. It is not because the King sleeps or the angels have taken a vacation. It is because evil came to dwell among them and they had invited it in.

Did they not realize that it changed everything for the angels? Did they realize that before the fall, the angels did not spend their days fighting for the King's children? They had other jobs. The fall of humans had changed everything, not just things on the earth. Not just things for the humans but for everyone.

He doubted they ever gave much consideration to how the fall had impacted the angels. He doubted they gave much consideration to how the angels watched over them every day, how they grieved and celebrated with them. How they fought so that the King's children would always have a way out of temptation, only to see them choose what was evil over and over again.

Aegeus's heart ached as he thought of the endless sacrifices heaven made for these humans, guarding them against foes who had once been friends. Even now, memories of those he'd once loved crept in—comrades turned dark, bound in evil beyond redemption. He wondered if the humans could ever understand how the fall had shattered everything, even for heaven. And while they hated the evil that now consumed those who had fallen, it still grieved all of heaven to see someone once so holy and pure now so covered in evil, with no hope of restoration. Watching them change from a holy, heavenly being to a demon was agonizing.

For just a moment, Aegeus let Seneca enter his mind. It had been many years since he had allowed himself to think of Seneca. The look in his eyes when he had fallen. The terror he experienced almost immediately once separated from the King. The sight of seeing the Light of God removed from him. Looking into Seneca's eyes and knowing that his brother had become his mortal enemy.

The memory was so powerful. He had to shake it from his mind. He tried to tune back in to what the women were saying. They had moved on. Aegeus had missed what was said. He felt himself reconstructing walls that he had begun taking down.

"Of course, King Saul was depressed because God himself sent a tormenting spirit to him," the Twelfth was saying. "That is actually a little scary. But what I find fascinating is that the demons still seem to have access to God."

Aegeus understood why people wondered about this, but of course, he also understood that everything in all of creation had access to the King. There would come a time when that was no longer true, but during this age, there was nothing that did not have access to the King. Separation from the King was separation from all hope, all Light, all that was good, replaced by suffocating in darkness, evil, and hopelessness—eternal torment. The real question was whether or not they took advantage of having access to the King.

The women ended their time with prayer, and each of them headed back to her respective office. The Eleventh and Twelfth walked down to the faculty lounge to get a cup of coffee. Several faculty and staff sat in the room eating a late lunch and talking when the Eleventh and Twelfth came in. A tall, thin woman was saying, "I just don't think you can be an alcoholic and be a Christian."

The Twelfth felt a rage she had never known pulse through her. She willed herself to stay silent. Her hands began to tremble. She went to the coffee kiosk and selected a light roast from the cabinet.

A stocky man sitting next to the woman added, "I know what you mean. I am always amazed when people claim to be Christians, but you can tell from their lives that they aren't. Like you said, alcoholics, drug addicts, Democrats." The group all laughed.

The Twelfth's rage grew even stronger. She willed the coffeemaker to brew faster. What was wrong with it? The Eleventh stood beside her, frozen in place. *Water, it must be out of water.* The Twelfth took the tank off and went to the sink to fill it. The group at the table continued.

"I mean, how can you call yourself a Christian if you're having an affair?"

"Or if you are gay," another added.

"Do you think you can be a Christian if you are a gossip?" The Twelfth swung around and said it before she even realized what was happening.

The group looked at her, a little stunned. "Or what about if you're judgmental? Can you be a Christian and be judgmental? What about liars? Are they excluded? Can you be a Christian and be a liar? How about sinners? Surely, you can't be a Christian and still be a sinner." The words poured from her mouth. Her hands shook at her sides. Her Light blazed from her and filled the room. The air crackled from the power of the King.

"You know those are different," the stocky man said.

"How?" she shot back.

"It's just different. Telling a lie is different then having an affair. You can't say it isn't." He felt secure and justified in his position.

"It is different to us, as humans, but to God, it is sin. All of it. And sin is a separator. But how dare you be a separator too? How dare you put a hurdle between anyone and the cross? How dare you tell anyone that they must remove all sin from their life before they can approach God?

"Who are you to say what struggle they will have? Just because you become a Christian, you don't just stop sinning. You don't suddenly get over it. The only difference between them and us is that we have hope. God fights for us. We have stepped out of the darkness and into the light. But our struggle does not end.

"There is no sin on this earth that a Christian hasn't committed. None. We are just as evil as anyone. And you have no right to say that anyone can't be a Christian because of their sin.

There are plenty of Christians who struggle, and you should be ashamed for putting barriers between them and God.

"It is only with God's help that they have any chance of ever winning against their struggle, and that is true no matter if their struggle is greed, lust, alcoholism, addiction, or pride."

She stormed from the room without her coffee. The Eleventh caught up with her in the hall.

"Hey, are you okay?" She asked, breathlessly.

The Twelfth stopped and turned back toward her. She let out an exasperated sigh.

"Can you believe that? There is no way to finish that sentence that is correct. You can't be a Christian if? Seriously? There is nothing that can finish that sentence that would be correct. Nothing." Her anger had started to subside, but it had not left her.

"Well...you can't be a Christian if you won't accept Jesus." The Eleventh said cautiously.

"Well, yeah, that." The Twelfth said smiling, her anger subsiding as quickly as it had come on.

"I'm a Democrat," the Eleventh blurted out. The Twelfth gave her a confused look.

"What?"

"I'm a Democrat." She said it again as if it were a confession.

"What does that have to do with anything?"

"One of the things he said was you can't be a Christian and be a Democrat. But I'm a Democrat." She said it with such simplicity, such purity.

The anger evaporated from the Twelfth. She smiled at the Eleventh.

"Well . . . I guess I can overlook that." She smiled wider. She couldn't care less what political affiliation someone had. The Eleventh was her friend; the idea that they could not be friends or that she would judge the Eleventh based on political affiliation was ludicrous.

"I'm serious, some people do tell me that—that I can't be a Christian if I'm a Democrat." She looked a little anxious.

The Twelfth just shook her head, a smile spread across her face.

"You know that's crazy, right? You're my friend, and that's all that matters." She squeezed the Eleventh's shoulder gently, letting her know she was in her corner, no matter what.

"Of course, it's the Republicans who aren't Christian." The Eleventh winked as she said it.

Chapter 50

The Wednesday group gathered once more at the home of the Second and the Third, a refuge from the cold, damp evening. A warm fire crackled in the large stone fireplace, casting a soft glow across the room. Kfir couldn't resist flicking the remote to turn the flames off and on whenever the Second and Third left the room. He grinned like a child each time the fire roared to life, marveling at how humans could summon warmth with a single push of a button. But as the others arrived, Aegeus shot him a warning glance, and he reluctantly set the remote aside.

The group members settled in with familiar ease, eager to reconnect and find strength in each other's company. Although a shadow of discouragement lingered from the Strongman's recent messages, the warmth of their gathering softened it, and quiet murmurs soon turned into deeper, comforting conversation.

The group had decided on a stone soup dinner, a tradition that brought a little warmth and simplicity to their gathering. Each had brought an ingredient to add, and as they gathered, they dropped their offerings into the simmering broth: shredded, spiced chicken from the Twelfth, small red potatoes from the Eleventh, celery and carrots from the Third. The aroma of fresh bread from the Eighth mixed with the scent of garlic, basil, and oregano, filling the house with a warm, inviting fragrance—a shared meal that was, for them, a taste of comfort and unity.

In the open floor plan between the kitchen and living room, they gathered, chatting easily as they shared stories from the week. Nearly a year had passed since the group first came together, and in that time, they'd forged strong bonds. These weekly meetings were a source of support, laughter, and grounding, and each member was eager to see the others, knowing they had a safe space, to be honest and find encouragement. Between work, family, and battles against unseen forces, these evenings became their anchor.

The angels listened closely to gather their collective knowledge about the college and the impact of the Strongman's messages. The group had established a rotation to determine who would attend his weekly service. The one who went filled in the rest of the group each Wednesday.

But their discussions of the Word were the ones that the angels most enjoyed. The angels had started bringing their own snacks, and they would also eat and discuss the Word, but of course, the angels had the advantage of having stood face-to-face with the King.

Listening to the group discuss the Word, Aegeus found himself intrigued by the different ways they wrestled with its meaning. He'd only ever known one interpretation—the King's way. But for the King's children, the Word was like a prism, refracting into different shades and meanings. He understood now why they struggled; the Word was their lifeline, a guide to a King they could not see. But he could see, too, how some used it to build walls, prizing it over the Spirit meant to guide them.

After the fall, when the children could no longer see the King, they needed a way to do so. The Word gave them that way. But the King had never intended them to use it to beat each other—a weapon they wielded against each other. And he certainly never intended it to replace the Spirit. It was a looking glass through which they could be introduced to him and their desperate need for him. Aegeus found that many in the town worshipped the Word above the King. They prized it over the Spirit.

Aegeus watched the group settle into their familiar seats, noting the easy banter and comfortable laughter that filled the room. He'd seen how the weeks together had woven an invisible net of trust among them, their conversations dipping from light to serious without hesitation. Each Wednesday, their camaraderie seemed to grow, and the warmth of it touched even him, a silent observer.

But even in this familiar circle, Aegeus noticed the way the Fifth's gaze often fell to her hands as though searching for answers in the creases of her palms. Her smile was always ready, but Aegeus sensed the effort behind it, the way it faltered just at the corners, her laughter often a beat behind the others. He noticed how her voice softened each time she shared her thoughts, as if uncertain they were worth hearing. Even her laughter, quick and bright, faded a little too soon, the echoes of insecurity casting a shadow over each smile. She carried unseen weights, burdens of her own making, and he wished he could show her her worth as the King saw it.

As the group's conversation flowed around him, Aegeus sensed the weight each person carried. The relentless presence of demons throughout the town had intensified, and those gathered here were feeling the strain more than ever. Aegeus felt the oppressive weight of darkness that seemed to thicken with each passing week. Demons swarmed around everyone connected to the twelve, their malevolent whispers seeping into thoughts and dreams. The town itself was steeped in shadow, making it difficult at times to discern where one battle ended and another began. Aegeus observed each person's quiet burdens as the room filled with easy conversation and laughter. Their unseen weights were like threads weaving them together, but he could see how those threads were stretched thin under the pressure of the Strongman's influence.

He turned to Kfir and Berhanu and exchanged a solemn glance before nodding. It was time for their own updates. Moving to a quiet corner, they shared the recent reports, knowing each story reflected a battle that was only intensifying.

"The Eighth's wife left him again: Berhanu began, his voice heavy with the memory of it. "She told him via text before she jumped on the back of a motorcycle and sped out of the town to start a new life—one free from all the sadness and sorrow that filled the town. But the farther she got from the town, fewer and fewer demons covered her until finally, she was alone with her own thoughts"

Aegeus sighed, the news settled like a stone in his chest. He knew too well how the demons played on such despair.

"But as soon as the demons left her, she called the Eighth and sobbed into the phone, asking his forgiveness. Ayo was with him when the call came in, but she had not been needed. The Eighth could feel his wife's anguish and shame through the phone. He went to her and brought her home. She had not been gone more than four hours. Since then, they had been going to counseling outside the town, and while things certainly were not perfect, they had begun to repair their marriage."

As Berhanu recounted the Eighth's struggle, Aegeus's hands clenched involuntarily. A simmering anger rose within him—not at the Eighth's wife, but at the demons gnawing at her heart, tearing her down until all she could do was flee. How he wished he could reach through the darkness that surrounded her and let her feel the King's love as solidly as he felt it himself.

"The Second and Third are exhausted," Kfir noted. "The demons have turned their attention to overwhelming their students. It's kept them working long hours, with little time to rest or be together."

Aegeus glanced over at the Second, noticing the subtle slump in his shoulders, the way the Third rubbed her temples when she thought no one was looking. Their steadfast spirits remained, but the weariness was evident.

"They've started talking about retirement," Kfir added.

"But the Spirit revealed the true issue to them," Berhanu interjected. "They're refocusing now, setting boundaries to protect what's most important."

Aegeus felt a glimmer of reassurance. "Good. They'll need their strength for what's ahead."

Meir spoke softly about the Eleventh. "She's been battling shadows from her past. The Strongman's words have reopened old wounds."

Aegeus looked toward the Eleventh, recalling moments when her light had dimmed, her gaze distant. He sensed the heavy cloak of shame and fear she wore, afraid that if others saw her fully, they would turn away.

"She's convinced she's not worthy," Meir continued. "We've been trying to reach her, but it's been difficult. She needs to know she's seen, known, and loved—regardless of the past. Her husband and the First have helped," Meir added. "She's started counseling and is on medication. There have been improvements."

It seemed to be something that all of them struggled with—the feeling of not being good enough. Aegeus wondered what it was they weren't good enough for. They were good enough that the Lamb died for them. What more was there?

"Let's continue to support her," Aegeus said firmly. "Her fight is far from over."

The Eleventh's struggle with depression was only made worse by the Strongman's declaration that depression was a lack of faith. The Eleventh sank even deeper into depression until she did not want to get out of bed. For many weeks, Meir went to the Eleventh morning after morning and coaxed her from the bed, but it became harder and harder to accomplish.

The angels coordinated encounters for the Eleventh to assure that her soul was getting fed and that Meir would continue to have something to work with. Eventually, her husband, with considerable help from the angels and the First, convinced her to seek help. She had been prescribed an antidepressant, and she had gotten better. The combination of medication and counseling had served her well, and she seemed to be well on the way to recovery.

Aegeus had caught a flicker of hesitation in Berhanu's gaze as he described the Fifth's insomnia and a tightness in Meir's voice as she spoke of the Eleventh's struggle with depression. They were all feeling the weight of this mission, fighting to keep their charges afloat while the Strongman's influence deepened every wound. The shared difficulties hung in the air between them, unspoken but understood, a reminder that even angels bore the burden of this fight.

"The Fifth continues to shut us out," Berhanu said, a note of frustration in his voice. "She refuses our help."

Aegeus's gaze shifted to the Fifth, who was laughing softly at something the First had said. Yet he saw the shadow behind her eyes, the fatigue in her movements.

"At night, the demons plagued her with nightmares," Berhanu continued. "She's stopped sleeping to avoid them."

Aegeus felt a deep concern. "But without rest, she can't endure this indefinitely."

"Exactly," Berhanu replied. "We need to find a way to reach her. But when she stopped sleeping, the demons stopped coming."

Aegeus nodded, determination hardening his resolve. "We'll keep trying."

The Twelfth, like the Fifth, did not need the demons' help to torment herself. They swarmed her husband, her children, and her students instead. Her days at work were long and filled with anguished students fighting the demons they could not see. A day did not go by that a student wasn't in her office crying.

She shared in their anguish and helped carry their burdens, but it left her so emotionally empty that she had little to offer her own children when she got home. Her husband saw her exhaustion and picked up more and more of the responsibilities at home.

But instead of seeing this for what it was, a loving act of kindness, she interpreted it through the lens the Strongman had taught her to use. She began to see it as evidence of her failings as a mother and wife. She convinced herself that her husband was not happy because she was not the right kind of wife. She tried desperately to put aside her own opinions and do whatever he suggested, but it made them both miserable.

Once tensions were high in her marriage, she began to crumble a bit around the edges. She ramped up her own self-loathing—no demons required. She tried so hard to fit into a mold she didn't believe in and didn't agree with, all the while counseling student after student not to do that.

Because of all the discussion on the role of women, women who did desire to be stay-at-home moms felt as if they were doing something wrong. The Twelfth encouraged all of them to follow the passions the King had given them, to seek first his will for their lives, and to listen for his voice.

The discussion of the Twelfth caused Aegeus to feel a pang of both admiration and frustration. She was fighting bravely, supporting her students even as her own spirit wore thin. But how much longer could she keep this up? His jaw clenched as he thought of the Strongman's poison seeping into her thoughts, twisting her husband's kindness into proof of her own supposed failings. He could see the weight she carried but was powerless to lift it for her. The lines of fatigue etched on her face, the way her smile didn't quite reach her eyes. It all spoke of a soul stretched too thin.

"She's carrying so much," Kfir murmured.

"And she's turning her struggles inward," Aegeus added, frustration edging his voice. "She mistakes her husband's support for evidence of her own failings. The Strongman's lies have taken root within her."

"The Ninth's questions have helped the Twelfth begin to find her way," Meir said, glancing toward the Twelfth, who was sharing a quiet laugh with the Eleventh. "They've been spending time together. The Ninth is so young and so full of questions."

Kfir leaned in. "What was it that helped?"

"The Ninth wanted to keep her maiden name when she married," Meir explained. "She feared it might be disrespectful to her fiancé—something the Strongman put in her mind, of course. But the Twelfth challenged her on it. She reminded the Ninth about Barzillai, the man in Ezra who took his wife's family name. The Ninth looked up the verse, and it was settled for her. Seeing the Ninth find strength in that verse gave the Twelfth a spark of clarity. She realized that following her calling, even if it didn't fit the Strongman's mold, was where her purpose lay."

Kfir's eyes softened. "Sometimes it only takes a small truth to counter so many lies."

"The Tenth grows more distant," Kfir noted, concern evident. Aegeus frowned.

"He's still avoiding the Twelfth?"

"Yes. His avoidance is deliberate, and it's isolating him. He's resisting our guidance and the whispers of the Spirit."

Aegeus sighed. "That leaves him exposed."

"Temptation is high," Kfir confirmed. "We've intervened where we can, but he's teetering."

"Perhaps the Fourth's prayers will reach him," Aegeus said thoughtfully. "We must remain vigilant."

"And the First?" Kfir asked, shifting his gaze to the other side of the room. "He looked wearier than usual tonight."

"He's been shouldering the worst of it since the latest round of sermons," Berhanu said, his voice tinged with frustration. "The Strongman has declared that mental health issues need no science, only Bible verses and repentance. This week, he even added a directive for the First's counseling department."

Kfir frowned, his wings twitching with tension. "What kind of directive?"

"All counseling is to center on 'finding the sin issue,'" Berhanu replied, his tone darkening. "And any violations of the code—drinking, smoking, even relationship struggles—are to be referred for discipline. Medication is only a 'last resort for extreme cases.' The directive was blunt, without compassion, as if the First's staff were enforcers instead of healers."

Kfir clenched his fists, his frustration almost as tangible as his loyalty to the King's children. "How did the First respond?"

Berhanu's lips curved in a faint smile. "He deleted it without a second thought—and told his staff to do the same. He knows they're called to bring comfort, not condemnation."

A quiet relief washed over them all as Meir murmured, "The First stands firm."

They exchanged a shared look of resolve, knowing each of them had a role in supporting the twelve as they wrestled with the Strongman's influence. For now, it was enough.

Chapter 51

Students quickly adjusted to this new threat, and the number of students going to the counseling center dropped dramatically. Only the most severe cases continued. The First spent his days facing the shadows of broken spirits—eating disorders, addictions, and the deep wounds of childhood abuse—each case a reminder of the heavy burden these students carried.

Many of them had lost faith that God was paying attention. The First prayed for them before and after each session, and when he felt the Spirit led him, he started to help them rebuild their faith along with their tattered souls. He prescribed medications when medically warranted.

The Strongman reported the great success of his counseling plan week after week by sharing with the campus that the number of students needing counseling was down. This, he told them, was evidence that his approach worked.

He did not mention that the number of suicide attempts was up or that across-campus, grades were down. He did not mention that morale was eroding or that enrollment for the next year was dropping. Or that a pervasive unease crept into every classroom and dorm. In the Great Hall, he only celebrated how well his plan was working.

The First worried that, eventually, the mental health department would close, but he was wrong. It was not the Strongman's intention to close the center but to replace the licensed counselors and psychiatrists with nouthetic counselors. The First shared his fears with the group, describing the latest upheaval: licensed psychiatrists and counselors were being replaced with untrained nouthetic advisors. The Strongman's new decree meant that women could no longer counsel male students, restricting the few remaining voices of compassion.

Aegeus looked around at the small group of friends. Not quite a year ago, they had been strangers. He had gotten to know each of them well over the last year; in some ways, he knew them better than they knew themselves. They were all so magnificently flawed, so deficient. Their journey was so full of bumps and failures. And yet, they were perfect. Each of them covered by the Lamb, filled with the Spirit, and a reflection of the handiwork of the King. He marveled at the beauty of it. Their brokenness had become their strength. They had found their own brotherhood.

He looked around at his brothers, those he went into battle with every day, and he realized that they were not so different. The King's children also went into battle together every day, and they, too, needed a brotherhood to support them in their battle.

In some ways, their battle was more difficult than Aegeus's because they could not see their enemy. Aegeus found himself wishing that he could walk beside them and show them how to wield the Light of God as their shield. If only he could speak to them directly, even for a moment, he felt certain he could prepare them for the battle that lay ahead. Suddenly, he better understood why the King had sent the Lamb.

Chapter 52

"How was work?" the Twelfth's husband asked, kissing her lightly and handing her a knife intended for the fresh vegetables on the counter. She sat her workbag down and began chopping vegetables while he cooked lamb and made what appeared to be Tzatziki sauce.

"Gyros?" She wasn't sure why she asked. What else would it be? But she asked.

"It just sounded good to me."

"How was work?" he repeated. Lowering the heat on the lamb so it didn't cook too fast.

"Interesting. Always interesting. I honestly love that I work somewhere where I can pull my Bible out during a meeting to reference it. I love that I can pray with my students and speak freely of my faith. But wow. Sometimes, I just want off the crazy train."

She shredded cabbage and carrots while she talked. How could she even explain what it was like?

"Something happen today?" he asked, reaching around her for another cucumber. He enjoyed chatting about their day while they cooked. Something about pairing the intellectual with the tactile resonated with him.

"My day was full of the same story in a million different ways. Everyone that came through my door thought they were the only one who didn't have it all together. They all carried some great burden they were afraid to tell anyone for fear of judgment.

"This female/male thing is out of control. Girls tell me they have no hope of a successful marriage because they're not virgins. It's just ludicrous.

"Girls telling me their husband of three weeks is more interested in porn than them. Or that their husband never spends time with them because he is too busy with video games. And if she says anything, he tells her he is in charge and she needs to submit to his authority. Females rejecting marriage altogether because they have been told it is about them giving up their dreams to help their husband fulfill his." She sighed as she thought through all the hurting people who had walked the path with her today. She said a quick prayer of thanks that God had seen fit to send them to her, and she prayed for each of their situations even as she recapped the general ideas to her husband.

"They tell them that a woman's job is to help a man accomplish his goals?" Her husband stopped cooking and stared at her, baffled. She nodded her head. "What about her own goals? And what about unmarried women? What message are we sending them?"

"Precisely." She appreciated that he understood.

"What about women married to horrible, horrible men or women married to men who aren't Christians or widows? Have they no more purpose?" he went on.

His mind could not wrap itself around what type of man would need to make a woman believe she had no purpose other than to cater to him.

"As I recall," he went on, "there were three curses in the garden. Work would become actual work, there would be increased pain in childbirth, and woman would desire man, but he would rule over her, indicating there would be a power struggle. Now, correct me if I am wrong here, but we have medication to help ease the pains of childbirth. Does anyone at your work say using that medication is sinful?" He had stopped cooking to look at her.

"Not that I know of," she said with a smile.

"Do any of them claim that having a job you are passionate about—one that does not seem like 'work'—is sinful?"

"No."

"What about if you have a job that doesn't actually require you to do work that is all that hard? Is that sinful?"

"No. I haven't heard that."

"Why then have we picked the one saying a husband will rule over his wife and decided that men not ruling over women would be sinful and somehow in violation of God's plan?" He paused for a moment and then had to turn back to the lamb that was now filling the house with its aroma.

"Oh, I can explain that. The punishment was the woman desiring her husband. See, God created man first, so that instantly made man in charge. Woman accepted this completely until the fall." She sliced the vegetables a bit more aggressively than was necessary.

"First, I don't see that anywhere in the Bible. Second, I don't think anyone mentioned that to Eve. If she were clear about the fact that Adam was in charge, then she would have consulted with him before eating the fruit. He was standing right there with her. And part of her sin would also have been that she usurped her husband's authority.

"And if he were supposed to rule over her, wouldn't the first sin truly have been his failure in leadership? I mean, if he was in charge, shouldn't he have stopped her from eating the fruit, making a leadership fail the first sin? Where, before Genesis 3:16 does God mention man ruling over woman?"

"The idea is that man was created first, and thus, he has dominion over woman. And, of course, he named her, further solidifying his dominion over her." She sounded exhausted even as she said it. He could sense her exhaustion, and knowing her well, he understood how trying this must be for her. He turned her toward him and looked into her eyes.

"Tell me the problem with that," he pressed.

"The problem is that animals were created before Adam. So, creation order seems meaningless. Someone had to be first. And, as far as naming, Hagar named God when she was in the wilderness. This did not give her dominion over him. And, of course, Adam didn't actually name her until after the fall. It is a silly theory." Moving it from her head to her heart was the issue.

"I wish I could convey how stressful it can be," she lamented. "The women are so subjugated and yet so strong at the same time." She paused.

"Isn't that the way of women?" He asked, stroking her cheek. In her eyes, he could see the pain that she felt for these women, for the students, for the young men who would one day be husbands and fathers.

"I am exhausted from it, and this issue comes up every day. Every day. I wish they would just quit talking about it already. Like I said, some days I just want off the crazy train." She looked down at her shoes. She was tired.

"What does the Father tell you?"

"Honestly?" she hesitated, ashamed of her answer. Her husband smiled back, waiting. "I haven't talked to him about it too much. The whole topic makes me so upset I just want to walk away from all of it." There, she had said it.

"From God?" He knew the answer already, but he asked anyway. Aegeus leaned in closer; he did not know the answer, and he was eager to hear.

"No. From the church. I love God. I love being with God. I love feeling him and hearing him. But this whole 'women's role' conversation makes me feel like less. It makes me angry and hurt. God tells me what he wants me to do. God directs my path—not some man in a pulpit. Did God just create me so I could have babies and take care of you?"

The pain in her eyes was evident. Her questions did not upset or offend him in any way. On the contrary, he felt offended for her.

"If I were a woman," he began, "and I was told that getting married meant I had to be in the background for the rest of my life, I would stay single. If I were a single woman and were told that my purpose in life was to get married and have children, I would feel purposeless. If I were a woman who could not have children, I would feel purposeless. If I were a woman whose husband could not give me children, I would wonder how I made such a poor choice in a spouse. If I were a widow, I would wonder what point there was in me still living. So, I ask you this: who would benefit from silencing women? God or Satan?"

He kissed her gently on her forehead and then walked away, leaving her alone with that thought.

Aegeus watched as her husband walked away to put the meal on the table. Her face showed an internal struggle. Her Light burned bright, and he hoped she would listen to the Spirit. She hesitated only a moment, turned her face toward heaven, and then joined her husband in setting the table and rounding up the children.

Later, in the cool of the evening, when dinner was over and the dishes were put away, the Twelfth put on a light sweater and walked out on the deck. Aegeus followed her. She stood soaking in the night air.

It was a particularly beautiful night. The crickets chirped, and the lightning bugs made everything seem magical. She thought about the crickets. Their sound was comforting, and yet, it was a desperate cry for companionship or an angry warning to aggressors. Despite that, it sounded beautiful to her. It made her wonder if her own desperate cries sounded beautiful to the King.

She looked up to the stars, and tears began to well in her eyes, but she fought them back—she was too worn to cry.

"Where are you?" she whispered, her voice barely breaking the night's silence. "You brought me to this place. I feel like I am wandering in a maze. Like you have given me an impossible task and abandoned me here." She wrapped her sweater more tightly around her. Aegeus stood motionless as he watched her. Prayer was a holy thing. He felt her words like echoes of a wound that had somehow touched his own heart. Her prayer was raw, a holy cry that made his spirit ache. He stood in silent witness to her anguish.

"They call me a rebel," she whispered, her voice breaking. "I did not come here to battle but to heal. And I don't want this battle. I am too tired. I feel so lost in this; I am not even sure I am fighting on the right side. I just know that they are destroying these women, and they're doing it in your name. Where are you? Why have you given me this task? I am not right for this—I can't be objective and passive. I can't remain silent like they keep telling me women should be."

She paused for a moment, and Aegeus thought perhaps she was done. The air crackled from the prayer, and he remained still, not wanting to move. It was so raw, so honest. It caused a stirring in him that he did not quite understand.

"God, why this? Why this issue? Why me? I went from being the most conservative person in the room to the most liberal. What changed? Not me. You moved me; you brought me here. I expected it to be different. I don't want to be in the middle of this. Who am I? I have no authority to speak on this topic. I am no expert. These people have years of biblical training; they have been to seminary. Who am I? Why won't you help me keep my mouth shut? God. Please."

She dropped her head for a moment, still as stone. "Please, God. I can't," she whispered, voice quivering. The weight of her decision pressed on her like a heavy cloak. Sinking into a chair, she let the quiet settle. Night cradled her in its stillness as the hum of distant crickets played softly.

Aegeus watched, unmoving, his heart thudding in his chest. Each breath felt tight as if the air itself quivered with her plea.

At length, she rose and walked to the edge of the deck. Gazing across the moonlit yard, she spoke again, her words clear and resolute. "Not my will but Yours. I'll do whatever You ask. I'll pay any price—just grant me courage, strength, and wisdom. Guard my lips so I speak only truth."

Her sincerity rippled into the night, and Aegeus swore he could almost hear it echo among the stars. An odd tremor coursed through him, neither fear nor pain but a stirring of pure loyalty. Something in her fervent prayer splintered the last of his defenses.

As her words lingered in the silence, Aegeus moved toward her as if drawn by an invisible pull. He stepped closer. The weight of his purpose settled on him as he prepared to say words it had taken him centuries to say. The final shred of his old resolve melted away as he stood before her, close enough to sense her trembling breaths.

His voice was steady with a newfound conviction, but he spoke softly. "I am Aegeus. Warrior of the King, and I will fight for you."

Neither of them moved. Aegeus stared into her eyes, aware that she could not see him but wishing that she could. A hush fell over the yard. For a moment, even the crickets quieted as though all creation held its breath at the promise binding them together.

Chapter 53

God strolled through the meadow. He paused under the great tree, resting His hand against its trunk. A current of light flowed from Him into the bark, causing it to shimmer. As though drawn by His touch, the tree leaned subtly toward Him, its leaves rustling in whispers only He could understand. A smile curved His lips as the radiance climbed from the trunk up into the branches, igniting the leaves with shifting colors and prompting fresh fruit to sprout. At a short distance, Michael stood watching the wondrous scene in quiet awe.

"Michael, you bring me news of Aegeus," the King said without turning around.

"I do," Michael answered as he joined the King under the tree, excitement tinging his voice. The King looked out over the meadow toward the city.

"Which of all the flowers is your favorite, Michael?" the King asked.

"The M. longipetala," Michael answered, eager to tell the King about Aegeus but knowing not to rush.

"Ahh, the Evening Stock—that is a fragrant one," the King acknowledged. Before he had finished saying it, the meadow was filled with them. Michael's wings shifted, rustling softly, as he bowed his head, marveling at the effortless beauty before him. He took a long, deep breath and savored the aromatic scent.

"They are beautiful," Michael said.

"There is beauty in all that is not evil if you know how to look," the King responded. He walked away from the tree, which seemed to cry out for him as he stepped away. The King stopped for a moment and smiled as if listening to a message from the tree.

Then, he continued with a slow, easy walk back toward the city. The King was never in a hurry. He was never late and never early; his timing was always perfect. When you walked beside him, your timing also became perfect.

"What news do you bring of Aegeus?" the King asked.

"He understands your love for your children." Michael was excited to make the report. The King stopped walking and looked at Michael, a smile spreading across his face in celebration of Aegeus's progress. The King's smile radiated, his joy spreading like sunlight across the meadow. For a moment, the flowers seemed to bloom even brighter, as if they, too, rejoiced in Aegeus's awakening.

"I knew the Twelfth could reach him." He smiled. "Aegeus will make an excellent Archangel. And how does she fare?" he asked, referring to the Twelfth.

"The seed has been planted. And she wrestles with it."

"When the time is right, Michael, she will discover her true self, what I created her to be, and it will be glorious."

Chapter 54

Finals week loomed as the academic year came to an end. The Twelfth stood at the sink, looking out at the clear evening sky. Stars shimmered overhead, and the air held a hint of warmth, a reminder that summer was just around the corner. She was washing the dinner dishes. The warmth of the water soothed her raw nerves, and the faint scent of lavender rose with the steam. Soft music played in the background, but it barely masked the lingering silence from dinner. She scrubbed a plate a little too long, trying to find solace in the routine.

Dinner had been difficult. The kids were riled up, her husband was a little cranky, and her patience was long since gone. She had lost her fortitude with one of the kids and fussed at them more harshly than she intended. As a result, no one else spoke for the rest of the meal.

She scrubbed the last plate absently, her eyes unfocused, replaying the dinner in her mind. The harsh tone she'd used echoed in her head, twisting her stomach with regret. Lately, even small moments spiraled out of her control, as if the weight of every burden she carried seeped into her voice. She needed to do better, be better, but tonight, the quiet house just made her feel small and worn out.

As she finished the dishes, she thought about the papers that needed to be graded and the e-mails still in her inbox. She had a full night of work ahead of her; grading was definitely one of the disadvantages of being a college professor. She poured herself a cup of coffee, got her workbag, and settled into her favorite chair with a stack of papers.

Halfway through the third paper, her shoulders tensed. The phrasing was too polished, too familiar. She opened her laptop, knowing what she would find but hoping to be proven wrong. A quick Google search should do it.

The woman with the wild red hair silently entered the room, her face serious. She sat down beside the Twelfth and laid her hand on the laptop. A Facebook notification popped up; the Seventh had shared a photo. The Twelfth, avoiding the issue with the paper, clicked the notification. Facebook was a great distraction. The picture was of the Seventh and the Fifth outside a Mexican restaurant.

The Twelfth leaned in to study the picture. It had been taken about a week ago when they had all gone to lunch at Sombrero's, a Mexican restaurant in the next town over. The restaurant was having a trivia contest; the winner got free sopaipillas. The Fifth had won by a wide margin, and the Seventh had the lowest score, so they had taken a picture together. But in the photo, the opposite seemed true. The Seventh's smile covered her face, while the Fifth had sadness in her eyes.

The Twelfth "liked" the photo, closed Facebook, and went back to investigating the student paper. But the look in the eyes of the Fifth haunted her. She found herself distracted by it, trying to think of the last time a smile had reached the Fifth's eyes. She couldn't remember.

"Focus," she said aloud, trying to get back to grading; students could be vicious on evaluations if you took too long returning their papers. But she couldn't shake the feeling that something was wrong. She decided to Facebook stalk the Fifth and searched her name, but the Fifth didn't have a Facebook page.

Again, she redirected herself back to her work. She typed in the phrase she was questioning from the student's paper and immediately got a hit. She wrote down the name of the journal and the title of the article and then put a zero on the paper. She would do a more thorough check in the morning using the plagiarism software they had on campus.

She started working on the next paper, but her mind kept returning to the Fifth—that look in her eyes. The Twelfth Googled the name of the Fifth. But all the results pertained to a reality TV star with the same name. She jumped to the third page of results, but again all the results related to the reality TV star. She tried the seventh page of results—nothing. The woman with the red hair gripped her shoulder. At the bottom of the page, there were related search results, one of which caught her eye—an obituary.

Her eyes skimmed the lines of the obituary, at first with casual curiosity, then with growing dread. A soldier killed by a roadside bomb in Iraq. She read and reread the line, survived by his wife and unborn child. The name beside it stole her breath. It couldn't be. But the weight in her chest told her it was.

The Twelfth sat stunned for a moment, not believing what she had just read. She wanted to dismiss it as a coincidence, but her chest tightened. Her fingers hovered over the mouse, trembling slightly, as if afraid of uncovering what she already suspected. She thought back to the moment when they had been sitting together, and she had suddenly known that the Fifth had indeed experienced the deep love of a man. Her mind flooded with little moments, with looks and comments over the last year that told her that this man— this story—was the story of the Fifth.

The words on the screen blurred as her eyes filled with tears. She blinked them away, her heart pounding. "*Survived by his wife and unborn child.*" The phrase hung heavy in the air. Memories and fragments of conversation with the Fifth crashed into her thoughts, each one a whisper confirming what her heart already knew. "*How did I not see it?*" she whispered to herself, guilt tightening around her chest.

She stared at the screen for a long time, letting her mind work out the details and linger over memories that supported the theory that this man had once been married to the Fifth. Guilt slid over her. A dull ache settled in her chest. Flashes of the Fifth's quiet smiles, the way her eyes always seemed to drift elsewhere, replayed in her mind. *Why didn't I pay more attention?*

She looked back at the article, searching for additional hints or clues. *What about the child? Was it possible the Fifth had a child?* She put the man's name into Google. Articles about his death filled the page. She waded through them, searching for information about the Fifth or her child.

As she searched, she found more and more information until she finally stumbled upon a picture of the Fifth and her daughter. Several more hours of searching passed before she saw the article on the fire. She continued to tell herself it was a coincidence. *Who could carry such a secret?*

The Twelfth sat motionless, her mind racing. She felt such grief and sorrow for the Fifth. *How could she have carried this alone? Why didn't she tell anyone?* The memory of the Strongman's words twisted in her gut. She recalled the Fifth slipping away after each service, shoulders tense, eyes haunted. A wave of nausea rose, and she gripped the edge of the table for support.

She looked at the clock; it was after eleven. The Fifth did not sleep, but calling her this late seemed rude. She sent a quick text to the Fifth to check on her. There was no response.

The Twelfth looked at the long-since-forgotten papers and started to stack them up and put them back in her bag. The woman with the wild red hair moved closer, her presence a tangible weight. When she placed a hand on the Twelfth's shoulder, warmth spread, not comforting but demanding. Urgency crackled through her veins like lightning, ready to strike.

"Go," the woman with the red hair said emphatically into the ear of the Twelfth. Her chest tightened, breath quickening. Light flared, illuminating the corners of the room, and for an instant, everything stilled. Then, her heart pounded in her chest. She grabbed her keys, not understanding why but knowing she had to move.

She would head to the Fifth's house. What could it hurt to drive by? She needed gas anyway, so she decided to go by the gas station and then drive by the Fifth's just to make sure everything was okay.

The Fifth's car was not in her driveway. She drove through empty streets, the town's silence deepened by shuttered storefronts and darkened windows. Nothing stayed open past ten, and every moment she spent searching felt like time slipping away. Storm clouds were forming over the woods; she hoped to be home before the rain started. The Twelfth tried calling the Fifth—no answer. Panic began to set in. She made her way around the town, checking parking lots for the Fifth's car. The streets were empty, hushed by the promise of the approaching storm. The air was heavy, pressing down on her chest as she drove, each turn of the wheel feeding her anxiety.

The wind picked up, rustling the trees with a low, ominous whisper. "Please be okay," she murmured, heart pounding. At the edge of the woods, she spotted the Fifth's car—abandoned on the side of the road.

Why would she be out here alone? And this late? The questions rattled through the Twelfth's mind, each one more unsettling than the last. Suddenly, an inexplicable sense of urgency overwhelmed her. She parked behind the Fifth's car and slid out, the rain already drizzling as storm clouds loomed overhead like a shroud.

She tried calling again—no answer. Her grip on the phone tightened, her fingers trembling. "Where are you?" she whispered into the night, but only silence greeted her. The dread coiled tighter in her chest, the urgency inside her roaring like a siren.

What if she's hurt? Or lost? The Twelfth's thoughts raced. The Fifth never ventured into the woods without telling someone. She glanced at the dim treeline. Why here, of all places? The chill creeping up her spine did little to reassure her.

She took a step forward, forcing her fear aside. *I have to find her.* Even the crunch of gravel beneath her feet seemed unnaturally loud. Her clothes were already damp, and she shivered as the rain began to fall harder. Still, she moved toward the looming forest, fear and determination locked in a silent battle.

Bracing herself, she pressed the phone to her ear one last time. Nothing but static. "Please, God, let her be okay," she whispered, dropping her arm to her side. She drew in a long, unsteady breath and pushed into the darkness of the woods; each step fueled by the unshakeable feeling that time was running out.

Chapter 55

Haywood grabbed one demon and hurled it aside, only for more to leap onto his back, claws and fangs shredding his tattered wings. Meir emerged from the tree line in helpless horror, tears burning her eyes. She was no warrior—her gifts lay in healing and comfort—and a swarm like this would tear her apart before she reached the Fifth.

Haywood's blood splattered across demon faces, staining them with golden mockery. His once-majestic wings, now tattered and torn, sagged beneath the weight of the attack. Meir felt nausea twist in her stomach at the sight, and a helpless moan escaped her lips. Every instinct told her to run to Haywood, to shield him. She stepped forward from the tree line, posed to run into the fray unarmed. Haywood caught sight of her, and his eyes flashed.

"Nooo!" Haywood bellowed, voice ragged, warning Meir back "No!" he said again, sadness filling his words. Meir's entire being flinched. A scream of protest caught in her chest, but Haywood's glare was resolute. She understood his silent command: *Stay away, save the Fifth.* A sob choked her throat. Her breath trembled, tears gathering hot and urgent. She knew the Fifth's only chance lay with her, yet the agony of leaving Haywood was unthinkable.

She held his gaze, then driven by instinct, she took a step forward, determined to protect them both. Haywood mouthed the word, "please" before turning his head away from her. A sob choked her throat. She had to do as he asked, or the Fifth was doomed. Meir nearly buckled. The emotions pouring off him were raw and unfiltered—pain, resolve, devotion. He knew. He knew this would be his last battle, and his only plea was for her to save his charge.

The knowledge cut Meir to her core. She stepped behind a thick tree, tears pouring down her cheeks as she peered around the trunk. A jagged scream ripped from Haywood's lips when a destroyer bit into his neck. He threw it off with a snarl, only for another demon to drive a blade through his back. His blood sprayed in arcs, spattering demon faces like a grotesque mockery of golden splendor. Meir pressed her palm to her mouth to stifle a cry. She could sense his pain in the spirit realm—each wound another wave of suffering.

Talons further gashed open Haywood's wing, and a demon's claw snaked through the tear to grab the Fifth. With a roar, Haywood twisted, arching his body around her, refusing to uncover her despite the agony. "Stay back!" he growled again, seemingly to the demons, but Meir knew it was directed at her. More of an anguished plea than a command.

All she could do was huddle behind the tree, tears streaking her face, as she whispered a frantic prayer to the King: *Please, let his sacrifice mean something. Let the Fifth live.* His face contorted with pain, yet a fierce resolve burned in his eyes: *Protect her, no matter the cost.* Meir's heart clenched at his unspoken message. Meir nodded slightly to let him know she would do all she could, then she stepped back from the fray, tears pouring down her angelic face as she covered her ears, desperate not to hear the sound of the demons tearing him apart.

A destroyer clamped its jaws around Haywood's shoulder. He hurled it aside, only for another to drive a blade through his back. Meir pressed her palm to her mouth, stifling a sob. Pain radiated from Haywood in palpable waves she could sense in the spirit realm—his anguish, his fear, and beneath it all, his unwavering devotion to the Fifth.

His ragged breathing stuttered, yet he forced himself upright. A vicious slash tore into his side, and he groaned, but he pressed closer, wings curving to keep the Fifth hidden. Even as his strength ebbed, his devotion shone like a beacon. Meir shut her eyes, biting down on her lip to keep from crying out. Her wings trembled with the longing to fly to his side—yet she stayed hidden, every fiber of her being shaking with the effort. Her soul screamed at the cruelty of this final sacrifice, tears scorching her cheeks. She pressed a trembling hand to her heart, whispering over and over, *Please, let his sacrifice be enough. Let her live. Protect them both if it's Your will—but if not… spare her.*

A guttural groan rumbled from Haywood's chest, but he bent lower, using every last shred of strength to cover the Fifth. Meir could see Haywood's lips move in silent prayer, even as his bloodied wings drooped. His gaze flicked again to her hiding place. The pain etched in his eyes wrenched her heart, but there was also a grim acceptance. He had no regrets; he fought not out of duty alone but out of a deep love for the Fifth.

Meir bowed her head, trembling, wishing with all her might that she could tear the demons away and heal him on the spot. *I'm sorry, Haywood,* she thought, her tears falling freely. *I'm so sorry.* Haywood's eyes clenched shut in pain, and Meir stifled a sob against the back of her hand. *Please… please let him hold on just a little longer.* Squeezing her eyes shut, she felt the spirit realm shift as more demons flooded in. She prayed one last time, mustering every ounce of faith she had: *Let me save the Fifth. Let Haywood's sacrifice not be in vain.*

With that prayer echoing in her soul, she forced herself to keep still. The sound of ripping flesh and Haywood's ragged gasps would haunt her for the rest of her days, but she steeled herself for the moment she might act—and prayed the King would give her the strength to do what only a ministering angel could.

Haywood bent lower, his body even closer to the Fifth. Pain ripped through him, but his thoughts were only of the Fifth. He was pledged to her, and he would not uncover her. Every strike, every claw that raked his wings, was a price he willingly paid. He whispered a silent plea to the King—*let this be enough, let her live.* His devotion to her went beyond duty; it was love, fierce and selfless. Haywood's screams reverberated through the night. Each one was a knife in Meir's heart. She cried out in desperation.

"Aegeus!" The voice rang out, laced with desperation. Not far away, Aegeus and the Twelfth were locked in a fight of their own. The demon horde closed in, drawn by the clash of blades and the calls of angelic voices echoing through the darkness. The smell of demons choked the air—sulfur, and decay that set his senses on edge. He knew they were closing in.

The Twelfth stumbled over tangled roots, her breath ragged, every step a struggle. Branches clawed her skin, drawing blood that mingled with sweat. Fear and determination pushed her forward, each heartbeat hammering in her ears. She yelled the Fifth's name again, but no answer came. Each unanswered call tore at her throat, every rustling leaf or snapping twig fueling the dread that something terrible had already happened.

In his hurry, Aegeus failed to see the destroyer demon drop from a nearby tree. A sword sliced into his arm, and he gritted his teeth against the burning pain. He countered with a sweep of his blade and realized the destroyer was not alone. Angel swords sang through the thick air, and battle erupted around them as they fought toward Meir and the Fifth.

The Twelfth halted abruptly, eyes darting around as though sensing a conflict she couldn't fully perceive. Her eyes were wide with fear, and Aegeus wondered briefly if she could see the battle that raged around her. She called the Fifth's name once more, voice shaking. Darkness seemed to thicken in the trees, and her heart pounded as if warning her of an unseen threat. *Please,* she prayed silently, *let me reach her.*

Suddenly, destroyer demons lunged at the Twelfth, teeth bared, sulfur pouring from their mouths. Thick smoke billowed, blotting out what little moonlight remained. Panic clutched at the Twelfth's chest.

Aegeus slashed through the stifling dark, slicing one demon in half with a sickening hiss of searing flesh. The thunderous crack of a demon warrior slamming into a tree shook the ground beneath his feet. He caught only glimpses of the Twelfth through the rolling smoke. Another demon lunged at him; he rammed his sword deep into its chest. Black blood splattered the ground with a rancid stench. Muscles burning, he pressed on, cutting a path toward the last place he had seen the Twelfth, but the swirling haze made it impossible to see her for long. The weight of every strike reverberated through his bones. Somewhere behind him, Meir's voice rose again, more desperate than before.

A sudden flash of Light, then a scream. Another dazzling blast lit the woods. Aegeus blinked, momentarily blinded but able to hear the demons screech. The Twelfth had unleashed the Spirit's power, repelling those who tried to seize her. The smell of blistered demon filled the woods. He could just see her running, demons forced back by her Light. Pride stirred in him—but the feeling vanished at the sound of another tortured cry. Haywood. Aegeus surged forward, cutting a path through the enemy, every strike more ruthless than the last.

Demons were still emerging from the woods, piling on to Haywood. If he acted too soon, the Fifth would have no hope. He had to protect her until Aegeus arrived and Meir could minister to her. The demons shrieked in glee; with each blow, they landed a triumphant crescendo. His ragged breathing grew more labored, but Meir felt the flicker of his spirit still burning. She could sense his devotion, shining brightly in the darkness.

A choked roar escaped him as another blade pierced his side, and the onslaught intensified. Meir ducked farther behind the tree, lips trembling in silent prayer. She could only remain hidden, waiting for the instant when the horde's attention wavered—an instant that could save the Fifth. She hated her helplessness, but she clung to hope, relying on the knowledge that Aegeus was coming.

A savage shriek echoed through the woods as another wave of demons poured in. Haywood gathered his last reserves of power, muscles trembling with the effort. He locked eyes with Aegeus, who had just broken through the demon horde. Pain and pleading filled his gaze—*Save her.* He shielded her with every inch of his battered body, his wings curling protectively around her like a shield. Scores of destroyers swarmed him, tearing at his flesh. Broken feathers littered the ground; blood pooled around his feet. Yet he braced himself, refusing to leave the Fifth exposed.

Even from a distance, Aegeus saw the flickering of the Fifth's Light—so faint it was nearly lost. Haywood bent lower, whispering words meant just for her: *You are not alone. You have never been alone.* Though the wind tore his voice away, he prayed she would feel it in her soul.

The sight of his brother covered in demons was enough to stop Aegeus short. Blood poured from Haywood's neck and back. Despite his suffering, Haywood fought for the life of his charge.

Aegeus was still too far to reach them, but he propelled himself forward with a newfound ferocity. Haywood looked up, and their eyes met; he looked deep into Aegeus's eyes, his own pleading with him, not for his own life, but the life of the Fifth.

Haywood mustered all his strength and started to uncurl his wings. The pain of the task registered on his face. Blood dripped from every ragged edge, and the Fifth cowered beneath him, a gun trembling in her hand. He knew that this was her only chance. He would destroy the demons and give Meir and Aegeus enough time to save her. He stood tall one last time, a broken sentinel of light. As he stood up, the demons rushed to cover the Fifth, filling her with lies. Despondence and Guilt dug their talons deep into her, sulfur pouring from them in their frenzy. Haywood raised his body, strong and tall, and mustering the last shred of his strength. Offering up the last of himself to protect her, he used the Light of God to blast the demons from the woods. For an instant, the forest fell eerily silent.

Aegeus and Meir rushed forward, but Haywood's lifeless body hit the ground before they reached him. The Fifth stopped crying. Time seemed to warp around her. The weight of the gun in her hands, the memory of a child's laughter that no longer rang in her ears, each thought was a dagger. Meir flung her wings around the Fifth, trying to bring her back from the brink, her eyes were empty, lost in a sea of grief and guilt. Demons poured in once more, and Aegeus barked orders to the angels to form a barrier of swords and wings. He fought with renewed ferocity, blocking the demons from reaching Meir and the Fifth. Swords drawn, the angels served as a wall of light against an ocean of darkness.

Meir searched the Fifth's soul for anything to hold onto—any spark of hope, any anchor that might pull her back from the edge. The darkness pressed in, heavy and unyielding, and each second that passed felt like sand slipping through her fingers. She couldn't fail—not now, not when every heartbeat counted.

"Help her!" Aegeus yelled over his shoulder.

"I'm trying!" Meir's voice quivered with panic. "She's barely holding on—she hasn't been feeding her soul well. I'm searching for something—anything to anchor her."

Closing her eyes, Meir reached deep within the Fifth's memories, pushing past layers of despair. Years of guilt and shame weighed the Fifth down, the death of her daughter festering like a wound she had never allowed to heal. Meir rummaged frantically through recollections of family, scripture, fleeting moments of warmth—scraps of hope hidden under the crushing darkness.

The thunder of swords and demon shrieks rolled through the woods. As the Fifth lifted the gun, Meir's presence tugged at her heart, but the darkness had taken root too deeply. Her finger trembled on the trigger, a tear carving a path down her cheek. Her pain was so raw, so overwhelming.

Meir waded past the pain, past the self-hate and loathing. There was so much blame, such sorrow. Her wings quivered as she pushed desperately deeper into the Fifth's memories. Each image cut like a knife—pain, loss, guilt—layers upon layers of darkness. 'There must be more,' she pleaded internally, tears streaming down her angelic cheeks. *Please, show me something—anything.*

The Fifth had been feeding her soul guilt and shame for many years. She had worked to punish herself for the death of her daughter. She had buried it so deeply and refused to even speak of her daughter. She had kept the secret, and it had been killing her.

Meir found memories of the Fifth's family and brought them to the surface. She flooded the Fifth with encouragement, words from her youth, favorite Bible verses, and words from the eleven.

"Meir!" Aegeus yelled as he battled the demons. The horde pushed against the angles with a pulsating evil. Aegeus dug his heel into the earth leaning his full weight into pushing them back. He had to buy Meir time. More angels engulfed the woods. The clash of swords sounded like thunder throughout the town.

Sounds of battle filled the woods. Then, with a hollow click, the Fifth pulled the trigger. Time seemed to slow. Meir felt the hot spray of blood cover her, but the reality of what had happened took longer. The Fifth's body slumped against Meir, the gun tumbling from her lifeless fingers.

A roar of triumph erupted from the demons, who scattered skyward in celebration. The Twelfth burst into a small clearing just as the crack of a gunshot split the night. She froze, her pulse pounding in her ears. A strangled cry left her lips when she saw the Fifth's body collapse to the ground.

"No... no," she rasped, stumbling forward. She wanted to believe she'd heard it wrong, that it was just another twig snapping, but the metallic odor of gunpowder lingered in the air. Kneeling beside the Fifth, she fumbled to press her fingers against a pulse that wasn't there.

Her mind spun, unable to reconcile the sudden silence that followed. "Why—?" she choked out, tears blurring her vision. Time felt sluggish and merciless; her breath came in short, ragged gasps. The faint rustling of leaves around her only intensified the hollow ache in her chest.

"I should have been here," the Twelfth whispered, guilt stabbing deep. A gentle breeze rustled nearby leaves, the only sign of Meir shifting closer, silently sharing in the Twelfth's desperate vigil. Their grief merged in the cool darkness—one seen, one unseen—both mourning a life that slipped away before their eyes, leaving only a broken sob in their wake. Her anguished cry merged with the angels, a chorus of grief that rose to the heavens.

Aegeus fell to his knees, the earth cold and unyielding beneath him. His cry pierced the heavens, raw and primal, echoing the agony of every life lost. Tears streaked his face as he spread his arms, a broken plea to the King for strength and meaning in the midst of so much loss. All around him, angels bowed their heads, swords lowered in defeat, as the final echoes of the demon horde's celebration faded into the darkness.

Meir clung to the Fifth's body, the warmth fading beneath her fingertips. The world blurred as hot tears streamed down her face. She cradled the Fifth's body with trembling hands, her own breath ragged with grief. Blood soaked into her robes, but she hardly noticed—it was the cold stillness of the Fifth that consumed her. A strangled sob escaped her lips, a raw testament to the battle lost and the soul now beyond her reach.

'Not like this,' she whispered, her voice breaking. Each tear that fell mixed with blood, a bitter reminder of what she had failed to save. Tears dripped down Meir's face, splashing onto the Fifth, whose blood she now wore.

Aegeus trembled as he knelt on the unrelenting earth, the ground beneath him soaked with blood and tears. He felt each heartbeat slow, the crushing silence swallowing him whole. Around him, angels dropped their swords, the weight of defeat pressing them to the earth. And in the center, Meir's anguished cries tore through the darkness—a lament that pierced the heavens.

Chapter 56

The demons took to the skies in celebration of the death of the Fifth. Titus sat atop the church steeple watching, pleased with himself. It had not been easy for the destroyers and taunting demons to reach her; Haywood was a formidable guardian. But the Eighth had seemed the higher priority, so the angels had focused on him, which allowed Titus and his demons to focus on the Fifth. It was easy once he learned about her husband and daughter. Titus savored every broken sob, every moment she crumbled under the weight of her memories. He had whispered her failures in the dead of night, painting guilt over every cherished memory until only despair remained. This victory was personal.

On a foggy day in April, during her junior year in college, the Fifth had been in a fairly minor car accident. The fog had reduced visibility, and as a result, she did not have enough time to avoid hitting the small gray truck crossing the road in front of her.

The sound of crashing metal filled the air, and her airbag smashed into her face, breaking her nose. She was otherwise uninjured. She had hit an Army man.

She was whisked away from the accident with little contact with him, but he sought her out at the hospital to make sure she was okay. They dated for three years and married during her time in graduate school. It was—the kind of blessing that made her believe in second chances, in love that heals broken things. But love wasn't armor strong enough to hold against fate's cruelty. They were happy when, after five years of marriage, she learned she was pregnant. In the third month of her pregnancy, her husband received orders to Iraq. He was killed in action five months later.

The Fifth gave birth to their daughter three days before her due date, less than a month after burying her husband. When she first held her daughter, the world seemed to hold its breath, and for a moment, every crack in her heart healed. The baby's tiny hand curled around her finger, and she whispered promises she was determined to keep—promises to keep her safe, to love her enough for two parents. She loved her child more than she could ever have imagined—she was all that the Fifth had left of her husband. The girl grew and served as a great source of joy to her mother. She had her father's eyes and his smile, and each day, the Fifth felt as if she could still see just a small hint of her husband.

When her daughter was seven years old, the Fifth went on a date with a man she had known for some time. She had not been on a date since her husband had died and had no real desire to go, but her friends had encouraged her to do so. And so, she had reluctantly agreed. She made arrangements for a friend to come over to watch her daughter, who begged her not to go.

The Fifth arrived home to find her home in flames, her daughter and friend lost to the fire. When the flames devoured her home and her daughter, the world fell apart again—this time irreparably. The heat of the flames seared the night air, and the acrid smoke clawed at her lungs as she screamed her daughter's name. It was the smell—the sickly, cloying scent of burning wood and fabric—that would haunt her forever, seared into her memory more deeply than the fire itself.

She shattered that day, fracturing into a million pieces. She poured herself into her work, never discussing the fire or her daughter. She simply could not face it. She could not say it out loud. In Platitude, anonymity was supposed to be a balm, a chance to start anew. But silence became its own curse, cutting her off from any hope of healing. No one asked about her past, and she convinced herself she preferred it that way—until the loneliness grew louder than the silence. No one knew of the pain that she carried so deeply inside of her—pain that had erased who she was, leaving only broken pieces of a person.

Day after day, as she listened to the Strongman make comments about how a woman's only purpose was to raise a family and serve her husband, she felt each shard of her broken soul stab deeper into her. What purpose did she have now? She had failed. What use was she to God? No fire could burn as hot as her shame and guilt, no night as dark as the pit she now lived in. And every word from the Strongman dug deeper into her wounds, whispering she was already beyond saving.

Ministering angels had attended to her almost daily, but she resisted them. She wanted to punish herself. Every time a ministering angel's Light touched her, it burned—not with heat, but with the weight of a forgiveness she couldn't accept. She shoved them away, clinging to her guilt as if it were all she had left of her family. Redemption was a luxury for those who hadn't failed so completely. She had nothing left but shame and guilt. What must her husband think of her as he looked down from heaven? How disappointed he must be that the only thing he left with her, the only piece of him left on this earth, their beautiful daughter—was no more because she had been so selfish to want a night away.

Now, she had every night away. What she would give to have the worst day with her daughter back. Being in Platitude, she had not told anyone about her daughter or husband because she thought it would be easier not to have to discuss it. But it also meant that she couldn't discuss it. Over time, that too, seemed like a horrible injustice that she should be punished for. So, she robbed herself of anything that eased her guilt. She could not forgive herself.

Titus let the final words of her story hang in the frigid air, savoring the bleakness of it. A crooked smile crept across his face, fed by the knowledge of her downfall and the roar of celebrating demons overhead. Then, with a slow exhale, he turned from his grim retelling, allowing the thrill of this moment—of the Fifth's demise— to pull him back into the now. The stench of sulfur and triumph still clung to the night, reminding him that her tragedy was complete, and their victory sealed.

As he watched the demons spiral higher in their macabre dance of victory, Titus traced a finger along the fresh wound on his arm. Pain shot through him, a bitter reminder of the cost—but it was a cost he'd pay a thousand times over for such a triumph.

Chapter 57

"Beautiful, isn't it?" Morax asked, joining Titus on the church roof overlooking the town.

Titus was not pleased to have his moment interrupted. He had won a great victory, and his demons were celebrating in the town. He wanted nothing more than to sit atop this church and watch.

"The town or the celebration?" Hopeful that his displeasure at being interrupted wasn't obvious.

Morax smiled and then took time to ponder the question before answering.

"Both, but I was referring to the town. The mountains are glorious."

For just a moment, Morax forgot that he was a demon. He forgot that long ago; he had made a decision that changed his course. He had chosen the Prince over the King. It had proven to be a mistake, one he would pay for for all of eternity.

But for a minute, he forgot all that and just soaked in the glory and majesty of creation. The mountains reached for the heavens, and the stream running through the town bubbled praise to the King. For just a moment, he forgot why he hated the hairless rats so much. Titus watched, intrigued to see Morax this way.

A crash rang out from the street below, bringing them both back to the present. Morax looked down to see a truck wrapped around a light pole. Demons covered the truck and the bystanders so that no one did anything to help the driver. They pulled phones from their pockets and bags and recorded the last breaths of the driver—it would make a great post on social media. All those phones and no one called for help, no one reached out to help, no one prayed. Titus looked at the scene and smiled. Oh, yes, he had done very well here indeed.

Morax watched, too. It was going to be a very good night for the demons. His earlier sense of nostalgia forgotten; he patted Titus on the back.

"You have done well, Titus. A promotion may be in store for you." It was a promise Titus longed for.

"Thank you, my liege. But the prophet still lives. Do we have plans?" Titus wanted to see the mission through, and he wanted to be the one responsible for destroying the prophet, if for no other reason than to gloat over Seneca.

"Seneca and Aegeus will meet in battle tomorrow. Once the angels are gone, we will have no problems destroying the prophet." Morax smiled at the thought of it.

What was the King thinking, sending a female prophet to this place? He laughed out loud. He knew the King rooted for the underdog, but a female prophet? Preposterous. Even without the demons, that was unlikely to work in Platitude.

"Where is the battle?" Titus asked, surprised by the news.

"Seneca has chosen the barley field on the backside of the campus." Morax laughed gently and shook his head in disbelief. "You should be impressed, Titus; you aren't the only one with artistic flair." Titus wasn't sure if he should be pleased that Morax had noticed his creativity or insulted by the comparison.

"I'm not sure I understand." The reference confused Titus.

"Many years ago, before Seneca lost the Light, he and Aegeus were friends. One might even say best friends. They were, along with others, assigned to fight alongside King David. Over time, each angelic warrior fought with a specific warrior of David's. Seneca was assigned Jashobeam, and Aegeus was assigned Eleazar."

"Aren't they two of David's mightiest three?" Titus asked, his interest piqued.

"Indeed. Your history serves you well, Titus. Having Seneca and Aegeus was what propelled them to be among the three. Things were going very well for them, and their victories were many. But the battle of Pas-Dammim would change everything.

"The Philistines and Israelites had met for battle in a field of barley. It was a sunny day with no clouds in the sky, and a cool breeze blew in from the north. The Philistines grossly outnumbered the Israelites. The battle was in their favor. The Israelite army fled. All except David and Eleazar. They stood their ground to battle, the two of them against the entire Philistine army." Morax smiled, remembering it.

"David never was one for standing down." Titus couldn't help but be impressed.

"Aegeus and Seneca remained in the battle—hundreds of angels did. As you can imagine, the fighting was intense. David and Eleazar fought back-to-back with the Philistines pouring in from every direction. They swung their swords with the might of ten men.

"A young Philistine boy, just able to swing his sword, rushed onto the battlefield. He was young, but he was already a mighty warrior. He pushed and shoved his way toward David.

"Today would be the day the boy earned his stripes. He would kill King David. But he was just a boy, and his resolve was not quite as strong as he wanted the others to believe. He hesitated for a moment, just a moment. Seneca stood between the boy and David. The word from the King was to kill the boy. Like the boy, Seneca hesitated. As the boy raised his sword Aegeus stepped in and killed him. Instantly, Seneca lost the Light of God for his disobedience. The battle raged on around them, but Scneca dropped his sword, disbelief registering in his eyes. Aegeus stood before him. His best friend, his brother-in-arms, now his mortal enemy. Aegeus cried out to the King, but Seneca's choice had been made."

"Why didn't Aegeus kill him right there?" Titus asked, unable to fully understand the bond of that type of friendship.

"You would have to ask Aegeus that, but I suppose it isn't that easy to kill your friend," Morax spoke as one who knew.

"Seneca left the battlefield that day and retreated to a cave where he spent hundreds of years alone. Each day the darkness took more of him. Without the Light of God, evil began to overtake him. Hatred filled him; anger, pride, and self-justification consumed him. He emerged from that cave a demon."

"Seneca hates the demons," Titus stated matter-of-factly.

"Seneca hates that he is a demon," Morax corrected. "Seneca hates everyone now. He is one of our mightiest warriors. He fights with great hatred, destined to never again show mercy to anyone. He has convinced himself that Aegeus cost him his Light. He has deceived himself into thinking his punishment was unjust and that if Aegeus had not stepped in, he would have killed the boy."

"So, he has chosen a barley field for their final encounter." The significance finally settled on Titus. The field would surely cause Aegeus to recognize his old friend.

"Do you think Seneca will be able to kill Aegeus?" Titus had his doubts.

"Yes, Titus, I do. I think Seneca could have killed him many times, I believe he is playing with Aegeus as a cat toys with a mouse. He has waited many years to exact his revenge, and when Seneca sinks his sword deep into Aegeus, he wants to be sure Aegeus knows who it is that is killing him."

The two were silent for some time as they watched the demon revelry in the town. Car alarms rang out in the night, the sound of arguing muffled by the thunder of the angels' cries. The sound of the angels made the night perfect for Titus. The demons flew about in jubilation. Lies, Distrust, and Fear made their way from home to home.

"Titus, how did you know about the Fifth?" Morax could not help but be impressed.

"She was so filled with regret and guilt that it was obvious she had something hidden. The Strongman's words affected her in a way that was different than the others. I sent Grigori to research her past. He found her secret." Titus smiled again to be reminded of his success.

"We will maximize on this. I will have the Strongman speak to the college about the sin of suicide. I will have him say that it is unforgivable. We will use the Word to prove it. If we can make them believe she will join us in hell, it will make their grief even greater. It will make them fear the King. They will recoil from him. They will feel guilty in mourning her and become unsure of their own position."

Ah, yes, the rats were so predictable.

Chapter 58

Word of the Fifth's death flooded through the campus. Meir returned home to the King brokenhearted. Social media was flooded with opinions on the matter, most of them uninformed, too many of them hurtful. The story of real people was rarely as simple as a social media post made it seem. The Wednesday night group was shaken to its foundations. Visions of the Fifth lying dead in the woods filled her mind, each replay tightening around her chest with suffocating regret. 'If only' echoed relentlessly, a torment that gnawed at every corner of her resolve. A sense of helplessness seeped in.

The Strongman called an early-morning prayer meeting in the neglected barley field behind the campus and required all students, faculty, and staff to attend. The group met early in the morning to pray together before going to the field. They traveled together to the field for the sunrise service, but the Third stayed behind. She needed time alone with the King.

The Strongman stood tall on a crude platform at the field's center, a dark silhouette against the false dawn. His words dripped with conviction, but his eyes gleamed with something far darker—a malice meant to twist hope into despair. Thousands of demons lined up behind him. Thousands more took to the sky to secure the demon dome, sealing the entrance to the town. The sky grew dark and ominous, blocking out the sunrise. The smell of sulfur hung thick in the air.

Aegeus and his team stood opposite the Strongman and his demons. Hundreds of angels stood with them. The Twelfth stood on the right side of Aegeus. She was trembling slightly, and Aegeus found himself wishing for Meir or Lavi so that she could be comforted.

Aegeus unfurled his wings, wrapping one protectively around the Twelfth. He knew it wouldn't banish her fear nor erase the darkness that pressed in on them, but it was all he could offer – a shield made of hope and memory. The Eleventh stood wide-eyed, staring at the Strongman. For the first time, she could see his demon and all those who stood behind him. She leaned toward the Twelfth and whispered, "He is a demon."

"I know." Although she could not see them, the Twelfth could feel them.

"There are thousands of them," the Eleventh whispered, "and they don't seem to like you very much," she said, her voice cracking in fear. The Twelfth looked at the Eleventh, and for a heartbeat, her fear gave way to the Spirit, and a flare of Light shot from her, piercing the suffocating darkness.

The demons snarled and hissed at the presence of the prophet and the Light. The Twelfth glanced quickly around; concern and uncertainty filled her eyes. Aegeus leaned close to her, and although he knew she could not hear him, he spoke to her.

"You are a prophet of the King Most High. You have the power to call his army. You have the strength to defeat the enemy. Draw on the Light of God." For a heartbeat, he held his breath, searching her face for any flicker of belief, any sign that she might draw on the strength he now knew dwelled within her. He had hoped she would cast off her own ill-fitting role and step fully into the light of who she was meant to be. But uncertainty clung to her like a shadow; he nodded once as if to reassure them both. He straightened, his eyes hardening as he took in the mass of demons that loomed before them.

"You're not alone," he murmured. The words meant as much for himself as for her. With a final, steadying breath, Aegeus shifted his focus to the Strongman, who now raised his arms with calculated menace. Shadows thickened; the air charged with the weight of unspoken challenges. The Twelfth trembled beside him.

The Twelfth leaned toward the Eleventh. "Text the group; ask them all to pray." She whispered. The Eleventh nodded and pulled out her phone. She sent the text and began to pray as the Strongman began to speak.

"We have experienced a great tragedy on our campus. We have lost a faculty member, and our hearts ache for her family and friends. All year, we have discussed the devastating effects of sin on our lives. We have now seen firsthand the might of the evil one.

Depression is a mighty tool, but you don't have to let it take over your life. You don't have to fight that battle alone. This tragedy reminds us that we wake up every day and we fight a great battle not against flesh and blood but against the principalities of darkness!"

Some in the crowd cheered his comments; some cheered the excited way he yelled them out with authority. Thousands of tormenting and destroying demons encircled the field, eager for the opportunity to bring confusion and chaos to those in the field.

The Tenth stood within the crowd, heart hammering as he listened to the Strongman's words. A sudden urging pressed against his spirit—an unmistakable nudge from the King, compelling him to speak out. He swallowed hard, pulse thrumming in his ears. *Now,* the voice seemed to say. *Stand for truth. Confront these lies.*

His palms grew clammy. He wanted to open his mouth, to challenge the Strongman's twisted statements, but *what if he lost his job,* He wondered. And *how would I explain that to my wife?* He look at thousands of people standing throughout the field and felt paralyzed with dread. *I'm not ready,* he thought. *What if no one listens?*

For a moment, he drew in a breath, lips parting. He could feel the Spirit's fire blazing in his chest. But then his gaze flicked to the warped faces in the crowd, the sulfuric reek clinging to them, and fear drowned out his resolve.

Slowly, he closed his mouth. The roar of chanting demons closed in, and the Tenth, trembling, let the opportunity slip away.

Aegeus witnessed the Tenth's hesitation. A flash of disappointment rose within him, burning as fiercely as any blade. The Tenth had been chosen to confront the Strongman with words of truth; he was meant to undermine these deceptions. But now, as the moment passed, even Aegeus felt the weight of that missed chance.

Please, don't let this cost them everything, Aegeus prayed, forcing himself to refocus. Their window to stop the Strongman was closing, and they needed every shard of courage in that field. The Strongman continued.

"There are those that would have you give up your religious freedom and replace it with lies. They would tell you that it is okay for a woman to pass up marriage and children for her career. Do you hear that? Her career? That is selfish and rebellious; it is all about her and not about the Word.

"Acts that are selfish and rebellious lead to separation and uncertainty. You can see the results of such sinful thinking in this tragic situation. This poor woman had no leadership and no one to spiritually guide her through poor choices, selfishness, and sin. Look around you! Look around you and see who is standing beside you that wants to lead you into unrighteousness, who stands among you that is rebelling against leadership? Who among you is wading in the wages of sin? We must cleanse ourselves of the unrighteous; we must purge them from our midst; we must free ourselves from the clutches of death!" the Strongman's voice yelled out into the field.

The demons lunged into the throng with a frenzied roar, their forms shifting. Their snarls were a chorus of hatred that rattled bones and pierced souls. As they wove through the panicked crowd, the demons' touch left a chill that seeped into the skin, a promise of torment that lingered long after they passed. Confusion and Chaos weaved in and out of the crowd, touching the people as they passed. The fog slithered in like a living thing, dense and suffocating. It clawed at their throats and swallowed all light, leaving only the echo of the Strongman's voice. Each breath tasted of ash and despair, blinding them to everything but fear. They could only hear the words of the Strongman—lies intended to deceive and destroy them. Fear and Distrust joined Confusion and Chaos, shoving, and pushing the humans.

Tormenting demons took to the sky and began to fly through the crowd, shoving and pushing the people. The thick smoke added to the confusion, causing them to blame each other. Their eyes, blinded by the demons, searched the crowd to find the unrighteousness that the Strongman spoke about, to purge them from their midst.

Fear choked them as they clutched at their throats. Confusion flew low through the field, causing them to trip and fall. Panic ripped through them. Poisonous lies continued to pour from the Strongman, encouraging them to seek out the lost among them—the rebellious—and to bring them forward for redemption.

His lies caused the fog to grow thicker and darker. Destroying demons flashed through the field, starting fights among the people.

Aegeus and the angels surged forward, their movements precise and fluid, cutting through the swarm of demons with a chilling grace. The clash of ethereal blades against demonic claws reverberated like a storm of metal and thunder, sending shockwaves that rippled through the wild barley field. Sparks of blinding light erupted whenever an angel's strike connected, briefly illuminating the grotesque forms of their enemies—twisted shapes writhing with fury. The air thickened with the acrid stench of burning sulfur as defeated demons dissolved, leaving trails of ash in their wake. If they could stop the Strongman, the battle would be over. The smell of burnt demons filled the air. Aegeus battled his way toward the Strongman, who continued to spew his lies into the crowd. The Twelfth stood frozen in place. The Eleventh prayed fervently.

The Seventh had arrived late and stood on the far left of the field. As emotions began to rise and the people began to respond with a mob mentality, she soon found herself surrounded by a group of young college men.

"Purge the unrighteous among you; drag them to the cross; bring them forward so that we can be free of all sin! Search for them among you and bring them to me so that we will have life!" the Strongman screamed into the crowd.

The young men surrounding the Seventh began to converge on her. They recognized her as a friend of the Fifth. One of the men grabbed her arm. Confusion dug his talons deep into him. Anger latched onto his back and stabbed into his spine.

"You were friends with that professor—the one who killed herself. You must be among the unrighteous!" he shouted, dragging her toward the Strongman.

Heartbroken over what was happening and terrified of their intentions, the Seventh struggled to pull her arm free. The boys closed in on her.

Chapter 59

The Twelfth spun at the sound of a piercing scream, her eyes darting across the chaotic field. Bodies surged and collided, a tide of fear and fury. Screams mixed with the dull thud of fists and the desperate sobs of the fallen formed a cacophony that clawed at her resolve. About two hundred yards to her left, she saw the Seventh, who was surrounded by a group of males. The men were swarmed with demons, but neither the Twelfth nor the Seventh could see that. All they could see was the men dragging the Seventh to the Strongman. The Seventh fought with all she had. The Seventh's resistance was fierce—desperate strikes and kicks against overwhelming odds. There was no time to think. The Twelfth and the Eleventh locked eyes for a fraction of a heartbeat, a silent pact forming between them. Then they ran, adrenaline surging and prayers spilling from their lips as they pushed through the chaos.

The Twelfth ignored the protests from her legs and lungs as she pushed herself further into the chaos toward the Seventh. This was no time for hesitation. She whispered a prayer between ragged breaths, each word a desperate plea for strength. She stumbled over a fallen body and crashed to the ground. Feet pounded around her, a storm of kicks and heavy boots. Pain exploded in her ribs as she struggled to rise, only to be knocked down again. Through the blur of dust and tears, she saw the Seventh, blood streaking her face, her shirt torn. The Eleventh prayed even more fervently. She reached the Twelfth just as a large man fell over her. The Eleventh reached down and pulled her friend from the ground.

"There are thousands of demons," she shouted over the massive noise that filled the field. She looked desperately at the Twelfth. "You are a prophet! You have to do something!"

"I am not a prophet. And even if I were, I don't know what to do!" The Twelfth's voice cracked, raw with fear and doubt. But the Eleventh's gaze held steady, unwavering. For a fleeting moment, the weight of what she could be pressed down on her, heavy and suffocating. She tore herself away and pushed forward, her limbs aching, blood trickling from her split lip. Bruises were already forming on her face and hands.

The boys had knocked the Seventh to the ground. One of them was on top of her, trying to pin her arms to the ground. The Seventh fought, kicking and writhing. Panic and fury coursed through her veins, driving her to fight even as her strength waned. The Twelfth ran up behind the young man, and with all her strength, she kicked him in the back, right where she estimated his kidney to be. Pain shot through her bruised limbs, but she didn't relent. Each strike was fueled by raw determination, a desperate refusal to let darkness win. She knew this wasn't about strength—it was about survival, and she would fight with every last breath. The boy fell over enough that the Eleventh could reach the Seventh and help her to her feet.

The Twelfth did not see the fist until it struck her on the side of the face. Lights danced before her eyes, and for just a moment, she went deaf. Pain shot through her face, and she stumbled sideways, nearly falling. Stars burst before her eyes, and for a moment, the world went silent. She staggered, her hand instinctively flying to her swelling cheek, the pain radiating with every heartbeat.

She turned to face the man who had hit her. She was not foolish enough to think she could win in a fair fight; he was considerably bigger than her and half her age. But she did not intend to fight fair. She put up her fists, and he laughed at her. With all her might, she kicked him in the groin. He dropped to the ground and began to vomit.

The demon that had been attached to him let go and laughed at his misfortune. He quickly found another host and headed back toward the prophet. The prayers of the eleven that remained continued, and Light slowly began to seep into the field.

From the edge of the chaos, Titus's gaze fixed on the prophet, her vulnerability a beacon. He raised a hand, and hundreds of demons surged toward her—a dark wave of malevolence and fury. Some possessed human hosts, their eyes glinting with unnatural light; others, spectral forms of shadow and rage, rushed unimpeded through the air. He would see the prophet destroyed.

Chapter 60

"Aegeus!" The voice sliced through the chaos, desperate and raw, rising above the clash of steel and the cries of the fallen. He froze, senses straining for that single note in the storm of shrieks and moans. The battle raged around him—smoke and sulfur stinging his nostrils, each breath a jagged reminder of how fiercely the fight pressed on.

He heard it again: "Aegeus!" Sharper this time, more frantic. Something in that call yanked him from his focus on the Strongman, setting every nerve on edge. He didn't recognize the voice, yet the urgency pierced him like a blade. His gaze swept the battlefield, scanning the silhouettes of demons and dying light.

Then he saw her—the Twelfth, encircled by a horde. Their eyes locked. She couldn't see him, not truly, but the intensity of her gaze struck him as though she could. For a heartbeat, he stood still, the realization slamming into him: *She* was calling him.

Instinct surged. He abandoned his pursuit of the Strongman and instead charged toward her. The air crackled with heat and fury, the mingled stench of sulfur and scorched earth clinging to his lungs. Shadows twisted at the corners of his vision, their claws reflecting in the flicker of some distant flame.

"Aegeus!" She shouted again, voice ragged. He plowed forward, sword raised, tearing through the demonic ranks between them. The world narrowed to that single point: reach her before it's too late. Adrenaline roared in his veins, each step pounding the trampled barley underfoot.

He tore away one demon, then another. The sounds of battle—shrieks, steel on bone, the wet thud of bodies—merged into a single deafening note. But through it all, he kept hearing her cry, echoing across the field, driving him onward.

"Kfir! The prophet!" he bellowed, his voice cutting through the clash of combat as he passed Kfir, locked in a struggle with four demons. Determination drove him forward; he slashed through the swarm, his blade a blur of light and fury.

When he reached the Twelfth, a man cloaked in destroying demons had her by the throat, his grip tightening with lethal intent. The man's eyes were a void of darkness, his movements jerky and inhuman. Tendrils of shadow wrapped around his arms, guiding his grip with crushing force. The demons shrieked, feeding off his rage, their forms flickering in and out of visibility as they clung to him like a living parasite. Aegeus seized the man, tearing him away and hurling him across the field. The impact reverberated, a sickening thud against the hard earth. The man's body twisted unnaturally as the demons shrieked and clawed at their failing host before retreating like a black, choking mist.

The Twelfth staggered, clutching her throat as she gasped for air.

"Thank you," she rasped, each word a struggle. Her voice was raw, every word scraping like broken glass against her throat. Tears mixed with blood on her face, and her body trembled—not from fear alone, but from the realization that she had come so close to breaking. Aegeus stepped back, the shock etching deep lines on his face.

You can see me?" he asked, disbelief cracking through his battle-hardened exterior. Around them, chaos roared on, but for a moment, it felt muted. She nodded, pressing a hand to her bruised throat, struggling to find words. Her words—simple, strained, yet undeniably real—struck him harder than any blow. Humans couldn't see him, shouldn't see him. But here she was, staring at him with eyes wide with gratitude.

"How long?" he pressed, his voice low, raw with disbelief. He staggered under the weight of the realization—no human had ever seen him, let alone spoken to him outside of heaven. And now, her simple, hoarse 'Thank you' seemed to unravel centuries of certainty

"Since the woods," she managed, her voice gruff.

Suddenly, while Aegeus was still trying to process what was happening, a great warrior dropped to the ground behind him. The long-haired demon with the scar, his eyes calm amid the chaos. He smiled, not wanting to forget a moment of this—their last encounter.

"Aegeus, we meet again," he said in greeting. Aegeus felt a rush of familiarity—the feeling that you know someone, but you just can't quite place them. He turned to face the demon, putting himself between the warrior and the Prophet.

His eyes searched, and recognition struck like a blade to the heart. In an instant, he was back in another barley field, centuries ago, watching his closest friend fall from grace. The memory was seared into him—Seneca, once radiant with the King's Light, now dimmed and twisted. Aegeus had been too late then, deep in the throes of battle, only realizing the truth after he had killed the boy in protection of King David. His duty had compelled him to act. His heart had shattered in the aftermath. As soon as the boy's body fell to the ground, time seemed to stand still for Aegeus. He realized what had happened. His eyes met Seneca's for the last time. He watched as the Light of God was withdrawn from Seneca. It was a horrible sight to behold.

They had stood there in that field, looking at each other for what seemed like a lifetime. And then, in the blink of an eye, it was over. Seneca dropped his sword and walked away, disbelief washing over him. Aegeus watched him go, knowing there was nothing he could do. Eventually, he had turned back to the battle, trying to focus, trying to tell himself it wasn't real. But angels do not lie—not even to themselves. Aegeus slew thousands of Philistines that day, along with ten thousand demons. But no amount of victory could undo what had been done.

This day, in this field, Seneca waited patiently for Aegeus to remember, wanting to be sure that Aegeus felt the full effect of the memory. When Aegeus's eyes told Seneca he had returned to the present, he drew his sword.

"Seneca," Aegeus nearly whispered it. Aegeus's chest tightened, suffocating as he took in what Seneca had become—the twisted reflection of a friend who once stood in the King's Light.

"I have waited many years for this Aegeus," Seneca said, a snarl on his face. He twirled his sword in front of him. It had taken hundreds of years for Seneca to become completely evil with no hint of the angel he used to be. His love for Aegeus had been completely replaced with hate and blame. He longed for nothing more than to plunge his sword deep into Aegeus's stomach. He wanted to rip the wings from Aegeus's body so that, like Seneca, Aegeus could never fight for the King again.

"Seneca, I do not wish to kill you. But I will defend the prophet." Aegeus stood firm. He planted his feet, wings unfurling as if to shield both the past and present. Seneca's eyes, devoid of any warmth or recognition, narrowed in contempt.

Kfir arrived and stood by him. He planted his feet, a living shield of light and steel. Every fiber of his being was honed for this purpose—to protect the prophet and hold the line so Aegeus could face what lay ahead. Kfir would not waver.

"Prophet?" Seneca scoffed. "She is little more than a woman and not a particularly impressive one at that." And with those words, Seneca swung his sword at Aegeus. He was in no rush. There was no sense of urgency, only finality. Their swords slammed together, the sound of it blasting through the field. The voice of the Strongman grew louder and more ominous. Seneca clipped the side of Aegeus's face with his sword before Aegeus could dodge it. Golden blood gushed from the wound.

Aegeus dropped low to the ground to avoid another blow and swung his sword toward Seneca, which caused him to jump. Aegeus shot into the sky after him, each of them slashing and swinging at the other. Nearby, Kfir fought with unwavering ferocity, each strike a testament to his oath. The ground around him was littered with fallen demons, their twisted forms evidence of his resolve. He cast a fleeting glance at Aegeus, silently urging him forward as if to say, 'Finish this.

Aegeus missed a shot with his sword but connected his elbow to Seneca's face, sending him flying backward out of Aegeus's sight.

No longer seeing Seneca and knowing that Kfir protected the Twelfth, Aegeus headed for the Strongman. If they could kill the Strongman, the fight would be over.

He battled his way to the Strongman then shoved his sword through the Strongman's chest just as Seneca thrust his sword through Aegeus's back.

Aegeus let out a yell as his knees buckled, and he sank down, causing the sword to slice farther through him. With every shuddering breath, golden blood spilled onto the ground like molten light. Seneca withdrew his sword and wiped it across his own chest, covering himself in Aegeus's blood.

Aegeus stumbled forward, golden blood pouring from his wound.

"The mighty Aegeus has failed," Titus gloated. "Your effort is futile." With cold precision, Titus strode to the Strongman's fallen form, his touch causing the wounds to knit themselves closed. The twisted smile that spread across his face spoke of triumph—one final push to snuff out hope.

Aegeus turned toward Seneca, staggering forward, barely able to stand. His eyes met the demon he had once called brother, and he saw no hint of the angel Seneca had once been. He saw only pride and contempt. Aegeus took a deep breath, and summoning his remaining strength, in one swift move he shoved his sword through Seneca's chin and out the top of his head. Seneca fell to the ground, and Aegeus collapsed beside him.

"Aegeus!" He could hear the Twelfth calling his name from a distance. The sound of running footsteps drew nearer until they stopped. The Twelfth dropped to her knees on the ground beside him. Tears filled her eyes. Blood was crusted to her lip and flowing from near her eye. Bruises covered her neck and face. She took his hand in hers, her tears dripping onto his face.

"Aegeus," she repeated his name, a pleading in her voice.

"You are a prophet," he whispered. She nodded her head in response, emotion strangling her voice and leaving her unable to speak. She leaned her head against his chest and cried. Aegeus placed his right hand on her head, wanting to give her comfort. The battle raged on, the smell of impending doom all around them.

"Is this my fault?" She lifted her head and choked out the words. The question pained Aegeus.

"No." He felt the life dwindling from his body, and emotion choked his voice. Aegeus was not sure how to handle the emotions that overwhelmed him. He knew he should say something to her, something to comfort her, something she could hold on to in the days to come, but he could think of nothing worthy of the moment. Emotion surged within him, raw and unmanageable, as he searched for words—anything to offer her solace—but they caught in his throat.

"How sweet," Titus said as he approached. Aegeus looked up into his eyes. Titus drew his weapon and grabbed one of Aegeus's wings. Aegeus tried to pull them in and protect them, but he lacked the strength. Titus pulled the wing, wrenching it awkwardly out of place. He raised his sword to cut it off.

"I will finish what Seneca could not," Titus said to Aegeus. Titus raised his sword, intent on separating Aegeus from his wing. Aegeus braced himself for the blow, every muscle taut, but he had no strength left to defend against it.

Across the field, the Eleventh let out a strangled gasp. "Enough" she cried. She couldn't stand to see the demons do any further damage. Dropping to her knees in the barley, she clasped her hands and began to pray. One by one, others sank to the ground around her—some trembling in fear, some full of fierce determination. Their voices rose in a shared plea, blending with the Third's fervent cries storming the gates of heaven.

The Twelfth locked eyes with Aegeus, and the Spirit within her broke open—a surge of power, luminous and pure, flooding every fiber of her being. Fear evaporated, replaced by a burning certainty. The Light of God blazed from her, scattering shadows and igniting hope in those who still stood. Titus could not cross the barrier to touch her. She rose from the ground. I am a child of God," she declared, her voice ringing out with a strength she hadn't known was hers. She stood firm, arms spread wide, as Light poured forth. Words failed her beyond this simple, unshakeable truth—but it was enough. Across the field, the warrior's mark on Aegeus's chest began to glow, a beacon of hope amid the battle's turmoil. Flames ignited along the blades of swords, signifying the King's imminent arrival. The sound of marching filled the air—a rhythmic, unyielding cadence that shattered despair and sent tremors through the earth. Fog and darkness peeled away, fleeing before the King's presence as His Light blasted every demon from His sight.

Chapter 61

Aegeus walked as one with eternity on his side, his hands brushing softly against the wheat stalks as he moved. He closed his eyes, savoring the gentle touch—each head of grain a reminder of the frailty and tenderness of the King's children. Wheat was one of his favorites. The heads of grain on the stalks felt soft on his fingers; he closed his eyes and continued to walk forward, savoring the delicate brush of the plant across his hands. He let the warmth of the Light sink into his skin, the scent of lilac washing over him like a welcome embrace. Aegeus loved the scent of lilac. He breathed in deeply, letting it soak through him. He turned his face toward the throne room, allowing the Light and power of the King to wash over him and beckon to him.

Standing in the middle of the field, he closed his eyes and listened to the voices of heaven singing the praise of the King. He stood straighter, reaching his full height. His wings were tucked into the compartments on his back, where they fit when he did not need them. His hair blew gently in the breeze. Aegeus felt the rush of love and overwhelming joy that could only come from the King. He felt the light brush of power caress his skin as if every particle of his being was getting charged.

In the distance, he could see the glimmer of the city. He headed in the opposite direction, toward the large tree in the center of the field. As he walked, he took in every scent, every color, and every texture along the way. The tree stood tall and proud where it had stood for all time. The bark of the tree was rough and cracked in a way that was beautiful.

Carvings etched just beneath the bark caught his eye. It whispered secrets of the past and the beauty of the future. Its limbs extended in every direction, long sturdy branches. The leaves fluttered in the breeze making a sound like ocean waves. They called out their praise to the King.

Far to the east, he saw a new arrival. She stood near the gate, being welcomed by her husband and child. Aegeus smiled. He hoped Kfir was near enough to see it.

As he reached the tree, he was pleased to see the others were not yet there. Aegeus had seen two passes of fruit on the tree since he'd returned from Platitude. Today, he would stand under this tree and be honored by the King. Today, he would become an archangel.

He looked carefully at the trunk of the tree, its carvings beautiful and ornate. He ran his hand gently over them until his hand touched an area that felt warm to the touch. When his fingers touched it, a little shiver ran through him. Aegeus leaned closer.

The carving seemed fresh—new—and was in the shape of the ancient horn symbol. The horn represented the King's power, triumph, fierceness, and strength. He rubbed his hand over it again, and two things seemed to happen simultaneously as he did. He was sure he heard the tree whisper his name and the name of the Twelfth. And he felt a sting on the back of his left shoulder. When he looked, the symbol had appeared there, a permanent reminder of this battle and that his journey and the Twelfth's were forever intertwined in the King's purpose. Aegeus stepped back from the tree and turned to face the wheat. He closed his eyes and stood quietly, letting the gentle breeze blow over him.

"You look like you're in heaven," the King said, joining him under the tree. The tree reacted to the King's presence. The King walked to the tree and placed his hand gently against the trunk. Golden, sparkling light filled the tree, radiating from it like glitter. Aegeus knelt on the lush green grass before the King.

"I see you have received the mark of the horn.," the King smiled, his hand still on the tree. "The Twelfth now carries the mark as well," he said, stepping away from the tree. The King placed his hand on Aegeus's shoulder, filling him with the Light.

"Aegeus, your heart is heavy. Rise and tell me what troubles you," the King said gently.

Aegeus stood. "What became of the Strongman?" he asked.

"The Strongman fled the battlefield as soon as he saw that the mark of the warriors was glowing. He will eventually resign from the college and go to Washington, D.C. to provide spiritual guidance to the rulers of the nation."

The King waited patiently. He understood this was not what troubled Aegeus, but it was not in the King's nature to rush an issue.

"So, we lost?" Aegeus asked, his voice low and heavy with the weight of all that had been lost.

The King smiled. While he knew this was important to Aegeus, he also knew that it was not what was truly in his heart. "What was your mission, Aegeus?"

"To protect the Twelfth," he answered confidently.

"Did you do that?"

"I did. But . . .." Aegeus reflected on the final moments of the battle when Titus was positioned over him, poised to remove his wings. But the prayers of the King's children brought Light into the darkness. The Twelfth discovered her true self, emitting the Light of God and protecting Aegeus until the King arrived.

"Protecting you was the only way the Twelfth could ever embrace who she truly was. Knowing who she is is critical to the next phase of her assignment. You did well, Aegeus. We did not lose." The King beamed with pride.

He knew it had been close, waiting for the Twelfth to truly accept who she was, watching as Titus threatened to cut off Aegeus's wings. The army had been anxious as they waited. But the King knew; he understood the importance of timing.

"But what about the Strongman?" Aegeus hesitated, not understanding how letting the Strongman escape was winning.

"Aegeus, many of my daughters have felt rejected by the church. The Strongman and others like him have persecuted them and twisted my words for their own selfish purposes. Through their persecution, my children have started many home churches, and word of me has spread. What the Strongman intended for evil, I have used for good.

"My daughters have clung to me, but they cry out for deliverance. I have heard their cry, Aegeus, and I can bear it no longer. I have sent them a prophet. They must understand how much I love them. The eleven in the town will serve as a voice for my daughters. The battle has only begun."

"But the Tenth failed," Aegeus said, sadness seeping into him as he remembered the death of the Fifth. The King smiled.

"Yes, Aegeus, he did fail. But even that can be used for good. The Tenth will never forget what his cowardice cost. He is my child, Aegeus, and he has come to me for forgiveness, which I freely give. He will find his courage—in time."

The King understood how important timing was. Even as he waited now, understanding that the next question was the one that was dearest to Aegeus's heart. The next question was the one that mattered—the one that had transformed Aegeus into who he truly was. The King waited with anticipation for Aegeus to ask.

Raising his eyes to the King, Aegeus asked what was truly in his heart. "And the Twelfth—what becomes of her?"

The King smiled. Now they could have the conversation he had been waiting for.

Chapter 62

In the dim light of the old church, Morax, Titus, and the Strongman gathered, shadows clinging to their forms like a second skin. Titus, full of rage and covered in burns from the arrival of the King, looked around the church. He would miss it. Being in the presence of the King reminded him, briefly, just how far he had fallen.

For just a twinkling, he let his mind wander back to a time when he had walked the streets of gold. At one time, the King's presence would not have burned him, but instead, it would have filled him with power. The memory of it was too painful; there was no greater torment than separation from the King. Without the King, there was no true hope.

Instead, Titus clung to his anger. He comforted himself with assurances of revenge.

The Strongman stalked to the front of the church, ripping the Bible from the communion table and hurling it across the room., roaring out in protest. His anger consumed him. How had they lost? How could this have happened? They had planned so carefully; they had been patient.

The Strongman had been sure that this battle belonged to the demons. He knew that, ultimately, the King always won, but this battle should have been theirs.

Morax sighed heavily. He, too, needed a moment to recover from being in the King's presence. He looked at the Strongman. A fresh scar covered his chest, reminding him of how close things had been. Morax waited, allowing the Strongman to rage and Titus to smolder.

When they were done, he spoke. "We have lost a great warrior today. Seneca was mighty, and we will surely feel his loss to our mission. But we are not defeated. This battle may not have gone our way, but our prince is relentless. He knows the King's children well.

"Certainly, the war's next stage would have been easier if we had claimed the college. We are not done here. When we go, we will leave behind many demons and much carnage. We will bring in another of our own to continue our work. You have seen how easily we can distract the hairless rats. They will destroy each other over minor things, keeping them distracted from what the King called them to do: love one another."

Titus shivered at the very idea of loving one another. It disgusted him, yet he knew that nothing else would matter if the King's children ever truly got it right. He also knew that as long as he had breath left in him, he would never stop fighting against them—his hatred for them was deep.

He conceded that Morax was right; distracting the humans with theological differences would keep them powerless. Oh, certainly, there were some exceptions. There were those who had learned to hear the King's voice. They understood it was about falling in love with the King, not following a list of rules, not passing judgment, not condemning each other. Those were the powerful ones, but fortunately, their numbers were few, and it was easy to turn the right fighters against them.

Morax looked at the Strongman and continued, "When your contract expires, you will move into the next phase of our plan. Washington is primed and ready. We already have your replacement at hand. He will continue our work. Little has been lost here. An entire generation now carries the poison of our lies. It festers within them—each word a seed of doubt, each doubt a chain to keep them bound. The lies we have taught will remain with them, serving as fodder for the tormenting demons to use against them. They will perpetuate those lies for several generations. Regret, shame and Guilt will flood this place tomorrow, overwhelming them. The messages we have instilled will cause them to rot inside.

"We now know of the prophet. We know of her weaknesses, of which there are many. We will not relent.; we will destroy her. We will poison their thoughts with whispers of doubt— her voice dismissed as unworthy, her presence reduced to a target of scorn. We know their weak points; they will cling to surface judgments, never hearing the truth. We will choose the things we know work well—distractions about her being a woman, her looks, how she dresses, her hair, any little criticism will do to keep people from truly hearing her message.

"We have uncovered the others as well. We ripped open their scars, and that will not soon be forgotten.

However, these are not the only ones."

Morax pulled out the folder he had been carrying. "The King has many children—some more vulnerable than others. We will begin our exit from this place, but there are many other targets—teams are already deploying to find the names on this list. None are safe." He held the folder up.

Titus took the folder from Morax and flipped through it. It contained the names of all the King's children spread across the world. A sinister smile spread across his face.

Morax was right. This might not have been the victory they wanted, but it had also not been a defeat.

A Note from the Author:

I hope you enjoyed reading The Prophet and that, in some small way, it changed the way you view spiritual warfare. It was a fun story to write and wrestle with. Watch for additional content related to the book, including an angel guide, a study guide, and a discussion guide for book clubs.

If you enjoyed this book, I'd be honored if you left a review of it. Reviews help me get more visibility as an author so other readers can find the book.

Thanks for reading *The Prophet*, I hope you join me for the next book in the series, *The Seventh Angel*.

Don't miss the next book in the series, *The Seventh Angel*

The Seventh Angel, Prologue

The demon led Titus into the study, where Lucifer waited. An overflowing ashtray sat on the desk, still smoldering from a freshly extinguished cigar. The room was full of the holiest of all books. It was evident to Titus that Lucifer was searching the Word for something.

"My Liege," Titus offered in greeting, kneeling on the expensive Persian rug before his Prince.

"I assume you have a good reason for coming uninvited to my home, for interrupting me, and for usurping your position," Lucifer drilled. But Titus was not concerned by the harsh tone. He knew that what he brought would be pleasing to Lucifer. He would not have taken the risk otherwise.

"Yes, my Liege," he answered humbly. Being confident did not mean being arrogant. While Titus understood the value of the gift he brought Lucifer, he also realized he was in a precarious position. Lucifer was the prince of the earth; he was not to be trifled with. Titus would proceed with deep respect, never overtly revealing his betrayal of Morax or his own personal quest for power.

"Get up!" Lucifer snapped at him, irritation and disgust evident in his voice.

"I bring you news of Platitude," Titus offered as he stood.

"Platitude? The King's college we are taking over?" Lucifer asked as if he didn't already know.

"Yes." He paused briefly, observing Lucifer for any signs of anger. He saw only annoyance.

"What is your report then?" Lucifer prompted, visibly fighting agitation.

"There was a prophet at the college," Titus once again paused, giving Lucifer plenty of time to process the information. He cunningly laid his cards out for Lucifer to see and was instantly rewarded. A small ripple of excitement pulsed through Lucifer, chased back by a hint of fear that Titus would never acknowledge seeing. All who were wise feared the King. It was only right that Lucifer should as well. After all, who knew better than Lucifer what the King was capable of?

"Go on," Lucifer asked in a slightly softer tone, his interest piqued.

Lucifer listened as Titus filled him in on the critical elements of the battle in Platitude. Titus did, of course, leave out many key facts, facts he was sure would work against him. He would leave that bit for Morax. Lucifer listened intently, asking only what had become of each of the humans. Titus relayed what he knew, which wasn't much.

"Find them and destroy them all. But bring me the prophet alive," Lucifer ordered.